Love Will Tear Us Apart

The third *Stranger Times* novel

C. K. McDonnell

PENGUIN BOOKS

TRANSWORLD PUBLISHERS

Penguin Random House, One Embassy Gardens,
8 Viaduct Gardens, London SW11 7BW
www.penguin.co.uk

Transworld is part of the Penguin Random House group of companies
whose addresses can be found at global.penguinrandomhouse.com

Penguin
Random House
UK

First published in Great Britain in 2023 by Bantam
an imprint of Transworld Publishers
Penguin paperback edition published 2023

A CIP catalogue record for this book
is available from the British Library.

ISBN
9780552177368

Typeset in Van Dijck MT Pro by Jouve (UK), Milton Keynes.
Printed and bound in Great Britain by Clays Ltd, Elcograf S.p.A.

The authorized representative in the EEA is Penguin Random House Ireland,
Morrison Chambers, 32 Nassau Street, Dublin D02 YH68.

Penguin Random House is committed to a sustainable
future for our business, our readers and our planet. This book is made
from Forest Stewardship Council® certified paper.

Love Will Tear Us Apart

CHAPTER 1

Tristram Bleeker's mind went blank. Staring down the wrong end of a gun will have that effect on a man. His mouth was dry. His palms were sweaty. He found himself utterly incapable of summoning a single coherent thought.

Not that he had much experience of these things, but it was not a normal gun. Instead of the typical straight barrel, the muzzle of this one flared out like the bell of a trombone. He kept his eyes fixed down the centre line of it, as if he might discern the spark in the darkness that would herald the eventful end to his previously uneventful life. It was like looking into the nostril of an irritable dragon. One that could barbecue you with a single breath.

'Do I need to repeat the question?' asked the voice at the other end of the weapon. It sounded oddly weary, as if Tristram were the tenth or so person it had held at gunpoint that day and the process was becoming entirely tedious.

Tristram's lips moved but no words emerged.

The voice tutted. 'This is not going well.'

It wasn't. In these circumstances, the cliché was that your life should flash before your eyes, but that wasn't happening for Tristram. Instead, the first ten minutes of his interview kept replaying in his head, over and over, as if his mind were trying to process how things had reached this alarming state of affairs. He must've done something very wrong at some point. Tristram was good in interviews – everybody said so. He was personable, articulate and a master of brevity. He'd been warned to expect the unexpected today and, to that point, he thought he'd dealt well with the curveballs thrown his way. Then he'd found himself staring down the barrel of this weird gun.

'The question,' said the voice, sounding increasingly irritated, 'was . . . how well do you handle pressure?'

'I . . . I . . .' stuttered Tristram.

'Never mind. I think we have our answer.'

Tristram was dimly aware of the sound of one of the doors being opened behind him. A female gasp followed. 'Vincent!'

'I'm in the middle of something, Grace.'

'I can see that. Put that horrible gun away this instant.'

After what felt like a very long time, the dragon's head turned away and was replaced by the face of a man who looked in need of a shower, a shave, a decent meal and about a month's worth of sleep. It belonged to the individual who had been holding Tristram at gunpoint: Vincent Banecroft, editor of *The Stranger Times* and former Fleet Street legend.

The view of Banecroft's face was only a minor improvement on that of the gun. His eyes were sunken and dark. For a moment, his eyelids closed and Tristram wondered if perhaps Banecroft were about to fall asleep, but then they shot open again abruptly. A master of multitasking, Banecroft placed the gun down beside him, sneered across the table and lit a cigarette.

Grace, the friendly matronly black woman from behind the reception desk, appeared at Banecroft's shoulder, bearing a tray loaded with two mugs and a plate of biscuits.

'Sorry about that, Tristram. Mr Banecroft can be a little . . .'

'Insightful,' finished Banecroft.

Grace's brow furrowed. 'I am pretty sure that is not the word I was looking for.'

'It should have been.' Banecroft held aloft two sheets of paper, which Tristram recognized as his CV. 'Mr Bleeker here, who is applying for the role of assistant editor at this publication, has a first-class degree in journalism from the University of Leeds, followed by seven years' experience working for a mixed bag of publications, ranging from national newspapers to more specialist magazines, and it is his dream to work here because of his lifelong interest in the paranormal. His portfolio is frankly outstanding and his references so glowing that the reader is required to wear protective eyewear or risk permanent damage to their retinas while perusing them.'

'I know,' said Grace, before adding pointedly through gritted teeth, 'he is perfect for the job.'

'Exactly,' said Banecroft, as he dropped Tristram's CV into the wastepaper basket at the side of his desk then casually flicked cigarette ash after it. 'My point being – if it looks like a duck, walks like a duck and quacks like a duck, I find myself highly suspicious as to why it is applying for the role of the bread-loving aquatic bird we are so ducking desperate to fill.'

Grace's face scrunched up for a second before she shook her head. 'No. You have lost me.'

Tristram coughed and was surprised to realize he had recovered the power of speech. 'I think what Mr Banecroft is trying to say is that I am overqualified for the role.'

'No. I am not trying to say anything. What I am saying is that you are perfectly qualified for the role. Too perfect. Now, run along before I lose my temper, and do let your handlers know that if they try this kind of thing again, next time I will not take it in such good spirits. Speaking of which . . .'

Banecroft picked up the bottle of Irish whiskey that sat on his desk and poured himself a healthy measure, then kept pouring past the point of unhealthy all the way to death wish.

'There's clearly been a misunderstanding here,' said Tristram, trying to sound jovial. 'Nobody has sent me.'

'Right.' Banecroft patted the gun. 'Well, you've got until the count of ten before I shoot you. Then, if nobody claims the body after a week, I shall offer your corpse a full and grovelling apology.'

'Vincent!' exclaimed Grace. 'You're being unreasonable. Even for you – and that really is saying something.'

'Four,' announced Banecroft.

'OK,' said Tristram. 'I get it. You're testing me.'

'Nope. Five.'

Tristram failed to keep the edge of panic from his voice. 'What happened to one through to three?'

'I said what I was counting to, never said where I was counting from. Six.'

Tristram looked up at Grace. 'He's kidding, right?'

The woman gave an expansive shrug, which resulted in a

splash of tea spilling over the lip of one of the mugs. 'With the good Lord as my witness, I cannot promise that.'

'Seven.'

Tristram got to his feet. 'You people are crazy!'

Banecroft picked up the gun. 'Sticks and stones may break my bones, but Chekhov here will make you holier than Grace. Eight.'

'I will be reporting you to the police.'

Banecroft raised the gun while looking up at Grace. 'Holier? Do you get it? I thought it was quite good.'

'It was not,' said Grace.

'You've no appreciation of wordplay. That's your problem. Nine.'

Tristram turned and ran for the nearest exit. En route, he tripped over one of the many piles of books on the floor and crashed headfirst through the door. In his hurry, he'd left through a different door from the one he'd come in, and this was how he came to find himself sprawled on the threadbare carpet of an open-plan office area.

Three people were seated behind desks and drinking mugs of tea: a portly white man in a three-piece tartan suit, an East Asian man tossing a yo-yo up and down, and a black teenaged girl with purple hair, who didn't look up from her phone.

Tristram pointed behind him in the direction of Banecroft's office. 'That man is a monster.'

His words were met with a round of nonchalant nods. Then, the portly gent in the three-piece suit turned to his colleagues. 'I have to say, these new biscuits are a bit dry.'

CHAPTER 2

Grace opened her notepad to a fresh page as Banecroft slumped into the chair he traditionally occupied for these meetings. It occurred to her that if they lost any more staff, he would soon be able to stay in his office and they could go to him, rather than him having to stomp ill-temperedly out to the bullpen.

'Right,' Banecroft began. 'Let's get this parade of ineptitude kicked off, shall we? Grace – please do the honours.'

She spoke as she wrote. 'Weekly editorial meeting. Present – the staff of *The Stranger Times*.'

'Remaining staff,' muttered Ox under his breath, still fiddling with his yo-yo.

'What was that?' snapped Banecroft.

'I was just pointing out that we are the remaining staff. Since we lost Hannah.'

'Lost? We haven't lost her,' said Banecroft. 'She isn't stuck down the back of the sofa. She walked out on us and went scurrying back to the philandering phallus she was supposed to be divorcing.'

'Why, though?' asked Reggie, readjusting his waistcoat.

Banecroft threw up his hands in exasperation. 'We have gone

over this several times in the last three weeks. She just informed me she was leaving and then she left. All of you seem to be having difficulty grasping these two salient pieces of information.'

'But what did you say to her?' asked Stella.

'How is that relevant?'

She pushed her purple hair out of her eyes. 'Because, boss, you have a tendency to say truly awful things in the way other people have a tendency to breathe.'

Banecroft shot a look at the young girl. 'And yet, I am somehow seen as the kind of easy-going cuddly boss who can be slagged off in a meeting by an apprentice reporter and that reporter can inexplicably still expect to have her job at the end of it.'

'You can't fire me. You ain't got enough staff as it is. I'm currently second in line for the job of assistant editor.'

'Hang on,' said Ox. He pointed at himself and then at Reggie. 'Which of us do you think is below you on that list?'

'Both of you,' interrupted Banecroft with a shrug. 'Grace is clearly number one.'

The idea made Grace feel queasy. 'Don't you dare,' she warned. 'Perhaps you should just ring Hannah and apologize?'

'For what?'

'Everything,' said Stella.

'Anything,' offered Ox.

'Being you,' concluded Reggie.

'All right,' said Banecroft, leaning forward. 'First things first – you are all skirting dangerously close to mutiny. Second – as it happens, I have attempted to ring Hannah. Not, I hasten to add, to apologize, but rather to see if the woman has come to her senses. Her phone keeps going to voicemail.' His eyes scanned the group. 'Has anyone else had any luck getting hold of her?'

The paper's remaining staff avoided meeting his gaze. Grace had been trying Hannah's phone several times a day but had received no response beyond the single word – 'sorry' – that her former colleague had texted on the first morning of her absence. Grace knew for a fact that none of the others had had any more success.

Banecroft folded his arms as he sat back in his chair. 'That's what I thought. You can all keep pretending this is somehow my fault, but the reality is she walked out on all of us.'

Nobody had anything to say to this.

Since Hannah's shocking departure, morale in the office had taken a nosedive. She had worked there only a few months, yet had somehow become the glue that held them together. In the weeks that followed, the cloud of depression that hung over the place had manifested itself in the form of petty squabbles and hurtful remarks among the group. Reggie had even got into a disagreement with Manny, the perpetually relaxed Rastafarian who ran the printing press on the ground floor. Having an argument with Manny was like trying to punch a cloud.

Everyone felt as if they'd lost a friend. Worse than that was the unspoken realization that the person they thought was a good friend apparently wasn't. True friends don't just up and disappear out of your life.

'Now,' said Banecroft, 'if we're all done having our little tantrums, we have a newspaper to publish.'

'To do that,' replied Grace, 'we really do need an assistant editor.'

'We can muddle through for another week until an appropriate candidate comes along.'

'Really? Last week's edition had two page sevens.'

'And,' added Reggie, 'a crossword that had the clues from three weeks ago reprinted alongside the wrong puzzle.'

'Yes,' agreed Grace, who had been fielding irate phone calls about the error ever since. She'd had no idea that people took crosswords so seriously. There had technically been a death threat. 'Technically' because, as Ox had put it, the intersection in the Venn diagram of individuals who complete crosswords and those who firebomb buildings was either empty or humanity was already doomed. 'Not to mention the story about Mr Adam Wallace's ghost frequenting that lap-dancing club in Chinatown and inappropriately touching the ladies.'

'Ah,' said Ox. 'That makes sense. That geezer outside this morning . . .'

'Was the very much alive Mr Wallace,' confirmed Stella. 'Accompanied by his missus, who was proper vexed.'

'I admit,' said Reggie, 'that I received some very bad information regarding that story. However, while the reports of his death have been greatly exaggerated, I believe the ones about his behaviour are accurate.'

'Still, though – not exactly paranormal, is it?'

Reggie looked affronted. 'You can talk. At least I can spell. You submitted a half-page article about an unidentified frying object over Bolton.'

'That's nowhere near as bad as—' Ox stopped. He looked across the room at Banecroft, whose chin had dipped on to his chest and eyes had closed.

Of the many things worrying Grace, this was the thing that concerned her most of all. Vincent Banecroft had never been what you would call healthy, but in the last few weeks he had really gone downhill. Falling asleep mid-conversation had become a new and alarming trend. His distracted, listless air also alarmed her, and while describing Vincent Banecroft as being more irritable than usual was akin to accusing the sea of being more wet, he was. He really was. His fury, while often unjustifiable, had always felt as if it had some sense of purpose behind it. Now, however, it seemed entirely scattershot.

All that aside, the effects of whatever was going on were being felt on the paper itself. What she had begun to think of as the 'old' Vincent Banecroft never would have allowed all the recent screw-ups to get past him. It was as if he were only half here. Going through the motions.

Grace looked round and saw the faces of her other colleagues mirroring her own concern. Then Banecroft broke the tension by passing wind loudly. It appeared to wake him up, and his eyes flashed suddenly.

'Now,' he said, without missing a beat, 'if you've all finished, I would like to remind you that it is not your job to point out other people's screw-ups. As editor, that is both my job and my privilege.'

Stella folded her arms huffily. 'It's the job of the assistant editor to make sure the screw-ups don't happen in the first place. That's why we need one.'

'And we will get one, eventually.'

'I thought it was gonna be that woman who wore all the scarfs and smelled of patchouli oil?'

'We had a fundamental disagreement.'

'What a shock,' said Reggie, which earned him a particularly dirty look from Banecroft.

'The woman didn't believe in double letters.'

'I'm sorry?'

'Case in point – she didn't believe the word "sorry" should have two Rs in it. Said it was wasteful. Bad for the environment.'

This last statement was met with confused expressions all round.

'I don't—' started Stella.

'Not just that,' continued Banecroft as he placed his slippered feet upon the desk and tipped his chair backwards to balance on its rear legs. 'She also believed that capital letters were elitist and punctuation was divisive.'

A long moment of quiet followed as everyone in the room tried to figure out exactly how such rules would work. Eventually, it was Ox who broke the silence. 'Even for this place, that is odd.'

Stella raised her hand. 'What about that nice old dude who was in reception last week? Big white beard. Looked like Santa.'

Banecroft turned to Grace and raised an eyebrow. 'Would you like to field this one?'

Grace blessed herself. 'He said he could not work on full moons as he needed to make a' – her face twisted into a sour expression – 'blood sacrifice.' She blessed herself again.

'That's right,' said Banecroft. 'Looked like Santa but loved him some Satan.'

'But . . .' Stella faltered, 'he had leather patches on his elbows. Leather patches,' she repeated forlornly.

'And the bloke from this morning?' asked Ox.

Banecroft gave him a blank look.

'Really?' Ox continued in disbelief. 'Came flying out of your office, like, twenty minutes ago, claiming you'd threatened to shoot him?'

'Oh, that one. Yes, he was too good to be true.'

Ox looked at the others with wide eyes before turning back to Banecroft. 'What does that even mean?'

'Clearly a Trojan horse sent by our enemies in a transparent attempt to destroy us.'

'More fool them,' shot Ox. 'We don't need any help doing that.'

Reggie shifted in his seat and straightened his waistcoat. 'Do you not think that is, perhaps, a touch paranoid?'

Banecroft yawned before responding. 'Have you been here for the past few months? You can't be paranoid if you have documented proof that people are literally out to get you. There's still a dent in the wall from the werewolf and I can't be the only one who, every time I take a dump, remembers the hidden camera installed in the new bathroom by the loony cult?'

'Maybe,' conceded Grace. 'Or maybe you're finding fault with all the candidates because none of them are Hannah?'

'Yes, that's it. You've found me out. I'm in love with that woman I was constantly at loggerheads with.'

'Judging by the sarcastic tone you employed while making that statement,' she responded, 'I am going to assume you have never, ever seen a romantic comedy film.'

'Have you lot been eating brownies with the Rastafarian or something? Look, if it will stop you all clucking like tedious hens, as it happens, I have the assistant-editor situation in hand.'

Grace's eyebrows shot up her forehead. 'You do?'

'Yes. I'm going to ask Stanley Roker to come in for a chat.'

'Stanley?' echoed Stella. 'The fella you called the worst kind of tabloid-scribbling parasite? That guy?'

'Yes.'

'Stanley's all right,' said Ox softly.

'I'm not saying he isn't,' she replied. 'But he' – she bobbed her head in Banecroft's direction – 'said he wouldn't trust the guy as far as he could throw this building.'

'We don't need to like or trust him,' said Banecroft. 'You all liked and trusted the previous assistant editor and look where that got us. Stanley Roker is many things, and while several of those things are reprehensible, one of them is that he is an individual with extensive experience in the newspaper business. He may have written some fetid tripe over the years, but it has always been correctly spelled and fact-checked fetid tripe. Now, we need to move on.'

'Quite right.'

The staff turned as one towards the corner of the room from where the new voice had come, Banecroft doing so vigorously enough to send himself toppling back in his chair and on to the floor. One of his slippers liberated itself from his foot and hit him on the head.

He got to his feet and joined his colleagues in gawping at the woman who was sitting behind a desk on the far side of the room, peeling a satsuma. She was rotund, about sixty, and was wearing a wax jacket and deerstalker hat. Her face was heart-shaped with ruddy cheeks, and she looked as if she would be more at home tramping around her country estate with a couple of collies than sitting in a newspaper office in Manchester. By way of greeting she gave them a cheerful grin.

'Who the hell are you?' asked Banecroft.

'Elizabeth Cavendish the Third, but please call me Betty.'

To Grace's ears, she sounded similar to one of those useful posh people who appeared on TV occasionally. The type that owned a lot of land but were still happy to shove a hand up a cow's rear end if the situation required it.

'How long have you been sitting there?'

'Long enough.'

'And, more importantly, how on earth did you get in here without any of us seeing you?'

She shrugged, popped a segment of satsuma into her mouth and chewed briefly before answering. 'I'm a woman of a certain age. The world has got very good at ignoring us – Hollywood in particular. Unless you're Meryl Streep or Helen Mirren, you just have to hang around and hope someone needs a grandma at some point. And don't get me started on the gender disparity among newsreaders.'

'What?' said Banecroft.

'Should I pick any free desk?' asked Betty, waving a hand about. 'Or is there a system?'

'What?' repeated Banecroft, with the air of a man about to lose it. As soon as he got a grip on exactly what 'it' was.

'Sorry,' said Betty. 'I've got ahead of myself again, haven't I? I do have a tendency to ramble. I must apologize. Chitty-chatty Betty. That's what the girls called me at school. Children can be so cruel, can't they? One girl – Dorothy Wilkins – once stuck chewing gum to my seat. Horrible little thing. Wonder where she is now. Probably married to a government minister. All the worst ones are. Anyway, yes – with apologies to the frankly awful-sounding tabloid chappie you mentioned, I am the new assistant editor.'

'Over my dead body,' snorted Banecroft.

Betty wrinkled her nose. 'Well, that would certainly explain the smell.'

'Let me get this straight – you thought the best way to apply for the job was to sneak into the building, join a meeting to which you weren't invited, and then insult me?'

Betty looked genuinely perplexed. 'Have I insulted you? I mean, I'm fairly sure you've insulted most of the people in this room during the course of this meeting, but I don't recall me or anyone else insulting you.' She popped another slice of satsuma into her mouth and chewed contemplatively. 'What surprisingly thin skin you have.'

'Let me save you some time. You've definitely, one hundred per cent failed the interview. Now, will you be leaving of your own volition, or shall I get Chekhov to show you out? That is the name of my—'

'Blunderbuss,' Betty finished. 'Yes, I know. Very clever. That will not be necessary. I will be going nowhere, though, as I'm afraid you have crucially misunderstood something. I am not applying for the role of assistant editor; I have already been given it.' She pulled a letter from one of her jacket pockets and held it up. 'I have here a missive from this newspaper's proprietor, Mrs Harnforth, explaining as much. A copy of it has just been emailed to' – Betty pointed – 'Grace, is it not?'

Grace nodded.

'Hello. Lovely to meet you. I've heard only good things.'

'Impossible,' said Banecroft.

'Excuse me?' said Grace, affronted.

'Not you.' Banecroft gave a dismissive wave and focused his attention on Betty. 'You cannot be the assistant editor as I and I alone have the ability to hire and fire.'

Betty popped in another piece of satsuma. 'Entirely incorrect.'

'It is in my contract.'

'You do not have a contract.'

'I have a verbal contract.'

Betty raised an eyebrow and looked round the room. 'Oh dear. Do you have any witnesses to this contract, as Mrs Harnforth clearly doesn't remember it?'

'It was an implied contract.'

This earned Banecroft the double-eyebrow raise. 'Let's just let that phrase percolate for a minute, shall we?'

Banecroft stamped his foot. 'Fine. I resign.'

Betty nodded. 'While obviously we are very sad to see you go, the newspaper thanks you for your service. On the upside, you have to admire how dynamic and fast-moving an organization we are. I mean, I've only been here five minutes and I've already been promoted. Not a hint of a glass ceiling. How refreshing. The *Six O'Clock News* could learn a lot from us.' She tossed two final satsuma segments into her mouth, chewed expansively and gulped them down, before favouring the room with a benign smile.

Grace looked at her colleagues and then back to Banecroft. The vein in his forehead was throbbing. She had a sudden urge to flee the area and take every piece of breakable furniture with her.

Betty swallowed. 'I see you're still here. Shall we assume that resignation was merely a joke that didn't hit the mark?'

Banecroft spoke through gritted teeth. 'I wish to speak to Mrs Harnforth immediately.'

Betty got to her feet. 'I'm afraid that is impossible, but as I am here as her representative, I will be delighted to discuss your concerns.' She waved a hand in the direction of the door to Banecroft's office.

The two of them locked eyes for an uncomfortable amount of time. Any passing polar ice caps would have gone up in a puff of steam had they been unlucky enough to get caught between the pair. Betty held her smile throughout. Eventually, Banecroft took a step towards the office.

'Lovely,' said Betty, sounding cheerful. 'And look on the bright side – I am a massive fan of punctuation.'

Ghost Cancelled

In what is being claimed as a world first, the ghost of Arnold Franklin, long associated with the Frog and Trumpet public house in Stoke-on-Trent, is claiming that he has been cancelled. Through the medium of a medium, Mr Franklin was quoted as saying, 'I've haunted this pub for forty-seven years, ever since I had a heart attack while performing my gags during the open-mic night, and I'm very popular with the patrons. Then, this new landlady comes in – a woman, if you know what I mean – and next thing I know, she's calling in an exorcist.'

In response, publican Mabel Clarke, who has owned the pub for fifteen years, said, 'To be honest, he was just getting tedious. He does hilarious "voices", so he says, which I think are racist, but they're so hard to identify it's impossible to be sure. He spends most of his time in the ladies loos, and we had to stop hanging mistletoe because of his poltergeist pervery. That, coupled with the jokes. If I have to hear the one about the two nuns and the bar of soap again, I'll scream, but at least that one isn't offensive.

'He keeps banging on about how he can't say anything any more. The reality is, he's got nothing new to say. It's just the same four jokes over and over again. He says he takes the piss out of everybody, but we've asked every patron and, along with the nuns, "everybody" translates to women, black people and one-eyed dwarves.'

CHAPTER 3

The countryside thundered past in a blur, unobserved by Hannah as she stared out the window of the people carrier, lost in her own thoughts. With a pang of regret, she realized that at this time on a Monday morning she was usually in the weekly editorial meeting, attempting to assemble some idea of what that week's edition might look like from the trail of destruction Banecroft habitually left in his wake.

She blinked a couple of times. She couldn't think about that now. For better or worse, she had made her choice.

Seventeen days ago, on a Friday evening, she had been leaving work, heading home after another challenging week of getting an edition of *The Stranger Times* to print. By the time she reached her flat, everything had changed. She resigned the following day.

Last week, she had accepted an invitation from her not-quite ex-husband Karl to have dinner. Up until about a month ago, he had been trying constantly to speak to her after she had decided – admittedly at the last minute – that she did want a chunk of the money due to her from the divorce settlement after all. Her change of heart had been brought about by the realization that her *not* wanting it might give the impression that Karl deserved to keep it.

More importantly, she had realized there were several good causes she could support with it. It was nice to think that something good could come out of the years she had dedicated to their sham of a marriage. She also had to admit that a small part of her took a giddy delight in just how much it would annoy Karl.

He hadn't always been this way, but even before their split, she had been disturbed to realize that Karl had sold to himself a personal narrative whereby he had somehow clawed his way up from the streets to become a self-made man. As if a private education and a sizeable inheritance hadn't played a rather significant role in his success. It was all smoke and mirrors, as were their tax returns, which showed quite how ludicrous an effort Karl had gone to in order to avoid paying anything close to a reasonable amount of tax. She'd only seen the accounts for the first time as part of the divorce negotiations, and the more she thought about them, the more embarrassing it felt. To have been both married to someone who behaved like that and so wilfully ignorant not to have noticed. She'd stupidly assumed that his constant whingeing about freeloaders living off their tax meant that they were actually paying some.

She'd had no interest in engaging with Karl, as she knew he would pull every trick in the book to convince her not to give 'his' money away. It had therefore been a relief when the messages had stopped. She'd heard nothing from him for almost a month. When he'd got in touch again, he'd done something disconcertingly unexpected. He'd apologized. Karl never apologized. Until that point, Hannah had been entirely convinced he didn't even know what an apology was. What's more, it had been a proper apology.

Apologies were fast becoming a lost art form, thanks to the repeated warping of the concept. There was the 'I'm sorry if anybody was offended' apology; the 'I'm sorry that somebody thinks I said this thing that I didn't say' apology; and its near-identical twin, the 'I'm sorry if you misunderstood what I said' apology. There were numerous variations, but they all amounted to the fact that the person wasn't sorry at all.

Karl had been truly sorry, and not just about the money. It had been about everything. He'd asked her to have dinner with him one last time – so they could leave their marriage on good terms, at the very least. Hannah wasn't an idiot – not any more. The man had always been a superb liar, but something about this felt very different. Besides, in those few weeks of radio silence, an awful lot had happened, so she had gone to dinner.

Over the starter, he'd expressed regret for his appalling behaviour throughout their marriage. He was ashamed of the man he'd been and the way he'd treated her.

Over the main course, he'd explained how he was a new man after attending a retreat run by the Pinter Institute. It was the brainchild of Hollywood icon turned twenty-first-century new-age business tycoon, Winona Pinter. Pinter had been all over the press in the last few years, and hardly ever for her acting. While the mainstream media was thrilled to report on the latest Pinter frippery – be it space-scented candles or yoga studios for pets – they also did a sterling job of keeping her name out there.

Along with the products came the successful lines of food and books, followed by online courses, and finally, for the very, very lucky few, the retreats. They were exclusive, or to put it in more simple terms, obscenely expensive. So expensive that, much to the papers' annoyance, none of them knew exactly how expensive. Before being accepted on any of the retreats, delegates had to go through a screening process. Although the Institute denied it, of course, places were offered only to people for whom money was no object, or at least to those who liked to pretend it wasn't.

In truth, Hannah had found the entire dinner rather unsettling. Yes, it had been only one night, but Karl hadn't been Karl. Over the course of their marriage, Hannah had become numb to the fact that her husband's eyes would rove the room perpetually. After a while, she had wondered if he even knew he was doing it. It had therefore been very odd when he had shown zero interest in the waitress's low-cut top or in the other patrons as they walked about the restaurant. Back in the early days of their marriage, when she had brought up his behaviour, he'd assured her it was all in her mind. Looking back, she realized she'd allowed herself the soft option of accepting feeble explanations rather than standing up for herself.

With this version of Karl, though, his wandering eye hadn't been an issue. During one meal, he had quite possibly made more eye contact with her than he had during their entire marriage. What's more, he'd done so while owning up to being a narcissist who'd gone looking for self-worth in meaningless sex rather than trying to value himself and the people he truly loved. Hannah had been prepared for Karl's attempts to beg, cajole and manipulate her, as he had done many times before, but this had been either raw honesty or he'd found a depth to his acting abilities that Winona Pinter herself would have envied.

Before dessert she'd excused herself to visit the ladies' room. Without intending to, she'd stood behind a screen of Swiss cheese plants and surreptitiously watched the 'new' Karl from a distance. He had sat there, patiently waiting for her return, his eyes fixed on the table in front of him. He didn't even make an attempt to flirt with the waitress, something he would have previously done as automatically as breathing.

Over coffee, he'd floated the idea that maybe, just maybe, they could give it another go. Hannah had been reluctant. It had been Karl who had suggested that perhaps she take a little time to reflect on what she wanted from the rest of her life. Perhaps she could go on a Pinter Institute retreat too? Get her head together.

And so here she was.

She was jolted out of her reverie as the people carrier took a sharp right turn off the road and pulled up in front of a pair of large metal gates. Tall electric fences hemmed the estate boundary, and bore prominent signage warning just how un-fun a high-voltage shock could be. After a couple of seconds, the gates opened. To her right, Hannah looked out at the Pennines, just visible over the serried ranks of tall coniferous trees that crowded the road from either side. The Pinter Institute valued privacy, to the point that several square miles of forest surrounded it. The only way to photograph it was from space.

The property had been renamed Pinter Institute HQ, not least because the Institute was keen to disassociate it from its past. Hannah had spent a couple of hours last night digging into the history of the place just because they seemed so keen not to mention its previous name – Ranford House.

The Ranfords had achieved their wealth in the most old-fashioned of ways: conquest. The family had been high up in the British Army even before it was called that, and they specialized in making sure that when one of them was sent somewhere in anger, the next brother in line would follow directly behind to ask if anyone minded terribly if he were to take this bit of land that nobody – at least nobody of consequence – appeared to be using. In this manner, the Ranfords claimed chunks of every new territory that the British Empire acquired – plantations in America, mines in Africa, railways in India; they owned vast swathes of assets the world over. The Ranford system worked, although it did result in the occasional loss of a son or two, either on the front lines or at the hands of the odd local who was a particularly sore loser.

Keen to show off their immense wealth, the Ranfords had built Ranford House at the foot of the Pennines to take advantage of the family's well-known love of nature – chiefly, shooting or chasing it down with dogs.

If Wikipedia was to be believed, the place had a blighted history. During construction of the house, several of the builders had died in unfortunate accidents, which began the house's reputation for being cursed. Once completed, it was one of the most magnificent manors in all of Britain, although it seems the Ranford family rarely enjoyed life there. Lord Albert Ranford lost his young wife when she died in childbirth in 1896. The baby survived – their only offspring, William. By all accounts, the lord of the manor was consumed by grief, to the point that he all but ignored his son.

William was considered odd, and not just in the way most aristocracy is. He was expelled from Eton for 'ungentlemanly behaviour' – something that was almost without precedent. Later, his playboy years were briefly interrupted by a stint keeping up the family tradition for warmongering with a disastrous commission in command of a battalion during the Great War. A report sent back from the front by a superior officer contained the damning sentence, 'I have never met a man with less regard for the value of human life than William Ranford.'

While the young Ranford's military career led to a great deal of death and destruction, he returned home unscathed, and resumed being an embarrassment to his father in other ways. The pair were estranged for most of William's adult life, but they must have put aside their differences at some point, given that following the untimely death of his father, William became Lord Ranford. The elder perished in a bizarre hunting accident and reports stated that he died in his weeping son's arms.

The bad luck continued and two years later William was crippled after a fall from a horse. Following his accident, events took a darker turn. William became obsessed with regaining the use of his legs by any means necessary, and when medical science failed him, he began to explore other avenues.

Details became sketchy after that, drawing more on rumour than on reported fact. A young girl died at Ranford House. The family received a pay-off and the matter went away, but regular reports soon surfaced of strange goings-on and unusual individuals frequenting the place. A large number of staff, many of whom came from families that had served the Ranfords for generations, left and were replaced by outsiders. Then, the Second World War broke out.

William Ranford was hardly alone among the aristocracy in being a vocal admirer of Hitler, but most of his contemporaries did a far better job of rowing back their feelings once war had been declared. Ranford was far too rich to face internment or similar for his political leanings, but he was also far too stubborn to realign himself with prevailing sentiments. In 1942, his betrayal by one of his staff led to the discovery of what the press dubbed 'the stash'.

Ranford, convinced that Nazi victory was inevitable, had built up and concealed a vast stockpile of supplies on the estate, intended as a gift for Hitler, to assist the Nazi war machine once it landed on British shores. The discovery caused outrage and Ranford fled to Switzerland, to live out the rest of his days in exile. Ranford House was seized as an asset, and after serving time as a convalescent hospital for returning soldiers it was briefly a private school. It passed through a few different sets of hands before sitting empty for several years and then being taken on by its current owners.

As the forest at the side of the road fell away to reveal the stern Victorian grandeur of Ranford House, Hannah caught her breath. Framed by the mountains behind it, the house was far too big for anyone to need, and its walls were constructed from the kind of thick granite that could withstand a full-on artillery barrage. Gargoyles sat atop the crenelations, fighting off ivy as they gurned down upon the world. The immense sprawl of surrounding lawns was broken up by ornate water features – probably to give the peacocks and other fowl that roamed the place something to perch on.

The people carrier pulled up at the end of the long driveway where a dozen Pinter Institute staff, all dressed in black tops and white trousers or skirts, were lined up on either side of the broad steps that led to the main doors, ready to greet their latest retreat delegate. As soon as the vehicle came to a stop, its passenger-side door drew open.

A man who looked like a life-sized Ken doll approached and bowed his head. 'Hello, Mrs Drinkwater. I am your personal experience facilitator, Anton.'

Hannah opened her mouth to correct him but stopped herself. Willis was her maiden name, but given her reason for being here, Drinkwater was once again appropriate, even though it jarred.

She looked along the line of staff and their fixed expressions. Hannah had never been greeted by a welcoming committee before. It was a rather disconcerting experience. Like something out of *Downton Abbey*. She wasn't sure if she was supposed to shake everyone's hand or ignore them or introduce herself or bow or . . .

So consumed was she by her sudden social anxiety at how to handle this unexpected situation, she inadvertently left a lasting impression on everyone present. As she stepped out of the car, her heel caught the edge of the door sill and she faceplanted on to the gravel.

An excellent start.

CHAPTER 4

Stanley Roker was uncomfortable.

First off, he had been sitting, slumped down, in his van for several hours now, and kept having to stretch out bits of himself to stop them from falling asleep. His ankle, while ostensibly healed from the break it sustained when he was dropped from a height by a quarter-faced magical bastard who still regularly visited him in his nightmares, still ached like a bugger if he used it too much or too little. He had not kept up with his physio.

It being one of August's better days, the van was uncomfortably hot, all the more so given he couldn't roll down the windows because of his allergies. And then there was the fact that he was experiencing 'digestive discomfort' – mainly in the form of heartburn, although he had spent the last hour wondering if there wasn't some sort of field toilet he could install in the van. An empty Snapple bottle, while an invaluable tool of the trade, could only do so much.

All these factors were potential reasons for Stanley's discomfort but, while he tried to convince himself otherwise, they were not the root cause of his black mood. No. Stanley Roker was feeling uncomfortable because he was uncomfortable doing what he was doing. This was awkward because Stanley Roker was doing what Stanley Roker did best.

He was slumped in his seat to avoid being seen by the owner of the silver BMW across the road. It was currently parked up outside of the offices of a production company co-owned by a major celebrity. A fixture of Saturday-evening TV. Somebody you would recognize. Even if you had never watched any of the shows, you'd have caught the adverts featuring him, his celebrity wife and their three darling children hawking the implicit promise that if Middle Englanders started doing their shopping at a certain supermarket, they and their entire family would somehow become as stunningly attractive and as blissfully happy as Mr and Mrs Celeb. Stanley was staking out the offices because he had it on good authority that at some point that morning the aforementioned celebrity would nip out for a couple of hours and meet a man he had been seeing for several years.

Of course, the days were long gone when outing someone as gay was considered news in its own right. People still wanted to know – of course they did – however, all but the most unreconstructed understood that you couldn't admit to or, worse still, act on that instinct. Luckily, that didn't matter in this case. There was a wronged woman in the picture. A man violating the sacred bonds of matrimony. The gay thing was just incidental. It wasn't, but the point was everybody could pretend it was.

This was a great story in the Stanley Roker meaning of the words. That is, it was going to be an enormous payday, and one he very much needed, given he owed serious money to some serious people who were seriously weird. Being in debt to a supernatural gangster was playing havoc with his sleep. The dreams were something else.

Subconsciously, he rubbed his right shoulder at the site of the tattoo that wasn't really a tattoo. The windfall from this job would clear his debt to Ferry and there would be enough left over to mean that he could stop sleeping in the van. It was therefore particularly inconvenient for Stanley Roker to be having his first ever crisis of conscience.

It had been only a few months since the fateful night that had changed his life for ever. Stanley was a victim – one who had been lucky to get away alive. However, he had become convinced that in the broader scheme of things, he was on the receiving end of his comeuppance – for all the crappy things he'd done over the years. Karma was a bitch. These days, he spent a lot of time wondering if it was too late for his soul to be saved. Doing that while doing what he was doing right now was not a happy mix.

His acute discomfort was replaced by alarm as the passenger door of his van opened and a slender woman of around sixty, wearing a vintage burgundy coat, climbed in and slid on to the seat. Her hair was cut puckishly short and dyed a light shade of pink. Somehow on her it looked elegant.

'What the—'

'Hello, Stanley.'

'Who the hell are you?'

The woman offered a manicured hand. 'Alicia Harnforth, delighted to make your acquaintance. Although, as I am the proprietor of *The Stranger Times*, you have technically worked for me already.'

'No, I haven't.'

She raised an eyebrow. 'Come, come now, Stanley.' She reached into the inside pocket of her immaculately tailored jacket and, between two fingers, withdrew from it a slip of newspaper. She held it up. 'This first-person account of a night when the writer was mugged, and then offered help by a kindly nurse who took him back to her apartment when he refused to go to hospital, only for her to transform into a . . . What was it?' She unfolded the article and scanned the text. 'Oh, yes – a terrifying, arachnid-like demonic being intent on consuming her victim in every way imaginable. Very dramatic. That wasn't written by you, was it?'

'It was anonymous,' said Stanley rather feebly.

'From the public,' she replied, tucking the article back in her jacket. 'Thank you, by the way, for your assistance with that situation a couple of months ago. I appreciate it.'

'Yeah, whatever. What are you doing here? Scratch that – how did you know where I was? And come to that – that door was locked. How did you open it?'

'So many questions. In answer to at least some of them . . .' She casually twirled the index finger of her left hand and the empty sandwich wrappers, sweet packets, soft-drink cans and miscellaneous detritus that formed a thick layer in the passenger-side footwell rose in the air and casually floated into the empty doughnut box beside Stanley. Its lid then closed softly. 'There,' she said. 'That's better.' She looked round the van and tsked. 'Not that the whole thing couldn't do with a deep clean. Or being set on fire for the insurance money.'

Stanley folded his arms, determined to appear unimpressed. 'Did you just come here to offer your valeting services?'

'No. I've come here for two reasons: one, to help you, and two, to ask you to help me.'

Stanley nodded. 'I see. Bit of quid pro quo, is it?'

'Actually, no,' said Mrs Harnforth. 'I know you desperately want to track down the thing that attacked you, to prove to your estranged wife that your version of events is true. In that regard, I can tell you the creature you're looking for is called a Balarig. As you've experienced, it's a nasty beast that essentially works in a similar way to a black widow spider. If your wife had not interrupted you when she did, rest assured you would have experienced one of the most excruciating deaths imaginable. Unfortunately, Balarigs are masters of camouflage. The good news is there may be a way of tracking this one.' She reached into the other inside pocket of her jacket and produced a business card. 'This is the number of a gentleman called Jackie Rodriguez.'

'It says here he's a painter and decorator?'

'He is,' she agreed. 'A fair to middling one. He is also the finest tracker I've ever seen.'

'And let me guess – he'll help me if I help you?'

Mrs Harnforth shook her head. 'No. He will help you because I have asked him to help you. You really are a terribly suspicious person, Stanley.'

'I can't think why.' He studied the card again then met her gaze. 'So, what do you want my help with?'

'I find myself in the unusual position of needing to conduct an investigation. I mean, I have done many investigations, of a sort, but none quite like this. I would like to avail of your particular expertise.'

'And what expertise would that be?'

'I need someone who can find things out and who is prepared to circumvent the law in order to do so. Someone with a finely honed ability to identify points of weakness and how to take advantage of them. In short, I need you to be you, Stanley.'

He sighed. 'To be honest, I'm thoroughly sick of being me.'

'Well then, here's the good news – you will do the kind of things you have been doing for quite some time now, but on this occasion you'll be on the side of the angels.'

'Does that side pay well?'

Mrs Harnforth's laughter was soft and melodious. 'Depends how you define it. Not to rush you, but I'm afraid we're up against it, so I need you to start on this right away.'

Stanley tapped the business card against his knee.

'Stanley?'

'I'm thinking.'

'I'm sure you are,' said Mrs Harnforth, 'but that wasn't my question.' She pointed in the direction of a man exiting the offices opposite. 'I'm not the world's most avid TV watcher but isn't that whatshisname from that thing?'

Stanley looked at the man getting into the BMW, down at the business card and then back up again. 'That . . . is none of your business.'

CHAPTER 5

Banecroft had met Betty only a matter of minutes ago, but had already assembled quite a substantial list of things about her that irritated him. Leaving aside the fact that she had turned up to his meeting unannounced, seeming to appear from literally nowhere (something he found intensely annoying and had caused him to fall on his arse in front of his staff, which was more annoying still), she had then gone on to contradict him, overrule him and finally call his bluff. She had done all of that while eating a satsuma and failing to offer him or anyone else a single segment. Banecroft couldn't abide bad manners, at least not in other people.

As if that litany wasn't enough, she had given her name as Elizabeth Cavendish the Third. Banecroft had never met anybody of whom he felt the world needed two further iterations. Yes, Reggie styled himself as Reginald Fairfax the Third, but that was so obviously an affectation adopted by someone who had changed their name in order to leave a former life behind, that Banecroft let it slide. There probably wasn't even one Reginald Fairfax.

He allowed her to enter his office first, and she managed to reach his desk and pick up Chekhov before he had even closed the door. He added her possession of an annoying burst of speed to the list.

'Please do not touch things you do not understand.'

'What a terrible principle,' said Betty, not looking up from turning Chekhov over in her hands. 'How are you supposed to gain an understanding of something without touching it?'

'That is a valuable weapon.'

'Oh, I know,' she replied. 'It's a Balander Blunderbuss. Magnificent piece of engineering. That's why it's a shame to see it being kept in such shoddy condition.'

He snatched the firearm from her hands. 'Are you trying to annoy me?'

She held up a hand in mock defence as she sat down on the opposite side of the desk. 'I can't see how I would need to. Being annoyed appears to be your default setting.'

'On the contrary,' offered Banecroft. 'I have a gloriously sunny disposition. It's just that nothing good has happened in quite some time to set it off.'

'Dear oh dear, let's do something about that right now.' Betty pulled a brown paper bag from one of the pockets of her wax jacket and held it out. 'Would sir care for a jelly baby?'

'No.'

She gave the bag an encouraging jiggle. 'Are you sure? I've never seen anyone look angry while enjoying a jelly baby. It simply cannot be done.'

'Thanks, but I'd rather stay angry.'

Betty raised her eyebrows. 'Interesting statement that, don't you think? A man could do worse than ruminate on it.'

'Oh, good God,' he said, sitting down and placing the blunderbuss on the ground behind him, well out of Betty's reach, 'save us all from the amateur psychoanalysis.'

She withdrew the bag and dived her other hand into it. 'Fine. Have it your way.' She fished out an orange jelly baby and popped it in her mouth.

'It doesn't appear I'm going to have anything my way. And I should say thank you for gatecrashing my meeting and attempting to humiliate me in front of my staff.'

Betty placed a hand to her mouth and swallowed. 'That was certainly not my intention. However, if you expect people to cower in the face of this spiteful demigod act you have going on, you should anticipate coming a cropper every now and then. Some of us aren't easily intimidated, I'm afraid.'

'In which case, can I ask what it is that you do? More specifically, as you are apparently my new assistant editor, am I allowed to ask what your experience is in the newspaper business?'

'Well, I've bought a few over the years – copies of papers, I mean. In truth, not that many recently, but then it's rather a dying medium, isn't it?'

'It is,' agreed Banecroft. 'Personally, I think it's been going downhill ever since they started to allow individuals with no idea about newspapers to hold positions of power within the management structure.'

'Touché,' said Betty with a grin. 'I knew if you kept plugging away, you'd land a shot eventually. Well done.'

'Thank you.'

'And your point is well taken. While I'm happy to muck in and help anywhere I can, I certainly do not have your expertise, or even that of Reginald, Ox, Grace or Stella.'

Banecroft tilted his head at this.

Betty widened her eyes in innocence. 'It's just good manners to learn the names of the people you shall be working with.'

'I was about to ask how you knew them, but let me guess – Grace is still emailing reports to Mrs Harnforth?'

'Indeed she is. She has quite an interesting writing style.'

'I am familiar with it. Like a gossip columnist with Tourette's whose tic is to randomly name-check Jesus.'

Betty bobbed her head and chuckled. 'That's spot on. Can I ask, is Stanley Roker working here now?'

'On a freelance basis. I was going to change that, but the position I was considering him for has gone to someone far less qualified.'

Betty favoured him with a broad grin. 'An underqualified woman being promoted over a man. What a refreshing reversal of the norm.'

'To be fair, our previous assistant editor was female, but she proved to be . . . Seeing as you're now the assistant editor, can you come up with alternative word choices for "disloyal" and "flaky"?'

This earned Banecroft a raise of Betty's bushy eyebrows. 'You pretend otherwise, but her departure has really bothered you, hasn't it?'

'Back to this, are we? Would you like me to lie down on a couch, Dr Freud?'

'No, but a shower wouldn't go amiss.'

Banecroft folded his arms. 'You seem to be under the false impression that your duties include acting as my mammy. They don't.'

In response, Betty stretched out her arms and yawned. It was one of those full-bodied yawns that stops conversation dead until its completion. Banecroft had no choice but to sit there and endure it. He considered reaching his hand into his desk drawer for his bottle of whiskey, but he hesitated. He then got annoyed with himself for doing so.

Once she'd finally finished, Betty smacked her lips and rolled her head around her neck. 'Oh, speaking of my duties, Mrs Harnforth has also asked me to carry out a full audit.'

'Excuse me?'

Betty stared into her bag of jelly babies as she spoke. 'Off the top of your head, could you tell me whether this paper made a profit or a loss last month?'

'Neither. It broke even.'

She nodded appreciatively. 'Well done. Not on being correct, as you most certainly are not, but on being able to lie straight to someone's face like that, without deviation or hesitation. It's quite a skill. Would you like to take another guess?'

'I'm afraid we've all been rather too busy to spend the requisite amount of time counting pennies. Something you would have no appreciation of, I'm sure.'

'Let's see – you foiled the attempts of a rogue member of the Founders to usher his son into the ranks of the immortals, and had to defeat a Were as well as a demented practitioner in the process. Then, a few months later, you thwarted the scheme of a bothersome little cult to kidnap one of your employees while simultaneously dealing with an outbreak of vampirism – something that did not exist until a rather despicable group of internet daters and an ancient power colluded to create it. A busy week, that one. Have I left anything out?'

'We also had the bathroom redone.'

Betty tilted her head to the side. 'Of course you did. My apologies. Would now be a good time to give you a second chance at that jelly baby?'

'No.'

'Have it your way. So yes, in answer to your sort-of question, I understand what you had to deal with and, let us say, the "altered world" in which you now find yourself operating. Given the circumstances, rest assured that Mrs Harnforth doesn't expect you to be making an obscene profit. She would, however, like to stem the bleeding enough for this place to burn money slowly instead of it going up in flames all at once.'

'Lesson one,' said Banecroft. 'That is what is known as a mixed metaphor.'

'Indeed it is. Well spotted.'

'Although, speaking of blazing infernos, the electrics in this decrepit old church are so fried that it's only a matter of time before we have one on our hands. In the meantime, the lights staying on is not something we can take for granted. Thus far, a stoned Rastafarian with a wrench has somehow managed to fix things, but we may need to find a more permanent solution.'

'Ah yes, Manny – I'm looking forward to meeting him.'

'Do so at the right time in his . . . let's call it his "relaxation cycle"' – Banecroft caught himself doing the bunny ears – 'and he'll be thrilled with your offer of a jelly baby.'

'I'm sure that can be arranged. I will be chatting to everyone, as Mrs Harnforth asked me to take a look-see at how the entire operation is running.'

Banecroft picked up a pen from his desk and tossed it down again. 'So, to put it in layman's terms – you are going to come in here to poke your nose around in my business and second guess everything I do?'

Betty wobbled her head from side to side and pursed her lips. 'Not everything. Although I have to say, from the little I've seen, it looks like staff morale could be improved.'

'You should have seen how miserable they were before we upgraded the bathroom.'

'I'm sure. Given that, it seems even more surprising that your previous assistant editor left so suddenly.'

Banecroft leaned back in his chair, threw out his arms and spoke loudly to the ceiling. 'For the last time, it is not my fault if a wronged woman inexplicably decides to return to the narcissistic jackal in heat to whom she is married. If there is anyone at fault for that, there's a certain detective inspector in the local constabulary that I'd like to have sworn in.'

'Yes. One DI Tom Sturgess, I believe.'

Banecroft eyed her suspiciously. 'You really are very well informed. Grace has been working overtime.'

'With that in mind,' replied Betty, 'is there anything else you think I should know?'

Instinctively, Banecroft's mind alighted on the image of the ghostly form of Simon Brush sitting at a desk in the bullpen during the wee small hours. 'No.'

Betty gave him a penetrating look, which he found disconcerting. It was as if she were trying to read his mind. 'Are you sure?'

'I'm not here to do your job for you,' he responded. 'Although, seeing as it is apparent you have no idea how to be the assistant editor of a newspaper, I'd imagine I will end up doing just that.'

She stood up and gave him a broad smile. 'I think you'll be pleasantly surprised. I'm a quick learner and nothing much gets by me.'

'How reassuring.'

'Now,' she said, 'unless there is anything else, I think I should go about finding myself a desk and introducing myself to the rest of the team.'

'No. That's it, at least until I get hold of Mrs Harnforth directly, and she and I will have a very frank conversation, I assure you.'

'Do give her my best.' Betty walked towards the door but turned back as Banecroft spoke again.

'Actually . . .'

'Yes?'

'I think I will take that jelly baby now.'

'Too late,' she said with a grin, before slamming the door closed behind her.

He really did not like that woman.

CHAPTER 6

Tamsin Baladin's head shot up and she glowered at Dr Carter across the table. Her reaction was the result of Dr Carter's failure to stifle the irritating giggle for which she was known.

'I fail to see what is funny here,' Tamsin scowled.

'Oh, sweetie, I'm afraid it's you.'

'Excuse me?'

Dr Carter leaned back in her chair and skittered her fingernails across the highly polished desktop. 'You are a very intelligent woman, Tamsin, but you do suffer from the affliction that comes with it – namely, an underappreciation of the fact that other people are intelligent too. Vincent Banecroft is many things—'

'Chief among them – by your own admission, Doctor – a belligerent drunk.'

Dr Carter nodded. 'He is that, yes, but crucially, he is not only that. And it is worth remembering who he was before he was that.'

'A tabloid editor,' said Tamsin, making no effort to keep the disdain from her voice.

'Correction – *the* tabloid editor. He may not have had the highest circulation or the blah blah blah, but his was the paper that put the fear of God into those in power. Celebrity gossip and voyeuristic titillation might be what gets eyes on the newspaper, but he was always the one determined to do something with that attention once he'd got it. Do you have any idea how many ex-government ministers have Banecroft to thank for the *ex* part?'

'That's as maybe,' responded the younger woman, 'but he is now the editor of a two-bit weekly rag that reports on UFOs over Birkenhead and a haunted toilet in Falkirk.'

'Yes,' agreed Dr Carter, 'and I bet he still spotted your little Trojan-horse candidate for the role of assistant editor before he'd even sat down.'

'But Tristram was perfect for the role!'

Dr Carter giggled again, which earned her a second dirty look. 'Tristram? Really? You sent in someone called Tristram? You might want to take another look at that psychological profile.'

Tamsin folded her arms across her chest and Dr Carter saw a brief glimpse of what the woman must've been like as a child. She would bet everything she had that the word 'headstrong' had appeared repeatedly in her school reports.

Dr Carter liked Tamsin Baladin. No, that wasn't right. Dr Carter did not dislike Tamsin Baladin. While it had not been her idea to bring her into the organization, she could understand it. Tamsin was the CEO of Fuzzy Britches, the dating app-cum-social media empire that she and her brother had built from scratch. After the brother's creepy little side project had brought the pair to the attention of the Founders, the Council had decided that the sister could be very useful. There wasn't a company in the world that could hire Tamsin Baladin, but then the

Founders were offering her something far more enticing than mere financial gain. They were offering power. Real power. And, if Tamsin played her cards right, eternal life.

A long time ago, Dr Carter had taken the exact same deal. So while she neither liked nor disliked Tamsin Baladin, she loved what she represented. Yes, the woman had skills that they needed to assist them in their management of the modern world, but she was also being trained up to be Dr Carter's eventual replacement.

It had taken a long time – too long – but Carter was now finally at the head of the queue to become a fully fledged Founder. It was so close she could taste it. She'd got so used to feeling nothing that the giddy sensation of anticipation was unnerving. Soon, she'd no longer look in the mirror each morning and see a lesser version of herself than had been there the day before.

There were still issues to resolve, of course, but the path was becoming clear. When her day finally came, she would no longer have to spend hour after hour holding back the tide of time. Death itself would be cheated, and she would step away from managing the array of challenges that the Founders had to perpetually deal with in order to achieve their twin goals of secrecy and control. Some day soon, the Banecrofts of this world would be somebody else's problem. Not that there really were Banecrofts, plural. She'd say this for the man – he was his own unique little problem.

A red light above a large monitor on the wall of the office flashed to indicate an incoming call. Dr Carter turned to Tamsin. 'Remember the rules – only speak when spoken to, and I will handle everything else.'

Tamsin nodded.

Dr Carter turned her chair to face the screen and spoke in a clear voice. 'Answer call.'

The screen remained blank, but the light turned green to show the camera was now on. As always with these calls, the man at the other end remained unseen.

She forced a smile and bowed her head. 'Good afternoon, sire.'

'Is it?' barked the gruff voice at the other end. 'Let's see about that. I believe you were attempting to infiltrate *The Stranger Times*?'

Dr Carter and Tamsin shared a look of surprise. They had not informed him about that.

'That is correct, sire. I'm afraid it proved unsuccessful.'

'What? How?'

'As I've mentioned previously,' began Dr Carter, 'Vincent Banecroft is as difficult as he is unpredictable. It appears he sniffed out Tamsin's candidate.' She'd be damned if she was going to take the blame for what had not been her idea.

The disembodied voice made a noise somewhere between a sigh and a growl. 'So be it. Miss Baladin, how goes your training?'

'Very well, sire,' replied Tamsin. 'In fact, I feel I could take on more.'

'Yes, yes. Everyone always believes that. You will do what we tell you to do.'

Tamsin blushed. Dr Carter suppressed a smile. She could see her young apprentice was still not used to being spoken to in this manner.

'Of course.'

'And the situation with your brother?'

Tamsin tensed visibly. While she was useful, the Council

members considered her sibling to be somewhere between an embarrassment and an abomination. 'He is responding very well to treatment,' she managed hoarsely.

'Is he?' The voice sounded far from convinced. 'He certainly needs to.'

Having found himself on the wrong side of an ancient power, Tamsin's brother had turned the myth of the vampire into a reality when he was transformed into one himself. Seeing as the archetype came into being as an allegory for the Founders, one they profoundly hated, his existence was not something they were pleased about.

Tamsin cleared her throat. 'Regarding *The Stranger Times* problem, sire, I believe I may have identified another point of weakness.'

'We have no interest in following one failure with another. Although that bloody man is a nuisance.'

'He is,' agreed Dr Carter, keen to regain control of the conversation, 'but, as I previously mentioned, a useful one. Banecroft and his team assisted with the Roxy situation, and the Moretti problem before that.'

'Yes, Doctor, I am well aware of that. I am also aware that we engage and expect *you* to fulfil that helpful role, not some loose-cannon hack over whom we have no control. On a related note, I have spoken with the Council and raised your concerns about your recent visitor, and we are all in agreement. What he has planned does not constitute a breach of the Accord.'

Dr Carter leaned forward, too taken by surprise to keep the irritation from her voice. 'But, sire, how can it not?'

'Are you questioning the Council?'

'No, but sire—'

'But nothing. The decision has been made. You work for us. The Accord makes provision for direct interference only, and this is no different from your feeble attempt to infiltrate. Our guest is to be given every help.'

Dr Carter bowed her head and cursed silently to herself. 'Of course, sire. I apologize. I meant only that might be difficult given the . . . history.'

'Hmmmm . . . There is that. You're not exactly the man's favourite person.'

'All I did was carry out the Council's wishes, sire.'

'I am aware of that. Doesn't make you any more popular, though, does it?'

Dr Carter ran the tip of her tongue over her lips, desperately trying to think of a new angle, but she wasn't quick enough.

'I would be honoured to assist our guest in any way possible, my lord,' said Tamsin, earning her a glare from Dr Carter.

'I don't think that would be a good idea, sire—'

'Well, I do,' responded the voice. 'We need Miss Baladin to get out there and get her hands dirty. This is an excellent opportunity for her to do just that.'

'But—'

'But nothing,' snapped the voice. 'It is decided. Now, if you'll excuse me, I have a tee time.'

Dr Carter opened her mouth to speak, but the light on top of the monitor returned to red, signalling that the call was over. She spun her chair to look at Tamsin. 'What the hell do you think you're doing?'

'What?'

'Oh, please. Spare me the batting-your-eyelashes act. I virtually invented it. You know damn well what. I told you not to speak unless spoken to, and not to get involved.'

Tamsin shrugged. 'There was a problem, I offered to help. That's all.'

Dr Carter got to her feet and strode towards the door, shaking her head as she went. She placed a hand on the door handle but stopped and turned around.

'Word to the wise, Miss Baladin. Be careful what you wish for.'

Gone in a Flash

A Californian start-up is offering people a brand-new life, albeit only for a couple of seconds. As CEO Albert Graft explains, 'It is widely believed that in the moments before death, your whole life flashes before your eyes. However, what if you don't want to see your life again? At FlashLife Inc., we can implant a chip in your head that will be activated when it determines your vital signs are failing. It will then play highlights from an entirely different life to the one you've led.

'The idea is that the client gets a much-needed boost in self-esteem right before they shuffle off this mortal coil. Who doesn't want to remember themselves feeding starving children, having had a movie-star career or saving the planet rather than mis-selling insurance or defending chemical companies from illegal dumping?'

The scheme is not without controversy, however, as critics claim that many of the new-life options are drawn from the lives of real-life individuals. Lawyer Wilbur Willis says, 'It is an obvious violation of copyright. Greta Thunberg's life is Greta Thunberg's life, and she hasn't given permission for it to be put into the head of an arms dealer from Belgium.'

Theologians are also worried, given how the afterlife is more over-worked than ever. There is a real risk that the ethereal plane's equivalent of border control staff might quickly view a deceased soul's highlight reel to determine its destination, rather than running the proper checks.

CHAPTER 7

It took every ounce of Hannah's self-control not to reach across the desk and touch the face of the man sitting opposite her. As he flipped back and forth through the mountain of paperwork she had spent the best part of half an hour filling out, his expression was unreadable, but that could have been because he only had the one.

To describe his skin as 'smooth' didn't begin to do it justice. It looked as if he had never laughed or frowned in his entire existence. There wasn't a single wrinkle, blemish or sign of life anywhere on his face. He was like one of those toys that grown men collect and keep in mint condition by never taking them out of the box. She wanted to squeeze his cheeks, to see what they felt like, and also to confirm her suspicion that they would spring back into place immediately, possibly accompanied by a pinging sound.

Anton was of average height, slim build, with tightly cropped blonde locks over an olive complexion. It was impossible to tell if his skin colouring was natural or acquired, and his voice offered no clues. It was one of those accents that didn't belong to anywhere; you got it out of a sheer bloody-minded desire to have it.

She'd previously heard it only from maître d's in restaurants where the name of the establishment was just a symbol, and shop assistants in the kinds of clothes stores where the garments didn't carry price tags.

His teeth were perfect white veneers that made you realize that actual teeth are all some variant of off-white. His outfit was a black jumper with white slim-fit trousers – the same colour combination worn by every other member of staff at the Pinter Institute. It was a kind of uniformity without being an actual uniform, which felt somehow more oppressive. A uniform is just a uniform, something to indicate to guests that you are staff and not supposed to be enjoying yourself in any way. Everyone turning up to work as if they've chosen to dress similarly felt like one of those creepy matching-outfit couples had somehow become contagious. The only sliver of individuality Anton displayed was an odd-looking necklace made from smooth stones of various colours.

He finally looked up from the sheaf of documents and gave what was the closest thing he probably ever came to a smile. 'Are you sure you are OK now?'

'I'm fine,' lied Hannah, still drowning in the embarrassment of her pratfall landing upon arrival at the Institute.

'Very good. So, you're here to save your marriage?'

'No,' said Hannah truthfully. 'I'm here to take some time and decide whether I want to.'

Anton nodded his head sagely. 'Yes, yes, yes. I understand completely. All we ask you to do is embrace the process. We here at the PI pride ourselves on combining techniques drawn from ancient wisdom with cutting-edge science and highly developed psychoanalysis therapy to provide each person with a boutique experience customized to their every need. The mind, the body, the soul – each is equally important to the PI path.'

Hannah could actually hear the trademark symbol being added to the end of that statement.

'Just to remind you of the guidelines we have to maximize your experience. No communication with the outside world is allowed, so all mobile phones and any other devices must be left here, please, to be returned to you on your departure. All celebrants must wear the casual loungewear provided, unless receiving our spa treatments, for which we provide swimwear. They are all tailored to your body's needs, but do, of course, let us know *immediately* if there is even the slightest issue.'

The way he delivered this information, with heavy emphasis on the word 'immediately', you could be mistaken for thinking that slightly uncomfortable jogging bottoms could prove fatal.

'We, of course, encourage you to socialize with other celebrants where appropriate. We do, however, forbid any physical intimacy as it would interfere with the process.'

'Absolutely,' agreed Hannah. 'Plus, if I'm here to save my marriage, I probably shouldn't be bonking about the place.' She smiled at Anton to convey she was aiming for levity. The utterly blank expression she received in return made it abundantly clear that she had missed the mark.

'As I'm sure you know,' he continued, 'Winona Pinter is a wonderfully warm and caring person. She has a deep and abiding love of people. Having said that, she is also intensely private, so we would ask that if you come into proximity with her, do not speak to her unless she speaks to you first, keep eye contact to an absolute minimum, and there should be no physical contact of any kind under any circumstances.'

'Right. I might just play it safe and curl up into a ball if she enters the room.'

'Please do not do that. Winona may find it upsetting.'

The thought flitted across Hannah's mind that perhaps Anton was some form of artificial intelligence. It would explain his interpersonal skills, but not his overall look. If he were a robot, his creators would have made more of an effort to make him look human.

'Finally, I must remind you that stimulants of any kind are forbidden here, as we find they stop celebrants from really engaging with the moment.'

'Right,' said Hannah. 'Of course. I mean, not always, though . . .'

'I'm sorry?'

'Stimulants . . .' she continued, silently cursing her inability to keep her mouth shut when nervous. 'Look at conga lines.'

Anton's eyebrows rose the maximum amount they were able to – a centimetre. 'I don't follow.'

'Take conga lines, for example. There's something that nobody over the age of sixteen who isn't enjoying a stimulant – typically booze – engages in. Have you ever witnessed a sober conga line?'

Hannah worried Anton might do himself an injury as he attempted to rearrange his face into the expression of confusion he was clearly going for.

'Do you know what? Never mind. Just an idle thought. So, you should probably show me to your room – shit, I mean my room. My room. I meant my room. You and I should just be friends.' Hannah was actively considering falling on her face again. It was better than allowing herself to talk.

'Yes,' said Anton, in answer to no question. 'We must get a move on.' He looked at his watch. 'You are scheduled for your welcome colonic irrigation in twenty minutes, and we can't be late.'

'Right-o,' said Hannah, attempting to sound positive. 'No. Can't be late. Don't want to cause that to get backed up. I mean . . . If you don't mind, I'm going to stop talking for a bit.'

Anton nodded. 'As you wish.'

'Super.'

CHAPTER 8

Stanley Roker was all too familiar with disdain. After all, he had been a tabloid journalist for most of his adult life. A few years ago, there had been a newspaper article based on a survey that found tabloid hack to be the most disliked profession in Britain, comfortably beating lawyer, drug dealer, traffic warden – even politician. Not that it meant it was true, of course – the article had been in a newspaper.

Even among Stanley's journalist brethren, there were those who looked down their noses at him. He was known for specializing in the down and dirty. No scoop too low, no target off-limits, no depth to which he was unwilling to sink.

At that very moment he was being viewed not so much with disdain, as with suspicion verging on aggression. He was an un-identified lone man wandering round a children's play area. He couldn't blame the other adults present for glaring at him. He knew the world was full of monsters, even more so than they realized.

The sun was out and the playground was packed. Children were running about in the fading rays of summer accompanied by a cacophony of their excited squeals and shouts. Stanley found the noise grating but he appeared to be the only one. The parents standing chatting in groups seemed entirely oblivious. Clearly, you either built up an immunity to the din over time, or you just went deaf and were happy for it.

As he moved around the yellow-and-blue perimeter fencing, past the largest congregation of kids playing some elaborate game on the climbing frames that seemed to involve mostly arguing about the rules, he finally spotted the person he was looking for. The faux leopard-skin top was the giveaway; she had always had a penchant for animal print.

Cathy Quirke must have been mid-fifties by now and looked good on it; a grandmother among the group of mostly mothers with the occasional dad thrown in. Even from a distance, you could see the respect she commanded. People's eyes were naturally drawn to her, judging her reaction to whatever was being said. They wouldn't even know they were doing it. Cathy Quirke was just a natural born leader. Stanley had known that the first time he had laid eyes on her.

When she finally clocked him, her face dropped for the briefest of moments, but she recovered quickly. Stanley was also very used to people not being happy to see him. He passed the gate to the playground where a young boy, his face encrusted with chocolate and God knows what else, was being led out howling and screaming by a woman who looked like she was seriously regretting her historic contraceptive choices. Stanley parked himself on the bench the duo had just vacated and waited.

For the want of something to do, he pulled out the angling magazine he now carried with him everywhere and started reading. He had never been fishing and had no actual interest in the subject, but he'd picked up the magazine on the advice of his GP. Stanley's job meant he spent an enormous amount of time waiting and watching. In the past, he had filled the hours by eating, but it hadn't taken a trained physician to tell him he was a heart attack waiting to happen. Reading a newspaper was out and books were a no-go as the material couldn't be something that required sustained attention. And so the magazine it was. He occupied himself reading about men he didn't know, attempting to catch fish he didn't care about, for reasons he couldn't comprehend.

After a couple of minutes, somebody sat down beside him.

'Cathy, you're looking well.'

'Thanks, Stanley. There's a dead dog on the green over there that looks healthier than you do.'

He shifted on the bench. 'You were always direct.'

She pulled a packet of cigarettes out of her pocket and offered him one.

'Thanks. I don't.'

Cathy drew one out and lit it in a fluid motion. 'You look that bad, maybe you should start.'

'I don't remember you being this mean.'

She gave a humourless laugh. 'Well, maybe if you'd remembered that the last time we spoke, when you swore it would be the last time we spoke, I'd be in a sunnier mood. Having said that, when did she leave you?'

Stanley turned his head and looked at her properly for the first time. 'How did you even know I was married?'

'From what I recall of that last time I saw you – when again, not to harp on about it, we said it was going to be the very, very last time – you didn't look like this, and it's only been a couple of years. No wife, even if she hates his guts, is going to let her husband leave the house looking like you do, and anyone who has been single for longer than that time and is doing as bad a job of taking care of themselves as you seem to be, would be dead by now.'

Stanley folded his magazine and shoved it back in the pocket of his coat. 'You should look for a gig as one of those motivational speakers, Cathy. I think you're a natural. By the way, see that sign up there on the fence? This is a no-smoking area.'

Cathy blithely took another puff. 'If it weren't for me, they would have levelled this playground last year and we'd be sitting in the middle of a distribution centre for a car parts company. You want to bet anyone here is going to come over and ask me to put it out?'

'You were always very good at rallying support.'

'Yeah,' she agreed, flicking away some ash. 'Speaking of which, as far as anybody over there is concerned, I've come over here to check if you're a wrong 'un or not. Want to see how quickly I can get you chased out of here with pitchforks and torches?'

'This isn't what you think it is.'

'Well, if you've come here to ask me out, you probably should have made more of an effort.'

'Now, that's just cruel.'

'We first met because you were blackmailing me, Stanley.' Cathy's conversational tone dropped for a second, and an undercurrent of anger slipped through. 'Even Tom Hanks is going to struggle to make this into a feel-good rom-com moment.'

'I just . . . That little girl waving at us from the monkey bars. Is that your Sean's daughter?'

'Don't you—'

Stanley put his hand up. 'Honestly, I meant nothing by that. I'm not here to threaten you or go back on our previous agreement.'

Cathy scoffed. 'I think you'll find that just by being here you've already broken our previous agreement.'

'All right. Look, I get it. You've got no reason to trust me. Just hear me out and then, if you want me to, I'll disappear and you'll never hear from me again.'

She took another drag on her cigarette and sighed out the smoke through clenched teeth. 'Fine.'

The next words out of Stanley's mouth surprised him. 'For what it's worth, I'm sorry.'

Cathy leaned forward and investigated his face intently. 'Seriously, have you got six months to live or something?'

'No,' replied Stanley. 'Let's just say a lot has happened, and life has got pretty weird. I'm starting to feel like some of my chickens are coming home to roost.'

Cathy dropped her cigarette, stubbed it out with her shoe, and then picked it up again. 'Not to change the subject or anything, but does that saying make much sense to you? Don't people want their chickens to come home? In what situation do people want them going out into the big bad world to make a life for themselves?'

'No idea,' admitted Stanley. 'And, I promise this is just a question and not anything else, but how is Sean?'

'He's fine. Working as a builder now, would you believe? But he likes it. Couldn't get a job in IT for love nor money after everything that happened – not that he particularly wanted one. He doesn't even own a computer now.'

Stanley nodded. A hacking conviction would make most employers nervous. Sean's case had made the national press. Cathy had made sure it did. He'd been a newly minted university graduate when Special Branch had broken down the door to his mum's house at 5 a.m., arrested him on suspicion of being the hacker they had dubbed Hamlet (for reasons nobody understood) and dragged him away in handcuffs.

The charges being brought against him were several incidents of what the press dubbed 'hacktivism'. Among those incidents were posting proof that a major British bank was laundering money for the cartels; that a car manufacturer knew its SUVs were fitted with untrustworthy airbags; and that a prominent government minister was really doing the job part-time around his massive lobbying interests, while his Cayman Islands bank account grew fat.

Certain members of the press were all set to hold Sean Quirke up as a modern-day Robin Hood, but there was a problem with that narrative; namely, that the man in question maintained in the strongest terms that he was entirely innocent and knew nothing about these hacks. The government, on the other hand, claimed they were in possession of circumstantial evidence that proved beyond a reasonable doubt that they had the right man.

On one side, the might of the Crown Prosecution Service was being directed by a government keen to make a point. On the other, a confused young man and a mother willing to do anything to vindicate her only son.

Strangely, it was Sean's fanatical support of Manchester United that had proved to be his salvation. When the defence had finally managed to get hold of some of the information the government had redacted, it had been noted that a couple of the hacks had taken place when United had been playing at home. Initially, the defence had produced witnesses that backed up Sean's attendance at the games as a season-ticket holder, but that had been rebuffed, with the admittedly weak assertion that witnesses could be mistaken or that Sean had sent a lookalike in his place. Following an appeal, hundreds of photographs from the two fixtures in question were sent in by members of the public, and Sean's presence had been verified in several of them. Once Cathy had enlisted the help of a few footballers and an ever-increasing band of celebrities, the Crown Prosecution Service had seen which way the wind was blowing and dropped the case.

As far as almost everyone was concerned, that had been where the story had ended. It could only have been Stanley, searching for the unseen angle as always, who had come up with a surprising revelation. People just fill in the blanks, you see; they see what they expect to see. It had never occurred to anyone that while they undoubtedly had the wrong man, they had the right family.

A middle-aged single mum who had left school at sixteen, worked nights as a security guard at a bus depot and still lived on the sink estate where she'd been born. That didn't fit the profile at all. It was pure fluke that Stanley met one of the night cleaners at the depot, who mentioned how Cathy was always reading computer books. He had played a hunch, caught Cathy in a moment of weakness and she had confirmed the truth. She was Hamlet. If the appeal had failed, she was going to confess all. The only reason she hadn't before now was that she'd guessed, probably correctly, that the CPS would try to nail it on both of them.

Stanley had weighed it up. On one hand, it was a helluva story, but that story involved turning in a woman who had become something of a national hero. No paper would want to run it and the possibility of being caught in a backlash was real and considerable. On the other hand, assuming Cathy was someone who learned from her mistakes, she and her skill set could be an invaluable asset. And so she had proven to be.

After the demands of her previous hacks, the private email accounts of famous faces and their agents were a walk in the park. Cathy, complaining bitterly, had done Stanley's bidding – at least for a while. Then she had presented Stanley with evidence of everything she had done for him and explained that if he was ever to take her down, he would be going down with her. And that was how they had left it. It was also why Stanley no longer trusted technology.

Cathy lit herself another cigarette and then shifted her weight on the bench. 'Should I be asking if you're wearing a wire?'

Stanley shrugged. 'You and I, Cathy, we've got the luxury of mutually assured destruction. You're welcome to frisk me if you'd like.'

'No offence, but I'll pass. Delightful though I'm sure the experience would be.'

'Before we get to why I'm here,' said Stanley, 'can I ask the one question I've always wanted to know the answer to?'

'You can ask,' she replied. 'Doesn't mean I'll answer.'

'All you've done. All you're capable of doing. You took no money for yourself, did you?'

'No,' she said firmly, sounding genuinely offended. 'I'm not a thief. I've not got much, but what I have, I got honestly.'

Stanley nodded. 'You know, Cathy, you might be the most moral person I've ever met.'

Despite herself, she laughed. 'Don't get me wrong, but seeing as you're probably the most immoral person I've ever met, that might not be the big compliment you think it is. It's been fun catching up, Stanley, but while I hate rushing you, little Keeley has a dentist appointment this afternoon.'

Stanley pulled out his phone, which still had a pair of earphones attached to it. 'I need you to listen to a recording of a phone call.'

Cathy looked round then held out her hand. 'OK, you've got me a little curious.'

He handed her the earphones and once she'd put them in, he played her the one-minute-and-twenty-seven-seconds audio file.

When it was finished, Cathy took out the earbuds and gave him a disappointed look. 'Not gonna lie – pretty big anti-climax, Stanley.'

'Tell me exactly what you heard.'

Cathy gave him a little side-eye, then said, 'Somebody called

Thomas Mandeville – sounded like a posh old duffer – doing some phone banking, moving three hundred grand from one account to another. I'm guessing when you're doing that, the bank probably doesn't leave you on hold as long as mine does.'

'But *how* exactly does he do it?'

'I'm no expert—'

'Yes, you are,' interjected Stanley.

'But . . . Fairly standard stuff for high-value transactions. Man gives a password, gives an identifying number, and then they use voice recognition with all that "my voice is my password" stuff. Gives the date and then repeats the phrase, "May I have a cup of tea and a slice of cake, please." Those phrases are chosen at random too, you know – prevents anyone from using a sophisticated recording. The bit of chit-chat about the weather at the start, by the way – not strictly chit-chat. Another little step in verifying that they're talking to a real person. All standard security in high-end banking.'

'That's exactly what it was,' confirmed Stanley.

'Again, big deal.'

'Now,' said Stanley, 'what would you say if I told you that Thomas Mandeville died two days before that call took place?'

Despite herself, a smile played across Cathy Quirke's lips. 'That's impossible.'

'That's what my employer thinks too, but she's willing to pay you a good fee and guarantee your anonymity if you're willing to help us prove it.'

Cathy reared back and gave Stanley an assessing look. 'Your

employer? Why do I get the impression this isn't just another story?'

'Because it isn't. So, what do you say? Fancy looking into some twenty-first-century grave-robbing?'

He could see that she was tempted. 'I don't want to make another deal with the devil.'

'I know you don't have any reason to believe me, but on this one, I'm actually on the side of the angels.'

Cathy ran her tongue over her teeth and tapped a finger on the metal bench. 'Stanley Roker on the side of the angels,' she said finally. 'How does that feel to you?'

'Weird.'

'Yeah, I imagine it does.'

CHAPTER 9

Grace stood up and stretched out her aching back with a groan. Then, she picked up the tiny watering can she kept behind her workspace and gave Phillip, the eucalyptus plant she had recently added to the desk, a drink. She enjoyed talking to Phillip.

'God bless this mess, Phillip! Somebody dropping from the sky saying we have got to be audited. What a thing. What do I know about accounts? I only do what I do because nobody else will do what I do.'

Banecroft had informed her that Betty had asked to see the last ten years of the paper's accounts, along with all their receipts, as if it were nothing. As if Grace had that kind of thing just lying round the place. Admittedly, she sort of did.

It was Grace's responsibility to take care of petty cash, and to file the invoices and receipts. 'File' was a rather misleading word in the circumstances. There hadn't been any system before she started working there and she had not put one in place. She hated accounts. Just thinking about them made her come out in hives. The best thing about being employed at *The Stranger Times* was that nobody had ever cared about money in and money out; something she had realized after a few weeks on the job.

Now, she kept everything because she knew she had to do that. However, she simply shoved any relevant bits and pieces into a cardboard box, and when that was done, she stashed the box away and started filling a fresh box. Admittedly, this had become a growing issue. Box upon box was now shoved into every cupboard and hidey-hole in the Church of Old Souls, which was home to the offices of *The Stranger Times*. They'd recently found out they had a basement, but that already contained several boxes, so Grace had also filled her garage at home.

She looked down at the ragtag collection of boxes she had extracted from the various spaces in the reception area. They were just the tip of the iceberg, and they looked pretty shoddy, a situation not helped by the fact that a bottle of bleach in the cleaning supplies cupboard had leaked over three of them.

The Stranger Times did have an accountant. Hand on heart, Grace had long suspected that Honest Henry Harper was neither the world's greatest nor most trustworthy of bookkeepers. He had done their accounts for the last few years without asking for any boxes of invoices and receipts, which even Grace knew was shady. She also had a very strong suspicion that truly honest people don't feel the need to pre-modify their name with the word 'honest'.

Straight after Betty's request she had emailed him and received an out-of-office response that had simply read, 'I am away for a period, pending appeal.' She didn't know what that meant, but it did not fill her with confidence. She had the horrible feeling she was on her own with this.

Grace was also worried that, even if she found all her records, they weren't the greatest. There were the couple of times when she had gone to the supermarket to get teabags, instant coffee and biscuits, and had forgotten to get a receipt. To compensate for this, she had taken to shoving the empty packets into the box as proof of purchase. It had seemed like a good idea at the time, but then at the time, Grace had not been expecting somebody to come in and ask to see them.

And then there were Ox's expenses claims. He relied heavily on his illegible handwriting, meaning that Grace couldn't tell what he was claiming for and rarely asked. She reasoned as long as he kept it to a minimum, it all worked out. Admittedly, the fact that a few of the receipts attached to his claims appeared to be scrawled on betting slips from the bookies was something she, again, probably should have cracked down on.

Grace jumped and clutched her chest at the sound of a throat being cleared. She spun round to find a waif-thin woman with pinched features smiling awkwardly at her from the other side of the reception desk. The woman was wearing a green cardigan and a collection of beaded necklaces, which gave her a vaguely hippyish look. A strong smell of lavender accompanied her presence.

'Excuse me. I did not hear you come in,' said Grace.

The one advantage of the creaking floorboards in the building was that it made it virtually impossible for someone to arrive unannounced. At least it had until today. Either Grace was going deaf, or women had started to appear out of thin air.

'Sorry to bother you,' said the woman. 'I'm looking for Hannah Willis?'

'Oh, I'm afraid she is not here.'

'I see.' The woman fiddled with the beads on one of her necklaces. 'Do you know when she'll be back?'

'She actually doesn't work here any more.'

'Really?' said the woman. 'I'm an old friend. She told me to drop in to say hello any time. I thought she loved it here?'

Grace shrugged. 'So did we, but then she left us without even saying goodbye.'

'Gosh,' said the woman, before pushing her long black hair behind her left ear to reveal a long dangly earring that featured the golden silhouette of a rabbit inside a hoop of silver. 'But she's coming back, right?'

There was something about the way she asked the question that Grace didn't like. 'I'd hope so, but it doesn't seem likely.'

The woman leaned forward and lowered her voice slightly. 'Did she give any reason for leaving?'

'You know, it doesn't feel appropriate for me to be talking about this. Give her a ring. I'm sure she will explain it to you if you truly are an old friend.'

The woman's face seemed to harden around her fixed smile. 'Yes,' she said, reaching up to fiddle with her earring. 'I shall discuss it with her, but first I'd like to ask you a few more questions.'

'I don't think . . .'

Grace trailed off as the woman, with a practised twist of her fingers, set the earring spinning at an impossibly fast speed. 'It doesn't really matter what you think.'

★

Grace stared down at the boxes. It was as if she had walked into the room and forgotten what she had come in for. She was roused from her reverie by the sight of Stella's concerned face in her field of vision.

'You OK, Grace?'

She felt rather dazed. 'Yes, I . . . Sorry, I'm fine. I think. Just a bit tired, probably. I might need a nice cup of tea.'

'Sure,' said Stella, before adding with a smile, 'I'm pretty confident you think a nice cup of tea is the solution to most problems. Who was that woman?'

Grace patted her hand against her hair. She couldn't shake feeling rather discombobulated. 'What woman?'

'The woman you were just speaking to.'

She did her best to recall the past few minutes and felt oddly queasy. 'I don't know. I . . .' She blinked a few times as if trying to clear her head. 'I guess I didn't get her name.'

Stella nodded, now looking more worried. 'What did she want?'

As Grace had another go at remembering, all she got was the sickly sensation of her mind prodding an area that was inexplicably empty, like your tongue finding a gap where a tooth should be. 'I . . .' She put a hand against the reception desk to steady herself. 'I'm not . . . I think I need to sit down for a bit. I am feeling quite lightheaded.'

'Right.' Stella nodded at the boxes. 'It's probably from dragging these around,' she said, as she carefully guided Grace into the ergonomic office chair behind the desk. 'You should have just asked me or one of the boys. We'd have done it for you.'

Grace patted Stella's hand. 'Not at all. You are very busy doing your journalism now.'

'I'm never too busy to help you. You stay there, and I'll get you that cup of tea.'

'Thank you, dear.'

Stella gave her one last concerned look before heading across the room towards the kitchenette.

Grace returned her worry with a smile then looked down at her own hands. She stared at the gold of her bracelets and a confused wisp of memory floated across her mind before disappearing into the ether.

CHAPTER 10

Hannah stepped inside the dining room and was instantly struck by a queasy sensation in the pit of her stomach, which was only partly related to how famished she was.

School. That's what the place reminded her of. She had attended an all-girls college run by French nuns, and every time she thought of it, her overwhelming memory was of how exhausting it had been to navigate the ever-changing landscape of cliques, fights and arsenic-laced bitching. When it came to feuds, the Gallagher brothers were amateurs compared to the typical teenage schoolgirl.

The queasy feeling had been triggered by the unwelcome sight of the trio of stick-thin, sour-faced women with whom she had spent most of the day. They were sitting at a table in the corner and stopped talking when she walked in, making no noticeable effort to cover the fact that she had been the topic of their conversation.

The dining room was a mahogany-panelled affair containing about a dozen well-spaced-out tables with booths in two of the corners. A group of four older women was seated on the far side of the room, three men occupied one of the central tables, loudly debating something, while a quartet of solo diners, two men and two women, were at smaller tables either eating, reading, or doing both. Not one person made eye contact with Hannah. She quickly took a seat at the nearest table to the door and concentrated on the immaculate white tablecloth upon which sat a flower-shaped candle in a gold dish.

Her day to this point had been exhausting and mortifying in equal measure. After her pratfall entrance to the Pinter Institute, followed by her orientation meeting with the mannequin-like Anton, Hannah had been colonically irrigated, hot yoga-ed, mud-bathed and entombed in an isolation tank, before having her chakras realigned by an elderly man with an alarming squint who kept making a noise somewhere between a hum and a cat trying to clear a problematic hairball. The activity she had liked the most was definitely the isolation tank. It really was very hard to feel as if you were doing it wrong. Undoubtedly, the worst part had been the hot yoga experience.

There had been only six people in the class, including the instructor, Marshall, an athletic-looking American with a West Coast accent in possession of the annoying habit of nodding and pausing after every utterance, as if deliberately allowing enough time for the wisdom he was imparting to sink in. The trio of women now sitting in the corner of the dining room had been there, as had a short bald man who had spent most of the class doing his best to stop his glasses from slipping off his nose by pulling increasingly elaborate and alarming faces.

As Hannah was seemingly the only new attendee, Marshall had begun by running her through what the class would entail. He explained that the temperature in the room would be held at

40° Celsius and the humidity level would be forty-two per cent. Most other hot yoga was practised at a humidity level of forty per cent. He imparted this deviation as if it were an incredibly significant piece of information. The only thing going through Hannah's mind was how she was already very sweaty in several locations, and seeing as they hadn't even started yet, she had the sneaking suspicion that she'd have been just fine at forty per cent.

Marshall went on to explain that his classes were also made up of twenty-seven poses, which was one more than a traditional hot yoga class. Again, the solemnity of his delivery matched what Hannah guessed J. Robert Oppenheimer had achieved with 'Now I am become Death, the destroyer of worlds', following the detonation of the world's first nuclear bomb. And speaking of detonations . . .

In Hannah's experience, the human body is, at best, only ever partly under the control of its owner, and immediately after a colonic irrigation is never one of those times. She had farted. It had been a good one too, perfectly timed to coincide with one of the very few lulls in the plinky-plonky music that accompanied everything they did.

She had been in yoga classes when that had happened to someone else. Previously, it had been either ignored or laughed off. Not today. No, today, she had been stared at in revulsion by the trio of women, Marshall the instructor, and even the gurning sweaty man. Then, without saying a word, Marshall had rung a bell and his assistant had come running in, waving a brass thurible of strong-smelling incense, as if trying to exorcize a demon. Hannah's face would have turned bright red if it hadn't been so already.

Now focusing as intently as she could on the dining table in front of her to avoid making eye contact with anyone, Hannah jumped as a woman with a blonde bob and wearing stylish, thick-rimmed glasses suddenly pulled out a chair and sat down opposite her.

'Oh, thank God, new blood!' Her accent was Glaswegian and she gave a broad smile as she extended her hand across the table. 'I'm Moira. Pleased to meet you, hen. Fingers crossed you're not another one of these dry shites.'

Hannah shook the proffered hand and tried not to notice the fact that the rest of the room was now glaring at them. 'I'm Hannah,' she said, returning the smile. Social anxiety got the better of her and she glanced round the room at the sour expressions. At a guess, Moira's opinion of the other diners didn't come as a shock to the rest of the room, although that didn't make it any more popular.

'Charmed to make your acquaintance. I spent the afternoon in an intense session with Dr Dangle trying to sort my head out, so I'm guessing you were on your own with the *Mean Girls* cast reunion over there.' Moira nodded her head in the direction of the trio.

'Mostly,' admitted Hannah.

'Let me guess,' said Moira, playing her hand across the white tablecloth. 'They asked just enough questions to check you weren't somebody important and then they blanked you for the rest of the day?'

Hannah avoided giving an answer, but that was indeed exactly what had happened.

'Aye, I thought as much.' Without turning her head, Moira raised her voice another notch. 'Those three remind me of the velociraptors from *Jurassic Park*. Only the velociraptors were at least willing to open a door for themselves.' She lowered her voice again. 'If memory serves, one of them is a wife, one an ex-wife, and one a mistress. Not to the same man, although might as well be. Give a man enough money and he'd invariably collect at least one of each of those things. Quite depressing, really.'

Hannah clicked her fingers. 'I've just realized who you are . . .'

'Let me guess, I'm the straight-talking tubby lass who provides the comic relief?'

Hannah thought it an odd thing to say, not least because Moira was not overweight.

'No, you're Moira Everhart.'

Her new companion gave a sheepish grin. 'Guilty as charged.'

It had taken Hannah a while to put a name to the face, principally because she had never actually heard Moira Everhart speak. She had read a profile on her in a magazine, though. Everhart's shops had become ubiquitous. Fifteen years ago, stationery used to be, well, stationery. Pens. Notepads. Post-it notes. All very functional, unless you were a six-year-old girl OD-ing on pink everything, or a terribly serious businessperson in need of a pen that emphasized just how much money you had.

Moira Everhart's genius was in understanding how stationery can be so much more than stationery. A great notepad can be a mystical thing. The touch of it. The smell of it. The potential of it. The right stationery gets you writing things down, and committing pen to paper is the first step in getting stuff done. Stationery can be inspirational. Comforting. There's a certain magic to it.

The tone of the magazine profile had been slightly mocking because the journalist obviously didn't get it. Moira Everhart got it though, and so did thousands and thousands of other people, Hannah among them. In the space of a decade, by providing high-quality stationery to grown-ups, Everhart's had grown from a single shop in Glasgow, struggling to survive, into a multi-million-pound behemoth. Hannah often went into a branch when she had time to kill. There was something comforting about the smell of the place.

'I've always wanted to know,' said Hannah, 'what do you do to make the shops smell so good?'

Moira's eyes twinkled as she shook her head. 'We honestly don't do anything. When you have that much nice stationery in one location it just sort of happens.' She pursed her lips. 'Let me guess – you're the kind of person who loves to make a list.'

'Of course.'

'Me too. The amount of money we've spent on consultants over the years because my senior management are always so desperate to recognize, define and expand upon our customer base. The reality is, there are the people who like to make lists and there are the people who don't, and we appeal to only one of those groups.' Moira leaned back in her chair and gave Hannah an assessing look. 'So, if you don't mind me asking – what are you in for?'

'Excuse me?'

'None of my business, of course, so tell me to take a flying jump, but ye cannae help but wonder.' She waved a hand in the air. 'All sorts in here. There's your addicts: drink, drugs, food, sex, shoplifting, gambling, and a few other addictions people are a lot less likely to own up to, I'm sure. Then there are your midlife crises, divorces, bereavements – all of that. Not forgetting group number three: rich people with so much money they come somewhere like this because they literally cannot think of anything else to do. Nothing stifles the imagination as much as a shit ton of filthy lucre.'

'Right,' said Hannah. 'Well, I suppose I land somewhere in group number two.'

'I thought so.' Moira wafted a hand up and down herself. 'I'm afraid I'm here for the blindingly obvious.'

Hannah hesitated. Nothing was blindingly obvious, but it felt somehow rather awkward to point that out. Hannah, like almost everybody else on the planet, felt that she could stand to lose a few pounds, but most of the time, she didn't consider it to be that big a deal. Moira had already described herself as tubby, even though she definitely wasn't.

Before Hannah could think of anything to say, they were interrupted by the arrival of a waiter. Decked out in the de rigueur black-and-white ensemble, the man was in his early twenties and very attractive. Come to think of it, all of the staff that Hannah had laid eyes on so far, male or female, could have been mistaken for models – maybe not runway, but certainly higher-end catalogue.

'Good evening, ladies. My name is Serge and I will be your waiter for the evening.'

'Yes,' said Moira, not unkindly, 'and I know we have discussed this every evening, but you've been my waiter now for every meal I've had for the past two weeks. Do you think I cannae remember your name?'

'And as I have repeatedly said,' replied Serge, failing to keep the hint of irritation from his voice entirely, 'we are instructed to reintroduce ourselves on each occasion, so that the guests do not feel bad if they do not remember our names.'

'Personally, and maybe this is just the million nametags I sell every year talking, but I think you should feel bad if you don't remember somebody's name after two weeks.' Moira slapped her hands down on the table, causing the solid silver cutlery to rattle. 'Here's an idea. I will give you one thousand pounds if, for each of my meals over the next three days, you serve me while pretending to be a different celebrity every time, and I have to guess who it is.'

Serge gave Moira a world-weary deadpan look that was depressing to see in one so young. 'We are expressly forbidden to take gratuities from guests.' He turned to Hannah. 'Would *madame* like to see a menu?'

'No need,' interrupted Moira. 'I will have the creamy apples and pumpkin verrines to start, followed by the stuffed pheasant, and my companion will have the baked feta with sumac and grapes, followed by the sautéed sea scallops with caramelized apples and chicken livers. And do chuck in a bottle of Château Lafite plus anything you've got open in the fridge.'

Hannah hesitated. 'I thought they said at the orientation today that they collate all our medical data, preferences, allergies, and then give us each a customized diet thing.'

'That's correct,' said Serge.

'And this is exactly my point,' said Moira. 'There's no choice but they'll still print out a menu of what you're about to eat, show it to you, bring you the food, and then when you eat the food, they bring back the same menu and show you what you've just eaten. I sell stationery for a living and even I think it's a complete waste of perfectly good paper.'

Serge's irritated expression was making Hannah nervous. Clearly, Moira did not share her personal trepidation about pissing off someone who is about to handle your food. Before she could find a tactful way to express this, there was a change in the air. The buzz of conversation behind them didn't stop but the pitch of it shifted.

Hannah glanced over her shoulder to see Winona Pinter entering the room, flanked on either side by Anton – he of the expressionless face – and a woman Hannah had not yet met, who was wearing a long flowing blue summer dress and a pair of dangling earrings.

It was weird to observe a famous person relatively up close. Winona Pinter was stunning but also looked smaller, somehow less than the mental image Hannah held in her mind's eye. It was inevitable, she supposed, that reality could never live up to the projected and airbrushed image.

The air was rent asunder by a wolf whistle that caused everyone in the room to wince and turn their head in the direction of Hannah's table. Hannah whipped her own head round to see Moira drawing her fingers away from the corners of her mouth then waving energetically towards the new arrivals.

'Winona, hen, how's it going? Big fan. Always wanted to know what Hugh Grant's like as a kisser? I've a strong suspicion he's a bit of a dead fish, but I could be completely wrong and he's a real face-sucker. Any clues?'

Winona Pinter looked at Moira with the open-mouthed gawp of shock normally reserved for unexpected extra-terrestrials or the discovery of a loved one in flagrante with a barnyard animal. The woman with the dangling earrings shot Moira a look then whispered something in Winona's ear and guided her by the elbow into one of the corner booths.

'She mustn't have heard me,' said Moira, failing to suppress a grin.

'That seems spectacularly unlikely, *madame*,' offered Serge.

'Sorry, Serge, I forgot you were still here. Would you like to ask the question? You know, the one and only real question you're allowed to ask?'

If looks could kill, Hannah would be eating alone.

Serge cleared his throat. 'Would you like still or sparkling water?'

'Still, please,' said Hannah quickly.

'Same,' chimed in Moira. 'And whatever you're having yourself.'

Serge gave a smart turn and hurried off.

Moira giggled. 'Sorry, but . . . Don't make eye contact. Speak when spoken to. They can blow that right out of their arses. Good God, everybody here takes themselves so terribly seriously.'

'You're going to get me in trouble,' said Hannah, struggling to stifle a laugh herself.

'Well-behaved women seldom make history and all that. So, on to the important stuff – what's your favourite type of notebook? Lined or unlined?'

CHAPTER 11

Knowing it was a dream each time did not mean Banecroft could ever wake up from it. Only the location changed, the content did not. Sometimes it would be in the house he and Charlotte had bought in Battersea, on other occasions that holiday in Rome or that weekend away in Cornwall. The worst one was their wedding day. Regardless of the setting, things always played out the same way. It would start as a faithful rendition of the memory only for Charlotte to turn to him and say the same words over and over. *You have to help me. I'm in so much trouble.*

All the surrounding action would freeze. The guests at their wedding would be caught in their smiles and applause while Banecroft's beautiful bride stood there at the altar, excruciatingly out of reach, repeating her plea. *You have to help me. I'm in so much trouble.*

He tried to reach her every time. Even though he had long ago realized it was an utterly futile endeavour. An invisible wall separated them, and it was impossible to break through it. He'd scream until he was hoarse but there was never any indication that she could hear him. She would just cry and continue her entreaty.

At long last, tonight's nightmare released Banecroft and he sat upright on the put-up bed in the corner of his office. He tugged the sweat-soaked sheets away from him awkwardly. The room was in darkness, save for the wan moonlight that washed through the stained-glass window and painted a faint tapestry across the floor.

He used to have an old radio alarm clock but he'd broken it the week before, so he angled his wrist towards the light, enough to see from his watch that the time was just after three in the morning. Feeling wetness at the side of his mouth, Banecroft touched a finger to his lip then looked at it to confirm he was bleeding. He wasn't surprised. Last week, he'd awoken to find the knuckles on his right hand bloodied and swollen from where he'd apparently punched the wall in his sleep. These days, when he slept at all, he found himself drained rather than refreshed by the process.

At the faintest of sounds out in the bullpen he was on his feet. *Please God, don't let this be another false alarm.* It had been six days now. Six long days since the last contact.

He opened the door leading from his office and a wave of relief washed over him so strongly that he had to grab the doorframe for fear that he would be knocked off his feet. There, at the same desk as always, sat the ghostly form of Simon Brush.

Banecroft glanced towards the main doors to the bullpen, which were closed. Hannah had been aware that Simon's ghost had become an occasional visitor, but he wasn't sure who else knew. Banecroft had not shared the exact details of the meetings with anyone. He wanted them to remain private – a combination of necessity and shame. It had been a couple of months ago, just after all the nonsense with the vampires, when it had happened.

The change. Simon's ghost had screamed in pain and the voice of Banecroft's supposedly dead wife had come out of the apparition's mouth. Banecroft couldn't explain it, and clearly whatever was going on was hurting Simon, but the message was too important. Those words again. *You have to help me. I'm in so much trouble.*

He had always known, deep down, that Charlotte was not dead. Seeing the body had done nothing to persuade him otherwise. For reasons he could not express, against all logic and the weight of medical science, he was convinced that the cadaver that had been placed before him was not that of his wife. The pursuit of answers had cost him his job and, ultimately, what remained of his old life.

It had left him broken – devoid of the will to live and lacking any ideas as to what life going forward could possibly look like. Then Mrs Harnforth had brought him here to run this newspaper. Looking at the bare facts, it had been a massive step down from his previous role as one of Fleet Street's most feared editors, but the reality was that it had been a massive step up from the gutter where she had found him. Still, professional pride would normally have meant a sincerity to his resignation threat earlier in the day, but whatever happened now, he could not leave *The Stranger Times*. Not until he finally got some answers, and at the desk on the far side of the room, flicking through a copy of last week's edition, sat the only possible source of said answers.

He had to take it slow. Simon's visits had become infrequent since Charlotte's unexpected interjection, and those there had been were infuriatingly brief and devoid of any new information. There had been no further messages, and Simon had answered no questions.

Banecroft drew in a slow breath. It was crucial that he remain calm. Losing his temper would only cause Simon to disappear, and who knew when he would next return. He took a few steps forward and perched on the side of the desk, six feet from the ghost.

'Hello, Simon.'

Without looking up, the ghost responded. 'Are you aware that this crossword is all wrong?'

★

Stella felt extremely uncomfortable as she pressed her eye to the oversize keyhole of the double doors leading into the bullpen, which afforded her a decent view of the centre of the room. Part of her wanted to just go back to her room and pretend to be asleep. Her discomfort was twofold, and principally stemmed from the fact that she strongly disliked spying on somebody, even if, ultimately, her intentions were to help that person.

Not that she had any idea how to help. Still, something was wrong, really wrong, with Banecroft. Stella hadn't given voice to her worries because the person most likely to understand – Hannah – had up and walked out on them.

For the moment, she was keeping a watching brief and hoping that, at some point, a sensible course of action would present itself. Banecroft was putting on a good show, but he simply wasn't himself any more. He was becoming more and more distracted, and Stella knew why. She also knew that every time the ghost of Simon appeared in the office, she felt a pain above her right eye.

Something to add to the ever-growing list of things about herself that she didn't understand.

The other side of her discomfort was practical. The wooden floor was a bugger to kneel down on for any longer than a minute, so she remained on her feet and bent over to peer through the keyhole. Unfortunately, it turned out that position just transferred the point of discomfort from the knees to the shoulders. She was a young woman in her so-called prime; she might have to take some of that exercise she'd heard so much about. While she had done quite a bit of running in her life, none of it had been recreational.

Banecroft being Banecroft, spying on him was already a tricky proposition. In the time she'd known him, the man had shown a mix of incredible instincts and outright paranoia, both of which were a danger to her in her current endeavour. The last thing she needed was an added degree of difficulty, but there it was, literally camped out in front of Grace's desk in the form of a tent containing the slumbering Betty. The paper's new self-appointed member of staff hadn't said a word to anyone, just pitched a tent, as if camping in the office were the most natural thing in the world.

Earlier in the day, when Betty had introduced herself, she and Stella had participated in a rather stilted conversation. Betty had made a big deal of saying that if there was ever anything Stella needed to talk about, her door was always open. Stella had felt an overwhelming urge to point out that Betty didn't actually have a door, but thought better of it.

She didn't trust people easily, and was even less likely to do so now Hannah had walked out on them, but even if that hadn't happened, some wax-jacketed, jolly-hockey-sticks woman wielding a bag of jelly babies would be an unlikely candidate for a confidante. Stella had enough to be dealing with in her life – the last thing she needed was some rah-rah speech from a toff born with a silver spoon in their mouth.

While the location of Betty and her tent posed an obstacle to Stella's surveillance of Banecroft, the woman provided her own solution. She snored like a hog in heat, so Stella would know instantly if she were to wake up.

Stella held her breath as she watched Banecroft leave his office and slowly approach Simon. He stopped in the same spot he always did, doing a poor job of feigning nonchalance as he perched on the desk.

An odd sensation took over Stella, like her ears popping in reverse. She worked her jaw, trying to relieve whatever the new and unpleasant pressure was. She could still hear what was going on in the other room, but it seemed somehow more distant than before.

Every interaction between Banecroft and Simon followed the same basic script: Simon would read whatever material had been left on the table and Banecroft would make small talk about it before inevitably asking questions about his wife. Stella knew she couldn't have witnessed every time the pair had spoken, given that over the last few weeks Banecroft had started to refer to 'what Charlotte said'. Stella assumed it meant he had taken something Simon had said to be a message. It would explain his spiralling anxieties. Somehow, her boss's delusions about his wife still being alive had been given some credence and his obsession had taken an even tighter grip.

Stella didn't consider herself to be the kind of person who was easily spooked and yet, when a hand was placed firmly on her shoulder, she screamed. A proper scream. Full-throated, high-pitched – the whole shebang. She whirled round, blue energy crackling at her fingertips, to be confronted by the sight of Betty in a pair of striped pyjamas, holding her hands in the air and wearing a broad grin.

Betty looked down at Stella's fingers. 'Well, now, that *is* interesting.'

Stella quickly shoved her hands into the pockets of her hoodie. 'What the hell are you . . .' *Oh God, Banecroft*. She spun back around and bent down to look through the keyhole. She was mystified to see Banecroft still carrying on his awkward conversation with Simon, as if her scream hadn't happened.

She turned her attention back to Betty.

In response, the older woman twirled a finger in the air. 'Cone of silence. Terribly useful. It stops sound getting out, but you can also reverse it. Simply marvellous for avoiding spoilers. I'm still catching up on the last series of *Strictly* and I've started using the cone on public transport ever since that woman on the bus ruined *The Great British Bake Off* for me. I have to say those types of shows are a real weakness of mine. I've even started watching the sewing one and I cannot abide needlework.'

'What?' asked Stella, lost.

Betty wafted her hand in response. 'Sorry. Rambling again.'

Stella looked around. 'A cone of silence?'

'Yes,' said Betty, with a full-cheeked grin as she wiggled her fingers. 'I'm a little bit "hocusy-pocusy". Something I see we share, although I have to say' – she nodded politely in the direction of Stella's hands – 'I've never seen that before. We must have a proper chat when the moment is right.'

Stella paused, hoping to change the subject, and it was at that point that she noticed it – the distinct sound of a contented snore still emanating from the tent. She jabbed a finger in its direction. 'Hang on. I can still hear you snoring.'

Betty shrugged off the comment. 'That's a rather simple parlour trick. If you'd really like your mind blown, peek inside and you can watch me sleep.'

Stella had no idea how to respond.

As she stood there, at a loss for words, Betty pointed at the door to the bullpen. 'May I?'

Seeing as Stella couldn't think of one good objection, she stepped aside to allow Betty to hunker down and peer through the keyhole. She stayed that way for a good thirty seconds, during which Stella could still hear Banecroft endeavouring to make conversation on the other side of the door.

'Oh dear,' said Betty. 'This has been going on for quite some time, hasn't it?'

'How do you know that?'

Betty glanced back at Stella and chuckled. 'It still amazes me what people find amazing.'

Banecroft licked his lips nervously. 'I was just wondering if . . . if you had heard any more from my wife, Charlotte. Only, last time . . .'

He was taken aback when Simon raised his head and locked

eyes with him. It was the most disconcerting experience, to have someone give you a piercing stare while you can see through them to the window behind.

Simon's voice came out in a strained whisper. 'Maybe you shouldn't—'

Before he could say anything else, his eyes clenched shut and his mouth widened into a strangled scream.

Banecroft took a step forward. 'Charlotte, is that you?'

The translucent figure of Simon Brush vibrated in the air, the head spasming at an impossible speed, a picture of terrible agony, before resolving itself into a crumpled and weakened version of the original. It was still Simon but the voice that spoke through him was not.

'Lumpy, is that you? You have to help me. I'm in so much trouble.'

Banecroft fell to his knees on the opposite side of the desk, clenching the edge of it in his hands to prevent himself from trying to touch the figure. 'I'm here, Charlotte. Tell me what to do.'

Stella took an involuntary step back as Betty bolted upright.

'Heavens. That is not good. That is not good at all.' Betty looked at Stella as if she were only just remembering that the girl was there. 'You should go to your room.'

'But—'

'Now!' The sudden sharpness in her voice caught Stella by surprise. Betty threw out her hand and a clipboard that had been resting on top of Grace's desk flew across the room to land in it. As an afterthought, she clicked her fingers and the noise from her tent stopped abruptly mid-snore. She looked at Stella again. 'Move, girl. Now!'

'But . . .' Stella repeated, unable to process her own objection.

Betty lost her patience and waved her free hand irritably in Stella's direction. She looked momentarily flustered when her action resulted in the grand total of nothing happening, but then she rolled her eyes. 'I'm guessing you have one of the keys to this place about your person?'

Stella did. Of the many revelations of the last few months, the fact that the keys to the front door of the Church of Old Souls offered a degree of protection against magic was one of the more mundane ones. Banecroft had given her a key and had insisted that she keep it on her at all times. For several weeks, he had taken to carrying out random spot checks to verify she was doing so.

'Please,' said Betty. 'It is vital that I deal with this alone.'

Stella took several steps towards her room then stopped.

Seemingly satisfied, Betty raised her voice. 'Mr Banecroft, I have a question for you.' Then she threw open the double doors.

From Stella's vantage point she couldn't make out Banecroft but she could see the desk that was no longer occupied by the ghost of Simon Brush, or whatever had taken his place.

'Ah, there you are,' said Betty, striving to sound cheerful. 'A night owl like myself. I just have a couple of quick questions about these expense forms.'

Banecroft didn't say a word. The sound of his office door slamming was the only response.

CHAPTER 12

Grace took a deep breath to steel herself against the impending onslaught. Loon Day — as everyone insisted on calling it, despite her objections — was, in a word, challenging. The problem with throwing your doors open once a month to the general public was that the general public turned up. In fact, it probably wasn't fair to call the group of individuals waiting outside the doors of the offices of *The Stranger Times* the general public. If they were a fair sample of the population at large, then Grace could only worry about what that said about the fate of humanity. As a God-fearing woman, she believed that most people didn't really think that next-door's cat was a demon, that UFOs had kidnapped Justin Bieber and replaced him with a robot, or that a vagina could be haunted. As the growing list of subscribers to *The Stranger Times* could attest, reading about such stories was entertaining. However, meeting the sources in person could be downright exasperating.

This month had Grace particularly worried for several reasons. First off was Banecroft, who mostly tolerated this exercise at the best of times, and recently, well, he hadn't been himself. Initially, she'd assumed that he was taking Hannah's departure badly, but now it seemed something more serious than that was at play. His skin had developed a waxy sheen and, while his complexion had always been pale, he now looked a tad jaundiced too. She had suggested that perhaps he should see a doctor, but her recommendation had fallen on deaf ears.

Despite his abrupt and confrontational demeanour, he had always featured in her prayers, particularly since she had become aware of the tragic circumstances surrounding his wife's death. These days, though, she was praying for him more often as she had an uneasy feeling that he was desperately in need of it.

Given his more pronounced mood swings, pumping a day's worth of crazy into the building struck her as a potential recipe for disaster. And speaking of disaster, there was the second thing. Yesterday, Betty had been worryingly excited when Grace had explained to her what was due to happen the following morning. Looking forward to Loon Day could only mean that said individual either had not understood the concept or was more suited to being in the queue outside rather than dealing with it. Normally, Grace was a fan of enthusiastic people, but Betty appeared to be enthusiastic about all the wrong things. Such as checking how things ran or asking to see things like accounts and invoices. Grace had suffered a particularly bad night's sleep worrying about the audit.

Last but not least was the third thing: providing tea and biscuits for those in attendance on Loon Day. It was a core part of the service, but Grace was worried that she'd made a fatal mistake last month. The local supermarket had had an incredible deal on those luxury assortment boxes of biscuits. The really fancy ones where some of them are individually wrapped. It was such a good deal that it had actually been cheaper to buy a load of them instead of the ginger nut biscuits she typically went for.

As if that wasn't bad enough, she'd gone for a different brand of budget teabags too, and had inadvertently come across a greatly superior cup of tea. For the whole of the last Loon Day, she'd been inundated with positive comments about the refreshments. Previously, she'd been careful to keep the standard down to avoid giving too much of an incentive to attend. She had a terrible feeling her errors in judgement were going to result in this month being the most popular Loon Day ever – at least in terms of numbers. Its popularity with the staff would be inversely proportional.

As she walked down the stairs, habitually skipping the dodgy step fourth from the top, Grace admonished herself. What was she doing, convincing herself the day was going to be terrible before it had even started? That was no way to face a challenge.

When she reached the bottom of the stairs, she nodded to herself and threw open the doors. She looked to her right and was pleasantly surprised. The queue, if anything, was a bit shorter than normal. Then, she looked to the left and her heart sank at the sight of a second line of a similar length stretching around the building in the other direction.

'Why are there two queues?'

'There aren't,' said a tall, shaven-headed woman in her twenties at the head of the queue on the right. 'There is only one queue. *This* is the official queue.'

Her words were met by a worrying cheer from a dozen or so of the people standing behind her.

The short man at the front of the other queue snorted deri-
sively and spoke in a distinctly Northern Irish accent. 'That
so-called queue is an abomination. I've been here since seven
a.m.'

'So have I,' countered the woman. 'I was here first.'

'She wasn't.'

'I was.'

'We came through the gate at the same time and she threw her
bag at the door, claiming that meant she'd made it here first.'

'It does,' she protested.

'Really?' he snapped. 'How many Olympic gold medals do you
think Usain Bolt won by chucking his bag over the finish line?'

Some followers of the man on the left applauded this point,
while the followers of the woman on the right made dismissive
hooting noises, and in one case, blew an unhelpful raspberry.

'This is a queue, not the one hundred metres. Why don't you
sod off and take a hundred-metre sprint along an eighty-metre
pier, tubby?'

Grace, with a growing sense of dread, turned and checked the
sign on the door behind her. It read, in large letters, 'Q starts
here'. She was definitely going to add an arrow on it for next
month.

'Who are you calling tubby, baldy?'

The leaders of the two queues had now started to square up to
one another.

'Silence!' Grace barked. Her tone was severe enough to stop the
duo in their tracks, their jabbing fingers frozen in mid-air. 'Neither
of you were here at seven a.m. because I and the rest of the staff

got here at seven fifteen and nobody was here. And' – she pointed a thumb over her shoulder at the Church of Old Souls – 'need I remind you that you are standing in front of a house of God.'

'I thought this wasn't a church any more?' said the Northern Irishman.

'God is everywhere,' declared Grace, folding her arms with an emphatic jangle of her bracelets.

'Yeah,' came a voice from somewhere to the left, 'but which queue is he in?'

The smattering of laughter that greeted the quip quickly died out under the white heat of Grace's glare. 'Who said that?'

Several members of the queue attempted to hide behind each other while still trying to maintain their place in the queue, which was quite the unsightly spectacle.

The tall, shaven-headed woman cleared her throat and leaned forward. 'Actually, I don't recognize a monistic God.'

'You don't have to,' replied Grace. 'Just know that he recognizes you.'

Even she realized that her tone of voice was a tad more threatening than that in which the good news about the Lord our saviour should ideally be delivered. She needed to get a grip on the situation fast or the only report from Loon Day to feature in this week's – or any future – edition of the newspaper would be an account of the riot that she would never live down.

She clapped her hands briskly. 'Right. Both queues are legitimate queues.'

'How is that supposed to work?' asked the man who was indeed tubby.

'We are going to alternate.'

'Which queue goes first?' asked the bald woman who was probably going to hell.

'We'll toss a coin.'

Her decision was met with a chorus of grumbles but nobody could put into words a firm objection.

'Good,' said Grace. 'We will also need somebody to monitor the queues.'

She ignored all the comments that came in response to this and simply turned around and stepped back inside the vestibule. She hammered on the thick doors that had formerly led into the church proper, but which now opened into the newspaper's printing department.

After about thirty seconds, one of the doors opened and Manny's distinctive head of pure-white dreadlocks wrapped around a warm, if slightly vacant smile popped out.

'Grace,' he said cheerfully. 'Wha' g'wan?'

As the sweet-smelling cloud of smoke that accompanied Manny threatened to envelop Grace, she fanned a hand in front of her face with as much subtlety as she could muster. 'I need you to monitor a queue.'

Manny's face crumpled into a look of confusion. 'We no get you?'

'There are two queues of people outside. I need you to let one in each time somebody else leaves.'

'We like a bouncer?' asked Manny.

'No. Nothing like that. Although if anyone tries to push in, you will need to stop them.'

'Like a bouncer?'

'Not . . . Fine – like a bouncer.'

Manny thought about this for a few seconds then nodded. He opened the door fully and stepped outside. 'We happy to help.'

His appearance was met with a very loud cheer. Grace, her cheeks flushed, turned around and did her best to block the queues' view of Manny.

'Maybe start by putting some pants on.'

Two minutes later, Grace stood at the doorway explaining the system again to the now, thankfully, fully clothed Manny. She pointed back and forth between the two queues as she spoke.

'So, one from this side, one from that side, one from this side again, and so on.'

The shaven-headed woman pointed at Manny. 'Is he stoned?'

'How dare you,' said Grace, trying to pretend she couldn't see Manny out of the corner of her eye, nodding his head. 'He is on medication for an allergy.'

'Aye,' said the Northern Irishman. 'An allergy to not being stoned.'

The bald woman and he shared a hearty laugh but Grace gave them both a stern look. 'I'm glad to see the two of you getting on so much better. Think how much time your friendship will have to blossom when I send you both to the back of your respective queues.'

The pair both wisely said nothing to this.

Grace nodded then raised her voice. 'My associate here' – she pointed at Manny – 'is in charge of managing the queue. What he says goes. Pity the fool that crosses him.'

'No offence,' said the bald woman, 'but he's not exactly the most intimidating bloke in the world.'

'Believe me,' said Grace, 'you really do not want to see him when he gets angry.'

'Ehm, Grace . . .' began Manny.

'Not now,' she responded, patting down her various pockets. 'I'm sure I had a coin here somewhere.'

'But Grace?'

'Just a sec . . .' She looked up as Manny tugged on the sleeve of her blouse.

'What 'bout the lady?'

'What . . .?' Grace stopped and looked towards where Manny was pointing.

While she had been busy with crowd control, a rather glamorous woman had arrived and was now standing between the two queues. She looked familiar but Grace could not place her. A tall man wearing a dark suit and a very serious expression positioned himself behind her.

'Hello,' said the woman in a polite voice. 'I'm here to see the editor.'

'Right. Do you have an appointment?'

'No.'

The tall man in the dark suit leaned forward. 'This is Tamsin Baladin.'

His words earned him a reproachful glance from the woman Grace guessed was his employer. 'Thank you, Michael. I am well able to speak for myself.'

Grace's brain belatedly caught up with matters and it was all she could do not to gasp. Not only was this woman the million-aire, possibly billionaire, co-founder of the Fuzzy Britches company, but a few months ago said company had been involved in all of that drama with the vampires.

Tamsin Baladin favoured her with a warm smile. 'Trust me – Mr Banecroft will definitely wish to meet with me.'

'OK,' said Grace, trying to make up her mind about what to do with this new wrinkle in her already difficult morning. 'Very well. If you would like to take a seat upstairs in reception, I will be up presently to see if Mr Banecroft is available.'

A chorus of dissenting voices went up from both queues.

'How is she skipping the queue?'

'I want to see the editor too.'

'I've got an appointment.'

'How come my dating profile never gets any interest?'

'Shut. Up!' roared Grace, having just located the end of her tether. 'The next person to say anything will not be getting through this door.'

Even she was surprised by the total silence that followed her pronouncement.

She nodded. 'Good . . . Well, then.'

She stepped to one side and waved Tamsin Baladin and her associate through and into the building. Once they had passed, Grace returned her attention to the two heads of the respective queues.

'OK. I do not have a coin so we will be doing rock, paper, scissors. Best of three. I will be the final arbiter.' Without taking her eyes off the duo, she reached up and snatched the 'cigarette'

Manny had just placed between his lips and was attempting to light. 'You'll get this back at the end of the day. I will give you both the count of three.'

'Whoa, whoa, whoa,' said the Northern Irishman.

'Is it on three?' said the bald woman.

'Or is it one, two, three, and then go?' continued the Northern Irishman.

'Lord God, give me strength.'

E. T. Phones Homes

The 'spam' phone call has become a curse of modern life, but researchers from Manchester Metropolitan University looking into the epidemic of unsolicited calls have made an unexpected discovery. Project Manager Margaret Ashdown explains: 'Using state-of-the-art technology, we ran traces to investigate the source of these calls. We were extremely confused when we identified a signal originating from deep space.'

With the possibility of the source being extra-terrestrial, the researchers have been contacting recipients to find out what was said. Darren Waller, from Middleton, received one such call. According to him, 'This lady started asking how I was, then randomly asked me what I was wearing. I thought, *Hello! Here we go*, but then she spent twenty minutes asking me what shoes are. It was a real let-down.'

Other callers have reported being asked similarly probing questions, such as, *What is Belgium? Is football some kind of religion? Do people only have children if they're allergic to dogs?*

The government has reminded people never to give cold callers their address, bank details or any information about planetary defence systems.

CHAPTER 13

It was all quite amusing, really. Refreshing, in fact. As Tamsin Baladin sat there on the edge of a threadbare sofa in the corner of the reception area of *The Stranger Times*, she racked her brains trying to remember the last time she had been made to wait for anything. She was the CEO of a multi-billion-pound company, which meant that you didn't wait for anybody – other people waited for you. She smiled as she realized who the last person had been – Elton John. He'd been fifteen minutes late and had apologized profusely. Tamsin checked her watch; Vincent Banecroft had already beaten Sir Elton's record by three minutes.

The multi-billion-pound valuation of Fuzzy Britches was admittedly theoretical. A couple of months ago, Tamsin had caused a rather large stir when she had unexpectedly reversed her decision to take the company public. At the time, they had spun it by explaining that she and her brother had reconsidered as they were uncomfortable with the loss of control. They didn't want users of the site to find themselves overwhelmed by targeted adverts. Keeping it in private ownership, while welcoming in some select investors, would mean that the Fuzzy Britches experience could be preserved.

The reality was rather more dramatic. Tamsin knew that part of her appeal to the Founders was her company and its ability to exert massive, if covert, influence on public opinion. The move from being a dating app to being a social media platform was, after all, what made Fuzzy Britches so valuable. The Founders needed to maintain the unseen control they exerted over the world. They had found themselves flat-footed in a rapidly changing technological landscape and now she was their solution.

Worrying about what was being published in the newspapers in the age of social media was like trying to close the barn door after the horses had all been replaced by motorcars. What she brought to them was a sharp understanding of how this new world worked, and how it could be controlled. What they brought to her was simple – who didn't want to live for ever? Who didn't want to exert massive power? True power. The people who didn't long for those things existed, of course, and she was glad they did. A shepherd is nothing without sheep.

Tamsin looked at her watch again. Vincent Banecroft was quite possibly making a point, although given the surrounding chaos, she couldn't rule out that she had been forgotten. From what she could gather, the staff were preparing to receive the two queues of people waiting outside. As they shuttled back and forth, setting up tables and chairs, they kept stealing surreptitious glances in her direction. It was quite odd. They knew who she was, of course – most people did – but they would be stunned to find out that she knew who they were too.

One of Tamsin's primary responsibilities was taking over media management for her new 'partners'. Strictly speaking, *The*

Stranger Times didn't fall into her portfolio, but she had taken the initiative and had them looked into anyway. It made sense, given the nuisance they had been to her and her wayward brother.

There was Reginald, the rather portly waistcoat-wearing ghost-hunter. Ox Chen, the East Asian man with the scraggly beard and gambling addiction, who specialized in all things UFO. Grace, the receptionist/office manager who had met her at the door. She had also seen Manny, the Rastafarian who took care of *The Stranger Times'* in-house printing needs. It seemed an anti-quated way of doing things to her, but then the whole place didn't exactly reek of innovative business practices. She had even caught a brief glimpse of Stella, the teenage girl who was rather more enigmatic than her colleagues. Tamsin's enquiries about her past had thrown up little – the girl seemed to have appeared out of nowhere, apparently not having existed until she stepped through the newspaper's doors, which made her of great interest to Tamsin. She did enjoy a good mystery.

Of even more interest, and no small amount of annoyance, was the rather rotund lady who had introduced herself as the new assistant editor and then offered Tamsin and her bodyguard, Michael, a jelly baby. The woman was annoying because Tamsin had not known about her at all. When she got back to the office heads would roll for that. Information was like high-priced seafood – its value comes from its freshness. That was rather the point of this visit.

She looked down at the brooch fixed to the lapel of her jacket that did not go with her outfit and resisted the urge to fiddle with it. Her new mentor was watching. She hadn't met him yet – only his right-hand man. Taking this on was risky, not least because doing so had annoyed Dr Carter, but you didn't get anywhere in this world by asking nicely.

Grace reappeared through a door and threw Tamsin a rather flustered smile. 'Mr Banecroft will see you now.'

'Thank you,' said Tamsin, rising from her perch.

Michael attempted to walk ahead of her, but she motioned for him to stay back. Procedure be damned. While having your own security sent a message, having them walking in front of you sent the wrong message. It was the difference between projecting power and projecting fear.

Grace led them down a hallway lined on either side with damp-smelling cardboard cartons piled so high that they looked in danger of imminent collapse. She knocked on the door at the end of the hall then, after receiving a response of what could best be described as a grunt, opened it and beckoned Tamsin through.

It was a toss-up between what looked worse – Vincent Banecroft's office or Vincent Banecroft. The space smelled like the place where musty went to die, and everything, including the rubbish, was covered in a layer of dust. Everything apart from the bottle of whiskey sat on the desk, that is. The man himself sat behind it, pointedly making no effort to stand and greet his visitors. In his nicotine-stained left hand he held a cigarette, in his right a glass of whiskey.

Tamsin Baladin strode forward and extended her hand across the desk. 'Vincent Banecroft, I presume?'

'Got it in one,' came Banecroft's reply, as he sustained his refusal to join in on the handshake. Instead, he took a drag on his cigarette. 'Sorry. No touching. I'm a bit of a germaphobe.'

'Yes,' she said. 'I can see that.'

Despite the withering look she received from her boss, Grace could not resist cleaning off the visitor's chair before offering it to Tamsin.

'Thank you.'

'Can I get you anything?' Grace asked. 'Tea? Coffee?'

Banecroft wafted the cigarette in the direction of the back wall where Michael had taken up position behind his employer. 'Some peanuts for your monkey?'

Tamsin ignored the last remark and instead looked up at Grace as she took her seat. 'No, thank you. I'm fine.'

Grace gave a nervous nod, hesitated and headed back to the door through which they had just come.

'I'm fine too!' Banecroft shouted after her. 'Thanks for asking.'

The only response this elicited was the slam of the door in her wake.

'Ah,' said Tamsin, 'the famous Banecroft charm I've heard so much about.'

Banecroft flicked some ash into the already overflowing ash-tray on his desk. 'Let me stop you there. I appreciate it is literally your business, but I'm not dating right now.'

'I'm sorry to hear that.'

'Yes,' he continued in a mocking sing-song voice, 'I'm just super-focused on my career and, you know, living my best life.'

'I would drink to that, but I don't start on the hard liquor quite this early in the morning.'

Banecroft raised his glass in response. 'You don't know what you're missing. By the way, is your monkey normally this jumpy?'

Tamsin turned her head as Michael leaned forward and whispered in her ear. She rolled her eyes before addressing Banecroft again. 'I'm afraid Michael here is a tad nervous as there appears to be a firearm in the corner of the room.'

'What? That old thing?' Banecroft asked, pointing to the blunderbuss.

'Yes,' replied Tamsin. 'I'm sure it's just decorative.'

'Oh no, not at all. In fact, a few months ago, I had to use it to drive a stake at high velocity through the chest of a vampire, of all things. Not that I need to tell you about that, of course. I assume that's what you're here to apologize for?'

Tamsin furrowed her brow and pulled a most bemused face. 'I'm sorry? I don't think I understand what you're talking about.'

'Really?' said Banecroft. 'A sleazy little side project run by your scumbag brother resulted in you winning the race among IT companies to see who could successfully create actual vampires. I mean, I don't think anybody else was trying, but still, well done on breaking new ground.'

Tamsin laughed. 'Even for this publication, that is a wonderfully fantastical story. I'm surprised you haven't run it. Not to toot our own horn, but Fuzzy Britches is rather big news, and if you can prove that kind of revelation it would be quite the exclusive.'

She caught the delightful brief twitch of irritation on Banecroft's face as her shot landed. They both knew he had agreed to keep the matter quiet.

'I'm sure we will get round to publishing it one day,' he muttered sullenly.

'Excellent. I will inform our lawyers.'

'Lawyers and vampires? You really don't mind what company you keep, do you?'

Tamsin gave a practised, hearty laugh. 'We will have to add "good sense of humour" to your dating profile – when you finally crack and set it up.'

Banecroft threw back a large gulp of his drink and added the stub of his cigarette to the overflowing ashtray. 'So, if you're not here to offer the heartfelt apology – which, frankly, wouldn't even begin to cover the mayhem you caused – why are you here? I'm a busy man with a newspaper to run. You remember newspapers? Those things that existed back when people wanted actual news, as opposed to being happy believing any old bullshit they find on social media.'

'Oh, indeed. I am a big fan. Newspapers, vinyl records, Betamax tapes – I love all that vintage stuff. In fact, I'm here to offer to help you.'

'Thanks for the offer, but we don't really need a webpage.'

'Well, to be honest, you do, but that's not what I'm here to put on the table. You see, I have recently become a member of a group of . . . let's call them concerned local businesspeople, and we want to assist you in any way we can. In particular, in the area of content-sourcing. We have a great deal of resources at our disposal, and we would be happy to send some stories your way. We might also, possibly, be prepared to assist with any ongoing expenses the paper may be incurring.'

Banecroft raised his eyebrows. 'Concerned local businesspeople?' He looked up at the ceiling and nodded slowly. 'Concerned local businesspeople,' he repeated. 'That's a peculiar turn of phrase. Seeing as I'm guessing you haven't joined the Chamber of Commerce or the mafia, would one be correct in the assumption that we are referring to the Founders?'

'The group I'm referring to doesn't have an official name.'

'I'll take that as a yes,' said Banecroft as he started to slap his free hand against the top of his desk repeatedly. 'Consider that the sound of one hand clapping. Congratulations. You've joined up with bloodsuckers? Switching from being a thorn in their side to a pawn in their little game. Brava. Well done on graduating from being evil with a little "e" to evil with the full big capital "E". Screw it – evil with the whole thing in block capitals, six feet high. In neon.' He leaned forward excitedly. 'Did they offer you the whole "eternal life, give your soul to Satan" package?'

Tamsin kept her facial expression completely neutral. 'Again with the fantastical stories, Mr Banecroft? I do worry that your work may be affecting your judgement. What is it they say about if you have a hammer? Everything looks like a nail?'

'I don't have either. I do still have a stake, though. I thought it best to keep one handy after the last time I encountered your idea of being helpful.'

'Sorry,' said Tamsin. 'I may have got entirely the wrong end of the stick here. I thought you were having financial difficulties?'

'No, thank you. Our finances are in rude health.'

She nodded. 'Only, the lady who introduced herself outside said she was your new assistant editor. I assumed the old one moved on for a better financial package. I mean, why else would anyone ever give up the wonderful opportunity of working with someone like yourself?'

'Sadly, there was a difference in opinion. It was just two people with strong moral viewpoints who couldn't agree. I wouldn't expect you to understand, what with you being utterly devoid of any moral compass.'

'Didn't you used to edit a tabloid newspaper?' she said sweetly.

'Touché. And I should add, I'm sorry your preferred candidate for the job of assistant editor didn't get the position.'

Tamsin tilted her head quizzically. 'Sorry, I think you've lost me again.'

'Sorry,' Banecroft repeated. 'May I say you use that word a weird amount, seeing as I get the definite impression you have never been sorry about anything ever in your entire life.'

'Nonsense. This outfit cost about five thousand pounds and only a few minutes ago I made the mistake of sitting down on this seat. I'm regretting that already.'

'Five thousand pounds? Good to see evil geniuses can still get taken.'

Tamsin tsked and shook her head. 'I have to say, I'm a little underwhelmed by the whole Vincent Banecroft experience. The former dark prince of Fleet Street was rumoured to be quite the caustic wit. You seem to have been reduced to rather tired old insults and bizarre conspiracy theories. Are you getting enough sleep?'

'I am dreadfully sorry to disappoint, and I must apologize for my behaviour. Anyway, I interrupted you while you were trying to bribe me into allowing this paper to become a glorified mouthpiece for the monsters to whom you've literally sold your soul. Or were you finished?'

Tamsin shrugged. 'I think I must be, don't you? I'm sorry—Ha ha! That word again, but I am – I'm sorry this didn't go better. Perhaps that was my fault. Perhaps yours.' She got to her feet. 'Do be careful, though, Mr Banecroft. Don't believe everything you come across. In your line of work, it can be incredibly dangerous. In particular, be wary of believing silly ghost stories.'

Those final words hung in the room for several seconds as Banecroft became still. As the pair locked eyes, he appeared not even to be breathing. Eventually, he spoke in a quiet voice. 'Excuse me?'

Tamsin casually smoothed down the back of her skirt. 'Ghosts – all that nonsense. Just strikes me as believing that type of thing could get a man into all kinds of trouble.'

'What is that supposed to mean?'

'Just a word to the wise.' Tamsin's tone was breezy. 'Hamlet believed a ghost and look what happened there. Spoiler alert – pretty much everyone ended up dead. Anyway, I shouldn't take up any more of your valuable time.'

As she turned towards the door, Banecroft hauled himself to his feet. Michael stepped forward, his movement enough to stop Banecroft in his tracks.

'Is there something you'd like to tell me?'

'Yes,' said Tamsin, turning back. She jutted her chin downwards. 'Your flies are undone. Now, do get on with running this paper. I am such a fan.'

Banecroft went to say something, but before he could decide on what that thing should be, his visitor was back in the hallway with the cardboard cartons and her bodyguard was firmly closing the door behind them.

Tamsin Baladin looked down at the brooch and smiled. 'Did you get all that?'

Back in her office, Dr Carter drummed her fingers on her desk. Despite the fact that, technically, she was not involved in this side project for which Tamsin Baladin was now acting as a liaison, she had still insisted on being looped in on the feed for the concealed camera.

She had considered the plan of pretending to bribe Vincent Banecroft to be an utter waste of time, but no one had been interested in her opinion. She had tuned in half expecting to see him tearing Tamsin Baladin to pieces, but she had to admit, the woman had more or less held her own. He was certainly not at his best.

Tamsin wouldn't know it, but the information her new boss wanted had been garnered in the first few minutes of her visit to the paper's offices. Dr Carter knew exactly who Betty was, and the other people watching the feed would have known too. The woman's presence was nothing but bad news for their little plan. It meant that somebody had strong suspicions that something was amiss. They might not know what, but they would know something. Dr Carter and Betty went back a long way, and while she still couldn't be sure how much of the bumbling toff persona was an act and how much of it was real, the woman was a smart operator and you underestimated her at your peril.

Truthfully, Dr Carter had been happy. The presence of Elizabeth Cavendish the Third should have been enough to scupper this little dog-and-pony show once and for all. Then, at the end,

Baladin had rather pulled it out of the bag. Warning Banecroft away. That had been a stroke of genius, intended or not. Already on the hook, appearing to push him away was exactly what you needed to do if you wanted him rushing headlong to the place you wanted him to go.

This was about to get ugly. Very ugly.

CHAPTER 14

A fool's errand.

DI Tom Sturgess was under no illusion – that was what he was on. It was a missing person's case where the missing person had already been located. The precise definition of a total waste of time. Still, the sister of the non-victim knew somebody higher up and had kicked up a fuss. Knowing what a pointless exercise it would be, Detective Inspector Clarke had taken great delight in passing the case over to Sturgess. He had played up the 'woo woo' elements, as he so tediously referred to them, in order to make it seem as if it fell within Sturgess's remit. Not that the aforementioned remit was written down, or indeed even acknowledged anywhere by Greater Manchester Police. Heaven forbid! Sturgess was tolerated only because he gave the force somewhere to go with the stuff they did not want to deal with.

For years, Sturgess had been coming up against things that defied explanation. At least now, since the incident of a couple of months ago, he had the explanation he had so long searched for. The impossible is not what we thought it was. There is magic in the world and far more going on than most ordinary people could imagine.

In fact, the person on the street will go out of their way to rationalize the impossible by any means necessary. Take the aforementioned incident – vampires roaming the streets of Manchester. Never mind the public, police officers with thirty years on the force had seen things that were impossible to explain away, and yet they had done exactly that. As soon as the situation had been dealt with, Sturgess had been amazed to see otherwise good coppers convincing themselves that the party line – namely that the whole affair was the result of a couple of psychopaths trying to create panic – was what had really happened. It was as if the human mind couldn't stretch itself around some revelations, and so it found it easier to recast the facts to suit the world that it already understood.

Since then, Sturgess had been splitting his time between taking on new cases and revisiting all his old ones. He had an ever-growing list of questions and was working every hour possible to find answers. Nobody else wanted them, but he had to know. If he was honest, given that he'd sort of been in a relationship with Hannah Willis until a couple of weeks ago, when she had unexpectedly dumped him with nothing more than a brief text message of apology, he was throwing himself into his work with renewed vigour.

Previously, he had little of what you could call a life outside of work, and it turned out that living like that suited him better. Still, the last thing he needed right now was a pointless wild goose chase – but here he was. He was already unpopular with the higher-ups, so it made sense to play along with this charade, however futile it was.

He found a place to park up when the GPS told him he had reached his destination. Fitzgerald Street in Hale was a rather nice-looking tree-lined avenue of well-maintained four-bedroom houses that screamed middle class, middle management, two point four kids. Number twelve, his destination, had an Audi parked on the driveway and a neatly manicured garden where bees buzzed around in the mid-morning sunlight.

The front door opened while he was still halfway up the drive to reveal a petite blonde woman of about thirty in a smart grey business suit. She held out her hand and gave him a tight smile.

'Detective Inspector Sturgess. Pamela Dawson – thank you so much for coming.'

Sturgess shook the proffered hand. 'No problem.'

She welcomed him inside and closed the front door behind him. 'With apologies, I'd like to get straight to it. I'm afraid I'm due back at the town hall for a meeting in just over an hour.'

'Town hall?' asked Sturgess.

'Yes,' she said, the faintest of blushes playing across her freckled cheeks. 'I am a special adviser to the Mayor. We don't normally hold meetings there, but it's for a thing with other regional mayors.'

'I see.' And he did. It explained what he was doing here.

Pamela Dawson must've seen something in his face. 'Look, I'm not an idiot. I know what the police think. They confirmed my brother got on a flight to Majorca two days ago and you all think I'm delusional.'

Diplomacy had never been Sturgess's strongest suit, particularly when somebody had said exactly what he was thinking. He studied Pamela Dawson's face. Regardless of what he or anyone else thought, beneath her practised sheen of professionalism, he could see the wetness in her eyes, feel her nervous energy; the all-too-familiar signs of someone convinced that something terrible had happened.

'I'm here. I have an open mind and I want to hear what you have to say.'

She looked away for a moment then nodded. 'Thank you,' she managed to croak before clearing her throat. 'They tell me you deal with the more . . . unusual end of things?'

'Yes.'

'Good. Follow me.' She walked down the hall and stopped at a doorway under the staircase. 'It's only me and my brother living here. It's been just us for quite some time. My parents passed away when I was a teenager. This is where Tony spends most of his time.'

Pamela Dawson pulled open the door and flipped a switch. The sound of neon lights flickering into life at the bottom of the stairs reached his ears.

'After you.'

Sturgess inched past her and was forced to duck his head as he descended the creaky wooden staircase. As far as basements went, it was probably a pretty big one, but the boxes stacked up to the ceiling against every wall made it feel claustrophobic. An impressive workstation with three monitors ringing the keyboard sat in the centre of the room. In one corner, beneath the stairs, was an unmade bed.

Pamela noticed Sturgess's assessing gaze. 'Yes,' she said. 'This is a four-bedroom house and my brother insists on sleeping here.' She looked down at her feet. 'We spent an awful lot of time arguing about that. You have to understand, Tony is . . . different. Teachers suggested getting him tested when we were younger, but my dad wouldn't hear of it. He took it as people seeing Tony as something lesser, and nobody could convince him otherwise.

'For his part, Tony is, frankly, a genius. He found school boring, but his grades were mostly excellent.' She gave a sad smile. 'He was always terrible at languages, though. I don't think he ever managed an entire sentence in French. Now he's a software-testing specialist, and he's superb at it.' She gave a weak laugh. 'He makes more money than I do, and he never has to leave the house.'

She sat down on the second-to-last step and folded her arms. 'Unfortunately, that does mean he never leaves the house. He talks to me but, these days, I'm the only one he does talk to.' She nodded towards the bank of monitors. 'At least in real life. As he always says, he has a lot of friends online. At least, there were plenty of people he argued with – on forums or whatever. And then, there's that.'

Sturgess followed her hand as she pointed towards what looked like a noticeboard covered by a tatty white sheet.

'May I?' he asked.

She nodded.

He inched around the boxes and carefully removed the sheet to reveal a board filled with newspaper articles, printouts of website copy, photographs and a litany of Post-it notes. While the room itself was neat, the board was chaos, with layers of items pinned over the top of each other and notes scrawled in near-illegible handwriting.

Sturgess scanned the articles. UFOs have invaded Scotland, a dragon lives underground beneath Manchester city centre, the government has been replaced by robots, Australia does not exist, the Royal Family used to be lizards but they have now been superseded by another type of lizard, and so on and so on . . .

The sinking feeling in Sturgess's stomach grew heavier. 'Ah, I see. Your brother is a bit of a conspiracy' – he struggled to find the polite word – 'enthusiast?'

'You could say that. Thank you for avoiding the word "nut". Most people wouldn't be so kind.'

'Let's just say I've seen a lot of strange things in my job.'

Pamela nodded at the board. 'Do you think there's a chance that Beyoncé really is running the US government?'

'Probably not,' conceded Sturgess. 'But we live in hope.'

'Have you ever heard of a newspaper called *The Stranger Times*?'

Sturgess was taken aback by the question. 'I have.'

'Tony used to write a column for them under the name Dex Hex. I knew nothing about it until he told me recently. They dropped it a while ago, but he kept emailing them asking for it to be reinstated.'

'I see.'

'He said the editor there was difficult.'

Sturgess nodded. 'Difficult' did not even begin to cover it.

Pamela Dawson looked at her watch and took a deep breath. 'My argument is, Inspector, does any of this' – she waved her arm around – 'fit with the idea of a man who would up sticks and fly to Majorca?'

He looked around the basement. 'I see your point.'

'No, I don't think you do.' Sturgess was alarmed to see her wipe a tear from her eye. 'This is all my fault.'

'I'm sure it isn't.'

'No, it really is.' She gestured at the board again. 'He was so obsessed with all this stuff. I thought, if he got it out of his system, maybe he could, you know, move on with his life.'

Sturgess said nothing.

Pamela Dawson pulled a fresh tissue out of her pocket and carefully dabbed at her eyes before continuing. 'I challenged him – said that rather than arguing about this stuff online, he should do what he does so well. Test it. Look for proof, or the absence of it. Oh my God, I thought I was helping.'

'I'm sure you were doing what you thought best.'

'Maybe, but he was really excited recently. I mean, behaving oddly . . . All right, odder than usual. Said he was working on something big. Something that was going to shake Manchester to its very foundations.'

'And?'

'And now he's disappeared. More importantly,' she continued, 'Tony and I are all the other has. Even when we argue, he'll always come up to say goodnight. He's my big brother and he knows I'm scared of the dark. As silly as that sounds.' She sniffed. 'My point is – he doesn't just go off somewhere and not talk to me for three days.

'I went to a leaving do at work on Friday evening. I rang him at six o'clock and he was in good form, talking about cooking something, which was a rare event indeed. I got home three hours later and he was gone. No note. No message. He didn't even put the alarm on, and he was obsessive about that, believe me. That, coupled with him leaving all of this, his life's work, behind him – I'm telling you, Detective Inspector, it doesn't make sense.'

Sturgess gave Pamela Dawson assurances that he would look into Tony's disappearance, and she thanked him as she showed him out.

He wasn't really sure what to think. The facts were the facts, and even Tony Dawson's sister admitted he was a man who was mentally unstable. There was also definite evidence of him boarding a flight on Friday evening.

It occurred to Sturgess that he hadn't been told exactly what that evidence was. He expected someone had confirmed a visual ID from security footage at the airport rather than just relying on immigration records, but even as the thought crossed his mind, he also had a sneaking suspicion. If in doubt, assume the bare minimum had been done.

That wasn't to say Tony had not got on the flight. Maybe he'd been chasing up what he considered to be a lead. Majorca, though? It didn't feature in many conspiracy theories that Sturgess had ever heard of. The file said the Spanish authorities had been contacted but were unable to trace him. He'd cleared customs and promptly disappeared, without any footage to verify his identity due to a malfunctioning CCTV camera. Sturgess could follow up on that side of things too. Force the Spanish to pull their fingers out and give poor Pamela Dawson some news.

He was walking back to his car when he noticed the elderly gentleman from the house opposite, peering out of his window at him. Sturgess stopped. The file hadn't mentioned anyone checking with the neighbours either. Assume the minimum. He looked at his watch, remembered how sad and lonely Pamela Dawson had looked sitting on that second-to-last step, and headed up the drive.

Through the frosted glass of the front door, he could see a figure standing in the hallway. Sturgess raised his voice. 'Good afternoon, sir.'

'No, thank you,' a voice came back instantly. 'We are not buying anything today.'

'I'm not selling anything, sir. I'm Greater Manchester Police. Detective Inspector Tom Sturgess.'

This earned him a pause. 'Have you got identification?'

'Certainly, sir. If you like, I can push my warrant card through the letterbox for you to take a look?'

'Yes, please.'

Sturgess drew it out of his jacket pocket and pushed it through as requested. He waited patiently for about a minute until eventually the voice returned.

'How do I know this is real?'

He resisted the urge to roll his eyes, just in case the man was looking at him using the doorbell camera. 'You can, of course, ring Greater Manchester Police and check.'

The man did. Ten minutes later and after a call from Control to his mobile confirming Sturgess really was who he said he was, the man finally opened his front door, by which time Sturgess was thoroughly regretting the impulse that had led him there.

The old man's posture was that of a brigadier general and his walrus moustache was of the kind you only saw these days on painfully ironic hipsters. He gave Sturgess a steely stare from over his horn-rimmed glasses. 'How can I help, Officer?'

Sturgess resisted the urge to get 'Officer' upgraded to 'Detective Inspector'. 'The gentleman who lives opposite you at number twelve, Tony Dawson, is currently missing.'

'Is he? Odd fellow. Hardly ever see him. Never attends the neighbourhood watch meetings. His sister is pleasant,' he conceded. 'Was helpful in getting the speed bumps installed. The lunatics we have zooming through here trying to take a shortcut.' He pointed at Sturgess. 'Your lot should set up a sting operation.'

'Not really my department, sir. As I was saying, Mr Dawson has been missing since Friday evening and I was just wondering if you saw him that day, or anything peculiar?'

The old man narrowed his eyes and tapped his finger against his thigh. 'Friday, Friday, Friday?' He gave a firm shake of his head. 'Nope. Nothing happened on Friday.'

'You're sure?'

The man looked positively affronted by the question. 'Of course I'm sure. Now,' he said, before adding, against all available evidence, 'I'm a busy man, so if there's nothing else?'

Sturgess was only halfway through saying 'thank you for your time' when the door slammed shut. He was about to turn away when he noticed the video doorbell again. He looked down the driveway, directly at the door of number twelve, then back at the doorbell camera. He swore under his breath and rang the bell once more.

'Now what is it?' snapped the brigadier general, who was still standing on the far side of the door, taking a break from his incredibly busy day.

Following some negotiations, which involved Sturgess having to stand in the hallway in case he somehow gleaned the gentleman's laptop password from the sound of him typing, Sturgess was allowed into the front room while the man attempted to retrieve Friday night's doorbell footage from the cloud.

Experiencing some difficulty, he reluctantly let Sturgess drive on the assurance that he was only looking for the footage. Sturgess was given strict instructions not to access internet banking, which was a shame as Sturgess had definitely intended to do that, just as soon as he'd finished hacking into the Pentagon.

He eventually found the footage he was looking for and started scrolling through it rapidly. A couple of pizza delivery drivers came and went, and the brigadier general complained bitterly about the speed of the cars travelling by. Sturgess didn't want to get into the fact they were watching the footage at six times normal speed. Instead, he agreed and promised to bring it up with a division that Greater Manchester Police didn't even have. Mollified by this promise, the brigadier remembered his manners and went off to make his guest a cup of tea.

Sturgess was about to give up entirely when, at 8.27 p.m. on the recording, he saw something he was not expecting. He paused the footage and rewound it.

As he hit 'play', Sturgess couldn't believe what he was seeing. Six men appeared – three from each direction – dressed in full body armour and balaclavas, and converged at the door of number twelve. The figures paused for a few seconds then, having somehow gained entry, all but two of them disappeared inside and re-emerged less than a minute later. They had with them a man with his hands cuffed and a bag over his head, and they were pushing him out the door. A white van pulled up and blocked the view. When it departed a matter of seconds later, the street was once again empty, as if nothing had happened.

Sturgess rewatched the clip, then opened a browser, logged in to his email and sent the file to himself. Satisfied it had landed in his inbox, he stood up just as the brigadier returned with a tray bearing two cups of tea.

'Thank you very much for your time,' Sturgess mumbled, before rushing for the door.

'But . . .'

He had no time for niceties. He had seen the men in that footage before. OK, not necessarily those particular men and, come to think of it, there was no certainty they were all men – not that it mattered. What did matter was that those storm troopers belonged to the Founders and Pamela Dawson was right. Tony Dawson was not in Majorca.

Wherever he was, he was in a whole lot of trouble.

CHAPTER 15

Stella studied the piece of paper she had been handed. 'I don't get it.'

'What's not to get?' asked Ox, leaning against Grace's reception desk, but careful not to touch any of the growing pile of cardboard boxes on it. 'It's bingo.'

'I don't get what bingo is.'

'But . . . it's bingo.'

Stella brushed away the strand of hair that had fallen over her left eye and folded her arms. 'Are you just going to keep saying the word repeatedly on the assumption that it'll start making sense?'

'You've really never heard of bingo?'

'I've heard the word, but that doesn't mean I understand what it is.'

'But it's—'

Stella narrowed her eyes. 'Say the word "bingo" again. I dare you.'

They were interrupted by Reggie's return from the kitchen with a tray bearing three mugs of tea.

'I strongly advise you to stay out of there,' he said, with a nod over his shoulder. 'Grace is doing a lot of mumbling to herself.'

'About what?' asked Stella, taking her mug.

'I'm not sure. There was a bit about chocolate biscuits being the devil's work and how boxes were sent to test her. Just trust me – stay out of her way. She is in quite the mood.'

'Did you ask her what that Baladin woman was doing here?' asked Ox.

'No. See my last note regarding her mood.'

Ox scoffed as he reached for one of the mugs of tea, but Reggie drew the tray out of his reach.

'Why don't you go in there and ask her, then, if you're so brave?'

All three of them looked up at the sound of something being put down in the kitchen with considerably more force than was necessary.

'I might do . . . in a minute.'

'Quite.'

Keen to change the subject, Ox bobbed his head in Stella's direction. 'She doesn't know what bingo is.'

'Is that so?'

Ox nodded as much as he could while slurping tea from the mug he'd finally grabbed.

'Oh, don't you start,' said Stella. 'He's just done five minutes on how unbelievable it is. Like you two never don't know stuff.' She jabbed a finger at Reggie. 'You asked me last week what a TikTok was.'

'And you just said it was a complete waste of time.'

'I stand by that.' Turning to Ox, she said, 'And you asked me what a bae is.'

'It's where boats come in,' said Reggie confidently, setting down the tray and taking the last remaining mug.

'That's what I said!' exclaimed Ox.

'And you're both wrong. It means somebody's significant other.'

'Do we really need a new word for that?' asked Reggie.

'I'm not in charge of the language,' said Stella. 'Much as I'd like to be. If I was, saying LOL in conversation would be a hanging offence. Speaking of violent revenge, I need someone to explain bingo to me pronto, or I shall become properly vexed.'

Ox went to speak, but she raised a finger. 'Not you. You think repeating words is the same thing as explaining them. It's like trying to learn a language from a parrot.' She held up the A4 sheet of paper that Ox had given her. 'Reggie, how does this work?'

'Right,' he said. 'How normal bingo works is . . . you have a card with a selection of fifteen numbers on it and the bingo caller selects numbers at random between one and ninety and reads them out. You cross them out as they come up and when you get a line of them, you shout "line". And when you get all of them, you shout "full house" or "bingo".'

'Where's the skill in that?'

'There . . . isn't.'

'But why do people go and do it, then?'

'It's . . . I mean . . .' Reggie began, sounding less and less sure. 'People enjoy it, I guess. Now that you mention it, I'll confess it doesn't sound like that incredible a night out.'

'It's just random gambling,' said Stella.

Reggie went pale and looked at Ox, the man he had personally walked to his first Gamblers Anonymous meeting to show sup-port. 'Oh God, it is, isn't it? Maybe we shouldn't . . .'

Ox held up a hand. 'Don't worry about it. This is different. We're not gambling. I asked at my meeting this morning and we all agreed it was OK. Besides, this isn't like ordinary bingo. You've not explained it, you see . . .'

Stella waved the sheet of paper about. 'I've got it. We're using random stuff the loons blame for conspiracies, or whatever, instead of numbers. Once someone explained the concept, as opposed to just repeating the same word over and over, the rest was easy.'

Ox stuck out his tongue, and Stella did the same in return.

'Now, children,' warned Reggie, 'behave yourself or you'll be sent to bed without supper.'

'First one to a full house wins,' declared Ox. 'Or failing that, whoever gets the most lines. We've all got the same card, so who-ever completes each line first wins that line.'

'And this definitely isn't gambling?' asked Reggie.

'No,' assured Ox. 'It's just a way of making Loon Day slightly more bearable, especially as the winner gets a pass on doing it next month.'

'Hey,' said Stella, 'this is my first time. I might enjoy it.'

'It's possible,' agreed Reggie, 'but seeing as you get extremely annoyed by the two of us, I'm not sure you've fully appreciated how you'll feel having spent several hours being confronted by the Great British public. Case in point, there's a bloke in one of the queues outside with a duck on his head.'

'There's more than one queue?' asked Stella.

'Yes. I think that might have something to do with Grace's state of annoyance. She's got Manny down there directing traffic.'

'Manny?' chorused Stella and Ox.

'Best not to ask.'

All three turned their heads as Grace emerged from the kitchen clapping her hands together.

'Right, then,' she said. 'It is ten a.m. precisely. Time to open the floodgates. Everyone to their places, please.'

Without another word, Stella, Reggie and Ox took up their respective positions behind their assigned fold-up desks while Grace made her way downstairs. Soon, the battered sofa and the row of fold-out chairs along the far wall would be filled by people who had come to tell them their stories. Hundreds more, who had travelled from far and wide, would be waiting outside.

Stella busied herself rearranging her two notepads, egg timer and three pens so that they were positioned just so. Then she placed the bingo card surreptitiously to one side. Despite her attempts to sound world-weary, she was excited. She was going to be sitting here all day, looking for stories, like a proper journalist. All right, journalists ideally went out and found stories, but this was a start. She hadn't forgotten that Banecroft had mentioned sending her on a course, but he'd been distracted lately, and she hadn't wanted to hassle him.

She looked up to see a shaven-headed woman pulling out the chair opposite her and sitting down.

'Hello, so how can—'

'The ghost of my dead nana has possessed my goldfish.'

Stella picked up a pen. 'Right.'

10.02 A.M.

The man sitting opposite Reggie was giving him an unnervingly broad smile while nodding expectantly.

'So, how may I help you, sir?' Reggie began.

The man spoke in a rather high-pitched voice, just south of a squeal. 'Give it a second, it'll come to you. It'll come to you.'

'Sorry, have we met?'

'No. I mean, we have now. But no, not before now. Still, you'll probably get it . . .'

'Right,' said Reggie. 'I see.' He didn't.

The man pointed at his own face with the index fingers of both hands. 'Give it a second, it'll come to you. I'm sort of famous.'

'Sorry, I do have a simply dreadful memory for faces.'

'Not a problem,' said the man, looking only temporarily deflated. He pulled a neatly folded newspaper clipping out of his pocket and unfurled it. 'Perhaps this article from the *Bolton Gazette* of November 2010 will jog your memory.'

He held it up beside his face with an air of triumph, one that became decidedly incongruous when placed beside the headline, under which was set a picture of his similarly beaming face.

'Are you holding that the right way around?'

'What?' said the man. 'Course I am.'

'I see. Only it says, "Local man arrested for having sex with a cigarette machine".'

'That's me. Brian Dinsdale, at your service, but you can call me Smokey.'

Smokey thrust forward his right hand for Reggie to shake.

'OK,' said Reggie, studiously ignoring the hand. 'And you were caught, ehm . . . being intimate with a cigarette machine.'

'Not just one. Multiple.'

'Right.'

'I was young, playing the field. It is a condition known as cigaretteasexyopia.'

'I see. Has that been diagnosed by a doctor?'

Smokey snorted. 'Doctors? Doctors? What do doctors know about love? I mean, a lot of doctors still insist cigarettes are bad for you.'

'They definitely are.'

'Not the way I enjoy them.'

Reggie resisted the urge to grimace.

'Mine is a story of forbidden love,' continued Smokey.

'I suppose it is,' conceded Reggie. 'Technically . . .'

'There's no "technically" about it. I have turned my life into a movie script. Steven Spielberg is interested.'

'Is he?'

'Oh yes. I mean, I sent it six months ago and I've not heard back, so they're clearly giving it a lot of consideration. If he passes, I'm going to send it to Simon Mayo.'

'The DJ?'

'Yeah. He seems nice, and him and that grumpy fella do movie reviews. They're bound to know people.'

'Fascinating. Well, best of luck with it all. Thanks for . . .' Despite himself, Reggie stopped. 'Wait a second, aren't cigarette vending machines banned in the UK?'

'Oh yes,' agreed Smokey. 'That's what us screenwriters call a complication, you see. It can't just be boy meets cigarette machine, falls in love, the end, can it? I mean, who would want to see that? No, you've got to have obstacles – like how Romeo and Juliet are from warring families, or how Meg Ryan's character in *Sleepless in Seattle* is already engaged when she falls for Tom Hanks, or how she runs a little bookshop in *You've Got Mail* and he runs a big one, or how he's trapped on a desert island with a volleyball and she isn't even in that movie. Obstacles, you see. Obstacles.'

'I see.'

'So ever since the bloody government made my love illegal, I've been forced to go on holidays abroad to meet cigarette machines. Searching for my one true love. Tens of thousands of pounds I've spent trying to find Miss Right.'

'Would it not be easier to just buy a cigarette machine?'

Smokey gasped, the look of revulsion on his face plain to see. 'Buy a cigarette machine? Just buy somebody to love? There's a word for that.'

'Well, but . . .'

Smokey got to his feet and jabbed a finger in Reggie's direction. 'You disgust me! I want nothing more to do with this tawdry publication!'

'But . . .'

Before Reggie could say anything else, Smokey turned and marched towards the stairs, only turning when he got to the top to inform the entire room that Reggie was a pervert. The man with the duck on his head sitting on the sofa gave Reggie a wary look.

'And we're off.'

10.04 A.M.

The woman leaned forward and, subconsciously, Ox mirrored her body language. She spoke in a conspiratorial whisper. 'That Richard Osman . . .'

'The bloke from the TV?' asked Ox. 'Who writes the books?'

She nodded. 'That's him. He's very tall . . .'

Ox waited expectantly.

And then waited a bit longer before finally saying, 'And?'

'I mean *really* tall. It's not natural.'

'And you queued up to tell us that?'

She leaned back and gave Ox a haughty look. 'I could've gone to one of the national papers with this, but I'm trying to support local journalism.'

'OK, well . . .'

Ox's head snapped round as Stella shouted 'Line!' excitedly.

'She can't be . . .' He turned back to the woman sitting opposite him. 'Thanks for coming in.'

'I've got more,' she added quickly. 'That Warwick Davis, the actor who presents that quiz show *Tenable* . . .'

'I've got an idea where this is headed,' said Ox, 'but I just need to confer with my colleague . . .'

Ox reached Stella at the same time as Reggie did. 'See?' he said. 'I told you that I should explain the rules. She's clearly not understood them.'

Stella shot him a fierce glare before turning to the short, bearded man who was sitting nervously on the far side of her table. 'Mr Phillips, would you please tell my colleagues what you just told me?'

The man scratched at his facial hair nervously and glanced round before he spoke. 'Right. Well, I'm only coming to you because the mainstream media won't report it.'

Stella nodded as she pointed at the mainstream media square on her card without breaking eye contact. 'Of course.'

'Elon Musk and NASA are in cahoots, doing mind control on all of us using that 5G signal . . .'

'Good lord,' said Reggie under his breath. 'A line in one go.'

'Bugger,' muttered Ox. 'I had three of them.'

'What?' asked Mr Phillips.

'Nothing,' said Reggie. 'Just . . . that is fascinating.'

'You've not even heard the best part,' continued the man, before using his incisors to repeatedly gnaw at the bristles beneath his lower lip, in a move reminiscent of a hamster. 'They're using the whole thing to get us watching that *Masked Singer* programme.'

'Right,' said Ox.

'I'm sorry, that what?' asked Reggie.

Stella shook her head. 'It's a TV show where celebrities in fancy-dress disguises sing and the judges try to guess who they are. How am I the only person here with their finger on the zeitgeist?'

Reggie shrugged. 'Commiserations. And people watch that?'

'Yes,' said Stella. 'In vast numbers.'

'Good lord.'

Mr Phillips folded his arms and looked across the table huffily. 'Do you want to hear the big reveal or not?'

'Sorry,' said Stella. 'Please continue.'

'On the current series, the alien – well, she's actually an alien.'

'And why would—' started Reggie.

'Isn't it obvious? By the time she's done with her soulful rendition of Aretha Franklin with the odd well-judged bit of Britney or Adele, she'll have won not just the series but our hearts, and the public won't care she's from the planet Gragerdack.'

Grace, looking flustered, popped her head out from behind the boxes that had encircled her desk. 'What are you all doing standing around?'

'Oh no,' exclaimed Phillips. 'Is she with them?'

'I am with Jesus!'

This was not the answer he was looking for. Mr Phillips attempted to leg it before he'd even got to his feet, which resulted in him sending both the chair and himself flying. 'Elon Musk was Jesus in a past life!'

'Blasphemy!' bellowed Grace.

'You mark my words,' he said, scrambling upright and stumbling towards the staircase, 'they'll be eating your babies for Christmas dinner!'

Before anyone could respond to that, he was off down the stairs. Judging by the sound of it, he fell down most of them on his way to a hasty, if painful, exit.

The three of them stood there in silence for a moment.

Reggie sighed. 'I don't know what is odder – that a man just ran out of here screaming about Elon Musk and . . . who was it?'

'NASA,' supplied Ox.

'Yes, them – that all of the above are in league with baby-eating aliens in a TV programme, or that I recognized that gentleman because he came to fix our shower a couple of months ago.'

'I'd probably not ring him again,' said Stella.

'Are you mad? He turned up on time and fixed it in under an hour. He'd have to be trying to sell a baby-cooking recipe book before I'd get rid of his number.' Reggie leaned in and lowered his voice. 'Also, slight change to the rules. I suggest we don't shout out "bingo" et cetera – might be viewed as unprofessional. Perhaps just say "consultation".'

'Good idea,' said Ox. 'By the way, you know that Richard Osman?'

'Author, raconteur, televisual maestro?' asked Reggie.

'Yeah. Turns out he's tall. Really tall. And we've got an exclusive on it.'

'We might need to clear the front page for that one,' deadpanned Stella.

Grace cleared her throat pointedly.

'All right,' said Ox, 'keep your hair on.' He caught Grace glowering at him and wilted. 'Come on, you two. Back to work.'

'How long have we been doing this for?' asked Reggie.

Stella checked her watch as she sat back down. 'Six minutes.'

'Good God.'

She looked up to see the man with a duck on his head moving across to sit opposite her, picking up the fallen chair as he did so. The duck itself remained entirely nonplussed.

'Let me guess – you're a big Terry Pratchett fan?'

'No,' said the man, looking affronted. 'Why do you ask?'

'No reason.'

CHAPTER 16

Hannah shifted herself in the chair, endeavouring to find the optimum sitting position. She was beginning to think there wasn't one. In her experience, only furniture that was really cheap or really expensive could be this uncomfortable. She'd noticed as she sat down that the chair looked nice, but it quickly became clear that it had been designed for a species other than *Homo sapiens*.

The seat itself slanted backwards to draw you into it, but the backrest was curved in such a way that regardless of the angle at which you positioned yourself, it was always sticking into you. Maybe it would work with a load of cushions, or maybe you could simply stick the cushions on the ground, sit on them and warm yourself next to the fire you just built from breaking up the rest of the chair for kindling.

Speaking of the need for extra warmth, it appeared the office Hannah was currently in was being deliberately kept at a low temperature. Hannah was wondering if the chair was also a deliberate choice. In which case, it felt like this therapy session was nudging closer to a Guantanamo Bay experience than she guessed regular sessions normally did. Either way, the person responsible for the aforementioned choices was inevitably the woman sitting opposite her, Dr Sarah French.

After welcoming Hannah in and encouraging her to take a seat and make herself comfortable – ha! – Dr French had sat down opposite. She was at an unpleasantly close distance, to the point where their knees were almost touching, and had launched into a detailed explanation about why most therapy was entirely useless.

Glancing at the clock on the wall, Hannah could see that Dr French had been rambling for a good ten minutes now and there didn't appear to be any end in sight. Hannah had always thought therapy sessions were concerned with talking about yourself – was that not a big selling point? So far, the good doctor seemed to be more intent on focusing on what was wrong with Freud. It felt as if maybe he should be paying for this session rather than her – or, to be more exact, Karl.

Seeing as it was quite obvious that Hannah was required to be an audience for this part of the session, she took the opportunity to check out the woman sitting opposite her and the office.

It seemed to Hannah that Dr French had the distinction of being the only member of staff at the Pinter Institute for whom the black-and-white uniform combo wasn't compulsory. She wore a green cardigan and a collection of beaded necklaces over a floaty blue summer dress. She was stick thin to the point of being underweight. As Hannah's granny would have said, French would get blown away in a decent wind. The danger of this happening might explain her earrings – long dangly affairs featuring a golden rabbit suspended inside a silver ring – each of which looked weighty enough to act as an anchor.

On the wall behind her hung three paintings, if you could even really call them that. Each one was a large white canvas featuring a single dot of blue placed seemingly at random. Hannah guessed that it cost quite a lot to get that much of bugger all. On the upside, at least these pictures were better than the others that hung throughout the Pinter Institute.

Everywhere you looked were massive close-up photographs of smiling faces beaming back at you. Individually, they were fine. Over the top, but fine. Collectively, though, it was like being under constant assault from the shiny, happy people. As if they were all saying, 'Look, we're all happy – what's your problem?' She and Moira had giggled like schoolgirls about it over breakfast that morning. Moira had compared it to being stuck in a never-ending toothpaste commercial and now that was all Hannah could think of when she looked at those beaming faces.

While initially Moira had felt a bit much, the more Hannah got used to her, the more she liked her. Hannah had been here a day and so much of it made her feel like she'd signed up to join a cult, but Moira was a great big dollop of Glaswegian perspective, unafraid to point out that not only was the emperor not wearing any clothes but he was also aggressively waving his genitalia about.

Case in point, Moira had told Hannah in gleeful detail how she'd acquired a marker pen last week and had taken to drawing moustaches on those toothy grinning photographs. That is, until one evening she'd found that the potted plant she'd been using as a hiding place for the pen had been removed. She'd assured Hannah that, given there were cameras covering all the common areas, they knew what she'd been doing and yet, oddly, nobody had said a thing.

Moira had been there a fortnight and was actively goading them to throw her out. She could have left at any time, of course, but for reasons known only to herself, she seemed determined to be ejected officially, as a badge of honour. As if it would be a victory in her battle with the Pinter Institute.

Hannah snapped back to the present when she realized Dr French was finally coming in for a landing with her monologue.

'So that's what we're not going to do,' she said in a cloying voice, making eye contact again, 'but now let me tell you what we are going to do. The Pinter Institute method' – again, Hannah could hear the silent trademark symbol – 'encourages you to think of your issues, failings, anxieties, traumas as not being yours. We want you to think of them as belonging to someone else. Someone who is clinging to you. Dragging you down. Stopping you from becoming your best self. The rest of the world is telling you to take ownership of your problem. We are not. We are here to tell you that you aren't the problem, this other entity is.'

Dr French was looking at Hannah expectantly. She had no idea what an appropriate response to this was and so, in the absence of any better ideas, she just nodded and said, 'Right.'

'Yes,' continued Dr French, satisfied. 'I know it is a lot to take in, but all we ask is that you place absolute faith in the process and the results will speak for themselves. I'm not going to lie to you. It will be tough at times' – her hand sliced through the air as she spoke – 'but that is when you know we are making real progress. Trust the process. Any questions?'

'Actually, yes,' said Hannah. 'Last night I was woken up at three in the morning to meditate.'

'Yes?'

Hannah shrugged. 'I mean . . . isn't meditation supposed to make you relax? I was already asleep. Isn't that as relaxed as you can be?'

'No. That's the wrong sort of relaxed. We need you to be the right sort of relaxed.'

In other words, thought Hannah, *the beatings will continue until morale improves*. She opened her mouth then closed it again and looked down at the floor as she spoke. 'I guess that makes sense. Sort of. Does it mean I'm going to be woken up to meditate every night?'

Dr French gave a patronizing little chuckle. 'No. You will be allowed to sleep undisturbed tonight.'

'OK,' said Hannah, relieved. 'Good.'

'And from then on, you will be woken up twice a night.'

'But—'

'And now,' Dr French continued, her patience for answering questions clearly having run out, 'it's time we started focusing on you.' She pointed at Hannah's chest. 'Let's really dig in and find out what is going on in there.'

'Oh God,' said Hannah, giving a nervous grimace, 'here we go.'

'Relax,' said Dr French, raising her left hand to her earring and fondling the golden rabbit between her fingers. 'It won't hurt a bit. Trust the process. Let's start by finding out who you really are, you tedious, entitled bitch.'

Hannah drew back, genuinely shocked at the unexpected harsh words, but before she could say anything, French gave her fingers a practised twist and her earring started rotating at an impossible speed.

Hannah jumped as Dr French clapped her hands. 'OK, and we are done for the day.'

'What?' Hannah's head was spinning and she had a sickly feeling in her stomach. The room looked exactly the same, but something felt very different. It was as if she'd woken up from a dream only to find herself in the same location that she'd occupied in the dreamscape.

Dr French touched Hannah's knee. 'Are you feeling OK, Hannah?'

'Yes, ehm . . . I guess I am. Or am not. Feel a bit all over the place, to be honest.'

Her words were met with a knowing smile and a nod of the head. 'That's perfectly normal. We just had an intense session and it can be common for the subject to become so engrossed that they lose track of where they are. Still, though, I think we made some great progress discussing your relationship with your mother.'

Hannah didn't remember discussing her mother at all. Only now she did. It was as if French saying that had somehow put the conversation into her head.

Dr French stood up and gestured towards the door. 'As we discussed, we will pick this up again in our next session, but I'm happy with where we are already.'

Hannah got to her feet, glanced round for a second, then nodded. 'Right. OK. Excellent.' She took a few steps towards the door and stopped. 'And thank you, Doctor.'

'You are most welcome. Trust the process.'

As she closed the door behind her, the last thing Hannah saw was the smile falling away from Dr French's face as she turned around and headed back to her desk.

Dr French sat back in her leather chair and snatched up the bottle of hand sanitizer from her desk. She squirted a massive dollop into one palm and ran each hand around the other, muttering to herself as she worked.

'I cannot stand these people. Feckless idiots. Such a waste of my talents.'

When she'd finished, her hands now drenched in antibacterial gel, she took some tissues from the box on her desk and wiped her palms thoroughly before tossing the wad into the bin. Then she picked up the receiver of her office phone and dialled. The call was answered on the first ring.

'It's me,' she said. 'She checks out.'

French listened to the rasping voice on the other end of the line. She took a breath before answering its enquiries, making sure to remove any hint of irritation from her reply.

'Yes, I'm absolutely sure. I'm just done with questioning her directly, and yesterday I went into the offices of that silly little newspaper and confirmed that she really doesn't work there any more. Hannah Drinkwater is just another vacuous drone looking to offload the problems she's created for herself. She's a perfect candidate for the next step.' A wicked smile broke across her lips. 'Trust the process.'

CHAPTER 17

1.27 P.M.

Stella got it now.

As she nodded farewell to the man who was convinced he was being haunted by the ghost of Tom Cruise, despite the fact that Tom Cruise was still very much alive, she realized she truly got it now.

It wasn't having to talk to a man who was convinced he was the son of E. T., or the woman who believed the Japanese were messing with her knitting while she slept, or even the lady who thought she was receiving subliminal messages from *Cheers* reruns ordering her to run naked through her local library. It was all of it, one after the other. It was the unrelenting assault of crazy. That's what got you. Nobody is meant to deal with that much weirdness in one day. When the human mind is confronted with something inexplicable, it takes time to process it and eventually, your brain, even if it doesn't quite understand it, comes to terms with living in a world with that particular slice of insanity.

Loon Day didn't offer enough time for that, though. It was all, *Thanks a lot, your time is now up; next customer, please.* She could feel herself getting tetchy and not just because the man who claimed he could do impressions of famous dogs had tried to eat her egg timer. Along with people informing the paper of what they considered to be news, there was a definite air of a messed-up talent show to proceedings. *I think I've figured out a new way to eat a banana. I need to tell* The Stranger Times *about this.*

Reggie had shot Stella a concerned look when she had expressed her opinion a little too loudly that maybe, just maybe, if reruns of *Cheers* were encouraging you to run naked through a library, you should stop watching them. The woman had given her a confused look and explained that it was her favourite show.

She, Reggie and Ox had been at this for over three hours now and there didn't seem to be any end in sight. While this was her first experience of being directly involved in Loon Day, Stella had the distinct feeling that today was a lot more edgy than usual. Several people who supposedly had earth-shattering revelations to share still managed to find the time to complain about improper queue management, that the standard of biscuits had dropped significantly or that, in a few cases, they'd not even received their promised cup of tea.

Stella could sympathize a little on the tea front. Normally, Grace managed both the queue and the provision of tea and biscuits, both to the people with stories to tell and those lucky enough to be tasked with hearing them. Today, though, the service had been haphazard at best.

All morning Grace had been disappearing and reappearing with cardboard box after cardboard box, and now the reception desk was entirely obscured by a mountain of malodorous storage receptacles. The stench had a touch of sulphur to it, as if the paperwork had been stored in hell. Grace was normally a woman blessed with a sunny disposition, but at this moment in time, as she dug through the boxes with an increasing air of exasperation, she looked as if she were on the edge of losing it.

Stella was considering going over to check on her but the moment was lost as her next customer plonked themselves down in the seat opposite.

'Hi,' said Stella.

'Don't you "hi" me,' said the woman of about fifty who had a face like thunder under what was probably a fur hat, but given that Stella had already spoken to a rather nice man with a duck on his head this morning, she wasn't eliminating all other possibilities. The duck man, incidentally, had been that rarest of things – someone who went away with an answer. He was relieved to hear that he wasn't going crazy and Snickers bars really had been getting smaller. Stella hadn't mentioned the duck as he hadn't, and it had seemed oddly rude to bring it up.

'I would like to speak to a manager.'

'Wow,' replied Stella, 'you really don't like the word "hi".'

'What?'

'I mean, why do you need to speak to a manager?'

'I have a complaint.'

'I figured. And what is it exactly?'

The woman narrowed her eyes. 'What age are you?'

Stella dropped her pen and folded her arms. 'What age are you?'

The woman reared back as if she'd been slapped in the face. 'None of your business.'

'Right back at ya.'

The woman jabbed her finger on the table. 'I will not be spoken to in this manner. I want to speak to the editor.'

'I'd be more than happy to unleash him on you,' said Stella, 'but luckily for you he isn't here. Neither is the current assistant editor, as they've both disappeared somewhere for the day, lucky sods. So, your choice is between talking to me or coming back next month. I'm totally cool with either option.'

The woman said nothing for a few seconds. Instead, she pulled a series of faces that looked like she was trying to deal with a particularly difficult toffee. Eventually, she settled for a begrudging 'very well' and opened her handbag. She withdrew from it a copy of *The Stranger Times* from several months ago and held it aloft.

'In here, you printed a story about a woman marrying the M62.'

The woman left a pregnant pause, which Stella eventually filled with 'OK?'

'That is impossible.'

'Lady, if we rejected stories on the grounds of them being impossible, the weekly newspaper would become a once-a-month pamphlet.'

'That woman cannot be married to the M62 . . .'

The realization dawned on Stella. 'Let me guess . . .'

'Because I am married to the M62, and I have been for several years.' She waved the paper in her clenched fist. 'This is nonsense.'

Stella paused for a couple of seconds then shook her head. 'Yep, there it is. Every time you think you've reached peak crazy, something like this happens.'

'What is that supposed to mean?'

A thought struck Stella. 'Actually, if you'll stay here a moment, I'll just go and consult with my colleague who wrote that article.'

Stella reached Ox's table just in time to see him stabbing a finger in the direction of the young man with a green mohawk sitting across from him.

'You are a monster!'

'Agree to disagree,' said the man.

'I don't agree with that.' Ox noticed Stella in the corner of his eye and turned to look at her. 'You will not believe this guy.'

'I don't doubt it,' she replied. 'At this point I'm somewhere between believing everything and nothing.'

'Yep. Welcome to Loon Day.' Ox picked up the egg timer on the desk in front of him, which had just run out. 'Time's up. See you next month, Steve.'

The mohawk guy shared a quick fist bump with Ox, nodded a goodbye at Stella and headed off cheerily.

Ox lowered his voice. 'He believes that the Russell Brand remake of *Arthur* is better than the Dudley Moore original. I mean, what is the world coming to?'

'He came in to report that?'

'What? No. He came in to tell us that the fairies that live at the bottom of his garden have stolen some industrial-strength glue from his shed and he's worried they're getting high on it.'

'How did you get from that to the *Arthur* films?'

Ox leaned back in his chair and looked up at the ceiling. 'D'you know, I'm not sure.' He sat up again. 'You can't have got another line— I mean, "consultation"?'

Currently, Stella had two, Reggie one and, to his obvious frustration, Ox had none. This was despite Reggie having to admonish him for, as Reggie put it, attempting to lead the witness. He'd overheard one of Ox's customers complaining about why he kept asking if the ghost of her dead auntie had mentioned the Clintons at all.

'No,' said Stella, 'I haven't.' Although she had three and four on the remaining lines. All she needed on one line was FIFA and, Manchester being a football-crazy city, she was hopeful. 'What I have is a woman who is angry because you previously reported that another woman married the M62.'

'Is she offended by women marrying motorways?'

'Only ones she claims to already be married to.'

'Blimey, that really is a coincidence.'

Stella shrugged. 'Is it? I don't drive myself but I've heard it's a great motorway.'

'No. I mean, what are the odds? Carol, the previously reported motorway marrier is a regular. In fact, that's her over there.'

Too late, Stella realized that, Ox being Ox, he was speaking slightly too loudly.

The two women locked eyes across the reception area.

'Oh no.'

Stella, Reggie and Ox, having pulled their tables out of the way, looked on as the two women rolled about on the floor, bound in a mutual headlock.

'*Homewrecker!*'

'*Trollop!*'

'Someone should break this up,' said Reggie.

'Don't look at me,' replied Ox.

'Well, you started it.'

'It's two women fighting. Men can't get involved in that.'

Stella noticed Ox's pointed look in her direction. 'No way, José. I'm a minor. You want to send me into the middle of that?'

'You could always . . .'

'What?' she asked.

Ox lowered his voice. 'Use your, y'know – your thingy.'

'Good God,' exclaimed Reggie, before leaning in to speak in a whisper. 'Are you seriously suggesting she use the supernatural power that she can barely control to break up a scuffle in reception?'

'Well, when you put it that way.'

'And anyway,' said Stella, 'there's nothing stopping you from breaking it up, Ox.'

'How so?'

'You're gay.'

Ox's eyebrows shot up. 'How is that relevant?'

'I'm just saying, if you get stuck in there and a boob pops out or something, you could be all, like, don't worry, it does nothing for me.'

'That's homophobic.'

'How?' asked Stella.

'I'm not sure but I'll figure it out later.'

The two women continued to roll back and forth. Truth be told, locked in a clench as they were, it wasn't much of a fight. It was rather a stalemate with occasional insults thrown in.

'*Tramp!*'

'*Harlot!*'

Reggie nodded appreciatively. 'You don't hear "harlot" much these days, do you? Anyway – let's just wait to see if they blow themselves out.'

'They'd better,' warned Ox, 'and before Grace gets back. She will not be happy.'

They all took a moment to consider quite how unhappy Grace would be and a collective shudder passed through the group.

'Where is she, anyway?' asked Ox.

'Probably digging out more of those boxes,' answered Reggie. 'This audit thing has her at sixes and sevens.'

'*Floosie!*'

'*Slapper!*'

It said something about the quality of the fight that one of the men waiting to be seen went back to reading his paper.

'I tell you what, though,' said Ox, 'watching two supposed adults fighting over who is married to a motorway can't help but make you feel a little depressed to be single.'

'My word,' said Reggie. 'That really is a grim thought.'

Stella pointed down at the two women. 'I mean, you could ask one of them out if you'd like?'

'No, thank you.'

Ox gave Reggie a friendly jab in the ribs with his elbow. 'Picky!'

'Hey,' said Stella, 'seeing as we have this gap in proceedings . . . and it has come up a surprising amount already today, can either of you explain the supposed obsession the evil masterminds running the world have with eating babies?'

Reggie gave her a confused look. 'You would like an explanation for that?'

'I'm just curious about the logic of it. I mean, do they look at a toddler and think, "Oh no, I'm not eating that. Too chewy. Yuck!"'

'It's probably like veal,' offered Ox.

'I do not agree with that,' said Reggie. 'Veal, I mean. Although also the baby thing.'

'*Whore!*'

'*Skank!*'

Reggie tutted. 'This is deteriorating.'

Ox leaned in closer. 'Here's something that's really starting to bother me. We have people coming in and blaming all manner of everything for ruining the world. Elaborate conspiracies left, right and centre.'

'And?' asked Stella.

'And,' continued Ox, 'does it not strike anyone as strange that nobody has ever come in here and said, "Hey, there's this bunch of immortal megalomaniacs called the Founders that run the world and they can live for ever by sucking the life of the magical people that also happen to be knocking about the place."'

His words were met with silence.

Well, near silence . . .

'*Strumpet!*'

'*Tart!*'

'You're absolutely right,' said Reggie. 'That is . . .'

The door at the far end of the room slammed open and Grace appeared through it, struggling under the weight of two large boxes.

She looked down at the women rolling around on the floor. 'For all that is good and holy, what is going on here?'

'It's . . .' started Ox.

The man who was reading his paper saved Ox from coming up with the rest of his sentence by piping up. 'Those two women are having a scrap over who's married to the M62 and, ironically, it's causing a traffic jam.'

Grace tossed the boxes to the ground, causing a mini avalanche of paperwork to spill out. She strode across the floor, glaring at her trio of colleagues as she passed them. She stopped above the ongoing wrestling match. 'Stop that this instant.'

'*Jezebel!*'

'*Hussy!*'

Grace placed her hands on her hips. 'Hmph! They say that dust on your Bible leads to dirt in your life! You two had better be referring to each other. Stop this embarrassing display this instant or I shall be forced to call the police.'

'Wow,' said Ox. 'That was fast.'

Grace gave him a confused look then followed his gaze to the top of the stairs where DI Tom Sturgess was standing. He gave them an awkward wave.

'Is this a bad time?'

CHAPTER 18

DI Tom Sturgess found himself being unceremoniously plonked down into a chair in the main office of *The Stranger Times* by Grace, who then clutched her hands together and caused her bracelets to jangle.

'May I get you a cup of tea?' she asked.

'No, thank you.'

'Ginger nut biscuit?'

'Not for me.'

She leaned in and lowered her voice. 'Seeing as you are an officer of the law, I do have a few chocolate biscuits stashed away.'

'I'm afraid Greater Manchester Police have strict rules about not accepting bribes.'

As the alarm registered on Grace's face, Sturgess sagged a little inside. This was why he so rarely made jokes as invariably they failed to land.

'Oh no, I wasn't—'

Sturgess attempted a smile. 'I know. I was just . . . I'm fine, thank you.'

'If you're sure. And thank you again for breaking up that unsightly display.'

'No problem,' said Sturgess. 'You'd be amazed how many fights between women I've had to break up over the years. I'm still a bit confused as to what it was about, though?'

'Which one of them is married to the M62.'

Sturgess paused then puffed out his cheeks with a resigned shrug. 'Makes a nice change from the football, I suppose.'

Grace, already standing up straight, somehow managed to straighten herself further. 'And what help can *The Stranger Times* be to you today?'

'I'm here because a member of your staff has disappeared.'

Grace's face fell, then she tilted her head and gave him a sympathetic look. 'Oh dear, I am so sorry. I had assumed Hannah would have contacted you.'

'No,' said Sturgess quickly. 'I'm not here about that.' Not that a part of him didn't want answers on that score, too. It had been early days, but he'd thought their relationship had been going well, right until the bombshell text message.

'I'm afraid she has gone back to her philandering husband.'

'Really?' The question popped out before Sturgess could stop himself.

'I am afraid so,' continued Grace with a sad nod. 'Normally, I am all for the sanctity of marriage, but she deserves much better than that awful man.' She leaned in, touched Sturgess's shoulder and dropped her voice to a softer register. 'If it is any consolation, I was definitely Team Detective Inspector Sturgess on this one.'

Sturgess cleared his throat. 'Honestly, it's fine. That's not what I'm here about. Is Banecroft around?'

'He has gone out. As has our assistant editor.' Grace winced. 'Not Hannah – the new one.'

'Right.'

'She just started. She seems like a nice lady but I am not sure she is your type.'

'Again. I'm here about the missing member of staff.'

'Right. Well, I'm happy to report that we have a full complement of staff,' confirmed Grace, 'except for the woman who unexpectedly left and inadvertently broke your heart.'

Sturgess opened his mouth but, for the life of him, couldn't think how to possibly respond. After a couple of awkward seconds, he decided to ignore it entirely and plough on. 'You have an occasional column in your paper written under the name Dex Hex?'

'Yes,' said Grace, an air of suspicion to her voice.

'The man behind it has disappeared.'

He watched a confusing array of emotions pass across Grace's face.

'Right. OK. Right. I'll . . . I'd better get the others.'

'Would anyone like a cup of tea?'

It appeared to be her verbal tic – in any stressful situation, Grace automatically offered everyone involved a cuppa.

'We're fine, thank you, dear,' said Reggie.

She nodded and took a seat alongside him, Stella and Ox, all of whom were now sitting in a line facing Sturgess.

'We should try to not be too long,' fretted Grace. 'Manny is in charge of the queue and he is . . . currently quite emotional.'

'Yes,' said Sturgess, 'I'd imagine he is. I had to show him my warrant card to get past the duelling queues outside, and I think he may have misinterpreted the purpose of my visit. He felt the sudden need to rush to the toilet, and whatever he did there involved quite a bit of flushing.'

Detective Inspector Sturgess couldn't help but be a little bit impressed at the straight faces the quartet were managing to keep.

'He has a dicky tummy,' offered Reggie.

'Yeah,' said Ox. 'I'd imagine he is feeling proper sick right now.'

'I meant to say,' said Sturgess, changing tack, 'I don't need all of you for this, if someone needs to go outside and help him?'

'I am the office manager,' said Grace.

'I am technically the most senior member of staff present in the building,' said Reggie.

'I am actually the most senior member of staff in the building,' said Ox, as he and Reggie shared a look.

Sturgess looked at Stella, who simply shrugged. 'I just needed a break from talking to the nutters and this looked like it might be something.'

'I see,' he said. 'Well, which one of you would like to tell me about Dex Hex?'

He noted the look, or rather the non-look, from Reggie, who caught himself from turning towards Ox just in time.

'Nobody of that name ever actually worked here,' said Ox. 'It was just the pseudonym somebody used for the sporadic column we had that discussed the more bizarre conspiracy theories doing the rounds.'

'"Was"?' Sturgess queried.

'Yes,' interjected Reggie. 'Mr Banecroft terminated it in his first week on the job. He felt it didn't mesh well with the paper's goals.'

'Or to put it another way,' said Ox, '"Why am I paying somebody to come up with nonsense when I've got people turning up at the door with cartloads of it that they want to give me for free?" He didn't actually use the word "nonsense", but I've cleaned up his choice of vocab for this audience.'

'Thank you,' said Grace.

'But you didn't know who wrote the column?'

'We did not,' said Reggie. 'Dex Hex deliberately remained a mysterious figure.'

'Yeah,' agreed Ox. 'They just emailed in the column whenever the mood took them.'

'Was the person behind it paid for it?'

'They were,' confirmed Reggie. 'I don't know exactly how much, but I would hazard a guess that it wasn't a great deal. At the risk of denting the air of glamour around this place, none of us are particularly well compensated for our skills. But, as I said, it has been quite a while since we printed any of the Dex Hex columns.'

'I understand. Still, can anyone tell me how this mysterious person was paid?'

A pregnant pause fell, and was eventually broken by Grace. 'I would . . . have to check our records.'

'If you could, I would appreciate it.'

'I'll have to find them first . . .' There was an unmistakable air of dread in her voice.

'If it helps, the man behind the column was called Tony Dawson,' Sturgess revealed.

'Tony?' exclaimed Ox.

'You know him?'

'Yeah. He's an occasional hanger-on at UFO get-togethers and all that. Bit odd. I mean, quite a few people at those things are, but he was very shy. I don't think I've ever heard him speak. He's claiming to be Dex Hex?'

'He isn't claiming anything,' said Sturgess. 'He's been kidnapped.'

'No, he hasn't,' said Ox.

'You seem sure of that.'

'It's a publicity stunt. Must be.'

Sturgess shook his head. 'I'm afraid not.' He studied each of the staffers in turn, then reached down to his brown leather satchel and pulled out a laptop. 'I've got something you should see.'

He flipped open the device, set it on the nearest desk and played the recording from the video doorbell of 12 Fitzgerald Street. As the storm troopers appeared in shot, Grace gasped and held a hand to her mouth.

Once the clip had finished, Ox spoke first. 'Tony got kidnapped by the SAS?'

'That is not the SAS,' said Sturgess. 'Judging by your faces, one of you has seen them before.' His eyes came to rest on Stella and the other three heads turned sharply to look at her too.

She pointed at the screen. 'Those dudes work for the Founders.'

'Yes,' said Sturgess. 'So, my question is, what could Dex Hex aka Tony Dawson have done to attract their attention?'

'I've got no idea,' said Ox.

There was that non-look look again as Reggie tensed.

Sturgess sighed. 'I was afraid you were going to say that.' He decided that now was the point at which it was necessary to apply a little extra pressure. 'His poor sister is beside herself with worry.'

'But you know it's the Founders,' said Stella. 'Can't you just knock on their door and demand him back? I mean, you're the police.'

'Yes,' said Sturgess. 'The problem I have is – well, there are several problems, actually. First, they don't have a front door I can knock on. Believe me, I've been trying to contact Dr Carter, but I can't find her either, and, while you and I both know that the men in that video work for the Founders, it's not like I have any evidence that would allow me to escalate this investigation. Officially, the GMP are taking the line that this is all an elaborate prank.'

'But it isn't,' said Grace.

'I know. I am the one police officer in this town that doesn't need convincing of that fact. It's why I came here. I, or to be more exact, Tony Dawson and his poor sister, need your help.' He fixed his gaze on Reggie as he spoke.

Reggie lowered his eyes for a moment then cleared his throat. 'Inspector, could you give me a moment to confer with my colleague?'

'Sure.'

Without another word, Reggie stood up and made his way to a corner of the room. After a moment's hesitation, Ox stood up and followed him. Stella unashamedly watched their rather intense whispered disagreement while Grace smiled awkwardly at Sturgess then clapped her hands together.

'The weather is very appropriate for this time of year, is it not?'

'I suppose so,' said Sturgess.

'Very appropriate,' repeated Grace.

Sturgess watched as Ox threw up his hands before turning around and heading back to his seat, with Reggie in his wake.

'Detective Inspector,' said Ox once he'd sat down, 'if a hypothetical individual had potentially relevant information regarding this matter, could they give it to you under the assurance that said information would not be shared with the hypothetical individual's employer?'

'I'm not sure I followed all of that, but I think I can answer that by saying I'm here to get Tony Dawson back. I have no need to tell Banecroft or anyone else anything that doesn't help that happen.'

'Right,' said Ox. He glanced at Reggie, who gave him an encouraging nod. 'Tony Dawson wasn't Dex Hex.'

'I've seen the email account on his computer.'

'Yeah, it got hacked about eighteen months ago. I mean, he might have just guessed the password.'

Sturgess nodded. 'And how do you know this?'

Ox wrinkled his nose and winced. 'I was Dex Hex. I needed a bit of extra money, so I convinced our old editor, Barry, that I knew somebody who wanted to write a column about the most out-there conspiracy theories on the internet.'

'So, you wrote all the columns?' asked Sturgess.

'Yeah. To be honest with you, I used to make them up when I was pissed. I can't even remember most of them. The whole thing was meant to wind up all the online conspiracy nuts as much as anything. Make them look foolish by coming up with the most insane stuff I could think of. A bit of silly fun and a few quid. Somebody took control of the email address last year, but the column had been deep-sixed by Banecroft by then, anyway. Besides, what could I say? Someone is pretending to be the person I was pretending to be?'

'Oh, Ox,' sighed Grace.

'The fake Dex Hex – Tony Dawson – spent most of his time defending the weird bollocks I came up with in the online forums. I was, like, so what? I mean, it didn't seem like it was doing any harm.'

'I see.' Sturgess pointed at the laptop where the final image of the van driving away was still frozen on the screen. 'Well, I'm afraid your bit of silly fun got a man kidnapped by some very un-fun people. We need to figure out what you said to cause them to react like this, or there's a good chance nobody will ever see Tony Dawson again.'

Bean Caught Speeding

The world of performative charity fundraising is in turmoil today, after the record for pushing a human being in a bath full of baked beans from Land's End to John O'Groats has been utterly smashed. The 1,083-mile trip from one end of Great Britain to the other was undertaken by a team of eight employees from a well-known supermarket chain, all of whom were chosen at random as part of a morale-building exercise.

One of the employees, Dawn Teale, takes up the story. 'Well, we all asked for a pay rise and, as a compromise, the company told us we could do this, which, come to think of it, is not what we asked for. Anyway, we had a short ceremony down at Land's End when the CEO flew in on a helicopter, chucked the last tin of beans over Nina, and off we went. We were stunned when, just over two hours later, we turned a corner and boom, we were at John O'Groats. I don't know what happened, but it was definitely nothing to do with Nina.'

Team member Mark Finley commented, 'It was mental. We were only walking along, and it was like the whole of Britain sort of disappeared. It was definitely nothing to do with Nina.'

Team leader Karen Karenson stated, 'To be honest, I was really disappointed. I was trying to get everyone into a game of I spy – you know, to distract everyone from Nina pointing out how utterly stupid it all was and how we should just give the money to charity and blah blah blah, then suddenly, we're done. It was definitely nothing to do with Nina, though.'

When asked to comment, Nina – no last name given – confirmed with a smile, 'It was definitely nothing to do with me.'

CHAPTER 19

As Hannah stepped out into the early afternoon sunlight, she ruminated on the fact that she hated every phrase with the word 'casual' in it. Smart-casual? That just meant having to buy clothes you didn't really want to wear in or out of the office. Casual dining? In her experience that translates to "our wait staff are so bad, we're making them a feature". And as for describing a relationship as casual? She and DI Tom Sturgess had done just that. Their respective jobs clashed. Hannah was coming out of a long-term relationship; she had inadvertently found out that he'd never been in one. And then there was the fact that, unbeknown to Tom, a parasitic eyeball on a stalk was living in his head. Their relationship had more tension than most hostage situations. Casual it was not.

Then there was Hannah's current situation here at the Pinter Institute. The instruction she'd been given had seemed pretty straightforward: exit through the large double doors that lead to the vast lawns outside and casually walk over to the bench near the large fountain. She had been walking successfully for many years, but she found herself re-examining her technique. Trying to determine if she looked casual enough.

She attempted to throw in more of a hip sway and nearly

tripped over her own feet. For a few steps, she inexplicably threw in a finger click, like an ensemble cast member in an amateur production of *West Side Story*. Blushing, Hannah shoved her hands into the pockets of her tracksuit and gave up on nonchalance entirely in favour of upping her pace. As she walked, she whistled nervously, only stopping when she realized she had chosen the theme tune to *Mission: Impossible*. *Smooth, Hannah. Smooth.*

She slammed herself on to the bench with a sigh of relief, as if she had made it through another round alive in some unseen game of musical chairs. *Mission: Possible* accomplished, she looked around. It was a glorious late summer's day. The sun beat down on her face. Bees buzzed, birds tweeted.

The lawns were the size of half a dozen football pitches, and yet nobody was playing football. Over to one side, a group of about ten residents was being led in a tai chi class, while in the distance on the other side, another group was throwing a ball between its members in some form of trust-building exercise. *Oh God*, thought Hannah, *please don't make me do that*.

She was still feeling discombobulated after her session with Dr French. She had a memory of their time together, but it had an odd, dreamlike quality to it. A bit like she could recall having a conversation about her relationship with her parents, while also being convinced that said conversation had never happened. It was a deeply unpleasant sensation, as if she couldn't trust her own mind.

Hannah realized she should probably be doing something as she sat on the bench. Keeping her eye out for a signal, perhaps. She tried to look around surreptitiously. In the middle of the fountain, a buxom woman carved out of stone was shooting water out of her mouth and hands while cherubic children danced below her.

She'd been told to come to this spot exactly – out in the open with the treeline a good forty metres away – but she didn't know how she was supposed to meet somebody there, at least not without that person being seen, which would undermine everything. She watched a couple of pheasants walk by with their perpetual air of bewildered royalty, gabbling away to themselves.

Then the thought struck her – the bench. She'd been told to come to this specific bench. She focused her attention on the stone rendering of the woman spewing water for all eternity while she ran her fingers along the underside of the seat. Nothing. She bent down to tighten the laces of her trainers and scanned the ground under the bench. Again, nothing. Not even a piece of chewing gum. She sat back up, and that was when she noticed the rock a couple of feet to the left of the bench. Now that she'd seen it, it was obviously incongruous. There wasn't a single other rock about the place.

Slowly, she started to sidle along the bench.

'Hiya, hen.'

Hannah yelped and whirled around to find a sweaty Moira, hands on her knees, panting heavily while a muscular blonde man jogged on the spot beside her, looking ecstatically happy about something as he grinned at the world.

'Sorry,' said Hannah. 'You startled me.'

Moira pointed back over her shoulder. 'Did you not feel the ground shaking as I was pounding towards you?'

The jogger-on-the-spot chipped in, 'Come on, Moira – nearly home now. No pain, no gain. Feel the burn.'

She shot him a withering look. 'Jesus. What is it with fit people and tedious clichés?'

'Loving that energy!' he chimed. 'Let's put it into crushing the last part of this run.' He threw up his hand for a high-five.

Moira placed her hands on her hips. 'What have we talked about, Chad? You try to high-five me one more time and I'll shove that hand somewhere that'll mean you'll be able to tickle your own tonsils from the inside.'

Chad demonstrated an alarming lack of survival instincts by giving a hearty laugh and pointing to his still-extended hand. 'Bring it in.'

Moira shook her head in exasperation and turned to face Hannah, rolling her eyes in the process.

'But—'

'Adults are talking, sweetie. You stay there for a sec and flex something.' Moira gripped the back of the bench and proceeded to stretch out her hamstrings. 'It's like somebody bred a Hemsworth brother with the Andrex puppy. Have you just had your colonic irrigation?'

'What?' responded Hannah. 'No.'

'Oh, right. Sorry. I just saw you walking across the lawn and . . .'

Well, thought Hannah. At least she now knew for sure that her inability to walk casually was not just in her mind. 'No. I've just had my first session with Dr French.'

'Have you now? Dr Dangle as I call her. I don't care what anyone says, those earrings are a health and safety risk. She turns around too quickly and somebody will lose an eye. How'd it go?'

'Well, it's hard to say.'

Moira straightened up and the smile dropped from her face. 'Sorry, ignore me. What a spectacularly intrusive question, even for me.' She shook her head. 'Good one, Moira.'

'No, honestly—' started Hannah, before she was interrupted by the human Andrex puppy clearing his throat pointedly.

Without looking around, Moira raised her voice. 'You need to get that cough seen to, Chad. It sounds incredibly unhealthy.'

Hannah watched his perma-grin crack as the briefest moment of self-doubt crept in. 'Really?'

'Aye. Do it again and there's every chance it could prove fatal.' Moira flashed a quick smile at Hannah and patted her on the shoulder before running off. She shouted over her shoulder towards Chad. 'Come on, slowpoke. If you beat me to the finish line, I'll let you hump my leg for a bit.'

Hannah watched the duo head into the distance, then, after making sure nobody else was anywhere near her, she continued to slide across the bench towards the incongruous rock. As she casually stretched her foot towards it to drag it closer, a bird landed on the back of the bench and gave her a quizzical look.

'Hello, Mr Bird, how are you today?' she asked, as she reached down and picked up the fist-sized rock.

In her defence, while she did yelp and toss the rock in the air, she managed to maintain enough sense of her surroundings to avoid getting walloped by it on its descent. It wasn't the worst of reactions given Hannah's understandable shock when the bird answered her.

CHAPTER 20

It wasn't that Hannah didn't recognize the voice. In fact, it belonged to the person she had come to the bench specifically to speak to. She just hadn't expected to hear it coming from an eight-inch-long bird. She was no ornithologist, but she was pretty sure it was a starling.

'Mrs Harnforth,' she said, feeling ridiculous, 'is that you?'

'Oh good,' came the rich dulcet tones of the proprietor of *The Stranger Times*, 'you can hear me.'

The bird turned its head and gave Hannah a quizzical look, but its beak didn't move in sync with the voice. Initially, Hannah had thought the animal was mostly black in colour, but when she looked more closely, she could see the feathers on its chest were dark green and blue in places.

Hannah had met Mrs Harnforth in person only twice. The first time had been during her first week at *The Stranger Times*, when Mrs Harnforth had wandered in and explained calmly to Hannah and Vincent Banecroft that everything about how they believed the world ran was wrong, and then sauntered off again. The second time had been that fateful Friday evening a few weeks ago when Hannah had been walking home. A green Bentley had pulled up beside her, Mrs Harnforth's distinctive head of stylishly coiffed pink hair had appeared out the window and she'd asked, 'Have you got a second for a quick chat?'

Hannah had sat in silence on the back seat's plush leather interior as Mrs Harnforth had made her pitch. Hannah had been vaguely aware of the Pinter Institute before this – everybody was, given the media's obsession with Winona Pinter and her wacky ways – but she hadn't given it much thought. At least, no more thought than she had a Kardashian or a *Love Island* contestant. Nevertheless, she had been shocked when Mrs Harnforth had informed her that her soon-to-be ex-husband Karl had recently attended a retreat at the Institute. Before that point he'd shown no interest in self-reflection. Mrs Harnforth had explained that she'd been investigating the Pinter Institute for quite some time and was convinced there was something very, very wrong happening there.

'Are you telling me that Karl has joined a cult?' Hannah had asked.

Mrs Harnforth had pursed her lips. 'Not exactly. In fact, I think probably not at all. This is something different, and while I have some suspicions, we need to find out exactly what is going on.'

'Right. Well, this sounds like precisely the kind of thing Vincent would love to investigate so we can . . .' Hannah had paused when she'd noticed the look on Mrs Harnforth's face. 'What?'

The older woman had reached across and patted Hannah's hand. 'I'm afraid this is where the whole thing becomes rather sticky. Vincent can't know anything about this. These people are paranoid beyond belief, and the first sniff of a newspaper being interested in what they're doing, even *The Stranger Times*, they'll shut it down and move the circus somewhere else. That's not good enough. For reasons I can't fully explain right now, we need to know everything, and quickly.'

'But what can I do?'

'What we desperately need is somebody on the inside. Your non-ex ex gives us a way in – you.'

Hannah had spent quite some time thinking about it and she still wasn't sure what it said about her. On the word of a woman she barely knew, she'd given up the new life she had fought so hard to achieve. Was she eager to help or just desperate to be liked? Not only did she have to resign, but she also had to make sure everyone believed it was genuine, as Mrs Harnforth was convinced that the Pinter Institute would check it out. Even if it was for good reasons, just dropping everything and walking out on her friends had made Hannah feel sick.

She'd been half hoping that when she met the new Karl he wouldn't float the idea of Hannah attending the Pinter Institute but, as Mrs Harnforth had correctly predicted, he did. As she'd said at the time, groups like the Institute always target couples. Since then, things had happened fast, and Hannah still wasn't sure how she felt about it.

Karl had been undeniably different, but it also had been a change for the better. At the very least he'd finally mastered the art of maintaining eye contact with eyes as opposed to other areas of the body, or other people's other areas. What was the crime there? So far, while the whole place had been decidedly odd, there had been little that qualified as sinister. At least, not until her little chat with Dr French.

Hannah snapped back to the present when she realized that Mrs Harnforth was speaking to her again.

'Can you hear me OK?'

'Yes,' she responded. 'Sorry. I just wasn't expecting you to be . . . a bird.'

'I'm not a bird, dear. I'm just speaking to you via an electronic device attached to the leg of the bird.'

Hannah squinted and was mortified to see the small metal device, which, in hindsight, was rather obvious.

'Of course,' said Hannah, cringing with embarrassment. 'That makes more sense.'

The bird shook its head and flapped a wing. 'Not too bright this one, is she, Mrs H? Not too bright.' The voice was simultaneously gruff and sing-song, and on this occasion, the beak moved in sync with it.

'Gordon!' admonished Mrs Harnforth. 'Apologies for him, Hannah. While he is very useful, he is also rather rude.'

'Rude I am. Am I rude? Rude boy. I'm a rude boy.'

When Hannah heard it speak for a second time, the bird actually sounded Welsh.

'Right,' said Hannah, more to herself than anyone else. 'The bird can talk. Of course it can. This is my life now. It's arguably no less insane than a talking bulldog, after all.'

'She knows Zeke,' warbled the bird.

'I do,' confirmed Hannah.

'Not actually a dog, though, is he? Not really. Not really. Not really. Technically, he is still a man living in the form of a dog. Not the same. Not the same.'

Hannah realized who Gordon reminded her of – a mechanic that she had dreaded taking her car to for years because, while he was reasonably priced and did fix the thing, his persona was full-on geezer and he insisted on living up to it. Gordon spoke in a similar manner while also singing parts of his speech. It left you feeling as if you were being heckled by a chanting football crowd comprising one small bird.

'Yes,' interrupted Mrs Harnforth's disembodied voice. 'Technically that is true.'

'That's right. That's right. That's right,' chirped Gordon. 'Dogs can't talk. Most birds can't talk.'

'Only you and parrots,' said Hannah. She had meant it as an offhand, jovial remark but the bird's reaction was incredible. Its face had really no expression, and yet, it somehow conveyed an air of instant outrage.

Mrs Harnforth's voice came out as a little electronic sigh.

'Oh no.'

Gordon jabbed his head back and forward as his wings flapped in time, now in total geezer mode. 'What did she say? What did she say?'

'She said nothing, Gordon.'

'Yes, she did. Yes, she did. Parrots? Parrots cannot talk. All they do is impressions. Stupid impressions. Stupid impressions. Like a covers band. Playing 'Love Me Do' does not make you The Beatles. Make you it does not. A parrot can parrot the dead parrot sketch, but it doesn't make it Monty Python. It just makes it a parrot.'

'I understand,' said Hannah. She didn't, but she was possessed by that crushing middle-class anxiety that she had unthinkingly offended somebody.

'And don't get me started on owls,' continued Gordon.

'Nobody is!' interjected Mrs Harnforth in a pleading tone.

'I'll tell you what the problem with owls is.'

'Oh no.'

'People think owls, people think owls, owls people think are so clever just because people put glasses on them in a few cartoons. Suddenly they are wise. Then J. K. Rowling bigs them up – claiming they can deliver magical doodahs and whatnots. I'll tell you. I'll tell you, I will tell you – you give a letter to an owl, not only are you not seeing that letter again, but there's every chance you're down a finger too. Meanwhile, pigeons, pigeons, yeah. Been delivering messages loyally for centuries, often through enemy fire, basically won this country two world wars, and what are they treated as? Vermin! Flying rats. It's a travesty, I tell you, travesty it is, travesty.'

'Right,' said Hannah, glancing around to confirm there was nobody within earshot to hear a starling losing it.

'Moving on,' came Mrs Harnforth's voice.

'And as for ravens,' continued Gordon. 'Biggest shower of pricks you'll ever meet.'

'Oh dear,' said Mrs Harnforth, sounding entirely resigned to this unstoppable tirade.

'Ravens,' he persisted, 'think they're all that. All that. Mystical and ominous. You ever spoken to a raven? No, you haven't. Haven't you not. Dull as dishwater and surprisingly racist. I'll tell you who else is vastly overrated—'

'No,' said Mrs Harnforth, clearly having decided enough was enough. 'Gordon, you are here to assist me. Remember? The plan. We had a plan. We are going to stick to the plan. You will stop explaining things right this instant or I will have words with Agatha.'

Gordon opened and closed his beak several times before tilting his head back to give Hannah a haughty look. 'She started it.'

'And now it is finished.'

Hannah thought Gordon was going to speak again, but he turned his head away huffily. Hannah didn't know who Agatha was, but apparently, she held rather a lot of sway.

'Very well,' said Mrs Harnforth, sounding relieved. 'Now, how have things been going?'

Hannah ran through everything that had happened since she had set foot, or rather planted her face, outside the Pinter Institute. Mrs Harnforth listened in silence, so much so that Hannah occasionally wondered if she was still there. Gordon, on the other hand, was now looking at her with rapt attention, opening his beak to speak a few times but resisting the urge. Hannah was relieved about that. It had been a weird few days but having to explain colonic irrigation to an irritable starling might push her beyond the maximum weirdness threshold.

'And then,' said Hannah, finishing up, 'I came here, as instructed.'

'I see,' said Mrs Harnforth's voice, distorting slightly as it came through the speaker. 'So, you remember talking to this Dr French about your parents?'

Hannah hesitated. 'I think I do.'

'Yes, but something feels odd about it, doesn't it?'

Hannah nodded, relieved to hear that wasn't all in her imagination.

Gordon spoke again. 'She just nodded.'

'Oh, right,' said Hannah, remembering herself. 'Yes, it does.'

'Good,' said Mrs Harnforth. 'Well, the good news is, that's because you never actually had that conversation. This is exactly what we discussed might happen.'

'I see.' Hannah wasn't comfortable with a substantial deal of this, but if she had to pick the part that bothered her most, she'd plump for what Mrs Harnforth had referred to as the implantation. Once Hannah had agreed to the plan, Mrs Harnforth had sat her down and put her into a trance. It had been explained as a countermeasure. If someone was to go poking around in Hannah's mind, they would find only the cover story. It all felt horribly intrusive, both the idea of someone rummaging around in there and the fact that it was possible to implant a false narrative in the first place. Tom Sturgess and that thing living in his head, unknown to him, popped into her mind again. She felt a little queasy.

Another thought struck her. 'How do we know it worked? That she found the false memories you put in there for her to find?'

'Well,' replied Mrs Harnforth, 'you're here now.'

Her answer did nothing to make Hannah feel better. They had not discussed what could happen if the Pinter Institute discovered she wasn't what they thought she was. That was going to stay with her all day.

'They couldn't . . .' Hannah hesitated, but then decided to ask what she wanted to know. 'They couldn't have put something else in there, could they? I mean, aside from this talk about my parents that didn't happen?'

'Such as?' asked Mrs Harnforth.

'I don't know. More false memories or whatever. Maybe I like green beans now. I never liked green beans. Or maybe I loved green beans all along and now I just think I've never liked them. Or, I mean, you could put anything in there and . . .'

'It's fine, Hannah. I don't think they would have any interest in doing that.'

'OK, but you admitted you don't know what they're doing here, do you?'

'What's a green bean?' asked Gordon.

The two women simply ignored him.

'That's true,' said Mrs Harnforth in a soothing voice. 'I don't know for sure what's going on, but I have some ideas. I promise I will explain it all when the time is right. You'll have to trust me because – I can't say why, but time has become more pressing. We need you to look around tonight.'

'Wait,' said Hannah. 'Look around? How exactly? There are security cameras everywhere and the doors are on electronic locks.'

'Yes, but we believe we can get around that. We hope.'

'You hope?' repeated Hannah.

'Apologies – terrible choice of words. We are confident we can get around the cameras and the doors, et cetera. Our new team member is working on it right now. We will know for sure in a couple of hours. You said you were in room twenty-eight?'

'Yes.'

'Excellent. Be careful to hide the earpiece and pop it in at exactly midnight.'

'But . . . Hang on. What earpiece? What new member of the team?' asked Hannah. 'I mean, there's a team? Why am I being kept in the dark about what's going on? I think I need answers. Actually, I think I deserve them.'

There was no response.

'Well?'

Hannah turned to find she was talking to fresh air; Gordon had flown off.

'Oh, that's just brilliant. I really am just talking to myself now. Wonderful.'

She looked around in every direction then leaned her head back over the bench and closed her eyes. 'I am so tired.'

She sensed, more than heard, a flutter of wings above her and opened her eyes just in time to see a tiny object heading straight for her face. It bounced off her nose before landing in her lap. She picked it up. It appeared to be an earpiece wrapped in cellophane.

'Well, I guess that answers that question.'

She hauled herself up off the bench and started to walk towards the main building when she noticed the figure of Brad, the hot yoga instructor whose class she was currently missing, striding purposefully across the lawn towards her.

'Oh, brilliant.'

CHAPTER 21

Cogs raised a forkful of spaghetti to his lips, paused, then dropped it back on his plate uneaten.

'What?' asked Zeke.

'Don't you "what" me.'

'I didn't say anything.' Zeke's nose hovered over his dish of spaghetti.

'You pulled a face.'

'I did not.'

'You did.'

'I'm a dog.'

'Ah, but you aren't.'

'You know what I mean,' said Zeke. 'I've got a dog's face. It has a limited range of expressions.'

'Yeah, and there's one you use when you don't like something. Like a minute ago.'

'It's just . . .'

Cogs tossed his plate of spaghetti on to the deck beside his sun lounger. 'That's it. From now on, you can do the cooking.'

'I would if I could,' said the not-technically-a-bulldog who looked an awful lot like a bulldog, 'but I haven't got opposable thumbs.'

'Ooooh! Opposable thumbs,' mimicked Cogs. 'I'm thinking of cutting off my thumbs. It seems all they're good for is getting blamed for stuff. You've made not having opposable thumbs into a pretty sweet deal.'

'Calm down, drama queen. All I'm saying is, a little bit of seasoning for—'

An old mechanical alarm clock burst into annoying life at a deafening volume.

'For crying out loud!' Cogs silenced it by tossing his near-empty beer can at it, which resulted in the clock falling off the edge of the houseboat and into the canal.

He quickly got to his feet and addressed the water. 'Sincere apologies, m'lady.' He bowed and righted himself just in time to catch the alarm clock, which had come shooting back out of the canal and was now flying over his head. It was still ringing, although it sounded considerably more waterlogged. Cogs dropped it on to the deck, picked up a nearby hammer and, with a series of swinging blows, put the alarm clock out of its misery.

'Feel better?' asked Zeke.

'D'ya know,' said Cogs, standing back up, 'I really do. We need to get some more alarm clocks.'

'Well, that one died in the cause of reminding you it is now one o'clock.' Zeke looked up at Cogs's blank expression. 'Really?' Zeke nodded his head in the direction of the sheet draped over the washing line that stretched from one end of the houseboat to the other.

Cogs rolled his eyes. 'Oh yeah, that.' He sighed, then, with his free hand, pulled down the sheet. 'Roll up, roll up, roll up, and welcome to Cogs's House of Truth where . . .'

He stopped as he looked over the footbridge fifteen feet away that spanned the Bridgewater Canal where his boat was moored. The boat was positioned away from the shore for good reasons and a half-dozen of those reasons were currently standing on the bridge.

'Six of them!' he cried. 'Six,' he repeated, looking down at Zeke. 'We are getting dangerously popular.'

'Who is he talking to?' asked the man wearing an England football shirt at the front of the queue.

Cogs pointed the hammer in the direction of the man. 'Never you mind, sonny.'

'Sonny?' said the man. 'I'm older than you are.'

The woman who was with him shushed him into silence. Before she could speak, Cogs held up his hands.

'Whoa, whoa, whoa – before anybody asks anything, rules is rules. I'm sending the bucket across. Please give generously.' And with that, Cogs pulled the lever that sent a bucket jerking along a line across the canal until it bumped into the footbridge. 'Please place your offerings into the offering receptacle.'

Four members of the queue dutifully obliged. The man in the England top and the woman next to him were clearly a couple. At the back of the queue, a woman in a sun hat looked guiltily at the bucket then raised her hand.

Cogs pointed the hammer at the woman. 'You forgot, didn't you?'

She nodded.

'Then I'm afraid you're gonna have to come back next week. Like I said, rules is—' He was interrupted by the sensation of a bulldog tugging softly on the leg of his jeans. 'Excuse me for a moment.' Cogs bent down and looked like a man who was holding a whispered conversation with his dog, which everyone in the queue knew was impossible. After a few moments, he stood back up. 'Actually, if you wouldn't mind nipping across the road to Sainsbury's for a few things, you can come back and we'll fit you in.'

The woman gave a thumbs-up. Cogs recognized her as a regular and was gratified to see she was displaying an admirable adherence to the rules vis-à-vis not talking before you make an offering.

'OK, sweetheart. We need some garlic, basil, paprika, thyme, chilli powder and cinnamon . . .' Cogs looked down at the dog. 'What? Oh yeah, and some coriander and nutmeg.' Without another word, the woman departed on her errand.

'Excellent. Now,' said Cogs, pulling the lever the other way to retrieve the bucket, 'let's see what else we've caught in today's net.'

Cogs gave the contents of the bucket an appraising look. 'We have' – he pulled out a six-pack – 'a half-dozen cans of one of the more unimpressive mass-produced beers. Not a good start.' He dropped them on to the sheet that was lying at his feet. 'Next up . . . Hello – jackpot! Someone got the memo. A bottle of spiced rum – the good stuff too. We have a leader in the clubhouse.' He carefully placed the bottle on the upturned crate that was doing service as a table. 'And then we have . . .' He pulled out some vacuum-packed plastic packaging. 'Yes indeed. Some steaks. Now we're cooking with gas. Literally, we cook with gas. These will go down lovely, thank you very much.'

He wordlessly held out the package of meat in front of Zeke, who took it in his mouth and trotted off down below decks to place it in the fridge.

'And finally, we have . . .' He drew out a small cardboard package. 'Cigars.' He made no effort to keep the disappointment from his voice. 'Cigars,' he repeated. 'I don't smoke, and the dog has given up. These are a poor offering.'

He looked across at the bridge and saw a man in a suit opening his mouth to speak. Cogs held up his hands to silence him.

'That's not how it works. You make your offering. You cannot plead the case for the offering – the offering is the offering.'

Zeke reappeared from below decks and Cogs showed him the offering. 'Cigars. Can you believe that? Cigars. I'm not even sure what we could do with these . . .' He tapped the package against his goatee. 'I suppose we could trade them with Dipshit Dave for some diesel.' He looked back at the man. 'All right, I'll accept it this one and only time. Actually, come to think of it – if any of you are intending to be repeat customers, we can always use diesel.'

Cogs went to give the cigars to Zeke, thought better of it and shoved them into the back pocket of his jeans. 'D'ya know what? Forget what I said about the diesel. No offence and all, but the calibre of some of the people we get coming here, I'm not sure I'd be comfortable with them walking round with containers of flammable fuel. Feels like an accident waiting to happen.'

Cogs drew up a stool, sat down on it and rubbed his hands together. 'OK. First up – who was the rum?'

A man wearing a pork-pie hat raised his hand.

'Right,' said Cogs. 'You are up.'

'That's bullshit!' said the bloke in the English football shirt. 'We were here first.'

'It doesn't go in order of who was here first, it goes by order of tribute. Which offering were you?'

'We were the beer,' said his female companion.

'You will be third, and thank your lucky stars that cigar boy is here.'

The man in the football top went to say something, but the woman grabbed his hand to silence him.

'Right, then – first customer, step up and receive the truth, the whole truth and nothing but the truth because for my sins I cannot lie, and that is not an expression, that is a fact.'

The man with the pork-pie hat stepped forward and removed it. Before he could say anything, Cogs raised his finger for silence.

'Oh dear. Let me stop you right there. Yes, you definitely, one hundred per cent can tell.'

'But—' started the man, pointing to what even a blind person could probably guess was not his real hair.

'But nothing, mate. Look, you're the rum guy. We love the rum guy. Even if I could lie to you, which I can't, I wouldn't. That thing is a disaster. Either get it off your head or teach it to sing a showtune, because keep wearing it and you're in showbiz.'

'He's not wrong,' said the six-pack woman in a kindly voice.

The man's head dropped, he snatched the blonde hairpiece from it and went to toss it into the water.

Cogs leaped to his feet. 'Don't! She's already in a bad mood and that will not go well for you.'

The boat rocked on the calm water.

'She's in an entirely justifiable mood,' clarified Cogs.

The man wedged the pork-pie hat back on his head, shoved the hairpiece into the pocket of his jacket and walked off forlornly.

'Thanks for coming, though,' Cogs shouted after him. 'Anyone who knows his rum is always welcome.' He shifted his attention to Zeke. 'Why is it always the best ones we have to give the worst news to?'

The canine gave the closest thing he could to a shrug.

Cogs sat back down on his stool. 'OK – steaks, you're up.'

A slender brunette woman in her mid-twenties stepped forward sheepishly. 'I was just wondering if I could get a second opinion, please.'

'First, second, third – doesn't matter, darling,' offered Cogs. 'I am literally overflowing with opinions.'

The woman gingerly removed her trench coat and winced, as if she was expecting the worst. 'I was just . . . If you wouldn't mind . . . I mean, I already know, but . . .'

'It's all right, love. Take your time.'

She nodded and swallowed nervously. 'Right. Does this dress make me look fat?'

Cogs looked at her for a long moment, then down at Zeke before shaking his head and giving a sigh. He pulled his stool forward as far as it could go, and the tone of his voice changed from its normal strident delivery to something much softer. 'OK. Now, as previously discussed, as I assume you know by reputation, and as you've already seen, I can only tell the truth. OK?'

She nodded nervously.

'Good, because this is important. That dress does not make you look fat. Do you know why? Because you, sweetheart, are not fat. Either when you're wearing that outfit or indeed anything else. In fact, I'd say you're a little underweight. More importantly, if there is anybody in your life who is telling you that that lovely dress makes you look fat, you need to push them out of the nearest window and get on with your life. Do you understand me?'

She gave an awkward smile and nodded.

A soft growl came from beside Cogs's leg. 'But before you do that, my dog here would like to bite that person or persons somewhere extremely memorable.'

She laughed and shrugged her coat back on, before waving goodbye and hurrying off.

Cogs watched her go. 'This world,' he muttered. 'I just don't know.' Remembering himself, he clapped his hands. At that point, he also noticed somebody he recognized joining the back of the queue. He acknowledged their presence with a nod.

'OK, the six-pack couple – you're on.'

The woman pointed at her companion. 'I want to know if he is cheating on me.'

Cogs threw back his head and groaned loudly at the sky. 'Give me strength.' He stood up and spread out his hands. 'How many times do I have to explain this to you people? It is a simple concept. I' – he grabbed his chest with both hands – 'am a man cursed only to be able to tell the truth. I am not a mind reader. I cannot tell the future and I am completely unable to find your cat or tell you if he' – he pointed at the man – 'or anyone else who is not me, has been cheating on you. What you need, darling, is a lie-detector test or an STD clinic. I am useless to you.'

'See, Tiffany?' said the man. 'I told you I wasn't.'

'For the love of . . . Just to be clear,' said Cogs, 'I am also definitely not saying he hasn't cheated on you.'

'So, what *are* you saying?' asked Tiffany.

Cogs slammed the palm of his hand into his forehead repeatedly. 'This, right here, is why I drink.' He spoke loudly and slowly, enunciating each individual word, as if trying to make himself understood by an old and incredibly deaf person. 'I. Can. Not. Say. Either . . .' He stopped himself. 'Hang on a second. Mate,' he said, pointing at the man, 'can you please raise your foot?'

The bloke in the football top gave him a bewildered look but followed his instruction.

'Yeah,' said Cogs, 'that's what I thought. He's wearing socks and sandals. Again – this is not part of the truth thing, but I'd be amazed if he could find two women willing to put up with that kind of sartorial choice. Frankly, I'm stunned he found one.'

Football Shirt took a step forward and puffed out his chest. 'You want to watch yourself, buddy, or I'm gonna come over there and give you something to watch.'

'Give me something to watch?' repeated Cogs. 'God, even his threats are awful.'

'Right, that is it.'

Football Shirt moved towards the edge of the bridge.

'I would not try to swim over here, fella. You'll drown before you reach halfway.'

The man laughed. 'Rubbish. It's probably not even five feet deep.'

'Trust me,' said Cogs, 'that will be more than enough.'

The man started to take his top off, but Tiffany grabbed his arm. 'Oh, for Christ's sake, Darren. Don't be a complete tool your whole life. Come on – I'm going home.'

'He . . .' started Darren, but Tiffany was already stomping away. With one last look in Cogs's direction he headed after her.

'If we're lucky,' said Cogs, 'the two of them won't breed.' He raised his voice again. 'OK, cigars. Let's make this quick.'

'Actually,' said the man in the suit, 'I was here last week. I left you a copy of my novel?'

'Oh, yeah – I think I might have tried to blank that from my memory.' Cogs bent down and picked up a bound manuscript of A4 paper from the deck. 'This thing?'

'Yes,' said the man. 'So, what did you think of it?'

'Before we get to that,' said Cogs, 'can I ask – why did you set it in Ireland?'

'My muse spoke to me.'

'His muse spoke to him,' repeated Cogs. 'Have you ever been to Ireland?'

'I was in Dublin a couple of years ago on a stag do.'

'Right. Well, I've not been there for a couple of hundred years, but even I know that actual Irish people do not end sentences with the words "to be sure" or "so it is".'

'Well . . . it's obviously exaggerated for comedic purposes.'

'Which brings me to – I had no idea this thing was supposed to be funny. It reads like somebody attempted to tell one of those computer things to write a novel, and this is the conclusive proof that they can't.'

'You didn't like it?' asked the man, folding his arms and looking huffy.

'The words "I didn't like it" do not do justice to my sentiments. I only read the first two chapters, but it is the worst thing I have ever been in the presence of. It's basically a hate crime. If an Irish person were to read it, there is every chance they would come and find you and beat you to death with it.'

'Have you got anything positive to say about it at all?'

Cogs paused. 'I do. It was absorbent.'

'Do you mean absorbing?'

'No. I mean absorbent. We spilled a bottle of wine last night and it soaked up quite a lot of it. We also ran out of toilet paper but,' – Cogs waved the manuscript in the air – 'I didn't want this thing to come into contact with that area of my body. For avoidance of doubt I am saying I literally would not wipe my arse with it.'

'You could at least try to be supportive.'

'I can't. Again – I have to speak the truth. So later, when you think back on this chat and remember all the horrible things I said – absolute truth. You know they say everyone has a book in them? You have disproved that theory.'

The man in the suit jabbed a finger at him. 'I'll have you know my wife thought it was hilarious.'

'Well, she is either the most loving woman in the world or, and this is my guess, she's having an affair and is shagging somebody else during whatever limited time you have given to writing this.'

The man drew himself up to his full height. 'You, sir, are a philistine.'

'I've met several Philistines and, overall, they were quite nice people. A couple of them were hilarious. A trait you do not share. Or, to put it in words you will understand – you are dreadful, to be sure, so you are.'

The man stomped off down the bridge, only stopping at the end to shout, 'You will be hearing from my lawyer!'

'All right!' returned Cogs. 'But if he's written a book and it's anything like this thing, tell him he's going to have to bring an awful lot of rum.'

Cogs tossed the manuscript back on to the deck. 'Later,' he said to Zeke, 'we'll open the rum, cook the steaks and burn this abomination.'

'Lovely,' said Zeke. 'But before that, don't forget we have a guest.'

'Oh, right. Sorry.' He turned to the remaining man on the bridge. 'Mr Banecroft, do come aboard.'

CHAPTER 22

Cogs punted the houseboat towards the shore.

'Mr Banecroft, I hope you appreciate the special treatment you are receiving. Only VIPs get to come on to the boat.'

'Yes,' replied Banecroft, 'I feel honoured. Although, I would have felt slightly more honoured if I hadn't had to wait for the dog-and-pony show to finish.'

'Well, rules is rules. Once I've accepted the tributes, I've got to do my thang, as the kids say.'

As the boat bumped against the shore, Banecroft stepped down on to the deck. 'I'm pretty sure the kids haven't said that for about twenty years.'

Cogs took a step back. 'I see somebody is in a good mood.'

'I don't have time for chit-chat. I need your help.'

'All right. As you know, I am always at the service of *The Stranger Times*. A big fan of your valuable work. You just need to pop a little tribute in the old bucket there.'

'I haven't brought anything. Let's consider this a rebate from last time. Remember, when you gave me and my staff that truly awful advice?'

Cogs dropped his oar. 'Hang on! Easy does it, tiger. I told you the truth. Vampires hadn't existed until that point. I told you what I knew, and as you bloody well know, I cannot lie to you. Can you believe this?'

The question was aimed at Zeke. When no answer was forthcoming, Cogs glanced in his direction and did a double-take. Zeke was at the far end of the deck, crouched on his hind legs. His front paws were extended, his teeth were bared and he was emitting a low growl.

'What the . . . What's wrong with you?'

'Smell. Bad. Bad smell. Smell bad.'

Cogs narrowed his eyes and looked between Banecroft and Zeke. He'd never seen his friend act this way before. 'Now, now, Zeke. We have a guest. Let's not be rude. And what's with the Tarzan impression?' He pointed at Banecroft. 'Cheetah. Friend.'

Zeke maintained his position, his top lip quivering over his bare teeth, his eyes wide.

Cogs turned back to Banecroft, his unease growing by the second. 'Sorry. Zeke seems to be having a bit of a moment.'

'Whatever,' snapped Banecroft. 'I don't have time for that. You need to tell me all you know about ghosts.'

Cogs scratched the back of his neck. In his limited dealings with the editor, the man had never been sweetness and light, but something did seem off. Cogs regarded himself as a pacifist – mainly because he wasn't any good at the other thing – but he felt his hands growing tight. Running wasn't an option but the jittery sensation in his legs didn't know that.

'I don't know that much about them. I mean, you gotta realize, it's an enormously big world, and it's not like we fae types hang out at, you know, magical parties. I've seen a couple of ghosts – they're essentially echoes of things that have passed on, but that's all I've got. Gnomes, however – I know an awful lot about gnomes. Pull up a chair and pour me a drink. I can bend your ear off talking about gnomes.'

'I don't care about—' Banecroft began to bark, before catching himself. He looked like someone who was putting a lot of effort into keeping themself under control. He tried again, more calmly. 'I need to know about ghosts.'

'What in particular?' asked Cogs. He tried to look Banecroft in the eyes. Maybe it was a trick of the light, a shadow from the man's overhanging mop of hair, but there was a darkness there. More than a lack of sleep. A lack of something far worse.

'Can they . . . Can they be taken over by another spirit? By . . . someone who is still alive?'

Cogs glanced again at Zeke, who was still maintaining his un-Zeke-like aggressive posture. 'I . . . If I'm honest with you – and, as you know, that's all I can be – I don't even understand the question. I'm not the man for this.'

'Fine,' snapped Banecroft. 'Who is?'

'Ehm . . .'

'There are people who can contact the dead, right? I know there are an awful lot of charlatans but, logically speaking, if there are all those people pretending that they can do it, there must be some who actually can.'

'There is,' said Cogs. 'Yes.'

'Right. Where can I find one of them?'

'I . . .'

'What?'

Cogs felt himself grimace. 'I don't want to tell you.'

Banecroft leaned in until Cogs could feel his breath on his face. 'Excuse me?'

'Look, why don't you sit down and tell us what's going on?'

'I'm not here for a chat.'

'It's just – you don't seem to be yourself, Vincent.'

'What I am is a man who needs some help. Now, are you going to help me or are you going to keep blathering on?'

Cogs eyed Zeke, hesitated, then looked back at Banecroft. 'No offence, guv, but I think I'd like you to get the hell off my boat.'

'So, you can help me, but you won't?'

Cogs folded his arms. 'Yes. Not right now, not like this. Maybe you should come back when you're feeling better.'

Banecroft nodded. 'Understood. I appreciate your point. Sorry for wasting your time.'

There was something about the way he spoke that Cogs didn't trust. 'OK,' he said, unsure of exactly what was happening.

Banecroft pulled his phone out of his pocket and, before Cogs could react, took his picture.

'Hey!'

'Sorry,' said Banecroft. 'I just need it for the story.'

'What story?'

'The one that will appear on the front page of *The Stranger Times* this Friday.' Banecroft drew a line in the air with his hand, laying out a headline. 'The man who can only tell the truth. Sub headline – and his talking dog.'

Cogs's eyes widened, scandalized. 'You wouldn't dare!'

'Wouldn't I? As far as I'm concerned, the world is divided into two kinds of people – those who can help me, and those who can be stories. You get to choose which you are. I imagine you'll have one hell of a queue here on Friday. You might want to put up some of those ropes. You could move location, of course, but I'm guessing it's hard to hide when you have to stay on the water.'

'You need to calm down, Banecroft.'

'No, what I need is the name of someone who can help me. Now, are you going to give me that or not?'

A couple of minutes later, Cogs sat down heavily on his sun lounger.

'That was—' started Zeke.

'I know. I know. I bloody know. I shouldn't have given him a name. And you,' he said, turning to look at his companion, 'what the hell was going on with you? You were acting weirder than he was.'

Zeke lay down in front of him. 'I don't know how to explain it in human terms. He smelled off – really off. Like rotten meat. Something is seriously wrong there.'

'Yeah, I . . .' Cogs shuffled awkwardly and pulled a cardboard packet out of his back pocket. 'I mean, it doesn't seem like that big a deal in the scheme of things, but for the record, I've only gone and sat on the bloody cigars.'

The bell tolled.

'Hello,' said Zeke. 'Look who's back.'

'Right, that's it.' Cogs leaped to his feet. 'I told you to f—' The invective stalled on his lips and he apologized to the woman nervously holding up a bag of groceries recently acquired from Sainsbury's. 'Sorry, love. Sorry. Thought you were someone else.'

Stephen King – Plagiarist?

Iconic author Stephen King is facing an unusual claim of plagiarism in the California Courts. The suit is being brought by one Roger Withershall, citing his book – *Whoops-a-daisy: Mr Crabtree Goes to Vegas* – as the plagiarized work. It was published two years before King's seminal work, *The Shining*.

Withershall contends that *'The Shining* contains all the same words that appear in *Whoops-a-daisy* – they're just in a different order. The hardest bit of writing is coming up with the words. I contend all King did was read my book, reorder the words, take out the bits with the stripper and the koala, substitute them for a haunted hotel, and *voilà*! He's been cashing cheques ever since.'

Mr Withershall previously captured the attention of the media when trying to get off a DUI charge by claiming that 'beer and bread are basically the same thing'.

CHAPTER 23

Stella looked down at the tabletop in front of her and groaned. It had already been a long day. In truth, she hadn't minded being pulled off Loon Day duty. It had been fascinating, infuriating and more than a little overwhelming, and she wasn't sure several more hours of it was something she could take. She had never been what you could call a people person – mainly because her experiences in life up until she had joined *The Stranger Times* had not left her with a positive impression of people.

Reggie had reassigned her because Stella was the closest thing the paper had to what he rather grandly referred to as an archivist. In practical terms, it meant she had spent her first few months with the newspaper attempting the Sisyphean task of collating every edition of the paper into a coherent library.

The Stranger Times being *The Stranger Times*, there was no online repository – the result of the previous editor Barry's fear of all things digital. So Stella had dug out any and all the old editions of *The Stranger Times* she could find round the office, and had unearthed lots of random crap along the way, including the manuscript for a version of the Bible that featured an awful lot more nudity than the original. Nobody even seemed to know when the paper had come into existence, and a Google search produced a stunning amount of bugger all. She had found one raggedy edition that made reference to the Berlin Wall going up and how a man in Didsbury was trying to raise money to build something similar between Liverpool and Manchester.

While she would never admit it, and had moaned relentlessly about the process, Stella held a little glow of internal pride that she had somehow assembled a complete collection of *The Stranger Times* stretching back to 2008, barring the 2017 Christmas edition, which she couldn't locate anywhere. It was before her or Banecroft's time at the paper, and when she brought it up with Reggie, Ox and Grace, none of them claimed to recall said edition. The only reason Stella knew there had been one at all was because Barry had felt moved to include an editorial in the following week's paper that apologized for it.

Still, that one mystery aside, her library meant that this afternoon she had been able to locate and photocopy each and every one of the Dex Hex columns that had appeared in the paper. DI Sturgess's theory was that while attempting to prove one of the bizarre conspiracy theories the columns contained, Tony Dawson had stumbled upon something that upset the Founders. While scanning the articles herself, Stella had been tempted more than once to agree with Ox's initial reaction that Sturgess's theory was nonsense, but then she'd remembered that footage of Tony Dawson being dragged out of his house and had kept looking. Besides, despite Stella's natural distrust of those in positions of authority, Sturgess had always seemed all right, and Hannah had trusted him.

Her mood was not helped by the fact that she had been banished to the basement to carry out this task. Ostensibly it was because it was where the 'new' photocopier was, which Hannah had picked up at a closing-down sale of a solicitor's office. The thing was possibly older than Stella and considerably more temperamental.

The real reason she was down here was that if Betty were to find out that Ox had been scamming a second pay cheque, he'd lose his job. If Banecroft were to find out, Ox would quite possibly lose his life. When she'd started this process, Stella had one hundred per cent not wanted either of those things to happen. After spending the afternoon in the dank, miserable basement, she was now, at best, fifty-two per cent in favour of Ox's continuing existence as either an employee or a member of the human race.

She hadn't noticed the smell the last time she'd been in the basement, so it had either developed considerably more 'personality' over the last couple of weeks, or the presence of a vampire huddled in the corner the last time she'd been down here had proven enough of a distraction for her not to have appreciated the full magnificence of its awfulness. If such conditions weren't enough, the room benefited only from the anaemic light of one bare light bulb, so she was getting eyestrain on top of everything else.

The double doors opened, flooding the room with dazzling evening sunlight. Stella turned and shielded her eyes.

'So,' said Ox, 'this is where you've been slacking off all afternoon?'

'Ha, ha. Hilarious.'

He fanned his hand in front of his nose. 'Man, this place is rank.'

'Is it?' she said. 'I hadn't noticed.'

'Is that sarcasm?'

'Is that sarcasm?' mimicked Stella.

'I'll take that as a yes.'

'Come on, children,' said Reggie, who had followed Ox through the doors. 'I don't think I have it in me to break up my fourth fight of the day.' He turned and, with a squeal of protesting metal, closed the doors behind them and plunged the room into what now seemed like a near-total darkness after the brief incursion of natural light.

'There were two more fights?'

'Oh yeah,' said Ox. 'The first one was about which planet the prime minister is from.'

'Out of curiosity, was anybody guessing Earth?'

Ox raised an eyebrow. 'What do you think?'

'What was the other fight about?'

Reggie moved across to stand beside her. 'Would you believe it – the use of video technology in football? Ironically, both parties belatedly realized they'd been agreeing with each other the whole time, but by that point, one of them had used the other's head to put a noticeable dent in the wall near the stairs.'

Ox leaned against the table, causing it to creak alarmingly. 'Is it my imagination, or are people becoming more stupid? Or just more mean?'

'I have a sneaking suspicion,' said Reggie, 'that people are getting more scared. It tends to bring out the worst in them.'

'Speaking of the worst,' said Stella, 'I can't help noticing that I've been stuck down here all afternoon, and neither of you two has thought to bring me down a cup of tea, a biscuit, maybe even just a glass of water.'

Ox and Reggie exchanged a guilty look.

'We are unforgivable beasts,' conceded Reggie. 'I apologize, and I shall get you whatever your heart desires this instant.'

Stella waved away his offer. 'Don't worry about it. I fully intend on getting out of this room in a minute, and Ox can take over after I've given my report.'

Ox folded his arms. 'Why are we still acting like this is my fault?'

'Because it is,' said Reggie. 'And because you created Dex Hex to write nonsense articles that only got printed because Barry, God rest him, was a naive fool. Whether you like it or not, while what happened after that isn't what you intended, it is all fruit from the tree of your deception.'

Ox's chin fell to his chest and his response came out as a half-hearted mumble. 'Tree is a bit much. It was a shrub at most.'

'Anyway,' said Stella, 'here we are.' She gestured at the folders on the table. 'As requested, save the infamous Christmas 2017 edition' – she looked between the two men and was disappointed by their lack of reaction – 'here is every one of the Dex Hex columns. Twenty-seven in total. I've created four folders containing copies of each of them, so there's one for everybody and one for DI Sturgess too, if he comes back. There was no rhyme or reason to when they appeared – sometimes there were three a month, at other times there wouldn't be any Dex Hex columns for months.'

Ox shrugged. 'If I'm honest with you, it all depended on how much I owed at the time.'

'Once I found them all,' continued Stella, 'I set about dividing them into two piles – pile A: columns that were utterly ludicrous and couldn't possibly be what we're looking for. And pile B: columns that could be of some use to us.'

Reggie pointed at the table. 'But there's only—'

'One pile?' interrupted Stella. 'That is incorrect. The one you can see there is pile A – the complete nonsense pile. Pile B is that massive space beside it. In other words, and feel free to take this as a compliment, Ox – every one of these columns is insane drivel. I'm amazed you could come up with this much crap.'

'To be fair, I was pretty drunk when I wrote a lot of them.'

'Incredibly, I find that easy to believe.'

'There must be something?' asked Reggie.

'Look for yourself. Maybe the Royal Family really are all shape-shifting panda bears. Frankly, it would make them a lot more lovable. Or perhaps the entire city of Wolverhampton really doesn't exist, and it's all an elaborate front for a plutonium-mining operation. Or perhaps Elvis really is running a chip shop in Stoke?'

'Are you sure that's one of mine?' asked Ox.

'According to the article, he's living there because he's on the run from the US government, which has been taken over by the Roswell aliens.'

'Ahhhh,' said Ox, 'that sounds more like it.'

'Then there's the giant invisible robot in Stockport, the house in the middle of the M62 where Tupac and Biggie Smalls now live, and, of course, the dragon living in a massive cavern under the centre of Manchester.'

Reggie nodded. 'I take your point.'

Stella reached out and placed a hand on the shoulder of each man. 'And I have total faith that the two of you are the ones to figure this out. Now, if you'll excuse me, I'm going upstairs to hunt for the remaining biscuits and to see if I can wash the smell of this place off me. If you need me . . . Actually, just don't need me.'

Five minutes later, Stella was on her knees with her head buried in the back of the kitchen cupboards, trying to locate Grace's hidden biccie stash. She could just find the woman herself and ask, but Grace had last been sighted hunting for yet more cardboard boxes. So engrossing was Stella's search that the sound of her own name being loudly barked made her slam the back of her head into the roof of the cupboard.

'Ouch!'

'Oh dear,' said Betty. 'You rather caught yourself a nasty one there, didn't you?'

Stella drew herself back out and into the room, and scowled at the assistant editor, who was beaming down at her.

'Thanks for noticing.'

A brown paper bag was shoved in front of Stella's face. 'Strawberry bonbon?'

'No, thanks—' Stella stopped herself. 'What am I saying? Yes, please.' She thrust her hand in and took three.

'That's the spirit.' Betty withdrew the bag and took a sweet herself. 'Where is everybody?'

'Reggie and Ox have left for the evening.' It wasn't technically a lie, if you accepted the admittedly shaky premise that the basement was not officially part of the office. 'Grace is . . .' The honest end to that sentence was 'quite possibly losing her mind', but seeing as it was Betty's audit that had brought this on, Stella went with '. . . around here somewhere'.

'What about Vincent?'

'Has he not come back yet?' asked Stella, genuinely surprised.

'Apparently not. At least he isn't in his office. Is that unusual behaviour for him?'

For reasons she wouldn't be able to articulate, Stella felt uncomfortable with this line of questioning. It was as if it were somehow disloyal to admit to Betty that Banecroft's behaviour was deteriorating. She settled for, 'Well, he's a pretty unusual dude.'

'Indeed. I'm worried about him,' said Betty. 'After what I saw last night, I mean.'

In the rare spare moments she'd had today, Stella had found herself thinking back to the night before, when Banecroft had been trying to talk to the clearly distressed spirit of poor Simon. 'What was going on there?'

'I'm not entirely sure,' admitted Betty, 'but trust me, it wasn't good. On the upside, I've been doing a spot of investigating too, and I think I've identified the source of the problem. Would you be up for helping me with something this evening?'

'OK, I mean . . . I guess.' She couldn't think of a reason to refuse, although she'd have been very happy to do so. 'What kind of something?'

'Excellent,' said Betty, rubbing her hands together and ignoring Stella's question entirely. 'We'll leave here at about midnight, and it could take a while, so do try to get some sleep in beforehand. You're going to need your energy.'

With that, Betty headed back out of the kitchen.

'Hang on. You've still not said what we're doing?'

She turned round. 'It wouldn't be a surprise if I did, though, would it?'

'I'm fine with that. That's why I keep asking. I know how questions work.'

'Such a clever girl.'

'That's a compliment, not an answer.'

Betty waved a hand. 'Marvellous. Looking forward to it,' she said with a twinkle in her eyes, 'and don't forget to bring a shovel.'

Stella shouted after Betty's back as she disappeared down the stairs. 'A shovel? Why do I need a shovel?'

CHAPTER 24

Stanley was trying to concentrate on his food but the woman sitting opposite him on the sofa was fidgeting constantly and it was getting on his nerves.

'Can I just—' she began.

'No,' said Stanley.

'But—'

'No.'

'What if—'

'No.'

She stamped her foot irritably. 'You don't even know what I was going to say.'

Reluctantly, Stanley looked up from his meal. It was going cold, and it hadn't been that good to begin with, but the takeaway was the only place willing to deliver to the picturesque little cottage halfway up a mountain. It was the nearest location they could secure to the Pinter Institute, which put them in the middle of nowhere as far as Stanley was concerned. Apparently, most people on romantic getaways to the country don't order a Chinese. It was one of the many reasons Stanley had never been on a romantic getaway, although in hindsight, it occurred to him that maybe he should have done a lot more things like that back when his wife was, well, still willing to be referred to as his wife.

The woman sitting opposite him was not his wife and seemed entirely happy with that arrangement. He got the definite impression Mrs Harnforth was not used to being told to wait for anything.

He lowered his fork. 'OK, what were you going to say?'

Mrs Harnforth looked over at the closed bedroom door from behind which the greatest hits of the Beautiful South were playing on a loop for the third time.

'I was just going to suggest that I pop in, say hello and welcome Cathy to the team?'

The woman had a voice fit for continuity announcing on Radio 4, and the result was that everything she said sounded infuriatingly reasonable, even if it directly contradicted the very thing you'd previously agreed. It was the same ability that would probably allow her to put on a sackcloth and somehow make it look stylish, whereas Stanley could make a suit crease just by picturing himself in it.

'Right. And you wouldn't be planning on asking her how she was getting along hacking into the security system at the Pinter Institute?'

'No. I mean, is it possible it would come up naturally in the conversation? Yes.'

Stanley nodded. 'That's what I thought. Leave her alone.'

Mrs Harnforth jutted her chin. 'You do realize I am the one in charge here?'

Stanley picked up his fork again. 'Not of this bit. You got me to take care of this bit' – he nodded towards the closed bedroom door – 'and I got Cathy to take care of this particular bit of this bit. That is what she is doing, and believe me, these hacker types are incredibly temperamental. You do not want to go disturbing them while they're working. She's probably in one of those whatchamacallits – flow states.'

'But it is already eleven o'clock.'

'And you definitely do not want to go reminding them of the time.'

'We told Hannah we would be in the system by midnight.'

'Actually, *you* did.'

'Only because you told me it was possible.'

'And it is, or Cathy wouldn't have told me it was possible. And I'm sure she's in there now, making it possible. What she doesn't need is you sticking your nose in, messing with her' – Stanley waved his hand in the air – 'mojo, or vibe, or whatever they call it.'

Mrs Harnforth gave a curt nod to concede the point reluctantly then diverted her attention to his plate. 'Should you be eating that?'

Stanley's heaped fork hovered in front of his mouth. 'What?'

'I thought you said you were going to be eating more healthily.'

'This is more healthily. It's got chicken – chicken is healthy. It's got chow mein in it. Chow mein is healthy.'

'Really?'

'The Chinese are a very healthy bunch of people. It's one of the many reasons they're going to end up running the planet.'

'No offence to the Chinese, but would a few vegetables kill you?'

'There *are* vegetables in here. They're in among the noodles. That's the whole point. It's like a camouflage thing.' Stanley was genuinely offended, not least because this really was one of the healthiest meals he had eaten in quite some time. There were identifiable green bits in it. He was about to point out that, for a while, he'd only eaten desserts, but he had a feeling it would not help his case much.

Mrs Harnforth lowered her voice. 'Are we sure she's up to this?'

Stanley set his plate down on the coffee table grumpily and gathered up the sheaf of printouts that were sitting on the occasional table beside him. 'I only picked her up this morning, and she's already got us a list of all the Pinter Institute guests from the last three years. Nobody else has got that, and believe me, I asked around.'

'How is that going?'

'I've pulled in every favour I can think of, or just flat-out hired people, and all this lot is being looked into.' He set the papers down next to him on the arm of the chair. 'So far, I've got reports on three guests from a few months ago.'

'Why didn't you mention this before?'

'Because,' said Stanley, suppressing an annoyed belch, 'you arrived just after my dinner did. Everybody is entitled to a dinner, you know. It's one of them basic human rights.'

Mrs Harnforth stood up and made a beeline for the printouts beside Stanley. He placed his hand firmly on top of them to stop her from taking them. She stood above him with her hands on her hips and glowered.

'Has anyone ever told you that you're not a team player, Stanley?'

'All the time. It's why I so studiously avoid being part of a team. Has anyone ever told you that you're a bit of a control freak?'

She folded her arms. 'Not twice, no.'

'With all due respect, Mrs H, you are too petite to carry off the intimidation act.'

Mrs Harnforth gave a flick of a finger and Stanley watched dumbfounded as his dinner plate floated and hovered in the air just below the ceiling. 'Only if you consider intimidation in terms of physical size. Rest assured, Stanley, there are a lot more variations on the word "power" than you realize.'

Stanley looked up forlornly at his levitating dinner. 'Do you know, up until a few months ago I didn't know magic really existed, and every time I've seen it used since then, it's always been to hurt me. Some crazy spider woman almost kills me, some nutter monk with a tattooed face drops me from a height and breaks my ankle, and now this.'

'Oh, don't be so dramatic.'

Mrs Harnforth returned to her seat as Stanley's dinner drifted down serenely and landed in his lap. He looked at it and set it to one side. 'I've lost my appetite. So, would you like that report now?'

'That would be wonderful.'

Stanley sat back in his armchair and scratched his armpit. 'OK. Fine. The three guests I've got info on so far: Martin Blake, fund manager with a pill addiction – seems like he's been clean since he left. Simone Finkel, depression – seems a happy bunny now. Margaret Gunther, teenage daughter of the Gunther glass empire, self-harming and other issues. These days, happy as a pig in shit – you should see her Instagram stories.'

'I see.'

'Not what you were expecting?' asked Stanley. 'That they seem to be helping people?'

Mrs Harnforth tilted her head. 'I'm more concerned with the how and the why, but let's not jump to any conclusions with just a small sample size.'

'Fair enough. Would you like the good news now?'

Mrs Harnforth raised an eyebrow. 'You've located a nearby health food shop?'

'Good God, no. But what we have located is the owner of the offshore bank account from that phone call made by Thomas Mandeville two days after he died.'

'Really?' Mrs Harnforth leaned forward.

'Yes. I told you Cathy is superb. The beneficiary was one Anton Lasherf, real name Anthony Lester, who is the "personal experience facilitator" – whatever the hell that is – at the Pinter Institute. He's up to his eyeballs in debt, and however he managed this, I'd bet he didn't do it with anyone's approval. An organization this clever wouldn't do something like that and then place the money directly into one of their staff member's personal accounts. If I'm any judge, Anton has gone way off the reservation, which makes him useful to us. I'll pay him a visit first thing in the morning and, fingers crossed, we'll then have our own man on the inside.'

'Are you sure that is the best approach?'

Stanley turned his head away and looked out the window at

nothing much. 'You might not like it, but how you get answers is by squeezing. If you don't have the stomach for it . . .'

Mrs Harnforth shifted in her seat. 'I didn't say that.' She glanced down at his plate. 'Would you like me to heat that up for you?'

'This place hasn't got a microwave.'

'Would it shock you to learn that I don't need one?'

'Would it shock you that, given my experiences with magic, I'm not wild about someone using it on my dinner?'

Mrs Harnforth held up her palms in surrender. 'Have it your way. Now, if you'll excuse me, I need to use the facilities.'

'Second door on the left.'

Mrs Harnforth made a half-hearted feint to follow Stanley's directions, then opened the door to Cathy's room.

'Oh sorry, you meant the other left.'

'There is only one left,' said Stanley resignedly.

Cathy, with three screens set out in front of her, was sitting in a leopard-print dressing gown, painting her toenails. 'Hiya. I'm assuming you're the woman in charge, then?'

'I am indeed. Mrs Harnforth.'

'Cathy Quirke. Charmed, I'm sure.'

Mrs Harnforth strode forward to offer a handshake, but Cathy waved her freshly painted fingernails by means of explanation.

'Right, of course.'

Mrs Harnforth stood there awkwardly and looked at her watch while Cathy went back to painting her nails.

'I could hear voices outside,' Cathy said, 'but I didn't want to interrupt in case you weren't who I thought you were. Stanley is an extremely lonely man. I thought there was a good chance he might have hired a hooker.'

'Thanks very much,' shouted Stanley from his seat in the front room.

'No judgement here,' Cathy shouted back, before looking up at Mrs H. 'And if you were one, I'm sure you'd be super-expensive. Like proper top drawer. So much so that I'd be hitting Stanley up for a raise in the morning.'

'Yes,' said Mrs Harnforth. 'Quite. Anyway, not to disturb you while you are in your flow state, but do you think you'll be able to gain access to the Pinter Institute's security systems tonight?'

'Oh, that? I did that, like, an hour ago. Would have been two but, word to the wise, next time you're getting a base for something like this, hard-wired fibre-optic broadband should be top of the shopping list, as opposed to lovely views of the countryside.' Cathy sniffed the air. 'Oh, is that chow mein? I'm hungry enough to eat the arse off a horse.'

CHAPTER 25

The *tick*, *tick*, *tick* of the clock on the wall behind Hannah felt like a fingernail scratching at the base of her brain. One minute to midnight. She'd been lying in bed for two hours pretending to sleep, and disciplining herself not to check the time too often. She didn't think there was a camera in the room, but she couldn't be sure. It probably was just a smoke alarm, but you never could tell.

The earpiece that had dropped from the sky earlier in the day was now clenched in her sweaty fist under the pillow. After her catch-up with Mrs Harnforth, achieved via the unlikely medium of Gordon the irate starling, she'd temporarily dodged Brad, the yoga instructor, by claiming she needed to go back to her room to use the loo. It had given her enough time to stash the earpiece in the leaves of the large ficus plant in the corner. It didn't feel like the greatest of hiding places, but the rules of minimalist design aesthetic to which the rooms adhered – in particular, the almost absolute lack of furniture – meant that her options were limited.

When she returned, she had been confronted by both Anton and Brad about her unacceptable divergence from her schedule. Hannah had expected the intimation that she was suffering from a bit of tummy trouble would be enough to get them off her back.

How wrong she was. Apparently, the Pinter Institute had its own faecal analyst on the staff – poo being an invaluable diagnostic tool when it came to optimizing the performance of the human body.

While explaining this, Anton's alarmingly plastic face became the most animated Hannah had seen it. She was informed that Tupperware containers would be provided in her bathroom for her to capture all bowel movements from hereon in. Hannah hadn't passed one since, and she was pretty sure the prospect of having to sit down with Anton and the faecal analyst to go through things was enough to ensure she was possibly never going to pass another one in her entire life.

She was worried, and not just about the possibility of a faecal inquisition. When going undercover had first been suggested to her, it had felt glamorous and exciting. In reality, it was making her a nervous wreck. During her orientation session, Anton had made it clear that roaming around the building at night was strictly against the rules. It was why the doors had electronic locks that sealed the rooms at ten o'clock. He had gone to great lengths to explain how this was *definitely* not like a prison, while failing to differentiate it from a prison. Beneath all the meditation, correctly aligned chakras and whale song, Hannah was coming to realize that the entire Pinter Institute operated in a permanent state of paranoia.

The thing was, while she wanted to think of herself differently, Hannah was not naturally one of life's rule breakers. She was a good girl. She had been head girl at her school. While everyone enjoyed the secret thrill of the idea of being a renegade, she had been the one telling the other girls that it was still possible to have lots of fun while obeying the rules.

She glanced up at the clock again. Three . . . Two . . . One . . .

Hannah removed the cellophane wrapping from the earpiece and surreptitiously popped the gadget into her right ear. For a couple of seconds nothing happened and then there was a beep followed by a female voice that she didn't recognize.

'Hello, Hannah. Can you hear me?'

'Ehm, yes,' she whispered. 'Sorry, who is this?'

'I'm Cathy. We haven't met.'

Now that she'd heard more of the voice, Hannah picked up the strong Mancunian accent.

'After a lot of discussion,' Cathy continued, 'we decided I should be the only voice you hear. Think of me as your fairy godmother. Mrs Harnforth and Stanley are here too.'

Hannah was surprised at the mention of Stanley but decided against saying anything. 'Is there a camera in my room?'

'No, you're fine. Nobody can see you.'

The tension in Hannah's shoulders eased a little, and she sat up. 'That's good. Thing is, I did try to explain this earlier on, but they've got these electronic locks on all the doors, which means I . . .'

She stopped at the sound of a soft clicking noise and looked across the room to see the light on the door lock had gone from red to green.

'Like I said, I'm your fairy godmother. Your wish is my command. Fancy going for a little stroll?'

★

Hannah took a deep breath, opened the door to her room and leaned out to steal a glance up and down the hallway. It was empty, save for the massive photographic portraits of smiling faces that were now under-lit by soft orange lights that provided the only illumination in the otherwise dark hallway. She took a step out.

'There you go,' said Cathy's voice in her ear. It had a calming quality to it that Hannah liked. 'And we're off,' she continued. 'Just so you know, there's a security camera at the end of the hall that you're appearing on right now.'

Hannah slammed herself back against the door.

'Sorry, sorry, sorry,' said Cathy, sounding embarrassed. 'I just meant, I can see you, but don't worry, nobody else can. I've looped the feed to the security system. They're just watching an empty hallway.'

Hannah relaxed and felt slightly embarrassed. 'Right. That makes sense.'

Cathy gave a nervous little laugh. 'My bad. I could have explained that better, couldn't I? I'll try to be a bit more careful in future.'

'OK. And I'll try to be a little cooler.'

'It's a deal,' said Cathy. 'My point is, I can see all the security cameras so I know where all the staff are, and I can direct you around them.'

'Right.'

'For example, right now I can tell you that the two night security guards are currently in their office. One of them is FaceTiming his girlfriend, and the other one is putting way too much faith in a pair of tens in a game of online poker.'

Hannah felt the tension in her chest ease a little. 'Good to know.'

'I got you, OK? Just let me guide you and this will be a walk in the park.'

In the background, Hannah heard a male voice. 'Can we move this . . .' The rest was lost in what sounded like a microphone being covered up. A couple of seconds later, Cathy's voice returned. 'Sorry about that. Just had to cancel my subscription to *Mansplaining Monthly*. If you're ready to go, Hannah, I'm going to explain the plan of attack for this evening's soirée?'

'OK.'

'Great. You're on the fourth floor of the east wing at the moment. That's where most of the guest rooms are. The west wing is home to the offices and some staff quarters. The main building is the big reception area and some of the exercise studios, plus the dining hall. We've noticed that there aren't any cameras in a basement in the west wing and only two members of staff have clearance to access it, which is interesting, don't you think? Fancy taking a look?'

It was eerie, tiptoeing along the corridors in funereal silence, save for the occasional direction or word of encouragement from Cathy. Hannah passed one room from which incredibly loud snoring was emanating. From behind another door came the sound of somebody crying. The only other noise was the soft swish of her Institute-issue trainers as she moved across the plush carpet. She trained her eyes straight ahead as the ubiquitous portraits of massive smiling faces took on a sinister appearance when underlit. It was as if their eyes were following her, judging her as she broke the rules. On the upside, Cathy's disembodied voice was having a much-welcomed calming effect. She sounded like someone who knew what she was talking about. Even if she didn't, Hannah was glad for the company.

Smaller corridors, like tributaries, branched off the main hallway at regular intervals, leading to yet more rooms. It dawned on Hannah that this place must have far more capacity than it was currently using. She'd noticed that while she seemed to see the same couple of dozen people in her classes and at mealtimes, there must be other people she never seemed to encounter. Possibly this was by design, to keep contact between the guests to a minimum. Regardless, she didn't think this place was going to run out of space any time soon.

Cathy guided her from the east wing to the west wing, via a couple of security doors that magically opened on her approach, and then down a couple of flights of steps to the first floor. This wing was noticeably different. In place of the photographic portraits were old oil paintings; the kind Hannah supposed might have come with the property. The occasional water cooler and functional-looking cupboard added to her sense that this was a place of work. The paint on the walls was also considerably more faded here, which highlighted the fact that the guests were never meant to see this part of the building.

At the top of the stairwell leading down to the ground floor, Cathy's voice in Hannah's ear became more urgent. 'Stop!'

Hannah froze, afraid to make a move.

'OK. Walk to your left and position yourself behind that large potted plant.'

As she hurried, Hannah spoke in the lowest whisper she could manage. 'What's going on?'

'This is one of those things that's gonna sound a lot worse than it actually is.'

'Cathy?'

'One of the guards is currently doing a sweep of the ground floor. Looks like standard procedure. He isn't— Crap. Scratch that – he's coming up the stairs.'

Hannah looked around her, panic pulling at her every nerve. 'What am I going to do?'

'Just . . . Hang on.'

'But—'

Hannah heard a soft clicking noise to her left and noticed that the small light on the handle of the nearby door had changed from red to green.

'In there,' hissed Cathy. 'Now.'

Hannah did as instructed, stepping as quietly as possible into the darkened room. She closed the door behind her softly and watched as the light on the electronic lock went from green to red.

Hannah stood rooted to the spot.

While the room was dark, it wasn't unoccupied. As her eyes adjusted to the light, she could make out a large figure in the bed at the far end of the room. She held her breath. Thankfully, the only sounds in the room were the slow, sonorous snores of what appeared to be a large man deep in sleep.

'Oh bugger,' said Cathy in her ear. 'That room isn't empty, is it?'

No shit, Cathy.

Outside the door, Hannah could hear the slow footsteps of somebody sauntering through a no doubt tedious and mundane task, whistling very softly to themselves as they went.

'Just stay calm,' Cathy whispered. 'We'll have you out of there in a second.'

Hannah bit her lip to stop from screaming as the figure in the bed spoke. 'Feel the burn . . .'

Brad. Bloody Brad. The man even dreamed of workouts.

After what felt like an eternity but must have been just thirty seconds, Hannah watched with relief as the little light on the door turned from red to green again.

'Coast is clear,' Cathy whispered.

She stepped out into the hallway and closed the door behind her with the delicacy of a bomb-disposal expert. She stood stock-still, half expecting alarms to start blaring or shouts to greet her re-emergence. Nothing happened.

'Well,' said Cathy, 'that livened things up a bit, didn't it?'

Hannah turned to look up and down the blissfully empty corridor, and finally let out the breath she'd been holding in. 'You could say that.'

'Let's get you down those stairs, then.'

The rest of Hannah's journey down to the ground floor of the west wing was mercifully uneventful. Following Cathy's directions, she eventually found herself standing in front of a large metal door.

'This looks like a bank vault or something,' she whispered. 'Do we have any idea what's down here?'

'No,' came Cathy's response, which was followed by a

pregnant pause. 'Look, to be completely straight with you, we don't have a clue. It's listed as an old wine cellar on the building schematics, but this feels like an awful lot of security for a few bottles of plonk.'

'You've never met my almost ex-husband. He got a lock for the wine fridge because he didn't trust the cleaner.'

'He sounds like a real prince.'

'Yes. I have terrible taste in men.'

'Don't we all,' said Cathy. Her tone changed to one of distinct irritation as she spoke to someone off-mic. 'We are. I'm getting to it.' Then the friendly manner returned. 'Sorry, Hannah, my backseat drivers were just reminding me that the clock is ticking. Now, I'm going to open the door, but remember, you're just taking a look-see. You see anything you don't like, you turn and run. I have got your back. Anything goes wrong, Mrs Harnforth would like you to know that the cavalry will be ready to charge in ASAP.'

Hannah knew that was supposed to make her feel better, but it really didn't. It just made her feel more exposed.

'OK,' she said, trying to sound a lot more confident than she felt, 'let's find out what they're hiding.'

CHAPTER 26

Stella took a deep breath and tried to focus on enjoying the nocturnal sights and sounds of Manchester as they rolled by outside the car window, but she was finding it difficult. She didn't know where she and Betty were, but that wasn't exactly surprising. She spent most of her time locked inside an old church, so it wasn't as if she had a great deal of geographical knowledge of the area.

In that regard, at least in theory, it was nice to be out and about. It was just the details of the out and about that were proving challenging – in particular, the fact that she fully expected to die in a fireball car crash, and the circumstances of the accident would unfairly confirm every crappy sexist stereotype about women's driving.

If anything, Betty drove like a man. A man possessed. A man possessed of a death wish. She threw the supposed car around a corner at an ill-judged speed and Stella closed her eyes. Any second now.

'Stella, dear girl. Please do me the kindness of not digging your nails into the door handle. You are going to leave a mark on poor Betty.'

'If you're so worried about your car,' snapped Stella, 'then why don't you get it another wheel?'

Betty sighed ostentatiously, while nimbly swinging the car past a drunk bloke who had stopped in the middle of the road to admire the vehicle. 'For the last time – it is only supposed to have three wheels. It is a Reliant Robin. A British classic.'

'Classic just means old, and the reason it's British is that nobody else in the world ever wanted to buy such a thing. Does it even have airbags?'

'I don't think so.'

'I figured. You usually put them in right after the fourth wheel. Cars have four wheels, you see. It's an extremely good design. Basic physics dictates that a wheel at each corner is the optimal arrangement because of, well, I don't know. I don't know that much about physics but . . . Forget physics. It's basic common sense.'

'But what about a sense of romance?' asked Betty.

'There's nothing romantic about a car.'

Having said that, as it happened, one of the tsunami of nutters Stella had had to deal with as part of Loon Day had been very romantic about cars. So much so that he was banned from most of the dealerships in Greater Manchester.

'And come to think of it,' Stella continued, 'what kind of narcissist names her car after herself?'

'Betty is not named after me,' said Betty. 'She is named after a different Betty. In fact, her full title is Betty Two.'

'Are we spelling that t-w-o or t-o-o?'

'Either works.'

The vehicle swerved an alarming degree as Betty executed an

overtaking manoeuvre around a late-night bus. It was just after midnight on a Tuesday night/Wednesday morning, so when they'd left the office a few minutes ago, there had still been quite a few people about. As they headed out of town, the larger groups of people gave way to lone individuals and pairs, either walking with a considerable amount of purpose or with none at all.

'Can I ask again where we're going?'

'I'd rather not say. It'll sound bad out of context.'

'What does that even mean? It's not out of context. Answering the question "Where are we going?" with the name of the place we are going to is decidedly *in* context.'

Betty's reply to this was a noise that only posh people make. As if a word had got stuck in their throats and they were trying to shake it free by wobbling their jowls. She followed it up with, 'Where is your sense of adventure, girl?'

'Adventure? Romance? These all feel like the kind of words you'd use to bamboozle the gullible. I got in the not-quite-a-car, didn't I? That was adventurous in itself. It's just . . . It now dawns on me that it is the middle of the night and I'm in a . . . let's go with "vehicle" with somebody I met for the first time only yesterday, there are a couple of shovels and a large mysterious suitcase on the back seat, and I don't know where we're going. It feels like we're on our way to dispose of a body and I'm worried that it might be mine.'

'Hmmm,' said Betty. 'When you put it like that, it sounds bad, doesn't it?'

'Yeah. So where are we going?'

'A graveyard.'

'OK,' said Stella, 'if you're not going to answer the question seriously . . .'

'I did. See, I told you it wouldn't make sense out of context. You'd better hang on, by the way.'

'Why do I—'

Before Stella could finish the thought, Betty wrenched the car into an improbably tight right-hand turn and mounted the pavement. Stella barely had enough time to take in the span of tall iron railings between two granite columns, with an ornate and imposing gate as their centrepiece, before the car was almost on top of them. She threw up her hands and turned her head, expecting a collision that didn't come. Instead, with a pained metallic screech, the gates flew open to admit them. Stella threw a quick look over her shoulder and just caught sight of them slamming closed again.

'How in the—'

Betty chortled uproariously and slapped the steering wheel. 'Oh, me oh my, that was jolly good fun. I was here earlier and set that up, but I wasn't sure it was going to work.'

They were now trundling along a gravel path with low hedges on either side, picked out by the headlights. Everything else was lost in inky darkness save for the faint glow of streetlights in the distance. Stella would have closed her eyes except seeing as she could see almost nothing anyway, it wouldn't have made much difference.

'You weren't sure it was going to work?' echoed Stella. 'What would have happened if it hadn't?'

'I presume we would have found out about that airbags thing. Anyway, it did work, didn't it?'

'That is not an answer. What—'

The end of Stella's sentence was lost as the car jerked violently, causing her head to bump against the roof. Betty's head was spared the same fate as her bulk was too wedged into her seat to be moved so easily.

'Oops-a-daisy,' said Betty cheerfully. 'I forgot about that step. Come to that, I think there are . . .'

The car bounced again. 'Yes, two of them. Thought so.'

The car swung around at a ninety-degree angle and came to a halt.

Once Stella had come to terms with the fact that she wasn't dead, she looked across at Betty, whose face appeared alarmingly demonic in the weak orange light from the dashboard.

'Was the handbrake turn really necessary?'

'Actually, it was.' Betty patted the dashboard. 'Betty's brakes aren't the best.' She slapped Stella on the knee jovially. 'Come on, then – let's get cracking.'

Stella stepped out of the car and looked around. 'Holy shit!' she said in a soft voice. 'We *are* in a graveyard.'

'Told you. Your generation – so cynical. They don't believe anyone.' Betty clicked on a torch she had produced from somewhere and nodded to her right. 'This way.'

Stella had a bad feeling about it all, but she duly followed. In her entire life she had only been in a graveyard once before, and that had been during the day. Under the cover of darkness, they were very different places.

Above the pair, the moon was skirting in and out of cloud cover and, as Stella's eyes adjusted to the light, she saw the outlines of gravestones of all shapes and sizes stretching into the distance. Dotted among the regular headstones, she could make out the larger shapes of commemorative statues, or oversized stone crucifixes.

Betty seemed to know where she was going and led them down a narrow path between the rows. Stella could hear her mumbling to herself. 'Seven down, five across. Seven down, five across.'

After they had passed what could have been seven rows, Betty took a left and walked towards the fifth gravestone. She turned to face Stella. 'Right, dear girl. Thank you for bearing with me. It's about time I give you the full explanation you deserve. As we both saw last night, poor Mr Banecroft is being visited by a spectre. That is one thing, but take it from me, one dead person does not speak through another.'

'Whatever it was is an abomination. Somebody is up to something very, very bad, and I'm afraid it falls to you and me to do something about it. I won't lie to you. It's not the most pleasant of tasks, but it must be done.'

Stella's horrible feeling cemented inside her, but for the sake of certainty, she felt moved to ask anyway. 'Where exactly are we?'

Betty didn't answer. Instead, she angled the torchlight to illuminate the gravestone before them. Stella read the inscription with a sinking heart.

Here lies Simon Brush. Gone too soon.

Stella licked her lips nervously. 'This is exactly what I was frightened of.'

Betty rubbed a hand up and down Stella's upper arm. 'I'm afraid so, dear. Now, be a good girl and go and get the shovels.'

CHAPTER 27

Hannah took a step back as the thick steel door swung open. There was an eerie absence of sound. A wide stairway leading down into total darkness was revealed and she managed a couple of tentative steps forward before having to catch her breath as motion-detecting lights clicked into life. The staircase was a modern-looking white-tiled affair scuffed with a flurry of muddy footprints heading in both directions. Clearly the Pinter Institute's cleaning elves didn't come down this far.

'What can you see?' asked Cathy.

'Nothing yet.'

Hannah made it down a couple of steps before whirling round at the feeling of a subtle gust of air against her hair. With no more noise than when it had opened, the door swung shut behind her.

'Don't worry about the door. It does that automatically. I can open it again, no problem.'

'You'd better be right,' muttered Hannah as she continued down the stairs carefully, her frame tensed, listening for the slightest noise in the darkness ahead of her. Halfway down, more lights sprang into life in the room below, revealing it to indeed be a wine cellar, with several old wooden racks stretching back to a stone wall at the far end of the room. A few bottles of wine were still dotted about the place, mostly covered in dust and looking all but forgotten. That was not to say the place was not in use, though. From the bottom of the stairs, the riot of muddy footprints stretched off to the right-hand corner and the wide mouth of a tunnel that sloped down into the darkness.

Hannah described to Cathy what she could see.

'Yeah,' said Cathy, 'that tunnel is definitely not on any schematic.'

'So, let's find out where it leads, then.'

Hannah moved towards the darkness and, this time, when the lights flickered on as they sensed her presence, she felt a lot calmer about it. 'OK. I can tell you the tunnel leads down to yet more tunnel. This thing must be long. It's reasonably steep too. I'll have to keep heading down to see where it goes.'

Cathy's voice in her ear was shot through with static. 'OK . . . A second . . . Need to . . . Something.'

'You're breaking up. I can't hear what you're saying.'

'Back . . . Nothing . . . Weird.'

Hannah tapped the earpiece in frustration, and when that predictably did nothing, she started moving back towards the stairs she'd come down. 'Can you hear me? Can you hear me now?'

As she neared the bottom step, Cathy's voice cut through. 'Yes, I can hear you. Is there somewhere you can hide?'

'What?'

'Just until we know what this is. It's a weird thing. Cameras in the east wing cut out a minute ago followed by a string of them cutting out through the main building and along to the west wing. Like a rolling blackout. It might be a built-in feature — some kind of device that stops certain people from being recorded.'

'What would be the point of that?' asked Hannah, panic rising in her belly again.

'I don't know, but I don't like it, and whoever it is, they're heading in your direction.'

Hannah started to make her way back up the stairs. 'Get me out of here.'

'No time. Where can you hide? Stay hidden for five minutes, then come back to where you are now and check in.'

'But—'

'Just do it.'

Hannah swore under her breath and retreated down the stairs, scanning the room as she went. She could head down the tunnel, but she had no guarantee where that would lead, if it even led anywhere. Her only other option was the scant cover offered by the wine racks.

As Hannah stepped off the well-travelled path, the smooth white tile abruptly gave way to uneven cobblestone, causing her to stumble. She reached the rear stone wall, wet to the touch with condensation, and looked back towards the stairs. She could see the staircase perfectly, which meant that anybody coming down it would see her too. Her heart thumped in her chest and her breath shortened as she was seized by the sickening sensation of being trapped.

She looked again in the direction of the tunnel. If she went that way, there was every chance she would be more ensnared than she was now. In the absence of any better ideas, she huddled in the corner and made herself as small as possible. As she felt the cool damp stone against her skin, a thought struck her. She reached across and grabbed a dusty bottle of wine from one of the shelves before retaking her position. If somebody discovered her, she would at least have a weapon to hand. She'd either fight her way out or waste some very expensive wine in her attempt.

After she'd been huddled there for a moment, the lights on the stairway flicked off again, followed soon after by the lights in the main cellar. The only source of illumination now came from the lights at the top of the tunnel. Not for the first time in her life, Hannah silently cursed herself for being such a damn people pleaser. Mrs Harnforth had come to her with what she had described as a vitally important mission that only Hannah could carry out, and she had been flattered. And now she had gone and got herself trapped.

Before she could berate herself any further, light spilled down the staircase chased by the sound of descending voices. Hannah suppressed a gasp of shock as she identified one she definitely wasn't expecting. It was distinctively Glaswegian.

'What the hell is down here?' asked Moira, her tone dripping with suspicion.

She was answered by Dr French. 'It's an exciting part of the facility that you haven't seen before.'

'Aye. Have you got a bag of sweeties and some puppies down here for me to play with? I didn't come down in the last shower, hen.'

'Trust the process,' came the distinctive voice of Anton.

'Pull the other one, Ken doll. I'd like to go back to my room now.'

Dr French sounded irritated. 'Hold her.'

'Hey, get your hands—' Moira was cut off in such a way that it sounded a lot like someone had slammed a hand over her mouth.

Hannah could make out the sound of her mumbled protestations gradually dying away as Dr French kept repeating the words 'trust the process, do as we say', over and over again. She shifted, torn between the urge to help her friend and the certainty that it would be a futile gesture.

A few moments later, pairs of feet coming down the stairs appeared in her vision. Dr French's and Anton's first, followed by Moira's. When Moira came into full view her expression was vacant – eyes dull, jaw slack – all her signature vivacity drained from her face. Two black-and-white-clad Pinter Institute staff members, both big blokes well over six feet in height, were bringing up the rear. They also wore blank expressions, but that might have been a permanent part of the package.

'I am sick to death,' Dr French moaned, bitterness replacing the artificial sweetness that normally suffused her voice, 'of having to use my powers to herd the sheep. Let's just drug them.'

Anton sounded like a man who was participating in a conversation he'd had quite a few times before. 'He says—'

The pair stopped as they reached the bottom of the stairs and noticed that the light at the mouth of the tunnel was still on. Hannah held her breath.

After a moment, Anton turned to one of the bruisers behind him.

His voice became a high-pitched screech as he flung a hand in the direction of the tunnel. 'Jesus H. Christ, Darren. It hasn't turned itself off again. I gave you one job! Can't you fix a simple light?'

'I did,' offered the big man.

Anton stamped his foot. 'Really? Am I having a stroke or something, then? A light staying on all day is terrible for the environment.'

The big man looked down at his feet. 'I'm not an electrician.'

Dr French turned around. 'I will not be using my gifts to wipe the mind of some insignificant tradesmen because you can't handle a simple task either. Sort it!' She spun back around, stomped across the room and headed down the tunnel. Anton followed. The two big men exchanged a look and placed a hand on each of Moira's shoulders. The Scottish woman offered no resistance, and they slowly followed in the others' wake.

Once they'd disappeared from view, Hannah waited for a few seconds before tentatively getting to her feet. What the hell was going on?

'Cathy?' she whispered.

All she received in response was a burst of static. She could hear the squabbling voices of the party fading away as they moved off. Hannah tiptoed across and when she was beside the mouth of the tunnel, she crouched down and risked a look. She could see their backs in the distance, over a hundred metres away now, as the passageway seemed to go down and down. She debated the next course of action with herself. Follow them? What good would that do? The chances of her getting caught were high and then she wouldn't be any use to anybody.

Reluctantly, she headed back towards the bottom of the stairs. 'Cathy?'

'Thank God.'

Hannah had never been so relieved to hear a voice in her life.

'You OK?'

'Yes, but I've just seen Moira – the woman I've become friends with – being brought down here like a prisoner. They've taken her off down that bloody big tunnel.'

'OK,' said Cathy. 'First things first. Let's get you out of there.'

'But what about Moira?'

'You're down there for recon, Hannah. You can't go chasing after her. You haven't got any back-up.'

'But . . .'

Mrs Harnforth's voice replaced Cathy's in her earpiece. 'Hannah, I understand your concerns but we have to stick to the plan. Finding out what is going on is the best thing you can do for your friend, and we can't do that if you're compromised.'

Hannah considered this for a few seconds then reluctantly came to a decision. She hated it, but Mrs H was right. 'OK. I'm coming out.'

'It's the sensible course of action,' Mrs Harnforth assured her. 'Don't worry, we'll do all we can for Moira.'

Feeling wretched, Hannah cast one last glance towards the mouth of the tunnel then started to climb the stairs. She paused on the third step as she remembered the bottle of wine she was still holding in her hand.

'Hang on a sec.'

She headed back down and placed it in one of the slots on the rack nearest the stairs. As soon as her fingers left the cool glass, an awful judder of anticipation passed through her – that brief moment when something hasn't yet happened but on some level you know it's already too late to stop it from happening. With a soft wet sound, the rotten wood at the back of the rack gave way and the bottle slid backwards. Tantalizingly just out of her reach, it seemed to fall in slow motion before, with a sickening jolt, the world sped up again at the sound of it smashing on the stone floor, the deafeningly loud sound tearing through the funereal silence.

'What's going on?' shouted Cathy, but Hannah was already taking the steps two at a time.

'Open the bloody door!'

Hannah abandoned all effort at stealth and rushed up the stairs as fast as her legs could carry her. She crashed through the first security door and then the second. Thankfully, she didn't meet anyone on her way, as she could only barely hear Cathy's shouted instructions over the pounding of her own heartbeat in her ears.

Before she knew it, she was back in the east wing with the grinning faces having taken on a mocking demeanour as they flashed by. She only stopped running when she was safely back inside her room, covered in sweat.

As she stood there, leaning against the door, her lungs heaving, she was only dimly aware that Cathy was still talking. 'I didn't . . . I didn't get any of that.'

'OK,' said Cathy, who now sounded a lot like a woman who was trying to stay calm. 'What happened?'

'The . . . A bloody stupid bottle of wine fell off a rack then I ran for it.'

'OK. Right. Well, the bad news is that two big baboons came running out of that door about a minute after you did, and they started searching. They didn't see you, though.'

'That's . . . good?'

'Yes. They've woken up a few more members of staff and they've all made their way into the east wing. They're going from room to room.'

'Shit,' said Hannah. She clutched her hair with both hands. 'Shit, shit, shit.'

'No, that's good news. It means they don't know it was you.'

'No, I get that, but the bottom of my tracksuit is covered in red wine.'

'You'd better wash it.'

'No kidding.'

There was the sound of movement on the other end, and Mrs Harnforth's voice came through. 'Hannah, you did really well.'

'I screwed up.'

'Rubbish. You adapted and you survived. That is the job. Did you see anything down there?'

'Not really. There's this big tunnel leading downwards to God knows what. Does that tell you anything?'

'Not a great deal,' admitted Mrs Harnforth.

'And . . . like I said, Moira – the woman I met – she was with Dr French, Anton and two big guys. She was . . . She wasn't happy, and then Dr French, I don't know, hypnotized her or something. They were taking her down the tunnel, but I don't know what the hell they were doing. Is she OK?'

'We don't know.'

'I . . .' Hannah didn't know what to say next.

'Look,' said Mrs Harnforth, 'if you want, we will come there and pull you out now. We can use the plan we discussed – when someone turns up and says there's a family emergency.'

'But we haven't found out anything yet.'

'True, but I don't want to put you in any more danger.'

'OK, but . . .'

'Hannah?' It was Cathy's voice again, cutting through. 'Sorry. Your friend – Moira. Is it Moira Everhart, by any chance?'

'Yes!'

'I'm looking at her right now.'

'Really?'

'Yes. She's . . .' Cathy sounded bemused. 'She's walking back to her room, looks as happy as can be. She's chatting cheerfully with the staff she's just passing.'

'Oh,' said Hannah. 'Are you sure?'

'Yeah.'

'I mean, she was . . . she was kind of a prisoner.'

'Right. Seems good now, though.'

'OK.' Hannah didn't know what to think. She was starting to doubt everything she'd seen. 'That's . . . odd.'

Mrs Harnforth came back on. 'Hannah, what do you want me to do?'

Hannah began to pace up and down the room.

'Hannah?'

'Screw it. I'm staying.'

'Are you sure?'

'Yes,' she said, feeling oddly euphoric. 'Have your bird friend watch. If I step outside and wave my left hand, get me out of here. And keep monitoring the earpiece. I presume this thing will work for a bit?'

'It's got three days' charge,' offered Cathy.

'Right. Good. Done. I need a shower.'

Five minutes later came a pounding on Hannah's door. Before she could reach it, it flew open.

'Hey!' she objected, pulling her bathrobe more tightly around herself. The two big guys from the basement were standing in the doorway. 'What the hell's going on? Can't a girl have a shower?'

'Sorry,' said Darren, 'we're doing a contraband search.'

'You're kidding?'

'I'm afraid not. Do you have anything to declare?'

'Yes. I declare this is absolutely ridiculous.' Hannah made a big show of rolling her eyes. She realized that focusing on being angry made it a lot easier not to appear frightened. 'Just get it over with, but rest assured, I'll be lodging a complaint in the morning.'

She stepped to one side and gave the duo access to her room, which they promptly set about searching in an efficient manner. Either they did this a lot, or they'd figured out a system because they'd already done so many rooms by this point. She noted the ficus plant got a particularly thorough inspection.

As Darren checked the linen basket, he picked out Hannah's

soaking-wet tracksuit bottoms, having been washed hastily in the sink.

'And?' demanded Hannah, glaring at him. 'Colonic irrigation can have some quite unpleasant after-effects. What's your point?'

His face reddened, and he dropped the bottoms as if they were on fire. 'Sorry,' he mumbled.

The pair headed for the door but just as they were about to leave, Anton appeared in the doorway, with a female member of staff in tow.

'Christ,' said Hannah, 'what now? An anal probe?'

Anton gave the tightest of tight grins. 'Not a full probe, no. Lauren here will need to check your person, though.'

'You're kidding?'

'Personal searches were covered in the induction form you signed.'

'Super. Just super.'

Hannah stepped into the bathroom where Lauren carried out a cavity search so thorough that, technically speaking, she got considerably further than Hannah's first two boyfriends ever did.

Having completed the search to her satisfaction, Lauren gave a curt nod and Hannah re-robed with a scowl. She returned to the bedroom where she glared furiously at Anton. 'Anything else? Ultrasound? X-ray?'

That not-quite-a-smile again. 'That will not be necessary. Enjoy the rest of your evening.'

'Like that's likely. Good night.' She grabbed the edge of the door as her uninvited visitors passed into the hallway. 'And don't go thinking you and that other weirdo are going to be sifting through my poo tomorrow. Not after this.'

She slammed the door shut and leaned against it, finally allowing herself to relax.

No, they would not be sifting through her poo tomorrow. She would, though, seeing as she had just swallowed her only means of communication with the outside world.

CHAPTER 28

Stella tossed another shovelful of dirt on to the growing mound before pausing to stand upright and stretch out her back. She had never dug a hole before, and it was proving to be considerably more challenging than she'd expected. Her brain had chosen to think of it as digging a hole and very definitely not digging up a grave, as otherwise she would most certainly start freaking out.

She dropped the shovel to the ground and examined her hands. 'I've got blisters. Actual blisters.'

'That's the stuff,' encouraged Betty from her position in an over-matched deckchair that creaked alarmingly every time she shifted her body weight. 'Good strong physical labour. Very character-forming.'

'Yeah. I bet that's what they said to slaves back in the day, too.'

Betty looked aghast. 'You didn't have to go there with it. You are so dark.'

'Maybe it's the blisters talking. Remind me again why you're sitting in the deckchair?'

'I'm taking a break. My hip is killing me. A young thing like yourself, you might find this hard to believe, but one day your body will start betraying you and breaking down in ways you can't even begin to imagine. Plus, I'm expending quite a bit of energy maintaining the bubble.' She moved her hand about in the air to emphasize her point.

Earlier, Stella had tested said bubble and, to be fair, the thing was impressive. It was based on the same principles as the one Betty had used the night before so the two of them could talk in the office without being overheard. However, this bubble also blocked light, meaning she could walk six feet in any direction, turn around and see . . . nothing. Meanwhile, back inside the bubble were two large torches to illuminate the space around the ground that they were digging up.

Stella sat down on the lip of the hole, her legs dangling over the edge. 'Yeah, like I said previously, the bubble thing is well impressive. I don't suppose there's any magic that could, you know, dig a hole?'

'Are you expecting that I can wave my hands and have the shovels start digging while dancing and singing a merry tune?'

'What are you on about?'

'*Beauty and the Beast*!' said Betty, sounding sincerely horrified. 'Don't tell me you have never seen any of the various versions of *Beauty and the Beast*?'

'Nope.'

'What kind of childhood did you have?'

Stella didn't look up from prodding the biggest of the blisters on her right hand. 'I'm not sure I had one. My earliest memories are just being in a sort of home where, in hindsight, I was treated more like a prisoner than a kid. Whenever I asked, they always told me my mother was going to come back for me. Here's the thing, though – I don't remember having a mother. Or a father. Or . . .' Stella suddenly felt very vulnerable. She'd never told anyone this much before, and she didn't know why it was spilling out of her now. She looked up to see Betty watching her with kind eyes.

'It's all right,' she said in a soft voice.

'It's not, though, is it? Grace and the others are always asking questions. They think I don't want to talk about my past, but the reality is, I don't really have one. At least not one I can remember. I don't even know when I was born. We had cake for Reggie's birthday a couple of months ago and I had to stand there, smiling, while trying not to completely lose my shit. I've never had birthday cake before. And I don't know what scares me more – the fact that that is one hundred per cent true or that I only recently realized it. As if whatever they did to me, I didn't have a life and I didn't even know.' She felt a wetness on her cheeks, looked up into the night sky and was shocked to realize she was crying.

There came a gentle tap on her shoulder and she glanced up to see Betty's hand holding out a handkerchief. Stella took it, wiped her eyes and blew her nose. 'Sorry, I've no idea why this is coming out now or why I'm telling you of all people.'

'I've got one of those faces,' said Betty. 'You should hear the bizarre nonsense people tell me at bus stops, and if I have to hear a detailed breakdown of another taxi driver's sex life, I'll scream.'

In spite of herself, Stella laughed.

'And don't worry, what is said in the bubble stays in the bubble.'

Stella nodded. 'Standard bubble rules.' A thought struck her, and she looked up at Betty warily. 'You didn't do something magical to me, to make me talkative, did you?'

'No,' Betty said in a kind but firm voice. 'I promise I did not. That would be a terrible invasion of privacy. All I've done is keep you up past your bedtime and coerce a member of Gen Z to do some actual physical labour. I'm guessing it's the shock of those two forces colliding that has had this unexpected effect on you.'

Stella sniffed and nodded. 'Speaking of magic and stuff, I don't suppose you can explain what I am? I mean this – whatever this thing is in me.'

'Extraordinary. That is what you are, my dear.'

'To be honest, I was hoping for something a bit more detailed than that. I've got some freaky power I cannot control, and nobody seems to know what it is, although some people wanted to kidnap me for— Well, I don't even know why, but let's assume it wasn't a happy reason.'

Betty heaved herself out of the deckchair and hopped down into the three feet of hole to sit beside Stella. 'When I said extraordinary, I wasn't just talking about your power. I meant you. You've been through everything you have, and then you ended up at *The Stranger Times*, which, by the way, I think was more fate than coincidence. Despite it all, you've turned into a fine young woman, and rather than exacting your revenge on a world that has treated you so poorly, you want to become a journalist, because you think the truth is important. And for all your protestations, you came here tonight because you know something is wrong and you want to help. I have no earthly idea what the power is that you hold, but never forget, that is not what makes you extraordinary.'

Stella ran the back of her hand across her eyes and sniffed. 'So, what you're saying is, there's no magical way to dig a hole?'

Betty nudged her playfully. 'I'm afraid not.'

Stella puffed out her cheeks. 'Feels like this magic malarkey is very good at doing stuff that isn't very useful.'

'Did you not see that thing with the gate earlier? That was pretty cool.' Betty furrowed her brow. 'Do people still say "cool"?'

'Yeah, but not like that.'

'I had a feeling.'

'Thing is, though,' said Stella, 'you're basically sitting there, eating a bag of bonbons—'

'Fizzy cola bottles, actually,' corrected Betty, holding out the bag. 'Would you like one?'

'No, thanks. I have a hard and fast rule about not eating junk food while engaging in grave-robbing.'

'For the last time, we are not robbing anything.'

Stella had been working deliberately with her back to the headstone as she found the sight of Simon's name too upsetting to look at, but she turned and regarded it again. 'Are you sure we need to do this?'

'No. I'm working on a hypothesis because, in all honesty, I've never seen anything like whatever is going on with this poor Simon chap, and I don't know how someone would go about making it happen. I'm not going to pretend otherwise. Even so, if I'm right, we're going to find something deeply unpleasant down there.'

'You mean worse than a dead body?'

Betty shoved her hand back into the bag of sweets and rummaged around. 'Trust me, my dear, when you do what I do for a living, you quickly find out there are far worse things in this world than death.'

Stella scrunched up her face. 'You do this for a living?'

'Not this in particular. You could call me . . . a professional problem-solver.' She nodded to herself. 'Yes, I like the sound of that. I have absolutely no need for a business card, but if I ever did, I think that's what I would put on it.'

'So, you're not really an assistant editor, then?'

Betty gave a sly smile. 'No. To be honest, I'm actually terrible at spelling as well as everything else.'

Stella smiled. 'Which means you were sent here for other purposes?'

Betty chewed her lip for a moment before answering. 'I'm not supposed to say, but yes. It's only fair I tell you, seeing as you have become my assistant . . .'

'Partner.'

'Junior partner, final offer,' countered Betty.

Stella shrugged. 'I'll take it, I guess. I've actually not had any journalism training, but an article I found online said that the most important thing is always to get the who, why, what, where, when and how. So, let's start with the who – as in, who sent you?'

'Like I said, Mrs Harnforth. Just not as an assistant editor.'

'Let me see if I can figure out the why,' said Stella, running her tongue over her lips. 'This can't be a coincidence.'

'No,' agreed Betty.

'But the only people who knew about Simon, other than Banecroft, were me and Hannah. I know I didn't tell anybody, and although I can't be sure, especially as she went well flaky at the end there, I don't think Hannah told anyone either.'

'That would be correct.' Betty leaned forward. 'Since the first time she met him, Mrs H knew that Mr Banecroft was convinced his wife was still alive. I know that doesn't sound like much, but it was the way he was convinced. There was something very unnatural about it. At Mrs H's request, I looked into it at the time but the woman was dead. I saw the body.'

'He just can't accept it?'

'Yes, but . . . It's hard to explain. Some bonds are powerful things and, at the risk of sounding like a greetings card, nothing is more powerful than true love. We kept meaning to do some further investigation, but there are an awful lot of other problems out there. It was on a list for quite some time, but it's an enormous list.'

'So, what changed?' asked Stella.

'I can't say how, because honestly I don't know, but I can tell you we received a message from an anonymous source that *The Stranger Times* was about to come under attack.'

'And you think that's what this is? Some kind of attack?'

Betty sat back and rubbed her chin. 'You must understand that the world you now find yourself in is full of people who will stop at nothing to get what they want. Love is a wonderful and terrible thing. It can lift you up and it can tear you to shreds. Behind all the bluster, the obnoxiousness, the bilious sarcasm, Vincent Banecroft is a broken man. If I'm right, somebody who really wants to hurt him has found a way. The open wound of his grief for the woman he loves has become infected, and the answer to how' – she pointed at the earth beneath her feet – 'might just lie down there.'

'Holy shit,' said Stella. 'That really is dark. Can't we just tell him?'

Betty shook her head. 'True love, remember. Nothing can get in the way of it. In short, he wouldn't believe us. It's not just that he's receiving messages or whatever. This thing has got its hooks into his soul. It's why we need to break the link.' Betty bent down, picked up the two shovels and held one of them out to Stella. 'So, junior partner, how about you and I put a stop to them?'

Stella took it. 'Let's dig.'

Gun Law

The US Congress has made history by approving the nomination of an AR-15 assault rifle to sit on the Supreme Court of the United States. 'Today is a great day for American democracy,' said Representative Ted Cruise-Missile. 'There are more guns in this blessed country than there are people. It is, therefore, shameful that it has taken this long to grant guns representation in the highest court in the land.'

This development, following so soon in the wake of last month's controversial decision by the Court to strike down the law of gravity as unconstitutional, has led some observers to question if the Court has entirely lost its collective damn mind.

CHAPTER 29

Stella looked down at the lid of the coffin and chewed on her bottom lip nervously. With both of them digging, it had taken them another forty minutes to get down deep enough. It had been less time than she'd expected, but that was because she hadn't thought it through properly. She'd calculated that their hole would need to be six feet deep, but of course that wasn't right. It would only be that deep if there wasn't a coffin already in it.

The varnished wood and brass fittings of the lid seemed remarkably unaffected by the several months it had spent underground. Once they'd cleared most of the dirt away, the thing seemed weirdly shiny. Stella knew very little about such things, but it still struck her as odd.

Then again, odd was all relative. On the other side of the grave to where she stood, Betty was busy unpacking the big suitcase she'd gone back to the car to retrieve. She was now rooting through it and extracting what looked to be a very random selection of items: a mallet, a weird African doll, a spice rack, a disturbing selection of metal spikes, a wooden box that concertinaed out into three shelves containing a selection of tiny bottles of various coloured liquids, what appeared to be a varnished lobster, a couple of stoppered clay pots that looked far too fragile to have survived in the case with all the other random crap, a large three-litre plastic milk container that held a blue liquid, a 500ml Diet Coke bottle that contained what looked disturbingly like blood, a teddy bear, a string of onions just like the ridiculous stereotype would have you believe you'd see around the neck of a Frenchman, a leather case containing surgical tools, a power drill, a small framed portrait of the scientist Isaac Newton, and something that looked an awful lot like a whoopee cushion. As if all that wasn't enough, Stella noticed that removing those items from the suitcase had not made it look any less full.

Betty clapped her hands together and gave the objects she had laid out to the side of the hole one last appraising look.

'Righty ho, I think we are ready to go. Oh, nearly forgot . . .'

She dived a hand back into the suitcase and, after a brief rummage, withdrew a large crowbar from it. Then, with an unexpected level of agility, she dropped to a crouch, spun herself round and eased herself into the grave in one fluid motion. Now only visible from the shoulders up, she looked up at Stella. 'You should probably take a couple of steps back, dear. We should expect the unexpected here.'

'Right.' Stella did as she was told.

'Expect the unexpected,' Betty repeated, before grabbing one of the larger metal spikes and shoving it into the pocket of her wax jacket. She grabbed the crowbar with both hands, ready to launch into action, but stopped herself. She relaxed her body for a moment and addressed the coffin. 'Mr Brush – Simon – we never met and, if I'm completely wrong about this, I do apologize, but I hope you understand that my intentions here are entirely honourable.' Having satisfied herself, Betty set her jaw, resumed her firm grip on the crowbar and bent down.

Stella didn't see what happened next, but she heard the multiple cracks of wood before Betty's head reappeared, still looking down.

'Oh my! That is . . . unexpected.'

Betty tossed the crowbar on to the ground then appealed to Stella for help. 'A hand, if you wouldn't mind, please.'

As Stella stepped forward, Betty shifted herself awkwardly and guided the coffin lid up to Stella, who duly pulled it out and laid it on the ground beside her. Steeling herself, Stella leaned forward and peered into the hole. She had prepared herself for the sight of a skeleton, or a decomposing body at the very least, and was taken aback by what she saw.

Simon was, well, Simon. He looked exactly like the odd geeky guy who had taken up position outside of *The Stranger Times* offices every morning, trying to convince Vincent Banecroft to give him a job. Even down to his glasses, which, as always, were taped up where they'd been repaired. It just seemed as if he were asleep – if people normally slept in a suit. But then there was the other thing. A harness that looked to be a mix of leather and chain mail was strapped around his chest and in its centre gleamed a large, orange, diamond-like stone.

'What the hell is that?' asked Stella.

'To be honest, I'm not entirely sure. Do you recall him wearing any particular bling when he was alive?'

'No.'

'I thought not. If it's what I think it might be, then someone has gone to a huge amount of trouble to do what they're doing.' Betty looked up at Stella. 'First things first, I should confirm this gentleman is the late Simon Brush, is he not?'

Stella nodded.

'Right. Then I'm going to need a bit of time to figure out what to do here.' She drummed her fingers against her chin. 'Yes, quite the pickle.'

After ten minutes, Stella sat down in the deckchair. Betty looked lost in thought as she continued to stare at the objects she had laid out at the graveside then back down into the coffin. It didn't seem like a good time to pepper her with questions.

Another fifteen minutes passed and Stella found herself studying the outlines of the surrounding gravestones. Her eyes had become attuned to the dark now and she could see a lot more. There didn't seem to be a set approach to the design of these things. Most of the graves had fairly ordinary stones with simple inscriptions. Some bore engravings of images. Others boasted statues.

She turned her attention to the stone rendering of a cherub perched atop a nearby headstone, a bow and arrow in its hands. When she looked across to her right, there was a very similar one, only this one was holding a lute. She supposed the similarity in design made sense. There couldn't be that many companies in Manchester that manufactured gravestones. That was when she noticed a third one.

She was about to say something when Betty gasped. The grave had lit up with an orange glow, strong enough to cause Betty to shield her eyes. Stella hauled herself out of the deckchair and nipped over to where the corpse of Simon Brush lay. The orange jewel across his chest was now blazing brightly.

'What the hell is going on?'

For the first time Stella saw what could be genuine fear in Betty's eyes.

'Nothing good.'

★

Banecroft lay on his bed, staring at the ceiling and chewing on the ruined remnants of his fingernails. Sleep was beyond him. He hadn't even attempted it since last night when that bloody woman had interrupted them. Charlotte had been trying to speak to him. She was all that mattered now. He was close. He could save her. He could end all of this.

The pillow beneath his head was damp with sweat. He turned it over and punched it irritably. Nobody understood. He just needed a chance. He just . . .

He heard a noise outside his office. Or did he? His mind was playing tricks on him. He'd already run into the bullpen three times this evening only to be greeted by the same empty room, mocking him.

He got up and moved across to the door quietly, holding his breath as he opened it. When he caught sight of the spectral figure of Simon Brush sitting at his usual desk, the air rushed out of him as if he'd been sucker-punched. This time, he didn't even attempt a casual approach. He raced across the room and crumpled to his knees across the desk from the ghost.

Words tumbled from his lips. 'Simon, Simon, Simon. I need to speak to Charlotte. Let me speak to Charlotte. Please. I must speak to Charlotte.'

The ghost looked up from the newspaper laid out on the desk and, for a moment, some small part of Banecroft was aware of the terrible sadness that lay in those eyes. Then, the mouth stretched painfully open and the head thrashed about at impossible speed.

Next came the scream. The terrible scream.

★

Betty stood with her feet balanced on either edge of the coffin as the body inside it flailed about.

'Do something!' shouted Stella, standing above her.

'I'm going to. I just need to figure out what the hell that should be.'

The orange light from the jewel faded slightly and, mercifully, Simon's corpse stopped moving.

'That's an improve—' Stella broke off as Simon's eyes opened. Only they weren't Simon's eyes. His actual eyes had been blue or brown, she didn't know – but they definitely were not blood red. And while they might have been a tad sparkly, they didn't glow ominously. 'I think I'm going to be sick.'

Betty drew the metal spike from her jacket pocket and snatched up the large wooden mallet.

Simon started talking, but the voice that came out was not his. His mouth moved, but a female voice emerged from it. 'Lumpy. You have to help me. I'm in so much trouble.'

'Oh, Lord,' said Betty.

★

'Anything, Charlotte,' said Banecroft. 'I'll do anything to help you. Just tell me what it is.'

The spectral Simon turned to look at Banecroft but spoke in his wife's voice. 'You have to help me. It won't be easy. They will try to stop you.'

'Nobody will stop me. I promise. I can save you this time. Just give me the chance.'

★

Betty hunkered down and placed the tip of the metal spike against the jewel. Her fingertip brushed against the stone and she drew it away quickly. 'Crikey, that's hot.'

'Are you sure about this?' asked Stella.

'Absolutely not. Stand well back.'

Simon's lips moved again and the voice continued. 'Come and rescue me. Save me from this place. There is a way.'

★

'Anything,' pleaded Banecroft. 'Just tell me what I need to do. Tell me how I can reach you.'

'There is a way,' repeated Charlotte. 'To find me, you need to . . .'

★

'Here goes nothing,' shouted Betty as she raised the mallet above her head and brought it crashing down. The spike drove into the jewel, which cracked under the force and emitted a high-pitched squeal.

Stella braced herself. Betty had just enough time to throw her arms in front of her face before the stone exploded with a blinding eruption of light and a wave of energy so strong it lifted her off her feet and threw her backwards out of the grave.

*

Banecroft blinked and the ghost disappeared.

He scrabbled to his feet. 'No! Charlotte. Simon. Come back. Please. Come back. No.'

A wail of anguish escaped his lips as he crumpled to the floor. 'No. Please. Come back.'

*

The explosion had also sent Stella stumbling backwards. She tripped over the lid of the coffin and ended up on her backside in the middle of someone's floral arrangement. She had no time to feel bad about that now. She picked herself up and raced over to Betty, who lay motionless on the ground.

'Are you OK?'

Betty eased herself up on her elbows, looked around and started to pat herself down. Bits of her clothing appeared to be smouldering.

'Well, I'm not going to lie. I could definitely use a stiff brandy.'

Seemingly satisfied that she wasn't about to burst into flames, Betty sat up fully and looked into the grave. All that was left were the remnants of the harness among a pile of dark grey ash.

'Is Simon . . .' started Stella, nodding in the direction of the coffin.

'He might not be looking as well as he did, but he's still dead. I now believe he is also, shall we say, his own man once again.'

'Right. Well, I suppose that's a good thing.'

'It'd better be. I'd hate to think this jacket got scorched for nothing.'

'Come on, let's get you up.' Stella began to help Betty to her feet but stopped at the sound of a grinding noise coming from behind her. 'What the hell is—'

Betty shoved her roughly to one side. Stella stumbled backward and watched in shock as Betty grabbed the two-foot-tall stone cherub that had leaped at her out of the darkness. She struggled with it for a moment before drawing her arms over her head and tossing it into the darkness from whence it came.

All attempts to understand what the hell was happening were pushed aside as the thought struck Stella that there had been more than one of the statues. She spun around just in time to spot another of the little blighters running at her, its lute still in its chubby little hand. Instinctively, she drew back her right leg and kicked the thing – something she instantly regretted as pain shot up her leg. It was as if she had just tried to drop-kick a boulder, which wasn't far from the truth. She hopped about for a couple of seconds before she was sent tumbling to the ground as the little boulder hurled itself at her, making a disconcerting *wheeee* sound as it did so.

Stella righted herself into a seated position just in time to see the demented little thing running towards her again. She grabbed its shoulder with her left hand then inadvertently slapped it in the face with her right as she attempted a two-handed grip.

The stone cherub threw her a hurt look before its features rearranged themselves into a sneer. From this distance its mouth, full of pointed, razor-sharp teeth, was clear. She howled in pain as it bashed its stone lute against the fingers of her left hand to free itself from her grip.

It leaped on to her chest, winding her, then stood there for a moment, its chubby little arms raised in victory before it tossed the lute away and made to lunge forward to bite her face. She grabbed it just in time, and its horrible little mouth snapped at the air in front of her nose.

As she held it at bay, it too grabbed on to her, bunching the material of her hoodie tightly in its fists. She tried to throw it away, as she had seen Betty do, but it wouldn't budge. They were trapped in something of a stalemate, except one of them was made from stone and didn't look like it was going to run out of energy any time soon.

It was at that point that Stella felt the power, the terrible thing, move inside her. She tried to hold it back but, with a sense of dread, she felt the horrible sensation of another pair of tiny stone hands grabbing at the right leg of her jeans. She was outnumbered. She glanced quickly to her left, afraid to take her eyes off the little snapping bastard for more than a second. She couldn't see Betty, but could hear the sounds of a struggle somewhere out of view.

The second stone cherub was clambering up her leg now, coming to join its buddy. She shook her limb about as much as she could, but her flailing had no effect. As her sense of panic grew within her so did the other thing. The power began to surge through her. Terrible, wonderful, irresistible.

She was losing her grip on the snapping and snarling cherub in her hands, and while she tried to buck her lower body to shake off the other one, her efforts were met with the sound of childish giggling.

Enough was enough.

'Screw it!' shouted Stella. 'You literally asked for this, you little shit.'

With that, she stopped trying to hold it back. As her hands started to glow bright blue, the little cherub stopped snapping at her and looked down in confusion.

'See ya!'

She felt a sickening jolt as the power surged through her. The cherub dissolved into dust as the bolt of blue energy shot into the night sky and lit up the clouds. She turned her body, trying to control it, but her movement sent the stream of blue light scything across the graveyard, accompanied by a snarling, ripping sound. It was as if the air itself was being torn asunder. Stones were sliced in half and a couple of small fires began to smoulder.

Finally, it stopped. Stella gasped for air, as if emerging from under water, where her body had been the plaything of a vicious riptide. She looked down at the fine layer of dust that now covered her hoodie and wondered belatedly what had happened to the second bastard little cherub, which was nowhere to be seen.

Betty's voice rose from the hole. 'Looks like they legged it. That was pretty bloody impressive, although not the most subtle of approaches.'

Stella's voice came out as a croak. 'Are you OK?'

'I am alive, but I'm also stuck in someone's coffin, so I have to say I've had better nights out.'

Stella struggled to her feet, limped over to the hole and peered down to see Betty firmly wedged at the bottom of it.

'Would you like a hand?'

'What gave it away? Quick as you can, please.'

Stella's left hand was still throbbing from the pain of being whacked with a stone lute, so she used her right one to assist Betty. Once she'd heaved her out, they both lay sprawled on the ground, panting. The back of Betty's jacket was covered in ash – bits of Simon Brush – but Stella decided that now was probably not a good time to bring that to her attention.

'What the hell was that?' she asked.

'An ambush. To be more exact, a booby trap. Sorry,' apologized Betty as she sat upright and held up a hand to her neck, 'I should have seen something like that coming. Whoever the swine is behind all this, they are both powerful and nasty.'

'Did I . . . That cherub thing. Did I . . .'

Betty must have guessed where Stella was heading and used her free hand to pat her junior partner's leg. 'You cannot kill what is not alive. Plus, you have a rock-solid case for self-defence there – no pun intended. Speaking of which . . .'

She drew her hand away from her neck and, through the gloom, Stella could see blood. '. . . One of the little blighters got me.'

Stella sat up to get a better look. 'It doesn't look too bad. We can disinfect it when we get back to the office.'

'Well,' said Betty, 'I'm afraid it's not that simple. I don't want you to panic, but things are about to get a bit . . . weird.'

Stella shook her head. 'They're about to get weird? Like, until now this hasn't already been the weirdest night of my life. We dug up my mate, my boss's dead wife started talking through his corpse, and then some small stone babies tried to bite my face off.'

'Focus, Stella. Focus, dear. You're gabbling and we don't have much time.'

'What do you mean?'

Betty pointed down at her right leg. From her foot to the middle of her calf had already turned to stone.

'Holy shit!' shouted Stella, scrambling backwards in horror. 'Why didn't you say something?'

'I was. It will actually be fine, just do exactly as I say. Go over there to my collection of tiny bottles and find one with a picture of a mountain on it.'

Stella was still staring at Betty's legs. As she watched, the stone slowly crept up over the woman's knee. Her left foot had also started to petrify.

'Stella!' barked Betty. 'Focus! Not much time. Bottle with a mountain on it. Liquid is yellowish in colour. Grab it. Now.'

Stella roused herself with a shake of her head and scrabbled on her hands and knees to where the wooden box concertinaed out into several shelves, each containing a row of small, old-fashioned medicine bottles. She snatched up bottles at random, staring at them in the torchlight before discarding them in turn. *Mountain. Mountain. Mountain. Come on, bloody mountain.* As she dropped one, its liquid escaped and caused the grass beneath it to smoke. 'Shit. Sorry.'

'Don't worry about it. Just find the one I asked for.'

Stella nodded and continued to pick up more bottles. After three further attempts she held one up excitedly. 'I've got it.'

'Good girl.'

Stella allowed herself to look back over at Betty, who was now lying flat on the ground, her entire lower half the same grey stone as the cherubs. 'Oh God.'

'Don't worry about it. Now, grab that big bottle of blue liquid and an onion.'

Stella did as instructed and hurried to Betty's side. The grey stone had now reached above the point where Betty's belly button would be.

'Quickly, pour all the blue liquid all over me.'

'Should I—'

'Just do it.'

Stella did as she was told. As she drenched Betty in the liquid there was a distinct smell of burning wood.

'Good. Now, pass me the onion.' Betty tried to extend her right hand to take it, but it wouldn't move. It too was now stone. Her left was still usable, though, so she grabbed the vegetable with that. 'I'm going to shove this into my mouth. Pour one drop of that other liquid on to it. Just one. After we're done, I'll be fine in a day or two. Just take me back to the office and keep me safe. Got it?'

Stella watched, horrified, as the stone reached Betty's chest.

'Stella, have you got all that?'

She met Betty's gaze and nodded.

'Good.' Betty shoved the onion into her mouth.

Stella fumbled with the stopper of the tiny bottle before managing to uncork it. The stone was inching towards Betty's neck now.

'God, how much is a drop?'

Betty didn't answer, just rolled her eyes.

'Screw it.' Stella tipped the small bottle and watched as a splash of yellow liquid hit the onion with a hissing sound.

Betty tried to speak around the onion. It was hard to make out, but it sounded like she was saying, 'Lie me down.' Before Stella could ask any more questions, Betty's face turned to stone before her eyes.

'Holy . . .'

Stella tentatively placed a finger on Betty's cheek. It was cold. Like a hard, lifeless rock.

She sat back on her haunches and took in all the paraphernalia that Betty had left scattered around the place; at the grave they had just dug up; and at the smouldering, shattered gravestones surrounding them. Then, finally, she looked back down at the statue that had once been the assistant editor of *The Stranger Times*.

'This is going to take an awful lot of explaining.'

CHAPTER 30

Reggie rubbed the heels of his hands into his eyes and leaned back in his chair. 'Good God, how long have we been at this now?'

'I don't know,' replied Ox. 'Time has lost all meaning. Having said that, it's three in the morning.'

Reggie raised his head and examined the pinboard they had dragged into the basement from upstairs. Managing to get it down the stairs was the only sense of achievement they'd enjoyed for the entire time they had been at this. On it were now pinned copies of all twenty-seven of the Dex Hex columns that had been printed in *The Stranger Times*.

Ox hopped from foot to foot in front of Reggie. 'I've got it. This time I've really got it.'

'Where have I heard that before?' muttered Reggie.

'What was that?'

Reggie raised his voice. 'Nothing. Fire away.'

Ox, wide-eyed, pointed both his index fingers at Reggie. 'We're thinking about this all wrong.' He waved a hand in the direction of the noticeboard behind him. 'We keep trying to figure out which one of these nonsense theories could have some truth in it. Hear me out – they're *all* true. It's you and I that don't exist.'

'OK, you're *Matrix*-ing again. I don't know what's worse about that theory – that this is the third time you've proposed it, or that the last time you suggested it I spent twenty minutes going down this particular rabbit hole with you.'

Ox threw his hands in the air. 'Fine, smart guy. Let's hear your big idea.'

'I still say our best bet is that the lost civilization of Atlantis is actually the Isle of Man.'

'And I'm telling you, the Isle of Man does not even qualify as a civilization.'

'You are so small-minded,' said Reggie. 'You think everywhere that isn't Manchester is shit.'

'Ha. That's where you're wrong. I happen to think Manchester is shit too. It's just less shit than everywhere else.'

'Well, at least we've found that new advertising slogan Manchester has been looking for.' Reggie shook his head. 'You are a tragic loss to the city's tourism board. If only you'd got a job there instead of here, I wouldn't be looking at this smorgasbord of utter drivel, trying to determine which bit of it got poor Tony Dawson kidnapped.'

'There you go again, implying this is all my fault.'

Reggie held up a hand. 'I wasn't implying this was all your fault. I was straight out saying it. This is all your fault.'

Before Ox could respond, they were interrupted by a loud banging on the doors to the basement.

Reggie jumped out of his seat. 'Who the hell could that be at this time of night?'

'I've no idea, but if it turns out to be King Charles confirming he really is descended from pandas, then I'll expect a full apology from you.'

'In the highly unlikely event it *isn't* him,' said Reggie, looking around the basement, 'we need to arm ourselves.'

'Arm ourselves?' echoed Ox.

'Yes. It's three o'clock in the bloody morning. It's not going to be somebody trying to spread the good word about Jesus at this time of night, is it?'

'It's me,' shouted a voice they both recognized. 'Now open the stupid door.'

Ox and Reggie hauled open the doors to find Stella leaning against one of the large wheelie bins kept there, breathing heavily. 'Took you long enough.'

Reggie rushed to her side. 'Are you OK? Hang on – how come you're covered in dirt? Dear girl, what on earth have you been doing?'

'I was . . . digging a grave.'

'What?'

'Well, technically, I was digging up a grave.'

'Oh,' said Ox. 'That's all right, then. You had me worried for a second, kid.'

'But why are you out of breath?' asked Reggie.

'I had to push Betty for the last half-mile. Broke down.'

'Our assistant editor has broken down?'

Ox shrugged. 'You say that like it's the first time it's happened. This place has had more assistant editors than I've had hot dinners . . . God, I could murder a hot dinner.'

'Ox. Focus,' snapped Reggie. 'Stella, dear, you're not making any sense.'

'Ha,' she said, turning away and beckoning them to follow her. 'If you don't think that's making sense, wait until you see what I've got to show you.'

Five minutes later, the trio were standing in the gloom of *The Stranger Times*' car park looking at the three-wheeler that Stella hadn't so much parked as just stopped pushing because she couldn't go any further.

'So then,' said Stella, finishing her recap of her eventful evening, 'I put all the stuff in the back of the car because it didn't come close to fitting back into the suitcase. Don't ask me why. I strapped Betty to the top of Betty Two and eventually managed to get out of the graveyard by using a crowbar on the gate. It's a minor miracle the police didn't come. Then I drove here, or at least I tried to. About a half-mile up the road, this clapped-out rust heap gave up the ghost and I had to push it the rest of the way. All in all, it's been a doozy of a night.'

'Is that a Reliant Robin?' asked Ox.

'Really?' replied Stella. 'I've just told you that the statue strapped to its roof is our assistant editor who was petrified after being bitten by a somehow alive stone cherub, and that is your first question?'

'I'm just saying you don't see many of them. They're a British classic.'

'Well, you can look forward to discussing that with Betty

when she . . . I don't know how you describe it. Reanimates? In one to two days' time. At least that's what she told me.'

'Can I ask,' began Reggie, 'how you got the statue on top of the car by yourself?'

'That's the weird thing,' started Stella, before stopping to correct herself. 'Sorry, that's about the four hundred and twenty-seventh weird thing – the statue isn't that heavy. It sort of floats.'

Reggie clasped his hands behind his back and swayed back and forth on the balls of his feet as he gave the statue a worried look. 'And we are sure she is going to be OK?'

Stella held up her palms. 'She seemed very confident about the prospect just before she turned to stone. Like I said, she told me she'd be all right in a day or two, and to just keep her safe until then. Then she said, I think, "Lie me down," but it was hard to make out because she had an onion in her mouth at the time.'

'Why did—' started Ox.

'She just did, OK? She just did. There has been so much weirdness tonight that if I have to explain even half of it, we'll still be standing here in two weeks' time. Now, I need the pair of you to help me get her inside without whacking her head off on a wall or something. So let's have less of the talky-talky, and more of the do-ey do-ey.'

'Who put you in charge?'

'Well, seeing as our current assistant editor is indisposed, I imagine I'll be moving up the chain of command pretty fast. Now help me with this because my next job is to have a very awkward conversation with Banecroft.'

'You'll be lucky,' said Ox. 'I was using the bog earlier when I heard him screaming and shouting. He then ran out of the building, got in his Jag and drove off like a bat out of hell.'

'Oh,' said Stella. 'That's probably not great either. Anyway, grab an end of Betty each and I'll undo the ropes.'

'Before we get to that,' said Ox, 'would you help settle an argument? Do you reckon it's more likely King Charles is a robot, a lizard or a panda?'

CHAPTER 31

Hannah poked at her breakfast with little enthusiasm. She wasn't much of a fan of omelettes at the best of times, and this morning she was feeling rather queasy. Several things could be blamed for that; after last night's disastrous reconnaissance mission, she had managed only a couple of fitful hours' sleep thanks to the adrenalin still coursing through her body.

Then there was the fact that she had been forced to swallow the earpiece. She knew it took between eighteen and thirty-six hours for a foreign object to pass through the human digestive system. She knew that because, six weeks ago, *The Stranger Times* had run a story on a man from Swansea who had decided to disassemble, eat and then reassemble his motorbike. When asked the obvious question why, he had replied that he was doing it for Comic Relief. It never failed to amaze Hannah how many crazy people got away with explaining their behaviour by saying it was in aid of charity.

Speaking of indigestible items, Hannah eyed the Pinter Institute Life Shake™ sitting beside her plate. Everyone got one for breakfast. As Moira had pointed out yesterday, for all the hype about the vitamins and minerals it contained, it tasted like old mattresses blended with mouthwash and just a hint of gravel.

Then there was the main reason Hannah was feeling so uneasy – Moira. Despite what Cathy had told her once she was out of the cellar, the last time Hannah had seen Moira, she had sounded as if she was being held prisoner – and worse, was then hypnotized to ensure her compliance with God knows what. Moira was also late for breakfast. It was very hard to be late for anything at the Pinter Institute, mainly because staff were always on hand to 'maximize your experience'. As Hannah well knew, in practical terms that meant you were under such strict supervision that an unscheduled bowel movement could trigger a team meeting.

Hannah was debating with herself whether, if Moira didn't turn up at all, she should just start kicking up a fuss there and then. Should she demand to see her to make sure she was OK? She might play it as being a concerned friend, but she would end up drawing a lot of attention to herself at the worst time imaginable. Maybe it was all in her mind, but the brusque service, minimal chat and furtive shared looks when they thought the guests weren't watching – Hannah had a definite feeling that the Pinter Institute staff were all on edge this morning. Far more so than previously. They knew that somebody had been sniffing around last night, even if they didn't know their identity, and the constant undercurrent of paranoia that permeated the place seemed much closer to the surface now.

Her internal debate was rendered moot when, much to Hannah's relief, Moira walked through the door. The first thing Hannah noticed was that she was no longer dressed in her Pinter Institute tracksuit. Instead, she was rocking a fetching burgundy suit and white blouse. The second thing was that she was positively beaming. As soon as she saw Hannah, her smile grew even wider and she made a beeline for her across the dining hall. As she closed in, Moira stretched her arms out wide and Hannah rose to greet her, only to be enveloped in a hug.

'Hannah, darling, there you are.'

'Moira, I was worried about you.'

Moira released Hannah, took a step back and laughed. 'Worried about me? Oh, bless you. No need to worry about me, hen. I have never felt better.'

'I can see that. I guess from the outfit that you're off home, then?' Hannah leaned in and lowered her voice. 'Finally getting out of this hellhole.'

'Oh no,' said Moira. 'I mean, yes, I am off home, but I will miss this place terribly. It did absolute wonders for me.'

'It did?' said Hannah, failing to keep the surprise from her voice.

'Absolutely. I mean, look at me.' Moira gave a twirl. 'I've never looked or felt better. I'm a new woman.'

'Great,' said Hannah blandly.

Moira's new outfit aside, she looked the same physically as she had the day before. Not that she looked bad on either day, but her change in attitude was remarkable.

'I have to say I'm a bit surprised, Moira. You weren't exactly the biggest fan of this place.'

Moira waved a hand, as if batting the idea away. 'That was the old negative me. Don't pay attention to that negative ninny.' She threw out both hands and all but sang at the top of her lungs. 'This place works miracles.'

Hannah didn't really know what to say to that. Instead, she looked around the room at the other diners, who had all stopped eating to watch the show.

Moira grabbed Hannah by the shoulders and beamed a wide-eyed smile at her. 'The Pinter Institute has changed my life, and it will do the same for you. Just trust the process. Trust the process.'

Hannah nodded while studying Moira's face. Not a hint nor a scintilla of sarcasm to be seen anywhere. She swept Hannah up in another hug and then she was off, waving and shaking hands with as many people as possible as she made a quick circuit of the dining hall.

Hannah looked over at the door and saw Dr French standing there, smiling at her. She returned the smile and then sat back down to her breakfast.

That had been a very unexpected kind of weird.

CHAPTER 32

Stella woke to the sound of her own name being bellowed from a distance. She had been having a rather unpleasant dream in which she was pushing a stone cherub in a buggy round Manchester Arndale shopping centre and it kept breaking free to bite people. A psychiatrist would have a field day with that one, even if she managed to convince them that the stone baby with sharp teeth wasn't a metaphor for anything.

'Stella!' came the shout again. It was Grace, sounding distinctly vexed.

'I'm coming,' she yelled back, looking round to locate the clothing she had wearily discarded the night before.

Grace was standing in reception, her desk now buried entirely beneath what looked like three layers of boxes, with a couple more cardboard cartons sitting at her feet. At this point, somebody could drive a truck at the reception desk and it would probably emerge unscathed. The way this week was going, Stella wouldn't bet against it happening.

'Stella!' Grace roared again.

'All right, all right, I'm here.' Stella stumbled into reception and pushed the hair out of her eyes. 'I see rehearsals for that performance of *A Streetcar Named Desire* are going well.'

Grace gave her a look. 'What?'

'Never mind. Pretty unexpected reference coming from me. I wouldn't have got it either. How can I help you today?'

'Are you being sarcastic?'

'No,' responded Stella quickly. Grace had views on sarcasm. 'I'm just . . . There was no need to shout.'

'I tried ringing you, but you weren't answering.'

'Ah. Yeah. About that.' She extracted the smashed remnants of her mobile from the back pocket of her jeans.

Grace's face fell. 'What happened?'

'It . . .' started Stella, before deciding on, 'broke.'

Grace was a worrier. If Stella told her the full account of how her phone had got smashed during a violent altercation with a pair of homicidal angelic statues, there was a distinct chance Grace would tie her to something to prevent her from ever leaving the building again.

'I can see it broke,' said Grace, her voice dropping. 'I got you that for Christmas.'

'I know and I'm sorry.' *It was the first Christmas present I ever received in my entire life.* 'I will get it fixed.'

Grace looked slightly mollified by this. 'Make sure you do. Now, where is everybody?'

'Everybody?'

'Everybody,' repeated Grace. 'It is nine o'clock. Reggie and Ox aren't here. You were still in bed. Mr Banecroft is not in his office.'

'Really?' said Stella.

She knew that was bad, but she didn't have a clue what to do about it. Betty had said that they needed to be diplomatic about the Banecroft situation, but that was before . . .

'Hang on, have you not seen Betty this morning?'

'No.'

'So you haven't been into the bullpen yet?'

Grace's bracelets jingled as she waved her arms. 'Of course I have.'

'Oh. Right.'

To be fair to Grace, most people probably wouldn't assume that the statue lying on the floor in the corner was one of their co-workers who had been literally petrified. Even for *The Stranger Times*, it was an unusual turn of events.

'Now, can you give me a hand with these boxes, please? There are more in the car.'

'But . . .'

Before Stella could say anything else, the sound of footsteps coming up the stairs heralded the arrival of Ox and Reggie.

'Good morning,' offered Reggie.

'And what kind of time do you call this?' asked Grace.

'Go easy,' said Ox, with a dismissive wave of his hand. 'We were here till all hours trying to figure out that bloody Dex Hex thing. For all the good it did us.'

'You have still not worked out for that nice DI Sturgess which one of your nonsense stories got that poor man into trouble?'

'We've been trying,' said Reggie defensively, 'but it's incredibly difficult to locate a lone nugget of truth in a veritable landslide of utter bunk.'

'So, ask the man.'

'What man?' Ox looked puzzled.

'The truth man. The man who tells the truth.'

'She means Cogs,' said Stella.

'Actually,' said Reggie, raising his eyebrows, 'that is a brilliant idea.'

'I know,' snapped Grace, picking up one of the boxes. 'I have lots of them, but hardly anybody ever listens to me round here. I am just the poor fool who has to find all the boxes because our new assistant editor wants to do an audit.'

'Oh yeah,' said Stella, remembering the rather important thing she had been sidetracked from revealing earlier. 'About that. Now, I don't want you to freak out but . . .' Stella opened the door to the bullpen and promptly freaked out. 'Where the hell is Betty?'

'I told you she wasn't here. I do not speak ill of people when they are within hearing distance. That would be unchristian.'

Stella held her head in her hands. 'She's gone. How can she be gone?'

'I have no doubt she will be back,' said Grace bitterly. 'Demanding to see receipts for things, as if I'm some kind of common criminal.'

'No, but . . . You don't understand . . .' She turned to the others. 'Do you two know anything about this? By which I mean, Ox – is this your idea of a joke? Where is she?'

Ox held up his hands. 'I don't have a Scooby. Why does

everyone always assume everything that happens round here is my fault?'

'Statistical probability,' responded Reggie.

Stella did a hurried tour of the bullpen, looking under desks that were in no way big enough to conceal the statuesque Betty as she lay in her hopefully temporary state.

'Erm . . . Stella,' said Reggie.

'Not now,' answered Stella, who was busy checking cupboards that were even less likely to contain Betty. 'I cannot believe I lost her. I had one job.'

'Stella,' repeated Reggie.

She continued to ignore him, opened the door to Banecroft's office and took a quick look round, before exiting via the other door and heading down the corridor back to reception. She then inspected the kitchen. 'Downstairs. Maybe Manny moved her or—'

'Stella!' barked Reggie with enough force that everyone turned to look at him, including Stella. He straightened his waistcoat. 'Sorry, but – could you come here for a moment, please?'

She walked over to where Reggie was standing by the doors to the bullpen.

'Thank you, Stella. Now, I would appreciate it if you tried to remain calm.'

'But she's gone.'

'The good news,' offered Reggie, 'is that she has not, in fact, gone. The bad news is . . . well . . .' He pointed up at the ceiling.

'Holy shit!'

'Stella!' admonished Grace. 'There is no need for that kind of language.' She walked into the bullpen and looked up to see what the fuss was about. 'Holy shit!' With a jangle of bracelets, she crossed herself three times.

'Grace swore,' said Ox excitedly, which earned him a clip round the back of the head from Reggie. 'Oi!'

'Sweet baby Jesus and all of his saints,' whispered Grace, 'what is that?' She pointed up to the statue floating about fifteen feet above their heads and bobbing against the high arched ceiling of the former church.

'That,' responded Stella, 'is our new assistant editor, who has been petrified. And I don't mean scared. I looked it up last night – "petrified" is the correct word for someone who has been turned to stone.'

'How has . . .' Grace leaned back against the wall. 'All of this insanity combined with looking up is making me feel dizzy.'

Stella patted her on the shoulder. 'You go and make yourself a nice cup of tea and I'll explain everything in a couple of minutes. OK?'

Grace nodded and headed off in the direction of the kitchen, already feeling on more familiar ground.

'Oh,' said Stella, slapping her palm against her forehead. 'I'm a bloody idiot.' She noticed the confused looks of her two colleagues. 'Remember when I said I thought she told me to lie her down?'

Ox clicked his fingers and pointed enthusiastically. 'Tie me down. She said, "Tie me down."'

Stella nodded. 'Where were you six hours ago?'

'Here with you, but I was a bit fixated on King Charles.'

Stella took another look at Betty, who was still gently bumping against the ceiling, then she turned and walked to the top of the stairs.

'Manny,' she shouted, 'I need your help. And bring the big ladder.'

CHAPTER 33

Stanley turned the apple round and round in his hands. This one was shiny. He had no idea if it would have any bearing on its taste, but it couldn't hurt. This morning, in his ongoing efforts to improve himself – or at the very least not die before the end of the week – he had decided to give fruit a go. He'd pulled the van over outside an honest-to-God greengrocer's and bought one of each variety of apple they had in stock, plus a couple of varieties of pear, an orange, a kiwi fruit and a banana. His taste test was not going well.

He'd started with the banana and, in hindsight, that was a mistake. He already knew bananas were all right. He should have held it in reserve, for no other reason than it would have been handy to rid his mouth of the taste of the pear.

He didn't even know how to eat the kiwi fruit and he was already thinking of giving it a miss. It was hairy. Since when was fruit hairy? He had occasionally eaten fruit before, although it'd mainly been on top of a slice of cake. Almost everything tasted wonderful on top of a slice of cake. You had to work really hard to mess that up.

Plain fruit, though, was proving to be very grim indeed. This shiny little bugger of an apple was his last hope. He took a bite.

Ten seconds later and he was out of the van dumping the entire bag's worth into a nearby bin. A man walking his dog gave him a look as he shoved the lot in while issuing the kind of sweary epitaph normally reserved for sex fiends or politicians. Judging by the man's facial expression, you rarely heard that kind of language at the posh end of Hebden Bridge, where they currently were.

Screw it, thought Stanley. Tomorrow he'd try vegetables.

As he hopped back into the van, his mobile was ringing. He snatched it up from its place on the dashboard.

'Hello, Cathy.'

'How's it going?' she asked.

He glanced at the blue door on the far side of the street. 'Nothing yet, but it is his day off. He might be having a well-earned lie-in. Speaking of which, how are things back at the Pinter Institute?'

'Testy. They've summoned the staff for a meeting in a couple of hours. Two big lads are guarding the door to the wine cellar and they've called in a highly paid IT security specialist to check their systems.'

'Is that going to be a problem?'

'He's currently reading last night's log files, which I doctored. Meanwhile, I'm inside his laptop. He's going through a messy divorce and it's about to get a whole lot messier as his wife's lawyer has just been sent a list of the places where he's hiding assets.'

'Blimey,' said Stanley. 'Remind me never to piss you off.'

'I think you've forgotten how we first met. Blackmail, et cetera.'

Stanley shifted in his seat. 'Sorry again about that.'

'Yeah. Say it like you mean it.'

'How's Hannah getting on?' asked Stanley, keen to move on to safer topics.

'She seems to be doing all right. Having breakfast and has just met that Moira friend of hers – the stationery mogul.'

'The one she said was being held prisoner last night?'

'Yeah. She looks as happy as Larry now, though. She's clearly off home today, running about the place, hugging everybody like she's just been selected to "come on down" on *The Price Is Right*. This must be one hell of a case of Stockholm syndrome.'

'Do you not believe Hannah?'

'I'm not saying that, but, well – what kind of explanation would cover what she said being true and what I've just told you?'

Stanley hesitated. As far as Cathy was aware, they were looking into the Pinter Institute because they were up to some dodgy financial stuff, possibly taking advantage of vulnerable people. He hadn't brought up the whole magic angle because, well, for one thing, this job was on a need-to-know basis, and second, he seriously doubted she'd believe him.

He was considering what to say next when circumstances rendered his decision unnecessary. 'He's out,' confirmed Stanley. 'Got to go.'

Whatever Cathy tried to say in response was lost as he ended the call. Anton Lasherf had just exited his house, turned right at the bottom of the path and was heading towards where his Audi was parked at the end of the street. This was exactly as Stanley had hoped and expected. While his broken ankle had more or less healed, it still hindered his ability to run, and it wasn't as if that had been a particular strength of his to begin with. Thankfully, that would not be necessary.

Stanley got out of the van and stood on the pavement, blocking the way. Anton glanced at him and then positioned himself to go around. Stanley took a step to put himself firmly in the other man's new path.

'Anton. Anton Lasherf.'

That got his attention. Anton looked directly at Stanley. 'Do I know you?'

'No. But I know you. You work at the Pinter Institute, don't you? Personal experience facilitator.'

It was hard to judge the man's reaction simply because his face was so smooth and fixed in place. He had had a great deal of work done and Stanley knew exactly how much he'd spent on it. It was how Anton had got himself into financial trouble in the first place. Not that Stanley was one to judge. He didn't care what anyone had done to themselves, but he did care about what knowing such things could help him achieve.

Anton lowered his head and took a firm step to swerve past Stanley. 'All press queries need to go through our PR team. I'm not at liberty to discuss anything.'

Stanley remained rooted to the spot. 'Are you sure, Anton? Or should that be Anthony Lester?'

Anton pushed past and quickened his pace towards his car.

Stanley raised his voice so it would carry after him. 'I'd rather not discuss Thomas Mandeville's generous donation to you with the press office, but I will if I have to.'

That stopped Anton in his tracks, but he didn't turn around.

'While the story of a rich man handing out wads of cash after he has died is a good one, if you speak to me off the record, I might just forget about it.'

Anton turned around slowly. He had the look of a bloke who thought he'd been about to fart only to discover something far worse had happened instead.

Stanley pointed across the road. 'There's a café on the corner. Fancy joining me for breakfast?'

Ten minutes later, the two men were sitting opposite each other in a greasy spoon café as the surly waitress plonked their order on the table. She looked like the last time she'd experienced joy had been at the tail end of the twentieth century, and she'd not much cared for it.

Stanley was having a full English, Anton a herbal tea. Herbal tea was not actually on the menu, but he had handed them a sachet containing the requisite tea bag. Stanley guessed Anton wasn't a regular here, and the staff seemed more than happy with that situation. The waitress had looked at the tea bag as if it had left her at the altar and never called.

As they'd waited for their food, Stanley had made painful small talk and deliberately avoided mentioning anything of consequence. They both knew he had Anton over a barrel, and it made sense to make him sweat a little. Stanley was a master of the squeeze.

As the waitress skulked off, Anton stared at Stanley's plate and threw the limited range of expression his face was capable of into a look of absolute disgust. 'How can you eat that filth?'

Stanley slammed down his fork with enough force that the café's only other patron, a bloke in a hi-vis jacket studying the racing form over bacon and eggs, looked across at them. 'Don't you start,' growled Stanley as Anton sat back as far as the faux-leather seating would allow.

'Look.' Anton glanced around surreptitiously. 'I don't know what you think you know, but I've done nothing wrong.'

'Fair enough,' said Stanley. 'If that's the case, I am very sorry to waste your valuable time, sir. We obviously have nothing to discuss. The door is just over there. Good day to you.' He picked up his fork and concentrated on his breakfast, polishing off half a sausage, a fried egg and most of the baked beans before looking up again. 'I see you're still here.'

Anton clenched and unclenched his fist. 'What do you want?'

Stanley forked the other half of the sausage. 'I would like to know what's really going on at the Pinter Institute.'

'I don't know what you're talking about.'

'Sure you do,' said Stanley, holding up the fork to admire the remainder of the sausage. 'Why can't fruit look like that?' He switched his focus to Anton. 'Let's start with what's going on down that tunnel in your wine cellar.'

Despite Anton's limited range of facial expressions, Stanley could see that was a direct hit.

'Look.' He noted how Anton's accent subtly changed. As if the stress of the situation caused his well-hidden Essex twang to resurface. 'You don't want to go messing with this stuff. You do not know who you're dealing with.'

Stanley bit off some sausage and chewed expansively before

picking up his cup of tea. 'If you're trying to threaten me, I really wouldn't bother. You should see some of the nutters—'

'I am not trying to threaten you,' hissed Anton. 'There are things going on that you can't possibly under—' He broke off when he noticed Stanley staring at the necklace he was wearing. 'What?'

Stanley pointed at the smooth stones that had started to glow with a pulsing yellow light. 'How are you doing that?'

'What? I'm not doing anything.' Anton's hand went to the necklace and then pulled away. 'Ouch.'

'What's happening?' asked Stanley, aware that he had now lost control of the conversation.

'They've . . . It's hot.'

'The necklace?'

'Yes,' snapped Anton, loud enough to attract the attention of the racing expert and the waitress. His hands flew to the back of the necklace.

'Take it off,' said Stanley.

'What the hell do you think I'm trying to do?' He fumbled with the clasp, a clear tone of desperation in his voice. 'It won't . . .' He tried to pull the necklace over his head but it had somehow become tighter and, try as he might, he couldn't drag it up further than his chin.

The waitress came over to their table. 'Is everything . . .'

The tempo of the pulsing of the stones increased and Stanley saw the unmistakable terror in the other man's eyes. At that point he realized it wasn't just the stones that were pulsing – so was Anton's entire head.

Stanley went to get up. 'Let me—'

You couldn't call it an explosion, as explosions are loud percussive noises. This sound was just weird and meaty. Anton's face remained frozen in shock but otherwise looked more or less as it had always done. What made that all the more extraordinary was the fact that the top of his head was missing. His head resembled a boiled egg that'd had the top sliced off, only unlike an egg, the contents of his skull had erupted and spread themselves over the widest area possible. Bits of his grey matter were on Stanley, the table, the waitress, the window, the ceiling. Everywhere Stanley could see.

Dumbfounded, Stanley looked down at the table in front of him and noticed that the entire top of Anton's skull, hair and all, was now sitting in the middle of his breakfast.

He stared at it for a very long second, and his mind only snapped back into focus when the waitress started screaming.

CHAPTER 34

Charlotte stood before him in her wedding dress, tears streaming down her face, her make-up running.

I'm in so much trouble. You have to help me, Lumpy. I'm in so much trouble. Why aren't you helping me? It hurts so much. It hurts so much.

Banecroft woke up, his heart racing, bewildered by his surroundings. After a couple of seconds, it started coming back to him. He was in his car, parked up on a side street in Stockport. He must've nodded off, his body exhausted after being denied sleep for days on end and gaining a brief victory over his mind's desperate need to stay awake. The clock on the dashboard told him it was just after midday. It was only then that he noticed the parking ticket stuck to the windscreen on the passenger side. Looking up, he caught sight of the female traffic warden glancing over her shoulder in his direction, before turning the corner and sauntering away.

He refocused his attention on his objective. Across the street was a hairdressing salon by the name of Braithwaite's Bobs. He'd been watching it all morning and noted that for the first time there was no queue. The middle-aged woman with permed blonde hair was chatting away happily to a customer seated in the chair.

She seemed to be the only member of staff and Banecroft was working on the assumption that this was Yvonne Braithwaite.

As Cogs had explained it, Yvonne Braithwaite was something of a Manchester institution; the women of her family being renowned for having 'the gift' for generations. Yvonne, however, had no interest in continuing that tradition. She had wanted to be a hairdresser. The thing was that, as she worked, she continued to receive messages from the great beyond. 'The gift' was not something that could be turned on and off at will.

And so it was that Yvonne would pass on messages to her customers. It was like the normal everyday chat you would get in any hairdresser's, save for the fact that some of the participants were dead. Possibly the greatest testimony to her abilities as a medium were the happy faces of her customers as they left the salon. Then, invariably, they would stop to re-examine their new hairdo in the window of the fishing shop next door and look a lot less pleased. He had already spotted two customers from that morning wave their goodbyes to Yvonne and then head straight into the other hairdresser's up the street for some serious damage control.

Banecroft wiped his brow. He seemed to be sweating constantly now, a fact that had nothing to do with the weather. Some small part of him knew that he wasn't himself. His mind seemed to be racing permanently, turning things over again and again without rest. He hoped that everything he had been told about this woman's abilities was true. Seeing as it had come from Cogs, it had to be, didn't it?

Cogs. For a brief moment, the tiny voice in his mind reminded him of how he had behaved, but he pushed it away. That didn't matter now. Nothing mattered except helping Charlotte. He looked across at the salon again. This was his last hope.

Yvonne Braithwaite waved her goodbyes to Doreen Marshall and turned to look around the salon.

'Right, then. Quick clean-up, time for a brew and then brush my teeth before I head off to the dentist.'

Yvonne had been in the habit of talking to herself throughout her life, although being a Braithwaite meant she was never that alone. She didn't think of it as a blessing or a curse – it was just there. It would be like getting upset at yourself for breathing.

The bell above the door rang and she turned to see a dishevelled man standing in the doorway.

'Sorry, love, I'm just closing because I'm off to the dentist. Also, I don't do men.' She giggled. 'I mean – well, you know what I mean. Barry Moorhouse has a barbershop just around the corner on Church Street. Our Alan goes there – never had any complaints.'

'I don't need a haircut,' replied the man, closing the door behind him.

She took in the unkempt bird's nest on his head. 'Well, you do, but have it your way.' He was making her nervous now. Something about him didn't feel right at all.

'My name is Vincent Banecroft. I'm the editor of *The Stranger Times*.'

'Oh,' said Yvonne. 'Good for you. By the way, your crosswords have been way off recently.'

'I need your help.'

'You don't want me. I'm no good at crosswords. I've just heard our dad complain about them.'

He took a step forward. 'I need you to help me contact somebody.'

Briefly, Yvonne considered pretending not to know what he meant, but it didn't seem worth it. 'I don't know what you've heard, but I don't do that.'

'You do. I know you do.'

She looked into his wet eyes. There was no denying how pitiful he looked.

'Please. Help me.'

'I'm sorry, love, but I can't.'

Something changed in his face, making it somehow harder. His bloodshot eyes burned into her and the pleading tone of his voice was replaced by a snarl of demand. 'Help me or I will put you on the front page of next week's edition.'

'Will you now?'

'Only if you don't give me a choice.'

Yvonne tilted her head. 'I think you'll find it's you who's not giving me any choice. You're a right mean bastard, aren't you?'

'I've run out of all other options,' said Banecroft. 'I will do whatever I have to. Just help me. Please.'

Yvonne moved past him and flipped the sign on the door from *open* to *closed*. 'Don't you dare blackmail somebody and then turn around and say the word "please". It's an abuse of the language.'

'I just—'

She walked towards the back stairs. 'Come on and shut up. Let's get this over with.'

Five minutes later, they were standing on either side of the small, pockmarked table in the kitchenette upstairs. Yvonne lit a candle and placed it in the middle of the table.

'We don't actually need that,' she said stiffly, 'but my nana was a big believer in the look of the thing. Sit down.'

Banecroft did as he was instructed, and Yvonne took the seat opposite.

'Right, then. Who do you want to contact?'

'Charlotte. Charlotte Banecroft. My wife. Only . . .'

'What?'

'She's not actually dead.'

Yvonne threw her hands up. 'I think you have crucially misunderstood what you are asking for, then. If she isn't answering the phone or she's blocked your number, that's not really something I can help you with.' She added under her breath, 'Not that I'd blame her.'

She'd be damned if she would cower before anyone, but something about this man worried her in ways she couldn't express. She was scared of and for him. It was as if he were trapped in a quicksand of despair and had grabbed on to her in a forlorn hope.

Banecroft cleared his throat. 'She speaks to me through another spirit. Simon Brush is his name.'

'That isn't how it works.'

'Just try,' he snapped.

Yvonne sighed. 'Fine.' She laid out her hands, palms up, on either side of the candle. 'Give me your hands.'

Banecroft complied.

Yvonne closed her eyes and steadied her breathing. 'OK, then. I can't guarantee anything, and it might take a—' She winced and drew back her head. 'Ouch! That's not . . .' Her eyes shot open. 'We need to stop this.'

'No. We can't.'

'It's just—' This time the pain caused her to double over and a low groan escaped from her lips.

'I'm sorry,' said Banecroft as he maintained a firm grip on her hands.

Yvonne tried to pull away from him, but he held on.

'I'm sorry,' he repeated.

The voice that came out of Yvonne spoke in a strained whisper. It was as if every word extracted a terrible cost. 'Lumpy. You have to help me.'

Banecroft leaned forward. 'I'm right here.'

'Find me.'

'Tell me how.'

Yvonne was wheezing now, tears rushing down her cheeks. 'Three words . . . Flesh. Loves. Enter.'

'I don't understand,' pleaded Banecroft, a cool wash of panic rising in his chest. 'Please, help me understand.'

'Flesh. Loves. Enter,' repeated the voice.

'But . . .'

Then, with a desperate surge of energy, Yvonne snatched her hands away and the connection was broken.

'No!' screamed Banecroft, scrabbling for Yvonne, his desperation electric. 'Just a little longer.'

She pushed the hair back from her face and glared at him from across the table. Blood was trickling from her left nostril and had reached her upper lip. She raised a shaking hand, unknowingly smearing the blood across her face before she pointed at the door. 'Get. Out.'

Banecroft got to his feet unsteadily, glanced at the door and then back at her. He paused, his head hung in shame. 'I'm—'

'Now!' she screamed.

He turned and ran down the stairs, three words rolling around in his tortured mind.

Flesh.

Loves.

Enter.

CHAPTER 35

Stella's neck was growing sore from looking up so much. She quickly took each of her sweaty hands off the ladder in turn, wiped them on her jeans and renewed her grip.

'We nearly got her,' shouted Manny from the top rung for at least the twentieth time. He was using a broom to guide the floating statue that was Betty towards him.

'Are we sure this is safe?' asked Grace, who was steadying the other side of the ladder.

'We've sent a stoned Rastafarian up a six-foot ladder to try to corral a floating statue,' replied Stella. 'This feels like the start of a weird Hallowe'en special of *Casualty*.'

'He is not stoned,' said Grace. 'He needs to take that stuff for his glaucoma. It is medicinal.'

Stella realized she was being deadly serious. She wasn't touching that one with a ten-foot bargepole, something they could really have done with there and then, but they were making do.

'We nearly got her,' repeated Manny.

Stella looked up again. This time, he really was close. He had a hand on the statue but it had the unusual trait of bobbing around a remarkable amount.

'Watch out below!' Manny dropped the broom and now had two hands on Betty's form.

'Brilliant, Manny,' shouted Stella. 'Now, try to guide her down carefully.'

'No problem. We— Whoa!'

Grace gasped as Manny lost his footing but retained his grip on Betty. The statue dipped a couple of feet but maintained its altitude as Manny dangled from the bottom of it and they started floating serenely across the room.

'Good Lord!' exclaimed Grace. She was standing behind Stella now, but the jangling of her bracelets confirmed she was blessing herself furiously.

'All right,' said Stella. 'Everybody stay calm.'

'We flying,' sang Manny. 'This beautiful.'

'OK, maybe panic a little bit more than that. I'm going to get my mattress for you to drop on to. Just . . .'

Stella watched in amazement as Manny started swinging his legs back and forth. Then, in a display of heretofore undreamed-of gymnastic ability, he swung a leg up and over and hauled himself up until he was sitting astride the still-floating statue.

'Or you could do that.'

'Manny,' shouted Grace. 'You shouldn't be riding around on top of that woman. It is not decent.'

Stella turned to look at her.

'What? It is the truth.'

Stella redirected her attention to Manny. His hands were now on the ceiling and he was grinning down at them like a child enjoying a see-saw.

'Well, his hands are on the ceiling, at least.' She raised her voice. 'You just hang in there, Manny. I'm pretty sure there's a rope down in the basement.'

'No problem. We chillin'.'

Stella hurriedly retrieved the rope, which she then threw up to Manny. After a near fall and some false starts, he managed to tie it around the statue. From there, despite the petrified Betty's unwillingness to play ball with gravity in any way, shape or form, they managed to pull them both back to terra firma and secured Betty to the six-inch-diameter metal pipe that ran along the bottom of the far wall. The thing looked so strong they all agreed it would likely still be there, even if the building fell down around their ears.

At that point, Grace gave a very confused Manny an excruciating talk about why you should not be hopping on top of women you'd just met, which was all too much for Stella, who excused herself.

Her lack of sleep was really starting to hit home. Ox and Reggie were off chasing their conspiracies, Grace could keep an eye on Betty, and Banecroft – well, she would just have to wait for him to come back and she would talk to him then. In the meantime, she needed a nap.

She returned to her room that wasn't really a room, given that it was the base of the church's steeple, and lay down on her unmade bed. She was too knackered even to get changed. As her eyes closed and she began to drift towards sweet oblivion, she sensed something in the room. In the absence of any better weapons, she snatched up her hairbrush, sat up and brandished it above her head, ready to unleash some serious haircare.

The ghostly form before her took a couple of steps back and waved nervously.

Stella dropped the hairbrush.

'Hello, Simon.'

CHAPTER 36

Reggie stood in the centre of the footbridge and turned to Ox.

'OK,' he said. 'Before we do anything, let's just agree. I will do all the talking.'

'I'm not agreeing to that.'

'And why not?'

Ox drew himself up to his full height. 'I'm just as important as you are. If anything, I'm more important in this area, seeing as I am the paper's resident conspiracy expert.'

'That's as maybe,' said Reggie, 'but you have never met Cogs before, and meeting new people is not – how can I put this? – the greatest of your many strengths.'

'What is that supposed to mean?'

'It means that on the ten-minute walk here, you got into a fight with a complete stranger.'

Ox threw his arms in the air as if appealing an egregious off-side decision. 'He was riding his bike on the pavement. A grown man and he was cycling on the pavement instead of in the desig-nated cycling lane.'

'I didn't say you were wrong. I was merely pointing out that your diplomacy skills are a tad lacking.'

'Totally unfair assertion. My message had to be direct and to the point because I had to shout after him after he cycled by.'

'It certainly got his attention, and I speak as the person who got hit by the orange he was attempting to throw at you.'

'And we're saying that's my fault now, are we?'

'Well, you did duck.'

Ox shoved his hands into his pockets huffily. 'Excuse me for having catlike reflexes.'

'Nevertheless, this one time, will you let me do the talking?'

Ox said nothing.

'I will take that as a yes.' Reggie reached down to pull up the rope to which a bell was attached. 'Cogs and I have only met the once, but I feel we have already bonded.'

Reggie rang the bell.

On the deck of the *Nail in the Wall* houseboat, Cogs sprang to his feet and peered around the sheet he had hung up to offer a bit of privacy. He took one look at Reggie and shouted, 'Absolutely not. No. Bugger off. You're barred,' before disappearing out of view again.

'You were saying?' said Ox, grinning broadly.

'Er, Mr Cogs, sir,' shouted Reggie, 'I think you might have me confused with somebody else.'

Cogs's head reappeared from behind the sheet. 'Are you the bloke from *The Stranger Times*?'

'Yes.'

'Then I am not confused. You're barred. Anyone who works for that paper is barred.'

'But you've not even met me yet,' shouted Ox.

Cogs offered him a jaunty salute. 'Charmed to make your acquaintance. You're barred.'

Zeke the bulldog made an appearance from behind the sheet too. He stood with his front paws on the side of the boat and gave them a quizzical look.

'Can I ask why we are barred?' tried Reggie. 'This isn't about the crossword, by any chance, is it?'

'No,' came the response. 'Although you really need to sort that out.'

'Too right,' chimed Zeke. 'Some of us really look forward to that thing.'

Ox pointed excitedly. 'The dog talked!'

Reggie spoke out of the side of his mouth. 'Shush. I told you the dog talked.'

'Yeah, but there's hearing about it, and there's actually hearing it in the flesh. See if you can make it say something else.'

'"Make it say something else,"' growled Zeke. 'The absolute cheek of it.'

Ox clapped his hands. 'It did it. It did it!'

'You are not helping,' snapped Reggie. He raised his voice again. 'Apologies for the crossword, but if it's not that, why are we barred?'

'You're barred,' said Cogs, 'because your bastard of an editor was here yesterday making demands and issuing threats. I do not give in to blackmail.'

'You did, though,' conceded Zeke.

'Whose side are you on?'

'Yours,' confirmed the dog. 'I was just pointing out that—'

'Shut up.'

'Speak. Shut up,' said Zeke. 'You people need to make up your mind.'

Reggie and Ox shared a concerned look. 'I'm very sorry about that. That doesn't sound like Mr Banecroft at all.'

Ox pulled a face and muttered darkly. 'Threatening people isn't exactly breaking new ground for him.'

'No,' admitted Reggie. 'But . . . he hasn't quite been himself recently.'

Cogs considered this. 'You're not wrong. I'd only met him the one time before yesterday, but he really didn't seem like the same guy.'

'Agreed,' said Zeke. 'Rotten meat.'

'Excuse me?' asked Reggie.

'Don't mind him,' said Cogs. 'But do bugger off, if you wouldn't mind. I'm not sure if I mentioned it but – you're barred.'

'Please. We wouldn't be here if it wasn't important.'

'Yeah. Everybody says that.'

'It is a matter of life and death.'

'And that,' said Zeke.

'A man has disappeared after trying to confirm some wild conspiracy theories he read in our paper.'

'Not interested,' said Cogs, and he disappeared back behind the sheet.

'He's been kidnapped by the . . .' Reggie paused. 'F-o-u-n-d-e-r-s.'

Cogs's head popped into view once more. 'What the hell do you think you're doing? We don't say the F-word, and we certainly don't spell it out.' He and Zeke looked at each other and shook their heads in disbelief. 'They're a cabal of immortals that wield incredible power, including the ability to spell. Did you confuse them with a three-year-old child?'

Reggie blushed. 'Sorry.' He drew a folder out of his bag. 'Please, if you could just look at these Dex Hex columns and tell us if there is anything in them that might have annoyed the you-know-whos.'

Zeke bounced on his paws excitedly. 'Oh, I used to love that column.'

'Thank you,' said Ox, sounding very pleased with himself.

'Yeah. It was like you'd given the village idiot too much caffeine and access to a web browser.'

'Oh,' said Ox, sounding rather less pleased.

'They're all right here,' Reggie said, holding the folder aloft. He dived his free hand into his bag again and pulled out a bottle. 'And I also have a bottle of spiced rum. The good stuff.'

'I don't care,' said Cogs. 'It's a no. And that is my final answer.'

Zeke hopped down and scuttled behind the sheet. Reggie could make out a brief whispered argument between the pair and, thirty seconds later, Cogs reappeared.

'OK, it turns out my final answer was not my final answer and we are prepared to advise you on this matter. Stick everything in the bucket.'

Two minutes later, once the sheet had been pulled back and Cogs had settled into a deckchair, a large rum in his hand, he began to take the photocopied sheets of paper, one at a time, out of the folder that sat on his lap. He read each in turn and then placed them in front of Zeke for him to do the same.

'No, no. I've no idea if the moon is a hollowed-out US military base, but it's been there for a long time, so I'm guessing that's a no too. I've never met King Charles, so I can't be sure if he's one of those. Or one of those. The Isle of Man?' He showed that one to Zeke and they both laughed. 'Atlantis? As if.'

Cogs pulled out the next piece of paper and the smile dropped from his face. He read it in full. Then read it again and bent down to show it to Zeke. They had a whispered discussion and Cogs got to his feet. 'We think we may have a winner.'

'Really?' said Reggie, trying not to sound too excited.

Cogs nodded and twirled the sheet he was holding around to show them. Even from a distance, Reggie and Ox could see which one it was and shared a disbelieving look. It was really saying something, but of all the absurd fantasies in the folder, this was the one Cogs was holding up. The one that had attracted the attention of the Founders and resulted in the disappearance of Tony Dawson.

Reggie could not find the words. Luckily, Ox could.

'You are shitting me?'

Comicon Ghosts

Comicon Manchester, a convention famous for attracting the most hardcore sci-fi and fantasy fans, has been left rocked by a series of ghostly sightings. It is believed the apparitions can be traced back to a tragic event that occurred a few years ago after the Best Costume awards party. Legend has it that an over-enthusiastic conga line took a wrong turn and somehow ended up in traffic outside the venue, with several contestants experiencing a disastrous coming-together with the number 27 bus.

Delegate Michael Dolan, who has attended every Manchester Comicon, claims, 'Initially, having the ghosts of Darth Vader, Obi-Wan and Yoda make an appearance – just like at the end of *Jedi* – was cool, but they won't stop asking what happened in the finale of *Game of Thrones*, and nobody wants to bum them out by telling them. Between that and the ghost of the Dalek who goes up to every food vendor to check if their menu is gluten-free, they're really more of a hassle than a feature.'

CHAPTER 37

As soon as Stanley's van pulled up outside the holiday home, Mrs Harnforth rushed out to meet him.

'Where the hell have you been?'

Without responding, he turned off the engine and opened the door.

She was standing there, hands on hips, her eyes boring into him. 'You're part of a team now, Stanley. You need to communicate with us. Answer your damn—'

She broke off as he stepped out of the vehicle and she got a good look at him. Her eyes widened and she stepped forward, her brow furrowed with concern.

'Oh my . . . What happened? Are you hurt?'

'No.' Stanley, his expression blank, pointed at the blood and other matter that covered a large part of the front of his shirt. '*This* is Anton Lasherf. He exploded.' There was no other way to put it. 'I had some wet wipes in the car, so I got most of it off my face, but I didn't have a spare shirt.'

Mrs Harnforth continued to take in Stanley, her face etched with worry. 'Are you quite all right?'

'Well, I was talking to the geezer then the top of his head blew off, and his brains and whatnot covered me and a large part of the café we were in.' Stanley turned his head to the side and spat on the ground. 'Sorry. Can't seem to stop doing that. My mouth was open when it happened and a bit of him went in.'

He felt a comforting hand on his shoulder. 'How did this happen?'

Stanley shut the van door and leaned back against it. 'We were talking. I was asking questions about the Pinter Institute. He was resisting, but nothing unexpected. Then this odd-looking necklace he was wearing – it had a few smooth lozenge-sized stones – started pulsating, and then *poof*!'

'I see. Where have you been since then?'

A wave of sudden anger burned away the fog. 'I was covered in a bloke. Literally covered. Sorry if I wasn't answering your phone calls as promptly as you'd have liked.'

'I didn't mean that,' Mrs Harnforth said, her voice softening. 'We were just worried about you. Especially given that, in the last hour, the Pinter Institute has gone into panic mode. All classes and whatever have been cancelled, and the guests have been sent back to their rooms. The staff have been running around as if the place is on fire. I can only assume that might be related to your unfortunate incident.'

'What is Hannah saying?'

'Nothing. Cathy is trying to reach her, but she's not responding. We know she's in her room, but not much else. We are picking up some odd noises through that earpiece, though. We think she may have had to swallow the thing to avoid it being found during the search last night.'

'Oh,' said Stanley. 'Ordinarily, I might find that a bit icky, but not after the morning I've had. What are we going to do?'

'Well,' said Mrs Harnforth, 'first things first. You are going to go and clean yourself up – preferably before Cathy sees you. We don't want her to freak out. Then we will have to have a meeting and decide on our next move.'

Fifteen minutes later, changed and showered, Stanley walked into the front room that Cathy was now using as her base of operations. Her table, with its semi-circle of monitors, was set up in the middle of the room. The large flat-screen TV above the fireplace seemed to be divided into six, each segment showing a different feed from security cameras in the Pinter Institute. Mrs Harnforth was seated on the sofa, her arms folded tightly as if restraining her hands from flying away. Her lips were twitching with words unsaid, and she was clearly stopping herself from asking questions or giving orders.

Cathy glanced up at Stanley. 'Oh, someone looks nice. Big date, is it?'

'Not exactly.'

'So, what happened in your meeting with Anton La-whatever? Mrs H is being coy about it.'

'He exploded.'

'Yes,' said Mrs Harnforth, giving him a pointed look. 'He got very annoyed, threw an entire milkshake over poor Stanley and left.'

'Oh dear,' said Cathy with a grin. 'Still, he's had worse.'

'You'd be surprised,' he said. 'That stuff gets everywhere.' If time had not been a factor, he would still have been standing in the shower. He'd discovered bits of Anton in his hair. He'd also spent several minutes throwing up. He desperately needed to occupy his mind with thoughts of something else. 'So, any updates?'

'Yeah. That Dr French woman just busted a shredder trying to feed too much into it in one go. Their IT expert is having a hell of a morning too. The servers he's trying to wipe are refusing to play ball, and he's getting some very upsetting phone calls from his divorce lawyer.' Cathy gave another broad grin. 'All things considered, it looks like the circus is getting ready to leave town.'

'It does indeed,' agreed Mrs Harnforth.

'Have you got what you need?' asked Stanley.

Mrs H shook her head. 'Whatever they are doing, I honestly still don't know what it is.'

'So far,' said Cathy, 'while these people all appeared to be a bit mental, it looks as if their techniques work. At least judging by how happy that Moira woman was this morning, they do, not to mention those patients from a few months ago you chased down.'

'Crap,' said Stanley. 'I just remembered. Razor, one of the guys I have looking into a bunch of the patients, tried to ring me when I was driving back. I need to check my voicemail.'

He stepped outside through the French doors and stood by the rockery while he first listened to his voicemail and then rang Razor to find out more details. Pinning the phone against his shoulder with his ear, he pulled out his notepad and started scribbling down details from Razor's report. He continued to spit on the ground intermittently in an attempt to get rid of the taste in his mouth that his brain was telling him was still there.

When he eventually joined Mrs Harnforth and Cathy in their operations room, he stood quite still and rubbed his hand across his forehead. He hoped he didn't look as pale as he felt.

'Well?' asked Mrs Harnforth.

Stanley sat down in an armchair. 'Razor is still checking on some other patients. A lot of them are hard to find out about. That's the trouble with rich people. They can be in any of a number of different countries at any given time, and it takes time to track them down and find a source willing to give you any information. Cash buys discretion. He's mostly trying to locate the ones who are still somewhere around London.'

'But he found out about some more, didn't he?'

Stanley nodded, pulled his notepad out of his pocket again and took a deep breath. 'Here we go. Edgar Pearce?' He looked at Cathy, who checked her records.

'About sixteen months ago,' she said. 'Was diagnosed with agoraphobia and social anxiety.'

'Full recovery of sorts,' said Stanley. 'Became quite the social butterfly. At a party in Cannes, he started dancing on the edge of a balcony ten storeys up, and then fell off.'

'Oh my,' said Cathy.

'Yeah. Razor is double-checking, but while there's nothing official, he spoke to a guy who said Pearce could be heard laughing all the way down. Tox screens showed he hadn't taken anything either. Moving on. Rebecca Nicholl — it says she was suffering from anorexia.'

Cathy nodded.

'She's currently in hospital. Just had a massive heart attack.

Apparently, in the two years since she was at the Pinter Institute, she put on over ten stone.'

'Good God,' said Mrs Harnforth.

Stanley kept reading. 'Brandon Johnson, gambling addict, is now a complete shut-in. Kevin Peters had issues with obesity. He has now been committed as he refuses to feed himself.' He looked up at the two women. 'Is anybody noticing a trend here?'

'Yes,' said Mrs Harnforth grimly. 'It appears the cure is worse than the disease.'

'Short-term solutions,' agreed Stanley. 'Long-term problems.'

'I don't understand,' said Cathy. 'Why isn't there uproar about this?'

Stanley closed his notebook. 'Because of the joys of confidentiality. The only reason we have information about who has been a patient at the Pinter Institute is because of you.'

'But,' she continued, 'I still don't understand how what they're doing can cause this to happen?'

'It's whatever they're doing that you can't see,' said Mrs Harnforth. 'The stuff that isn't in the brochure. In other words, whatever the hell is going on down that tunnel.'

'Any ideas?' asked Stanley.

'No, not really. We need more details, and time is running out.'

The three of them looked at each other for a long moment, then Cathy turned around to one of her screens.

'I'll keep trying Hannah.'

CHAPTER 38

DI Tom Sturgess opened the front door to his house and looked down at the letter sitting on the mat. Without bending down, he could tell it was from the water company and its red lettering was making clear their displeasure.

'Oh crap,' he said to it. 'I was going to pay you. I tried to pay you, in fact, but you never pick up the bloody phone. Don't go sending me angry letters.'

'You tell 'em,' said a voice that caused Sturgess, despite his years on the force and well-deserved reputation as a surly bastard, to yelp and involuntarily toss his bag of shopping into the air. He peered into the front room where the woman he knew as Dr Carter was sitting in his armchair, which she had turned to face the door.

She rolled out that highly irritating giggle of hers.

'For Christ's sake,' he said. 'What the hell was the point of that? There's no need for these sub-Bond villain histrionics.'

'Can't blame a girl for wanting to make an entrance.'

'I can if it involves breaking and entering.' He looked down at his shopping bag, the contents of which were spilling across the hall floor. 'There were a half-dozen eggs in there.' He pointed at her irritably. 'You owe me some eggs.'

'I'm just delighted to hear you're buying some proper food, Thomas.' She bobbed her head in the direction of the kitchen. 'A fridge full of condiments and something that was, I think, at one point, cheese. Full-on bachelor tragic.'

'Exactly how long have you been waiting here?'

'Long enough,' replied Dr Carter. 'I've hired you a cleaning service. They start next Monday at nine a.m.'

'I don't need a cleaner.'

She looked pointedly at every corner of the room then back at him and raised her eyebrows. 'Really?'

'I've been busy.'

'Don't I know it.'

'Well,' said Sturgess, stepping over his shopping to stand in the doorway to the front room, 'as it happens, I've been trying to get hold of you.'

'Don't I know it,' replied Dr Carter, holding up her phone. 'Sixty-seven texts, Tom. Stalker much? You've gotta give a girl a bit of room.'

'Not when her storm troopers or whatever you call them have kidnapped an innocent man. Does the name Tony Dawson ring a bell?'

Dr Carter shook her head. 'No.'

'Also known as Dex Hex? A one-time columnist for *The Stranger Times*.'

'Oh, him? You should have said. Not that I can really blame you for it, but this little nonsense couldn't be happening at a worse time. One loon stumbling into things that don't concern him is nothing in the grand scheme of things.'

'I disagree.'

Dr Carter met this with an eye roll. 'Yes, yes. Every life is sacred. We're all precious little individual snowflakes. Blah, blah, blah.'

'Sorry if I'm boring you,' said Sturgess flatly.

She nodded, as if accepting his apology at face value. 'There was no need to involve the paper. Those people have bigger fish to fry, and you are distracting them right when they really need to be alert. Some things actually are important.'

'What's that supposed to mean?'

She adjusted the jacket of her suit that probably cost more than his car. 'That's all a bit above your pay grade. Are you even sure this Tony Dawson fellow has actually disappeared?'

'It's funny you should say that,' said Sturgess. 'Two days ago, I went to see his sister, who was distraught because her agoraphobic, near recluse of a brother had disappeared off the face of the earth, except for a text saying he's gone to Majorca which, she said, was entirely unbelievable. I dropped round to give her an update today, and she seemed completely, almost unbelievably fine about everything. She now reckons her brother really has gone to Majorca, although when questioned about it in detail, she seems to have some rather alarming gaps in her memory.'

'Well, there you go, then. Everybody is happy.'

'Not me. And I'm guessing not Tony Dawson, seeing as I have footage of him being snatched by a squad of your goons.'

'I know,' said Dr Carter. 'And believe me, we are using that as quite the training moment. Still, his sister's fine about everything now, so all's well that ends well.'

'No, it most certainly is not. Something in those lunatic

columns he was obsessed with proving true led to your . . . let's call it "organization" snatching him. What was it?'

'Word to the wise, Tom – just let it go.'

'No, I won't.'

She let out an elaborate sigh. 'I know you won't. It's that tenacity that makes you useful. It's also the thing that makes you a massive pain in my arse. If I were you, I'd be careful to stay on the right side of that particular ledger.'

'Where is Tony Dawson?'

Dr Carter pointed a manicured nail at the sofa. 'Would you like to sit down?'

'No.'

'Fine, have it your way. You won't remember this but, just so I can enjoy saying it – learn to let something go every once in a while, would you? The fact that you can't, and that you're getting close enough to the truth, is why I'm here. Today is just a course correction, but one day, you'll get yourself stuck in the middle of something that I won't be able to save you from.'

'You're saving me?'

'Yes, from yourself.'

She uttered a word in a language that theoretically had been dead for several thousand years, the result of which was Tom Sturgess's eyes closed, his body went limp and he crumpled to the ground.

'I did try and warn you, Tom. There is just no talking to some people.' She raised her voice slightly. 'All right. Out you pop.'

A brief but unpleasant squishy noise filled the room, followed by the appearance of an eyeball on a stalk out of the top of Tom

Sturgess's head. Sturgess's eyes opened, although they weren't really his eyes any more. His body stood back up.

'And as for you,' said Dr Carter, 'you are supposed to be keeping him out of trouble.'

The eyeball on a stalk drew back as if offended by this assertion. A string of words then came out of Tom Sturgess's mouth that Tom Sturgess would not have been able to understand, given that they were also in the language that theoretically had been dead for thousands of years.

'Excuses, excuses,' replied Dr Carter, standing up. 'Just remember, if he becomes too much of an inconvenience, it's curtains for you too. Stay in control of him for the next couple of days and stay here. Don't answer the phone.' She took a step towards the front door and stepped delicately over the groceries on the floor. 'And for God's sake, clean that up.'

With that, she opened the front door and left.

Once she was safely out of earshot, the creature that was now in control of Tom Sturgess said more words in a language that has been dead for thousands of years, but in a tone of voice even small children the world over would recognize as sarcastic mimicry. With that, Tom Sturgess's body made its way to the sofa, slouched into it and picked up the TV remote. It flicked through all the channels until it found a repeat of the 1990s show in which people in swimwear saved other people from drowning by running in slow motion towards them. The eyeball on a stalk bobbed around excitedly.

Later on, it decided, it would order in a curry and check out what was on pay-per-view.

CHAPTER 39

God bless colonic irrigation.

Four words Hannah couldn't believe she was thinking. This was certainly a week of firsts. She assumed the colonic irrigation was responsible for the earpiece passing through her system so quickly. By her estimate, seeing as it was now 5.15 p.m., the device had completed its epic journey in just under seventeen hours. To be fair, its rapid progress might have been the result of yesterday's procedure, given that her internal transportation infrastructure was free of any traffic black spots, or it could just be that the food at the Pinter Institute had that effect on her.

Either way, she now held the earpiece in her hand. She had spent the last ten minutes cleaning it rigorously but she still found herself retching at the prospect of putting it back in her ear. She didn't even know if it would still work. It wasn't as if she'd had the time before she swallowed it to check with Cathy if what she was about to do would invalidate the warranty. Still, at least the Tupperware containers beside the toilet had come in handy.

She shuddered and shoved the gadget in her ear. After a couple of seconds, she heard a beep.

'Hello?'

'Hannah?'

A wave of relief passed through her at the sound of the voice on the other end. 'Cathy. Thank God.'

'Amen,' agreed Cathy. 'We thought we'd lost you. Did you have to . . .' An awkward pause followed. 'Do you know what, never mind. It's just great to have you back. Are you OK?'

'Yeah, I think so. They told us all to go back to our rooms hours ago, and the doors have been locked ever since. I've no idea what's going on.'

After a brief rustling noise at the other end of the line, Mrs Harnforth's Received Pronunciation replaced Cathy's Mancunian drawl. 'Hannah, wonderful to have you back. There have been some developments.'

Hannah listened in silence as Mrs Harnforth briefed her. Without going into much detail, she explained that the approach to Anton – who, it turned out, had been behind the inexplicable financial transfer from the late Thomas Mandeville – had been unsuccessful and that the Pinter Institute now knew that someone was looking into them.

'Hence the increased security?' asked Hannah.

'Yes, I'm afraid so.' Mrs Harnforth paused for a moment. 'We've also discovered some disturbing news about previous patients.'

Hannah listened in horror to the laundry list of lives going off the rails.

'Oh my God – poor Moira! And Karl, obviously.' She winced. They might be getting divorced but her ex should probably still have come into her thoughts ahead of the woman she'd known for only a few days.

'Yes,' agreed Mrs Harnforth. 'We need to stop this, but first we need to find out what "this" is. I'll be honest with you – obviously, the risk is greater now. Would you be willing to have another go at finding out what they are hiding down in that basement?'

'I'll do it, but you just told me they have guards on the door of the wine cellar, not to mention all the other staff. How am I going to get round all of that?'

Off mic, she heard Cathy saying, 'Just give me a few ticks.'

There was silence on the line for about thirty seconds before Mrs Harnforth exclaimed, 'Oh my.'

'What's happening?' asked Hannah.

'I don't know, but whatever technological magic Cathy has worked, the guards and most of the other staff have left their posts. They're heading back down to the ground floor.'

Cathy came back on the line, an unmistakable air of laughter in her voice. 'Yeah. I imagine they're all pretty upset. They've just received a text message from their employer telling them they're being made redundant without pay. That sort of thing will wind anyone up.'

A second later, Hannah heard a soft clicking noise in her room and the light on the door lock changed from red to green.

'Fancy stretching your legs?'

CHAPTER 40

Reggie stopped dead in his tracks so unexpectedly that Ox almost ran into the back of him.

'Something wrong?' enquired Ox.

'What did you say?' asked Reggie in a still, ice-cold voice that someone with a better sense of these things than Ox might have read as a warning sign.

'I asked if something was wrong.'

'Before that.'

'I just said it's unbelievable. And it is. It's unbelievable.'

Reggie's fists clenched and as he turned around Ox belatedly picked up on the tension.

'I know you think it is unbelievable. The reason I know this is that we have been doing this for seven hours now, and every five minutes, like clockwork, you have been saying it is unbelievable. You have said the word "unbelievable" more times than the band EMF, whose one and only hit was the song "Unbelievable".'

Demonstrating a lemming-like instinct, Ox opened his mouth to crack a joke.

'Don't,' said Reggie, jabbing a warning finger in his friend's face. 'Don't crack a joke about EMF. What I need you to do is to never

ever, ever, ever say the word again. I can't even bring myself to say it now – the word beginning with the letter U. That word. If you say it one more time, although I consider you a dear friend, I will rip off your left arm and beat you to death with it. Understood?'

Ox, because even lemmings are afraid of fire, nodded his head slowly.

'Thank you.'

When Ox spoke next, his voice was slow and calm. 'To return to something I said earlier, do you want to swing back to that camping shop and see if we can get some wellies?' he asked, pointing down at Reggie's shoes.

Reggie straightened his waistcoat and took a deep breath. 'No. Thank you. My brogues are already ruined. As are the trousers of this rather expensive suit.'

They really were too. The pair had spent the day traipsing around sewers, storm drains, anything they could find in the centre of Manchester that might lead to something below the city. Ox's trainers were similarly destroyed but he'd bought them off One-eyed Terry and they held no value, sentimental or otherwise.

'Still . . .' said Ox. 'Wellies?'

Reggie raised his hand. 'Absolutely not. I would rather give off the appearance of a gentleman who has fallen on hard times than of a buffoon who walks around the city centre combining a fine tweed with a pair of wellington boots.'

He then turned on his heel and set off again, dodging a couple of mums pushing prams on his way. They were walking along Watson Street, just to the east of the Great Northern entertainment complex with its cinema, restaurants and casino.

Ox fell into step beside him. 'It is' – he checked himself and quite possibly saved his own life – 'surprising, though. I mean, of all the crazy nonsense in those columns.' He unfolded the sheet of paper he was carrying. It was the one Cogs had picked out of the folder of printouts – *Is there a dragon living under Manchester?*

'Actually,' said Reggie, 'it has just dawned on me that he never actually said that bit' – he pointed at the word 'dragon' – 'was true.'

'Didn't he?'

'No. Incredibly, for a man who can only speak the truth, he didn't say whether there was one of them, or indeed, if they exist.'

'How did he manage that?'

'I don't know, but I've a sneaking suspicion it doesn't speak well of us as journalists. All he said was someone could get themselves in an awful lot of trouble poking around under the centre of Manchester.'

'Do you think we should go back and ask him a few more questions?'

Reggie stopped outside the entrance to the multi-storey car park. 'Let's try here first.'

Ox followed him inside. 'All right, but if it turns out a dragon has been sitting in a long-stay car park and nobody has noticed, I will find that' – he smiled at Reggie, whose head had shot around – 'inconceivable.'

Ten minutes later, Ox was doing something he had already done several times that day – namely, standing around trying to look casual while keeping a lookout. This was because the second-biggest revelation of his day had been that Reggie, whom he had known for many years, could not only pick locks but also carried upon his person a neat little kit to assist him in his endeavours.

Ox, despite lacking self-awareness in certain areas, knew instinctively not to ask about this new discovery, as it fell within the great unspoken expanse of dark space that was Reggie's past. So instead, he'd watched in quiet awe as a man resembling Rupert the Bear's librarian older brother had broken into and entered a fair few areas that, admittedly, nobody was especially bothered about anyone breaking and entering into.

They'd seen a lot of sewers, pumping equipment that they didn't understand, electrical equipment that they also did not understand but accepted might very well kill you if you touched it, and a room full of naked shop mannequins that had properly freaked Ox out. Reggie had also come up with the plan that if anyone were to confront them, they should explain that they were urban explorers, whom he'd read an article about in the *Guardian*.

At that moment they were in the sub-basement of the multi-storey car park and Reggie was picking the lock on a serious-looking metal gate. Behind it was a blue door bearing an unhelpfully vague sticker that simply read 'Danger'.

With a happy clink, the gate opened.

'You're getting faster at that,' observed Ox.

'Yes, well, I may have been a little out of practice.'

Reggie opened the gate and, with one last glance around to make sure they weren't being watched, he and Ox passed through it. As Ox pushed against the blue door, it unexpectedly gave way to reveal a narrow stone stairway poorly illuminated by grubby strip lighting. Somewhere in the darkness water was dripping. Without exchanging a word, the pair stepped inside, closed the door and turned on the torches they had bought earlier in the day.

Ox walloped his a few times until its flickering beam righted itself. 'This thing is supposedly brand new and it doesn't work. Livid.'

'In hindsight, maybe you should not have bought one from the bargain bin?' Reggie stepped forward with his considerably more powerful and reliable torch. 'I suppose I'd better go first, then.'

They descended the stone stairs carefully, as the rounded edges of the treads suggested they'd been there a long time, pre-dating such things as handrails. The walls on either side were cold to the touch and the light from the men's torches picked out runnels of water trickling down them.

They reached the bottom after what felt like hours, and emerged into what looked like a surprisingly large tunnel, forty or fifty feet in diameter. Reggie turned his torch first one way and then the other, illuminating nothing but empty tunnel in both directions.

'Interesting,' said Ox in a near whisper as they had swiftly learned how sound really travelled in such a space.

'What is?'

'This concrete looks almost brand new. It's also dry, which means, fingers crossed, there's less chance of a wave of sewage catching us by surprise again.' It really had been a very long day.

'Which direction would you like to travel in first?'

Ox shrugged. 'Dealer's choice.'

Reggie chose right and Ox followed. Their footsteps echoing around the cavernous tunnel did little to compensate for the unnerving lack of sound.

'Can I ask a question,' Ox began, 'without you getting mad?'

'Of course.'

'We've been so busy trying to find something down here. What's the plan if we actually do?'

'That's a good question. I suppose we tell DI Sturgess.'

'Yeah, but we've been trying to ring him for most of the day and he hasn't been picking up.'

'Well, presumably at some point he will start picking up again. Failing that, we can talk to Banecroft.'

It didn't escape their notice that in ordinary circumstances he would have been their first port of call.

'That'll mean coming clean about the Dex Hex columns.'

Reggie shrugged. 'I wouldn't worry about it. First, it was before his time, and second, you'll be delivering a big juicy exclusive at the same time. Besides, he's been a bit distracted lately.'

'What did you make of what Cogs said about him?'

'I don't know, but it's bad. When we get back, we should probably talk to the others. See if we should have, I don't know, some kind of intervention.'

Ox sniffed. 'I think I'd rather face the dragon.'

Reggie held up his hand for quiet and they both slowed to a stop.

'What?' whispered Ox.

'I thought I heard something.' They waited in silence for a few more seconds before Reggie started walking again. 'Sorry, must be my brain playing tricks on me.'

'Do you smell something?'

'To be honest, I'm deliberately trying not to. I can live with the darkness, but the smells . . .'

They both stopped dead as their torches simultaneously went out.

'What the—' started Ox.

He only got so far before blinding lights came at them from all directions, sending them spinning round in bewilderment.

'Hands in the air!' shouted a voice. 'Do not move.'

Before Reggie's eyes could fully adjust to the brightness, hands were on his shoulders and a swift kick to the back of his legs sent him crumbling to his knees.

As his sight returned, the first thing he made out was the business end of a machine gun aimed straight in front of his face. Someone pinned his arms behind his back and cuffed him before turning him over. Ox was on the ground beside him in a similar position. Surrounding them were half a dozen or so of the black-clad storm troopers they had seen on the video recording of Tony Dawson's abduction. Each was holding a gun and pointing it directly at them.

Reggie cleared his throat and attempted a smile. 'Hello, we're urban explorers. You may have seen an article about it in the *Guardian*?'

High-speed Encounters of the Third Kind

West Yorkshire Police have been left dumbfounded after clocking an unidentified vehicle travelling along the M62 at incredible speed. Traffic officer Raj Singh reports, 'I didn't see it so much as felt it. There was an incredible *whoosh* of air and I was, like, bloody hell, what just happened?'

Such was the object's speed that camera footage from 2.30 a.m. on 12 July couldn't accurately record it. However, Jonathan Marshall, a financial consultant, was stopped later that morning further up the motorway, having been caught travelling at 120 mph in his new BMW. When asked by officers at the scene why he was travelling at that speed, he claimed he'd slowed down to take a call. At the time of writing, authorities are still unsure whether the incident is proof of intelligent life on other planets or a distinct lack of it on this one.

CHAPTER 41

Hannah studied the thick steel door she had first stood in front of the night before. It had been considerably easier to reach on this occasion, thanks to all of the staff having been informed they were being made redundant via text message. The cloak of zealotry they'd all worn had long since been cast aside. Those members of staff she came across showed no signs of caring what the guests were doing, as long as they didn't dare ask them to do anything.

At one point during her journey to the west wing, she had run into a woman she recognized as one of the waitresses. She was coming out of one of the offices carrying an expensive-looking printer and a bag that looked heavy. Hannah guessed she was taking care of her own severance package. There was a moment when the girl considered pointing out to Hannah that she shouldn't be there, but then she remembered she didn't work there any more and therefore didn't care. Hannah had held open the door for her.

Mrs Harnforth's voice was now in her ear, all business. 'OK, Hannah. We know we will lose contact with you once you enter the tunnel, but Cathy is pretty certain that unless you go really deep down, we should still be able to track your location. Having said that, if you see something you don't like, run, and if we don't hear from you within thirty minutes, we will abandon the softly, softly approach and send the cavalry in to get you. OK?'

'Affirmative.' Hannah was endeavouring to sound a lot more confident than she was feeling. This had seemed like a much better idea when she'd been sitting in her room. Still, she was here now. 'Right. Open the door.'

The room on the other side was dark, which was good news. Hannah walked down the stairs and, as expected, the motion-detecting lights clicked on. The wine cellar looked more or less as it had done and she cursed the traitorous broken bottle still lying on the ground as she walked by.

'I'm entering the tunnel.'

All she received in response was a burst of static. She was on her own.

The tunnel descended at what Hannah estimated to be a fifteen-degree angle. She made her way along it at a normal pace, reasoning that, thanks to the motion-detecting lights, there was no point trying to be stealthy. Anyone coming the other way would see her a mile off.

The space reminded her of a hospital corridor, which was an unsettling thought, and an image from a film she couldn't remember the name of popped into her head. It was of rooms filled with people strapped to gurneys as masked doctors wheeled them out one at a time, no doubt to do something horrible to them elsewhere. Hannah hated horror movies, and she presumed she hadn't made it to the end of that one. She tried not to think about it.

The blankness of the walls was disorientating, and made it

hard for Hannah to keep track of how far she had walked. All she knew was that a new set of lights had clicked on ten or twelve times now, and when she looked back up the tunnel all but the last couple had turned themselves off again. This lighting system was no doubt good for the environment, but not exactly great for her nerves. She also tried not to think about how much solid rock must now be above her head.

As yet another set of lights clicked on, she stopped. Before her, the tunnel ended in a wall of sheer rock, and the only way forward was offered by a set of double doors on the right-hand side. It occurred to her that if these were locked, her journey down here would all be for naught. She had no Cathy now to magic it open. She pushed it gingerly and a wash of relief passed through her as it moved beneath her touch.

It led her into another tunnel. In contrast, this one was hewn out of solid rock and lit by orange ceiling lights, evenly spaced about six feet apart, which illuminated the path of the tunnel as it stretched on at an incline into the distance. Lights notwithstanding, Hannah couldn't see to the other end. Still, an incline was certainly better than a further descent, as she was really hoping to hear Cathy or Mrs Harnforth's voice again soon.

In the distance came a faint noise. At first Hannah thought it was running water, but as she continued her ascent and grew ever closer, she realized it was something else entirely. She stopped in her tracks. Human voices. Lots of human voices. Was it possible that after all this, she had gone full circle and ended up back in the heart of the Pinter Institute?

No. She wasn't exactly sure where she was, but unless

something strange had happened, she was certain she was well away from the main building and getting further away from it with every step. She couldn't imagine what these voices might be. Ranford House was in the middle of nowhere, after all. There weren't any other buildings for miles.

She resolved to keep walking, only now she did so crouched down and close to the wall, as if that offered some kind of protection. Up ahead, the tunnel finally began to level off and the voices grew ever louder. There was something unmistakably odd about them, but for the life of her, Hannah couldn't put her finger on what exactly that was.

'Cathy?' she whispered softly. 'Mrs Harnforth?'

No response. What she wouldn't give to hear a friendly voice. She unclenched her hands and splayed out her fingers in an attempt to release some of her tension.

She had almost reached the point at which the tunnel levelled off and she could see that it turned left. At that precise point the orange lights in the ceiling ended and the only source of illumination was an odd, blue-tinged glow from around the corner.

The voices had become very loud indeed, but still sounded strangely wrong. She crouched there for a couple of minutes, her head tilted, listening intently, trying to make out what was being said. It was impossible to pick out one voice from the multitude. Whenever she tried to focus on an individual, it seemed to drown in the sea of noise. At that point it dawned on her. That was precisely what was wrong. All the voices were talking at the same time. There was no back and forth. No conversation. It was just a constant babble of everyone vying against each other, desperate to be heard.

She tiptoed towards the corner and pressed herself against the cold stone wall. She closed her eyes and drew in a deep breath, noticing a bitter taste in her mouth as she did so. As she slowly exhaled, the thought struck her that, ironically, now would be a good time for some of that meditation the Pinter Institute was so fond of, and she had to clamp her lips together to prevent an adrenalin-soaked giggle from escaping.

Part of her wanted to know what was just out of view, but another part – the part you were never in control of as it was an instinct millennia in the making – just wanted her to turn and run.

She opened her eyes, steadied herself for a moment then stole a quick glance around the corner. She had been expecting to see a room full of people but there was no one there. At least, not the throng she had been anticipating. She waited a few seconds then risked a longer look.

Hannah found herself staring at what appeared to be an immense natural cavern filled with a multitude of sheet-covered objects. They were all rectangular in shape, about six feet tall and a couple of feet wide by a few inches deep. Like picture frames, perhaps. She fancied that she could see the bases of wooden stands poking out from beneath the cloth. The blue light in the cavern seemed to be coming from under the sheets and, with a jolt, she realized that's where the voices were coming from too.

A chill ran down Hannah's spine and her right leg began to tremble. She clasped her hands around it to steady it. Every fibre of her being wanted to flee back down the tunnel but she disciplined herself to remain still and carefully, methodically looked round the cavern to make sure she couldn't see anybody amid all the sheets.

When she'd satisfied herself that she was alone, for a certain value of that word, she raised herself to a standing position and crept forward. As she moved, the light shifted and she caught a flash of glass from beneath one of the sheets. Not picture frames. Mirrors. Under each and every sheet was a full-length wood-framed freestanding mirror, much like the one her mother used to have in her bedroom. She raised her arm to confirm that the hairs on the back of it were all standing on end. The palpable energy in the room, mingled with her own fear, gave her the distinct sensation of being a bug heading towards one of those electrical zappers.

When a sudden burst of static exploded in her ear, she actually jumped and her arms flailed involuntarily. She slammed her hand over her mouth to stop herself from screaming. You never saw James Bond doing that. When her heart rate had slowed to a brisk speed-metal tempo, she removed her hand and spoke as quietly as she could.

'Cathy? Mrs Harnforth? Can anybody hear me?'

Nothing.

'Anyone – can you hear me?'

Nothing.

'Shit!'

Hannah's heart sank, but then she realized that even though she couldn't hear them, it didn't mean that they couldn't hear her.

'If you can hear me,' she whispered, 'I went down the tunnel and then up another one, and I've now reached a massive cavern that has . . . I'm not sure, but they look like full-length mirrors – the freestanding kind – covered in sheets. Loads of them. There are . . . I know this sounds mad, but there are voices coming from them.' Hannah licked her dry lips. 'I'm going to investigate. I really hope you can hear me.'

Somehow it felt better to be talking. Even if nobody was responding, she felt less alone.

As Hannah continued to move forward, she finally began to make out individual voices. As she'd suspected, they weren't participating in a conversation, they were just pleading for someone, anyone, to help.

Well, she thought, *I'm anyone*.

'The voices,' she whispered, 'sound distressed. Terrified, really. I—'

Hannah stopped in her tracks. One of the voices sounded familiar with its distinctive accent. It was coming from under a sheet to her left. With another furtive glance to make sure she wasn't being observed, Hannah hauled the sheet off.

Some part of her brain, putting everything together in the background, must have had an inkling of what she was about to see, but there was the concept and there was the reality, and Hannah doubted anything could have prepared her for that. There, looking back at her from inside the mirror, was not her own reflection but that of Moira Everhart – only it wasn't. Her friend looked about six stone heavier and her eyes were puffy from crying.

Hannah stood transfixed, her fingers clenched between her teeth as she tried to comprehend the sheer awfulness of it.

'Hannah, hen, you've got to help me. Oh God, please help me. I don't understand what has happened. Where am I? Please get me out of here.'

Hannah's first attempt to speak came out as a garbled croak. She cleared her throat and tried again. 'Oh my God, it's Moira – only, it isn't. She's . . . different. What the hell is this place?'

Hannah clamped her hands over her ears as the din around her suddenly grew painfully intense, as a hundred other voices cried out for help too. She fell to her knees, as if pushed down by the wave of voices. When she looked, Moira's hands were clawing at the inside of the glass, trying to reach her.

Hannah did her best to be heard over the cacophony. 'Hold on, Moira. I'll get you out of there. I'll help you all, just—'

Her promise turned to a scream as a pair of powerful arms enveloped her and dragged her away. The world spun as she was lifted into the air and twisted around. Standing in front of her was Dr French and one of the muscle-bound henchmen she'd seen her with the night before. The other brute was presumably the owner of the arms that now restrained her.

The look of pure visceral hatred in the doctor's eyes was unmistakable.

'Silence!' the woman screeched.

In an instant, every noise in the room ceased. It happened so quickly that Hannah could hear its echo as it died away.

'You,' spat Dr French, her mouth in a snarl. 'You caused this.'

They all turned as an unfamiliar voice rang out impossibly loudly around the cavern. It was hoarse, older, male. 'Did she?'

Hannah looked up to a balcony at the far end of the cavern, which was now illuminated by a bright red light. There stood Winona Pinter, the supposed celebrity driving force behind the Pinter Institute, wearing the same blank expression as she had on the night she had not won an Oscar. Beside her sat a man in a wheelchair.

'From where I sit,' he rasped, 'I think there is plenty of blame to go around – don't you?'

Beside Hannah, Dr French immediately fell into a grovelling bow. 'Yes, your Lordship.'

CHAPTER 42

Flesh.

Loves.

Enter.

'You have to help me.'

Flesh.

Loves.

Enter.

'I'm in so much trouble.'

Banecroft felt the world sway around him. Everything else blurred into insignificance as he ran towards the location of the little pin on the map on his phone. As if things weren't tortuous enough, the damn thing was now running out of charge. Not now. Not when he was so close. Charlotte. She was all that mattered.

It had taken him so long. Too long. When he had fled Yvonne Braithwaite's salon, he had felt immediately guilty. Part of him had wanted to go back and apologize. To try to make it right. But he had no time. Charlotte. If he could just save her, then everything else would be fixed. The world would make sense again. He had bent over behind his car and thrown up nothing but bile. He couldn't remember the last time he'd eaten anything. Or slept beyond the few minutes when he occasionally blacked out. That done, he'd got in and driven away, eventually pulling into the car park of a McDonald's drive-thru to gather his thoughts.

He'd spent the rest of the afternoon in an increasingly exasperated frenzy, attempting to figure out what the message could possibly mean. All he had were three seemingly random words. He tried googling them in different orders, combinations and with any spelling variations he could think of. His searches threw up some reality TV show, a photography exhibition in Japan, a series of forty-eight biblical verses that he spent a futile hour trying to decipher, a twenty-five-year-old rom-com novel, an internet forum for IT professionals looking for love . . .

All of them led nowhere. They remained just three random bloody words. He had been all set to smash his mobile phone in frustration when it hit him like a bolt from the blue. Three random words. That was exactly what they were. He had slapped his hand against his forehead repeatedly. How could he be so stupid? *The Stranger Times* had even done an article on the bloody thing. The app that could guide you to any location on Earth using just three words. The paper had covered the story of the man from Bristol who was convinced that the three words tied to the location of his house were a personal attack based on a scandalous local rumour alleging he had an unhealthy obsession with trout.

Banecroft downloaded the app, typed in the three words, and

was shown a location of three metres squared that appeared to be a body of water on some open land in the Manchester suburb of Swinton. That couldn't be a coincidence.

His heart raced as he drove there, his hands shaking on the wheel all the way. He got as close as he could in the car, which meant he pulled up outside a sixth form college at the bottom of a broad, tree-lined cul-de-sac. He abandoned the Jag in a no stopping area and followed a dirt-track laneway between the college and another school until he reached a stretch of eight-foot-tall fencing bedecked with signs declaring it 'private property'. It was dusk now, the warm sun of the day bidding a pink-hued farewell behind scatterings of cloud to the west. It would be dark soon.

He followed the fencing, tripping on tree branches as he kept checking his location on his phone, and eventually found a gap between some trees where the thick wire mesh had been pulled away. In his haste, he ripped the left sleeve of his jacket on the way.

As the map had indicated, the space was large and green. Too wild to be a park and too lacking in fences to be used for agricultural purposes. Banecroft looked to his left and right. There were plenty of trees, but they stood in regimented lines, as if planted there by design. A golf course. It was a golf course, albeit one that was no longer in use. Fifty yards to his right, in the middle of what would once have been a fairway, lay the ashes of a campfire surrounded by beer cans.

Banecroft consulted the map again and headed across the fairway through a small copse. At the far side he caught sight of his journey's end. In truth, it was only a pond about forty feet across at its widest point, and the rusting shopping trolley poking out of its waters was its only feature. This didn't seem right. His elation at reaching his destination was souring fast and leaving a bitter taste in his mouth.

He called out Charlotte's name. Silence, save for the faint sound of a bird taking flight somewhere in the distance.

'Charlotte?' His throat felt constricted, as if hands were clasped around it.

As he stood alone in the fading light, he scanned his surroundings and saw nothing. *This couldn't be it, could it? What was this?* Tears filled his eyes as he shouted Charlotte's name again and again, a tide of desperation threatening to overwhelm him.

He stumbled towards the water's edge and fell to his knees.

This.

This was nothing.

It had all been for nothing.

He stared at the surface of the water, and in the waning light someone he did not recognize stared back at him. People live their lives cloaked in the mental image of what they used to be or what they thought they could be. In that moment, Banecroft saw himself as he truly was. A broken husk. A man he could pass in the street and not know. Sunken eyes, dishevelled hair, skin waxy pale. A dead man walking.

He sat back on his haunches. Too exhausted to move another inch. He didn't know where to go next, even if he could summon the energy.

As he rubbed the heels of his hands into his eyes, he sensed a subtle change in the air. He blinked his eyes open and tried to focus. Despite there being no wind to speak of, the surface of the water had started to move. Only a ripple at first, but it continued to build.

Banecroft sat there, his mouth hanging open, unable to process what was happening. As the water began to swirl, it called to mind a minor tornado he'd once seen in the dusty parking lot of a small-town 7-Eleven in Nevada while on a Stateside road trip. It had appeared from nowhere and dissipated just as quickly. The locals had barely acknowledged it.

This, though – this kept building. The water was spiralling more quickly now. Two, four, six feet in height it grew as it danced back and forth across the surface. His mouth dry, a lightness in his chest, Banecroft dared not breathe for fear of interrupting whatever had started. The spiral twisted faster and faster and faster, blurring the air around it, casting off a fine mist of cool water that kissed Banecroft's upturned face, and then . . . it stopped.

He blinked several times, unsure if he believed what he was seeing. There, in the centre of an unremarkable pond, in the middle of an abandoned golf course, stood a perfect rendering of his wife, sculpted from water. It smiled at him and spoke in the unmistakable voice of the woman he loved.

'Lumpy, you found me.'

CHAPTER 43

Hannah yelped as she was shoved unceremoniously on to the cold stone floor of the cavern. Pain shot through both her knees. The hands that had been restraining her began to pat her down roughly over her clothing. They moved to her hair, yanked it back and thick fingers wrenched the earpiece out of her ear.

'Ouch!'

'She was wearing this.'

'Destroy it,' barked Dr French.

Hannah watched as the tiny gadget was crushed beneath a massive boot. She and that earpiece had been through a lot together. In truth, it had been through a lot of her.

She looked up again to witness the surreal sight of the wheel-chair floating serenely across the vast cavern until it landed effortlessly on the ground in front of her. Up close, she was subjected to a better look at the man occupying it. He actually looked less like a man and more like a skeleton someone had taken a quick stab at covering in skin with the intention of coming back to finish the job later. His flesh hung loose in places around his neck and jowls. He couldn't have weighed more than a few stone soaking wet.

A shiver of primal revulsion passed through Hannah's body.

All her instincts suggested that this man should be dead. His full head of blonde hair should have looked completely ludicrous perched atop the liver-spotted cadaver beneath it, but then you reached the man's eyes; a vivid, ice-cold blue so full of malevolent life that Hannah had to look away.

She stole a quick glance back up at the balcony to where Winona Pinter had remained but now appeared to be staring at the wall.

'So, it seems we have located the source of our problems.' The man's voice sounded like the irate rustling of old parchment.

'Yes, your Lordship,' confirmed Dr French without raising her head from the deep bow she was still executing.

'And how exactly did she slip through your screening process?'

'I don't . . . I'm sorry. I don't know how she could have, my lord. I checked, I double-checked. I even went to the offices of that preposterous little newspaper. I don't understand how this happened.'

'Well, how wonderfully useful of you.' A growl of anger laced the man's every word. 'It now seems we will have to move this entire undertaking because you could not do one simple task. Years of planning and groundwork, ruined.'

Hannah watched his skeletal left hand reach forward towards Dr French, and Hannah braced herself for something awful to happen. The moment hung in the air before the hand returned to its resting place on the arm of the wheelchair.

'And as for you, young lady.' It took Hannah a couple of seconds to realize that she was now being spoken to directly. 'Who do you work for?'

'I . . . I don't know what you mean. I'm just a guest at the Institute and I got lost when—'

'Silence!' hissed the man. 'Do not waste my time with your pathetic lies. Doctor, what happened to Anton?'

'A man – someone we don't know – approached him and started asking questions, my lord. The fail-safe we put in place worked perfectly.'

'That is scant consolation when it turns out that you were the one we should have been worried about all along.'

'I can fix this, m'lord,' she pleaded. 'Just give me a chance.'

'You have had enough chances. And we were so close.'

'It's not too late. With the subject we already have in place—'

'Enough,' snapped the man. 'Do not matriculate your ineptitude by following it up with terrible counsel. Do you think this simpering fool and whoever spoke to Anton are working alone? Someone else will be behind this, and I warrant I know who. We will salvage what we can and move on.'

Hannah was surprised to see tears rolling down Dr French's cheeks. 'Yes, your Lordship. Sorry, your Lordship.'

'Your apologies mean nothing to me. Ready this one for the procedure.'

'Is that . . . wise, my lord?'

'You dare to question me, on today of all days?'

'No, of course not. It's just, if we have been compromised . . .'

'Then I want to know by whom exactly, and exactly what they know. This one will hold that information. We do not need or want to keep her, but her remnant will be useful for us to interrogate in due course.'

'Excellent. Although she has not been prepared fully.'

'What does that matter?' said the man. 'It's not as if I want her to live through it.'

Hannah tried to shift her body around, looking for a way to free herself and run, but the same powerful hands held her still.

The thought of pleading for mercy entered her mind, but when she looked into those eyes again, all she saw was the cold certainty that there was none to be had.

From Hannah's perspective, the next ten minutes seemed to pass both torturously slowly and painfully fast. Even if she had wanted to plead her case, one of the big baboons had clamped his hand over her mouth, so not only could she not speak but she also spent what increasingly seemed to be her last few minutes on earth enjoying the foul stench of tobacco ingrained in his fingers. It was not her only discomfort – blood trickled down her left leg from where her knee had split open when she was pushed on to the rock floor.

For the look of the thing, she kept an eye out for any opportunity for escape, but none presented itself. Stamping on the toes of your captor to gain release only works in the movies. Here, it would just guarantee a clubbing punch to her head. She was severely physically outmatched. The baboon may not have been the brightest, but she couldn't think of any way to get him into a pub quiz situation.

Part of her wanted to go out swinging but she found herself devoid of all energy, wrapped in a cocoon of despair. Maybe it was the lack of oxygen thanks to the baboon's massive stinky hand, but something in her wanted to just close her eyes and let it be over. Her last fading hope lay in Mrs Harnforth's final words to her – something about the cavalry coming charging in. With an ever-increasing sense of dread, Hannah found herself straining to hear the sound of horses' hooves that would never come.

Dr French and the m'lord in the wheelchair had moved away and were locked in intense conversation. Hannah could not make out the content of their discussion, but judging by the body language, the not-so-good doctor was having almost as bad a day as she was. Almost. The other baboon disappeared and returned moments later carrying a mirror identical to the others in the room. He placed it in front of Hannah. She looked up into his face and saw nothing. He displayed an almost preternatural level of disengagement from everything around him. She wondered if that was just how he was or if he had also been 'assisted' in some way. She really was beginning to hate magic.

Unable to resist, Hannah looked in the mirror. She seemed so tiny against the bulk of the baboon holding her. She glanced to her left and could still see Moira – or at least the distorted version of her – cowering in her frame. Hannah felt the bile rise in her throat as she realized that death – her death – would not be the end. Some part of her would be held like that – trapped in some unspeakably tortuous state for all eternity.

The prospect was enough to stoke a surge of energy from within. *Come on, girl. Pull yourself together.* Even if escape wasn't possible, there were worse things than death, and one of those was right in front of her. She had to find a way to fight because dying in the attempt might be one of the better results open to her.

She noted a hint of movement in the reflection and a ball of anger grew in her chest. The utter bastard restraining her was flexing his bloody muscles in the mirror. She was about to die and he was admiring himself. Whatever happened, she was going to find some way to inflict some pain on the bulbous little turd before this was through. It felt good to be angry. So much better than the alternative.

Dr French and the man in the wheelchair had finished their conversation and had returned their attention to Hannah.

'Very well,' he rasped. 'Let's get this over with. There is much to do and little time to do it in.'

As Hannah's gaoler pushed her forward towards the mirror, she put every ounce of her anger into struggling to free herself. The living corpse in the chair grabbed her too, and the grip of his spindly fingers around her wrist felt impossibly strong. It was as if Death itself held her in his grasp. With his other hand, he touched the mirror and an undulation passed through the reflective surface. The baboon then seized Hannah's chin and forced her head to the left, where Dr French was standing, a malevolent grin spread across her face.

Dr French reached up to one of her long dangly earrings and, in one deft motion, set it spinning. It turned impossibly fast. Hannah tried not to look, but the grip on her chin was too tight. She tried to close her eyes but as she strained to do so, her eyelids refused to move. Her face vibrated with the futile effort.

Soon, her whole being was consumed by a horrible, sickly sensation, as if all her willpower was being sucked out of her body. She felt her head droop . . .

The last thing she would hear was the monotone incantation of Dr French. 'Trust the process. Trust the process. Trust the process.'

And then, the mirror shattered, emitting a pulse of energy that sent all bar the man in the wheelchair hurtling backwards to the ground. Blissfully, Hannah felt the meaty hands release their grip on her, and she rolled away. She sprang to her feet and, in a moment of glorious reprisal, sent her right foot crashing into the prone baboon's testicles. *Flex that, you bastard.* She quickly stepped back, fists raised, ready to fend off whoever tried to grab her next, but nobody did. They were all far too busy looking at the person standing behind the man in the wheelchair.

Mrs Harnforth gave the ensemble a cheery wave. 'Oh, I'm sorry. Did I break your concentration?'

CHAPTER 44

Several miles away, in the garden of a picturesque holiday cottage, Cathy Quirke stood, lighting a cigarette with shaking hands.

Stanley stood behind her. 'Can I—'

'Shut up. Shut your big mouth, Stanley.'

'OK.'

She spun around and jabbed the cigarette in his direction. 'Don't you "OK" me. Don't you *dare* "OK" me. What the hell have you got me into, Stanley?'

'Can I just—'

'No. Shut up. I mean, first off – that Hannah girl goes down some weird tunnels and ends up in a massive cave where she says mirrors are talking to her. Like, mirrors full of people or something. I just assumed she'd dropped some acid or was having a stroke or something, but then, the woman we work for – the woman who *you* got me to work for – walks out of them French doors, blows a whistle, and a couple of hundred robin redbreasts swoop down, grab her and they all disappear off into the night. I mean – have I got all that right? Well, answer me.'

'You did actually tell me to—'

'And now I am telling you to speak. Speak, Stanley, speak. Have I got that right?'

Stanley shifted from foot to foot nervously. 'Actually, no.'

'Really?' said Cathy, tossing the cigarette she hadn't managed to start smoking into the rockery.

'Not to be pedantic,' began Stanley, 'but they weren't robin redbreasts, they were starlings.'

Stanley Roker, being Stanley Roker, had been hit by women several times in his life. Cathy Quirke gave a good account of herself by reaching number two on the all-time list with an extremely impressive right hook.

CHAPTER 45

The haggard figure in the wheelchair manoeuvred himself around to look at Mrs Harnforth.

'Alicia!'

'Willie,' she replied cheerfully, as if greeting an old friend.

'Do not call me that.'

Mrs Harnforth laughed. 'His Lordship, William Ranford — always so determined to make people respect you. As if that's how respect works. Still, congratulations on not being dead. You faked that well. That I will grant you.'

Hannah's mind raced. If this man was indeed Lord William Ranford, he must be knocking on for one hundred and thirty years old. She studied him again. It was believable. If anything, it looked like he'd had a hard life.

'How did you get in here?'

Mrs Harnforth nodded towards Hannah. 'I was able to get an approximate location on my colleague here, and from there we used a Russian spy satellite to locate the other entrance to your little hidey-hole.'

'Really?'

'No,' said Mrs Harnforth with a grin. 'But what makes you think I would explain my methods to you?'

She made a couple of hand gestures and Hannah shielded her eyes as a blindingly bright golden ring appeared in the air above them, making a loud sizzling noise as it hovered there.

Hannah turned her body as the baboon who'd been holding her struggled to his feet beside her, but all of his attention was on the main event. Dr French and the other henchman were already back standing, looking as confused as Hannah about what was happening.

Ranford strained to raise his voice and pointed up at the ring. 'What is the purpose of that?'

Mrs Harnforth shrugged. 'It's all rather dull and grubby in here, isn't it? What is it they say about light being the best disinfectant?'

'Always that same old arrogance.'

'Now, if that isn't the pot calling the kettle black. By the way, was that a rather dazed-looking Oscar-nominated actress I passed on my way in?'

'She is my bride.'

Mrs Harnforth turned to look at Dr French, an undisguised expression of revulsion on her face. 'I see someone has been busy.'

Dr French glared back at her. 'You will address Lord Ranford with respect.'

'No, I don't think I shall.'

As if acting on instinct, Dr French reached for her left earring. Before she could grasp it she screamed, as it was torn free from her ear and flew across to land in Mrs Harnforth's outstretched hand.

'I think we've had more than enough of that,' Mrs Harnforth declared as she deposited it in her coat pocket, then wrinkled her nose as she noted the bloodstain it had left on her fingers.

Clenching the digits of her left hand around her bleeding earlobe, Dr French pointed at Mrs Harnforth with her right. 'Seize her.'

The two henchmen looked at one another and then, without saying a word, turned and ran towards the entrance Hannah had come through.

'Oh dear,' said Mrs Harnforth. 'It is so hard to find good help these days, isn't it?'

'I don't need them,' snarled Ranford through tight white lips. 'You have made a terrible mistake and walked right into the centre of my power. Here, you are no match for me.'

'The problem with that supposition, Willie, is that I am standing directly in front of the source of your power.' She waved a hand at the mirrors arrayed around her, then casually wafted a finger in the air.

'Don't,' said Ranford, suddenly sounding weak. 'Please. You don't understand.'

'Oh, I think I do. It may have taken me too long to get there, but I now understand perfectly. *The Picture of Dorian Gray* was written as a warning, William, not a blueprint. Every one of these mirrors contains the remnant of a soul, each one stolen by you from a vulnerable person.'

'They wanted it.'

For the first time, Hannah saw anger in Mrs Harnforth's eyes. 'No, they didn't. They wanted help. This is not help. It might look like it for a brief time, but a distended soul cannot function in the world. Either you don't know that or, more likely, you don't care. You have been stealing life from people and then using them as glorified batteries to keep you alive.'

'You're one to talk.'

Mrs Harnforth's eyes narrowed.

'You don't understand,' Ranford said as he looked away. 'My research – I'm very close to being able to turn back the clock.'

'I don't care.' Mrs Harnforth looked around the room. 'Charlotte Banecroft. Where is she?'

'I don't know what you're talking about.'

Hannah was dumbfounded. There had been no mention of this before now. Banecroft's wife?

'Don't play the innocent, Willie,' said Mrs Harnforth. 'You can't pull it off. I'm guessing she was one of your earliest victims. Where is her remnant?'

'She's not here,' said Ranford.

'I can just start pulling sheets off until I find her.'

A harsh noise came out of Ranford's mouth. After a couple of seconds, Hannah realized it was supposed to be a laugh.

'Go right ahead,' he said with a grim smile. 'It won't do you any good.'

Mrs Harnforth locked eyes with him. 'Who did you give her to?'

'Not give. I got a really good price.'

'Who?' she repeated.

'Why would I tell you that?'

Mrs Harnforth lowered her head and Hannah saw her jaw working up and down, a clear sign of her frustration. After a few seconds, she looked back up again. 'Fine. Tell me who has her and I'll let you keep all of this.'

'Am I supposed to take your word for that?'

Mrs Harnforth dipped her hand into the pocket of her coat and withdrew a small ornate knife. 'My blood oath.'

Ranford leaned forward and ran his small black tongue over his lips before looking at Hannah. 'And the girl?'

Mrs Harnforth's eyes darted briefly in Hannah's direction before returning to Ranford. 'Your witch'— she nodded in the direction of Dr French — 'can wipe her memory.'

'Excuse me?' said Hannah.

'Silence!' hissed Ranford.

'Screw you, you creepy old bastard!' She looked directly at Mrs Harnforth. 'I don't want anybody messing with my memory ever again.'

Mrs Harnforth didn't even turn to look at her. 'Hannah, please keep quiet.'

'No, I—'

Ranford gave a wave of his hand and Hannah was cut off by her own two mutinous hands slamming over her mouth. She tried to move, but similarly found her feet unwilling to do her bidding.

'Silly girl.' Ranford turned his head to smile up at her. 'If you learn nothing in this world, know that you should never trust a Founder,' he said as he nodded towards Mrs Harnforth.

'If you are quite finished,' interrupted Mrs Harnforth, 'do we have an agreement or not?'

Ranford nodded. 'We do.'

'And need I remind you what happens if I give a blood oath and you then lie to me?'

'You do not.'

She bobbed her head. 'So, we understand each other.' She held out the blade with her right hand and then, with only the slightest wince, ran it across her left palm. She then raised it to show her fresh blood running freely from the wound. 'Provided William Ranford tells me everything he knows about the remnant of Charlotte Banecroft and the person to whom he gave it, I will leave this place, untouched, and never speak of it to another soul. My blood as my witness.'

A broad grin spread across Ranford's nightmare of a face. 'Excellent. A deal is done.' He drummed his hands excitedly on the arms of his wheelchair.

'No,' she said, 'it is not. Not until you fulfil your part.'

He nodded. 'It was an old friend of yours, in fact.' He paused and gave her a yellow-toothed grin. 'Dominic Johnson.'

Mrs Harnforth's eyes widened in disbelief. 'That's not— Why would he have any interest in her?'

'I don't know. Your kind rarely explain themselves to us mere mortals.'

'When did you make this deal?'

'A couple of months ago now.'

She nodded and spoke more to herself than anyone else. 'That makes sense.'

'So,' said Ranford, 'if that concludes our business, I believe you should be leaving.'

He turned towards Dr French, who was now holding a blood-soaked handkerchief to her ear. 'Take care of the girl.'

'I can't. She has taken my lure.'

Ranford waved a skeletal finger at Mrs Harnforth. 'Return it to her.'

'Of course,' said Mrs Harnforth, taking the earring out of her pocket and tossing it casually to Dr French, who snatched it out of the air as if it were a lifejacket.

Ranford turned to Hannah and favoured her again with his grisly smile. 'Do you see? She thinks she's so much better than the likes of me, but she readily gave you away as if you had no value.'

'Oh, William,' said Mrs Harnforth with the tone of somebody admonishing a disappointing child. 'Your problem – well, one of your many problems, really – is you have never understood the fundamental principles of magic.'

'You're picking a most peculiar moment to lord your abilities over me, Alicia.'

'You misunderstand. I actually meant stage magic. You know, the illusions conjured by nothing more than ingenuity.'

'Cheap parlour tricks.'

Mrs Harnforth shook her head. 'On the contrary. Even the simplest trick works on the basis of having an understanding of how the human mind works. The classic principles of misdirection, for example – how a bright shiny thing can be used as a distraction.'

She clicked her fingers and the golden ring above their heads disappeared. Hannah saw the precise moment when doubt entered Ranford's mind – as everyone bar Mrs Harnforth stared up into the darkness, his mouth formed an O of uncertainty.

Hannah heard the noise first. Chirping. The flapping of wings. Then, as her eyes adjusted, she could make out movement.

'What . . .' started Dr French.

'Starlings,' answered Mrs Harnforth. 'An entire murmuration of starlings.'

Ranford sounded agitated now. 'Get out, and take your minions with you.'

'Not my minions. My friends. Creatures of abundant free will. So, any agreement you may have with me does not cover them, and they take a very dim view of anyone being kept in cages.'

A lot of things happened at once, so much so that Hannah would never be able to piece it all together to her satisfaction. Ranford gave a bloodcurdling scream as the darkness seemed to come alive. Birds descended en masse and began to swirl around the four of them. Hannah felt feathers brushing against her from all sides amid the deafening thunder of hundreds of wings flapping around them and building to a crescendo.

She let out a scream as a pair of arms tackled her to the ground. She looked up to see Mrs Harnforth crouching over her, making a couple of quick hand gestures. The air around them shimmered, and suddenly, everything seemed more distant, more muted. It was as if there were an invisible barrier between them and the rest of the world.

Through the confusion of swirling feathers, Hannah could just make out Ranford attempting to stand. He teetered on his feet for a moment before crumpling to the ground. Orange light shot from his hands and a few birds fell to the ground, but they were a tiny proportion of the flock.

The rush of air sent several sheets falling from the mirrors. The figures revealed in each one began to bang and push against the glass, their screams adding to the cacophony. As Hannah watched, a fracture appeared in the mirror closest to her – the one holding the remnant of Moira. The crack spread rapidly, a spiderweb of tiny fissures racing across the surface. Then, after a moment's pause, it shattered entirely and an orb of orange light escaped from it.

It was like the first domino falling. Mirror after mirror exploded around them as the chain reaction took hold. In the chaos, Hannah saw more starlings falling bloodied to the ground, cut down by shards of flying glass as orange light after orange light joined the maelstrom.

Then, she noticed a pattern emerge among the chaos. The small globes of light had begun to gather around Ranford as he attempted to swat them away. His efforts were futile. As if responding to some invisible signal, the birds began to ascend, and now Ranford was alone, being lifted off the ground, swamped by the orange orbs.

'Please, no!' he begged. 'No! I . . . No!'

He rose into the air, his arms and legs stretched wide in a perverse star jump. Then, as those cold blue eyes grew wide with terror, he exploded into a mist so fine that nothing fell to the ground. What had once been Lord William Ranford floated away in the still-swirling wind.

The orange lights slowed for a few moments, dancing in the

air, before they shot straight upwards and ripped through the rock like a knife through butter. Within seconds they were gone.

Hannah lay there, stunned, until she felt a finger tap her on her shoulder. She looked up to see Mrs Harnforth standing above her, extending a hand to help her up.

'Well,' she said, 'that was all rather dramatic.'

CHAPTER 46

Hannah stood to one side and surveyed the destruction. The whole of the cavern was now illuminated by a ball of bright light conjured up by Mrs Harnforth. The floor was a sea of sparkling shards of glass mixed with wooden splinters. The light showed more of the cavern than had been visible previously, although there was not a great deal left to see. The frenzy of flying glass and whatever else had destroyed everything in its path. She looked up through the hole in the ceiling where the orange orbs had carved a tunnel straight through a mountain. Hannah reckoned that if she angled her head just right, she could see a patch of darkening evening sky above them.

On the other side of the cavern, Mrs Harnforth was now deep in conversation with a starling. Hannah assumed it was Gordon from the bench. Once they had finished, the bird flew off to re-join its flock, presumably heading out the same way it had come in. Mrs Harnforth, meanwhile, picked her way carefully across the sparkling floor. Amid the glass and splinters of wood were numerous feathers and spots of blood.

'How many did they lose?'

'I'm sorry?' said Mrs Harnforth as she drew close.

'The starlings. How many did they lose?'

'They don't view it in those terms.'

'Excuse me?' said Hannah, irritated by the tone of the response.

'They do not see these things as you and I do. While yes, they consider themselves as individuals in a sense, they view themselves as part of the collective first and foremost. They don't see it as death. To them, those birds are still with the murmuration. It, the collective, has been wounded, but nothing has died.'

Hannah folded her arms. 'Clearly my view of the value of life is out of step with everybody else's.'

Mrs Harnforth gave a sad smile. 'You have questions.'

'Yes, I do. Am I allowed to ask them or would it just be easier for you to wipe my memory?' She whirled around. 'Wait. Hang on, where's she gone?'

'Who?'

'Who?' she repeated, exasperated. 'Dr French. The woman with the earring.'

'Ah, her. She probably made her getaway when everything happened.'

'Shouldn't we go after her?'

Mrs Harnforth gave a dismissive shrug. 'She is small fry. Her master is gone. That's what's important.'

'Gone? Don't you mean dead? Or is he not really dead either?'

'No, he is. Not by my hand, though. What you saw were the remnants exacting their revenge on a man who had been torturing them – using them as glorified batteries, really – for his own gain. Brutal, it might have been, but they had that right.'

'What the hell were we doing here?' asked Hannah, throwing

out her hands. 'You told me we were investigating this place because people were being taken advantage of.'

Mrs Harnforth tilted her head. 'And they were. In the worst way I can imagine.'

'Yes, but not like this. You didn't—' She stopped herself, struggling to find the words. 'All of that stuff with Thomas Mandeville, when you played me that tape. Was that even real?'

'Of course it was. It turned out that it was Anton, the customer experience something or other, who was stealing his money. My assumption is that he arranged things so that the remnant of the late Thomas Mandeville made the call. He probably told him he would let him out if he did.'

'And will Anton, at least, be going to jail?'

Mrs Harnforth winced. 'I'm afraid not. Stanley approached him earlier today and his head literally blew up.'

Hannah threw her hands out in exasperation. 'Of course it did.'

'It will have been something Ranford put in place. He clearly didn't trust him.'

'Like you didn't trust me?'

'I'm sorry.'

'You lied to me.'

'Actually' – she paused and scratched behind her ear – 'technically, I didn't. Did I tell you all I knew, or all I suspected? No. But I'm afraid that is part of my job. I have to decide what people do and don't need to know.'

'Technically?' repeated Hannah, her voice rising. 'Technically? Well, that's just great. Do I get to know now, or should I just be happy that I'm no longer being used as a pawn in your stupid bloody game?'

The tendons in her neck were growing tight. She couldn't say exactly what she was angry at, but she found herself boiling with rage.

Mrs Harnforth gave her an infuriatingly calm look. 'Ask away. I will tell you all I can. You have indeed earned that.'

'Gee, thanks. OK, let's start here – what on earth is a remnant?'

Mrs Harnforth paused, held an elegantly manicured finger to her lips and began. 'It's probably easiest to think of it as a part of the soul. Like you split someone in two. One part can go out and live a normal life, in a manner of speaking, while the second part is trapped here. From what you told me, the Pinter Institute, through the therapy, conditioned people to see their problems as belonging to something other than themselves – or rather a version of themselves – to make it easier to divide them in two. The part here, the remnant, would have a perfect recollection of the person's life until the point of the split, but they would also be a crude representation of certain parts of the host's personality. People have attempted to use magic to do this kind of thing for centuries, although as far as I'm aware, Ranford was the first to do it on a grand scale, to other people, with the purpose of using the remnants as a source of power. Leaving aside the appalling morality of it all, I suppose you could say it was a clever enough scheme.'

'I'm not sure you're perfectly positioned to give lessons on morality,' said Hannah.

Mrs Harnforth said nothing to this.

'You were going to let that awful woman wipe my mind.' Hannah was annoyed to feel tears filling her eyes.

'Actually, I wasn't. I had to say that as I needed Ranford to believe that telling me what I needed to know offered him a genuine chance of getting out of this with what he wanted.' She pointed upwards. 'He wasn't going to. Once I'd seen what was happening, I had prepared for that eventuality.'

On an intellectual level, Hannah couldn't find fault with this, although she wanted to. 'What the hell was all that about Charlotte Banecroft? You never told me anything about that.'

Mrs Harnforth gave a nod. 'No, I didn't, and I apologize for the lie of omission. To give you the full truth, some friends and I have been looking into her death for some time, given Vincent's unshakeable belief that something wasn't right. After a lot of investigation, we discovered she had come to the Pinter Institute, and so we started poking around here.'

'So Banecroft is right?' asked Hannah softly. 'His wife really isn't dead?'

'No, I'm afraid she is. The remnant isn't an individual in its own right, just a collection of memories and certain elements of their personality. They can't change. They can't experience new things. Vincent knew – don't ask me how, but he knew – that his wife was not completely dead, which is true in a way. But she is also not alive.' Mrs Harnforth pointed at the sizeable gap in the ceiling. 'Those remnants, assuming their hosts are still with us, will go and rejoin them now that they are free. So your friend Moira will be her old self. So will your husband.'

Hannah surprised herself by laughing.

'Is everything . . .'

'Sorry,' said Hannah, holding up a hand as she struggled to stop the massive build-up of tension within her from finding a release. After a few seconds, she regained control. 'It just struck me as odd – that Karl, returning to his old self, would end up being a fantastic result. My life has become so utterly weird. It's hard to keep track of everything now.'

'I'm just sorry we couldn't keep his remnant, so you could use it as a witness in court.'

Hannah laughed again then found her mind turning back to poor Banecroft. 'So, when Ranford said that this guy, Dominic Johnson . . .'

Mrs Harnforth nodded.

'Him,' continued Hannah. 'He now has the remnant of Charlotte Banecroft?'

'Yes. And I believe he was using it as a hacker would use a virus, to get inside Vincent's mind and take control. All done via the medium of poor Simon Brush.'

Hannah's eyes widened. 'So when Simon appeared in our offices . . .'

'Initially, it was just the normal activity of a spirit with unfinished business, but at some point, yes, I'm afraid the poor boy was taken over and his ghost used as a cipher for an appalling assault. I'm not even sure what Johnson was hoping to achieve.'

'You keep using the past tense?'

'Yes,' said Mrs Harnforth. 'A few weeks ago, I received an anonymous tip-off that *The Stranger Times* was to be attacked in some manner, and let's just say by that point I had my suspicions, although I never would have suspected something quite like this. Luckily, the last I heard, my friend Betty, who I sent in as your temporary replacement, had discovered what was going on with Simon, and was endeavouring to break the connection.'

'Oh,' said Hannah, hurt. 'You replaced me?'

Mrs Harnforth smiled. 'Temporarily, I assure you. Betty would not want the position permanently, and I am entirely sure she and Vincent would kill one another within a matter of weeks.' She laid a hand on Hannah's arm. 'That place really needs you, now possibly more than ever.'

Hannah pulled away slightly. 'I have another question.'

Mrs Harnforth nodded. 'Of course you do. Let me save you a little time – yes, what Ranford said is true. I am a Founder.'

Hannah looked at her. Despite everything they'd just been through, Mrs Harnforth's appearance remained immaculate, somehow untouched by the chaos. Not a hair out of place, not so much as a crease on her stylish but functional green trouser suit. In this moment, Hannah wanted to be angrier than she was. 'But I thought you were fighting against them?'

'No. Nothing as easy as that. I am fighting to keep the peace. Trying to repay the massive unpayable debt that I carry with me every day of my life. I am drenched in the sacrifice of others, and I feel an immense shame at that, like you cannot possibly imagine. The only way I can even begin to make it right is to find a solution.

'The Accord was one step, one imperfect step, but all it did was stop the bloodshed. If things had carried on the way they were going, the Folk would be rounded up like cattle and the worst elements of the Founders would run amok. This way, I have given them a chance. An imperfect chance, but it was the best I could manage. In the meantime, the others and I are doing all we can to maintain the peace, while striving to find a better solution.'

Hannah didn't know what to say to all that. It was too much to take in at once. When she looked at Mrs Harnforth again, she felt her anger dissipating. Maybe the woman was still some kind of a monster but, right there and then, she didn't look it. She looked like somebody weighed down with guilt and trying to make the best of a bad situation.

Hannah cleared her throat. 'So, what now?'

Mrs Harnforth looked around. 'Well, I'd imagine I'm going to be here for quite some time cleaning up this mess and dealing with the rest of the Pinter Institute.'

'And what about Banecroft?'

Mrs Harnforth put her hands in her pockets. 'I need you to talk to him.'

'Me?'

She nodded. 'Betty, I assume, has dealt with the threat, but somebody needs to explain to the man what was being done to him and what it means. He has earned the right to grieve properly.'

'Are you sure I'm the best person for that job?'

'You might not think it, but I rather suspect that you are the best friend that man has in this world.'

'Wow,' said Hannah. 'I think I'm going to need quite a lot of time to process that statement.'

'Excuse me?' called a voice from the far side of the cavern. The two women turned to see the figure of Winona Pinter looking rather lost among all the debris.

'Oh, shit,' exclaimed Hannah. 'We completely forgot about her.'

'Sorry to bother you,' said Winona Pinter as Hannah and Mrs Harnforth hurried over to her, 'but I can't find my PA anywhere. I think I'm supposed to be on set but I don't know where make-up is. I haven't missed my call time, have I? I hate to keep a director waiting.'

Hannah and Mrs Harnforth exchanged a look before Hannah took Winona's arm and patted her hand. 'Not at all. You just come with me.'

As they walked, Winona looked down at the floor. 'Oh dear, a broken mirror. That will be seven years' bad luck for someone.'

CHAPTER 47

It was an odd sensation, watching a ghost as it sat there and read. Stella was lying on her bed while Simon's form was perched at the makeshift desk she had constructed for herself in her not-quite-a-room room. Its position at the base of the church spire meant that its walls were curved, something that rendered interior design a bit of a challenge, given the infuriatingly straight nature of the edges of most items of furniture.

As Simon moved on to the last of the three pages she had laid out in front of him, Stella bit her lip and resisted the urge to ask questions. She sensed the point at which he stopped reading, but he continued to stare at the page for what felt like an age. She reminded herself that time was relative, especially when you're dead.

Eventually, she cracked. 'You don't like it, do you?' she asked.

'No,' he said, before looking up and giving her a wide dimpled grin, his ethereal glasses somehow slightly askew on his face. 'I love it.'

Stella laughed with relief. 'Would it have killed you to say that a bit sooner?'

'Nothing can kill me – not again.'

Stella's face dropped, but then Simon gave in and giggled. 'The look on your face.'

'Ohhhh, you . . .' She picked up a cushion, threw it at him and watched as it passed right through his form, which caused Simon to laugh even harder.

Stella joined in and abandoned herself to her joy so much so that she began to struggle for breath. It was one of those explosions of emotion that is as much a release of pent-up tension as it is related to anything that has been said. She couldn't remember the last time she had laughed this hard. The place hadn't been that much fun recently.

Their revelry was interrupted by the sound of Stella's name being bellowed at the loudest volume possible by a woman with an impressive set of lungs.

'Oh God,' said Stella, glancing at the sheet of plywood that served as the door to her supposed bedroom. When she turned back, Simon was gone.

'I'm never going to get used to that,' she mumbled as she rolled off her bed.

Grace was standing in the middle of the reception area and looked like she was gearing up for another go at seeing how loud she could holler Stella's name.

'Relax. Relax. I'm here.'

'Could you not hear me calling you?'

'Are you kidding? People in Belgium could hear you calling me. There was quite possibly a landslide in the Himalayas directly attributed to you calling me.'

'And yet it took you this long to get here?'

Stella was about to continue their exchange, but noticed Grace's genuine agitation. 'Is everything OK?'

'No. Everything is not OK. Mr Banecroft is still not here. We have no idea where that poor man is.'

'Oh,' said Stella. 'Yeah, that is a concern all right. I'm not even sure where to look for him. He doesn't normally leave the office.'

'And as if that wasn't enough, Reggie and Ox are missing too.'

'Really?' Stella looked at her watch. 'Grace, it's just after seven in the morning. They wouldn't normally be here at this time anyway.'

'I know that, but I was trying to ring them both last night and nobody answered. They told me they would get in contact by the end of the day. Ox is Ox, but Reggie is very reliable.'

Stella nodded. Grace wasn't wrong. Ox was flaky at the best of times, but you could set your watch by Reggie.

'And the last thing they were doing was going off to follow up on those crazy conspiracies.'

'Oh, yeah,' said Stella. 'I forgot about that.'

'They went looking for a man who seems to have disappeared, and now they too have disappeared. That seems like an enormous coincidence to me.'

A thought struck Stella. 'Have you checked their desks? It's possible Reggie's phone ran out of charge, and Ox is out of credit more often than not. Maybe they dropped by and left a note?' She pointed at Grace's desk, or at least the approximate area where she assumed it still was. The entire thing was now buried behind cardboard boxes. Grace's storage solutions were now taking up over half of the reception area. 'It's not like they could have left a note on your desk.'

Grace nodded, happy for the hope, and rushed over to the bullpen. Stella followed her through to the empty space where the desks looked as they normally did – Reggie's neat and tidy, Ox's like a vacuum cleaner and a recycling bin had fought to the death over a takeaway order. There was no note on either work station.

Grace sat down on Reggie's chair and held her head in her hands. 'What are we going to do? Everything is falling apart.'

Stella made her way over and placed a reassuring hand on Grace's back. 'Hey now, come on. It'll be fine. They'll all show up. Give it an hour or two and we'll be laughing about this.' Even as the words left her mouth, Stella had a hard time believing them.

'Do you think so?'

'Absolutely.' She tried to sound as confident as possible. 'Just to be on the safe side, though, I'm going to—'

A loud cracking noise cut her off. Both she and Grace looked over to the corner where Betty's petrified form was still floating six inches off the ground, anchored to the pipes lest it make another attempt to break free of the Earth's gravitational pull.

A layer of stone was starting to fall away before their eyes. It was much like watching a newborn chick emerge from its shell, although Stella guessed the average chick didn't suddenly sit up, spit a root vegetable an impressive distance across the room, then retch and shout, 'I cannot stand ruddy onions.'

★

It took Stella and Grace a couple of minutes to get Betty back on her feet, and another couple of minutes of assisted walking to get her to the point at which movement seemed to return to her body more naturally. She then performed some simple stretches and thrusts before announcing loudly that she was off to the bathroom to have what she described as 'a prodigious micturition'. While she was gone, Stella did a quick google to confirm her suspicion of the word's definition.

By the time Betty returned to the room with a purposeful stride, Stella had decided that she needed to tell her everything. They had been through quite a bit together, and in a weird way they had bonded. None of that meant Betty wouldn't fire Ox when she found out exactly what he'd been up to, but it couldn't hurt.

'Good God, I needed that.' She slapped Stella on the back. 'Well done on getting me back here in one piece. It all got a bit sticky there, but you clearly handled the situation very well.'

Stella bobbed her head briefly. She didn't know how to take a compliment. She'd received so few of them in her life that she hadn't really practised her response.

Betty sat down heavily on one of the chairs and continued to do some stretches while she spoke. 'Am I speaking loudly?'

Stella and Grace nodded.

'Right,' she replied with no noticeable decrease in volume. 'It's the whole petrification thing. Throws stuff off a bit. Only temporarily, I'm happy to say. So, how are we? Actually, blow that – what day is it?'

'Thursday,' said Grace, happy to be able to contribute something to the conversation. 'It's seven fifteen a.m.'

'Is it? Interesting. And how is everything else going?'

'Not great,' admitted Stella.

First, she filled Betty in on the ongoing absence of Banecroft. As Betty listened, she tapped a finger against her lips.

'Hmmmm,' she said. 'That is a worry, but we broke the link with Simon. Theoretically, while we don't know exactly what they were doing to him or who was doing it, that should stop it. Given what was involved, though, it's possible Banecroft's lying low somewhere, processing it all. Nasty business.'

'I guess.'

Betty gave Stella an assessing look. 'Why do I think there's something else that you're not telling me?'

'Before I do, I'd like to remind you that I did sort of save your life.'

'Noted.'

'And while each member of this paper's staff is annoying in their own way, I really don't think we can afford to lose any more of them.'

And with that, Stella took Betty through the Dex Hex situation and the disappearance of Reggie and Ox. When she had finally finished speaking, Betty looked first at her and then at Grace.

'Why on earth didn't you tell me all this several days ago?' she asked.

'Because,' said Grace, 'you are the new scary assistant editor, sent here to shake things up. We assumed Ox pulling down a second salary was exactly the type of thing you would be looking for in your audit.'

'Audit? What audit?'

Grace leaned forward. 'Banecroft told me that you wanted to see the last ten years' worth of accounts.'

'Oh, that.' Betty laughed and waved Grace away. 'I just made that stuff up because I didn't want him to realize why I was really here.'

Grace's left eye began to twitch in the most alarming manner. 'What?'

Stella could see the plane heading straight for the mountain and decided to dive in and grab the controls in the hope it wasn't too late.

'OK, no need to talk about that now. Grace – I don't know about anybody else, but I'd love a cup of tea.'

Grace was still staring at Betty. Her lips were ashen.

'Or maybe you just stay here. Betty, do you mind stepping outside to the reception area with me for a minute?'

Betty gave her a confused look. 'Why would we—' she started.

Stella rushed over, grabbed Betty's arm and guided her towards the double doors. 'Now. Right now. Right this very instant.'

Once through the doors, she slammed them shut and leaned back against them.

'Have I said the wrong thing?' asked Betty mildly.

'You could say that.'

'What are all these boxes doing here?'

It said something that when Grace screamed, Betty had the common sense to look far more frightened than she had while being attacked by psychopathic fanged statues in a graveyard having just dug up a body.

★

Ten minutes later, Grace looked as if she had calmed down, at least relatively speaking. She was picking things up and putting them down with more force than necessary while muttering darkly under her breath, but it was still a definite improvement. The time to be worried was when she went deathly quiet. That was when you had to start subtly moving away anything and everything breakable with sentimental value – objects, pets, people.

Stella had given Betty a copy of the folder of Dex Hex columns, which she was now flicking through, making various harrumphing noises as she scanned them. Eventually, she held up one of them.

'Are you seriously telling me that this newspaper printed an article suggesting that dogs are aliens from another planet?'

'Yes,' said Stella.

'That is ridiculous. Cats? Maybe. It would explain their clear disregard for human life. But dogs?'

'Don't get bogged down in that. I need you to figure out which one of those theories might have got Tony Dawson and, we can now assume, Reggie and Ox kidnapped by the Founders.'

'Oh, that's easy,' said Betty. 'Not only that, I know exactly where to go to get them back.'

Stella and Grace shared a look, before Stella said, 'When were you going to tell us?'

'I hadn't finished reading all the articles,' said Betty. 'It would have been rude of me not to do so, after you went to all the trouble of putting them together.'

Grace shook her head in disbelief.

'Right,' continued Betty, 'where are the keys to Betty Two?'

Stella winced. 'I'm afraid she broke down.'

'Yes, she does that. There's a wonderful little fellow I can call to get her sorted out, but in the meantime, can anyone lend me a car?'

Stella looked at Grace, who shook her head firmly. 'Absolutely not.'

'Fair enough,' said Betty.

Grace stood up. 'I will drive you.'

'It might be dangerous.'

Stella was surprised when Grace marched towards the stairs. 'Good. Everybody else gets to go out and do these ridiculously dangerous things, whereas I remain stuck here looking for boxes, answering phones and making cups of tea. Enough is enough. Stella, stay here and hold the fort. Betty, come with me.'

Betty and Stella looked at each other in surprise as Grace strode down the stairs.

Betty leaped to her feet as Grace roared, 'Hurry up!'

CHAPTER 48

When Banecroft looked up he was shocked to see that it was somehow now morning. The dawn mist was clinging to the ground in a futile attempt to lengthen its stay under the light of the new day. He and Charlotte had talked all night. Talked and watched perfect renderings of their best memories together playing out across the surface of the water.

It had been truly magical, both joyous and torturous. Joyous because he was able to be back together with his precious Charlotte, the only woman he had ever loved. Torturous because he could not touch her.

There she was before him, rendered in exquisite detail, a living sculpture created entirely out of water. Every mannerism, every little quirk – the things you can never remember about someone but that you recognize on some deeper level when you see them.

It was her.

It really was her.

And yet he knew that if he were to reach forward and touch her, she would fall apart before his very eyes. What exquisite cruelty.

She looked across at him. 'Oh dear, somebody has got his thinking face on.'

'Sorry,' he said with a laugh.

'Any more of that, and I'll make you sit through my memory of that dinner with Peter and Jenny.'

'Do that and you'll have to fish me out of the water.'

She held out her arms. 'OK, but be warned – irony of ironies, I was never much of a swimmer.'

He nodded. That was true.

He looked away and then back again. 'This has been wonderful.'

'Yes,' Charlotte agreed, 'it has been. I've missed you so much.'

'And I you. I don't understand what this is, but as selfish as it sounds, this is not enough.'

She sat down cross-legged on the water and looked across at him. 'And this will not last for ever. They made that clear. This is only a stolen moment. Our last goodbye.'

Banecroft allowed his heavy eyelids to slip shut briefly and gave himself a moment. There was a weariness in his bones that no amount of sleep could ever ease, and his chest ached as if it might explode.

'I'm not ready to say goodbye.'

'Nobody ever is.'

Banecroft opened his eyes and scratched at his stubble irritably. 'I know you said not to ask questions, but I have to. Whoever is helping you do this; I need to speak to them. To see if there is a way.'

Charlotte's watery form leaned forward and pushed her hair out of her eyes in a way that melted his heart. 'What if I told you there was?'

His heart leaped. 'Really?'

'That's what they've told me. It won't be easy.'

'I don't care.'

'But if it works, we can be together for ever.'

'That's all I want,' cried Banecroft. 'All I've ever wanted.'

'And you will be helping her at the same time.'

Banecroft was confused. 'Helping who?'

'Wait until you hear.' She smiled. 'That's the best part.'

CHAPTER 49

On her third attempt, Grace reverse-parked into the only available space on Cambridge Street. She was happy with her final positioning, although a traffic warden might beg to differ.

'Finally,' said Betty.

'I am sorry, but parking in the city centre is very difficult at this time of the morning.'

'Let's go.' Betty opened the passenger-side door and almost took out a Lycra-clad cyclist in her haste. The guy was so busy concentrating on turning around to register his displeasure through the medium of sign language that he scraped against a parked car and decided to make a swift getaway rather than engage further.

'I just need to pay for parking.'

Betty was already striding down the pavement. 'No time. Just stay with the car.'

'I will not stay with the car,' said Grace firmly. 'I am fed up with being left behind.' She started to root around inside her bag. 'Oh no, I think I put my loose coins into the collection at church. Do you have any change on you?'

'No, I do not have change. More importantly, we are in the

middle of a dramatic rescue. You do not stop to pay for parking in the middle of a dramatic rescue.'

Grace slammed her bag shut and glowered at Betty. 'Fine. Sweet Lord forgive me. Let's go.'

Betty led them back up Cambridge Street and on to Whitworth Street West. When Betty slipped inside what looked like a newsagent's, Grace failed to conceal her surprise. The place was entirely empty save for an unusual-looking small man who was out on the shop floor stacking shelves. He resembled an ungifted child's drawing of a human brought to life. His legs were too short, his arms too long, his head too small and his neck was nowhere to be seen. He wasn't white but he also wasn't any other race either. He was a shade of brown not associated with any ethnic group or geographical area. People didn't question what he was because he walked and talked, and everyone knew that meant you were a human. At least, everyone who didn't know better.

'Are we stopping to get snacks?' asked Grace.

'No,' replied Betty, 'we are not stopping to get snacks. Having said that . . . Ooooh, wine gums.' She picked up a bag and placed them on the counter.

The man stacking shelves did an excellent job of ignoring them.

Betty lowered her voice. 'Do you notice anything unusual about this shop?'

'The service is appalling.'

'Anything else?'

Grace took a more considered look around. Having done so,

she could see that the place was indeed odd. All the shelves were stocked with just enough goods to give the appearance of being in use, but there were large empty spaces behind that first row of items that should be accommodating far more merchandise. Two four-packs of toilet roll sitting next to each other on a shelf that could hold twenty. Four Pot Noodles in a line with nothing behind them.

'It doesn't feel real. It is like someone has dressed it up as a set for a TV programme.'

Betty gave an appreciative nod. 'Good.'

'And there are two Sainsbury's, two Tesco and, I think, a SPAR all within a few minutes' walk of here. Why would anybody come to this shop?'

'That is precisely the point. They don't want you to come here. I'm sure some people walk in here and assume it's a money-laundering scheme, but it isn't.'

'What is it, then?'

In lieu of an answer, Betty raised her voice and shouted, 'Shop!'

The little man shot them a dirty look and continued slowly stacking boxes of teabags with the degree of care and attention normally reserved for brain surgery.

Betty dived her hand into her pocket and pulled out two pound coins. She slammed them on to the counter and held up the bag of wine gums. 'These are for the sweeties!' she bellowed.

'So you did have change for parking,' grumbled Grace.

'And,' continued Betty, 'I am going to need the key.'

The man didn't even look up. 'Toilets are for staff use only.'

'Not that key.'

He glanced over at them for only the second time. 'No idea what you're talking about.'

Betty sighed. 'Fine. Have it your way.'

She pocketed the packet of wine gums and, with one hand, took Grace by the arm. Then, she walked across the shop floor, calmly grabbed the little man by his collar and lifted him up with the other.

'Hey,' he yelped. 'You don't know who you're messing with.'

'Oh, I think I do.' And with that, Betty marched towards the back wall of the shop with the little man held out in front of her like a shield.

Grace braced herself as it seemed that her companion was about to run a man through a wall displaying a large poster that informed shoplifters they will be prosecuted. Just as the little man was about to make contact, the wall somehow dissolved and, before she could process what was happening, Grace was pulled through.

'My Lord,' she whispered, looking around her.

Ahead of them was a broad staircase leading downwards. Grace turned and observed the wall that, despite all recent evidence to the contrary, looked very much like a wall. She reached out and touched it tentatively. It was indeed a wall. She blessed herself.

Betty dropped the little man back on to his feet. He whirled round and jabbed an accusatory finger at her.

'There is going to be trouble,' he said in a high-pitched whine, before sprinting back through the wall that Grace had just re-assured herself was a wall.

'Right,' said Betty, waving a hand towards the stairs, 'let's go and find this trouble, then, shall we?'

The two women descended the stairs and found themselves in a large, well-lit tunnel that curved round to the right. Grace noticed a camera up on the wall that tracked them as they walked.

'I think somebody knows we are here.'

'I'm counting on it,' said Betty. 'Whatever happens, please stay right beside me.'

'What are you expecting to happen?'

The sound of running feet came at them from all directions.

'Pretty much this. Best put your hands up.'

Grace did as instructed as a band of figures in full combat gear and black masks seemed to appear from everywhere and sur-rounded them. Grace counted ten of them in total, all carrying some very serious-looking machine guns. Multiple voices bel-lowed at them to get down on the ground.

Grace attempted to comply, but Betty grabbed her elbow and held her up.

'We will remain standing, thank you kindly.' Her voice was firm, devoid of any panic.

Two of the storm troopers moved forward but then stopped dead. Their body language was that of confusion as they looked down at their feet, then at each other and finally back at their colleagues. They seemed unable to lift their boots off the floor.

Two more of the goons stepped forward and the same thing happened to them.

'Now,' said Betty, 'if we're all done shouting and waving our little guns about, I would like to speak to the woman in charge, please.'

CHAPTER 50

Stella had started to open cupboards at random. She was getting really annoyed now. The kitchen wasn't that big and it really shouldn't be this hard to find Grace's secret stash of biscuits. She was craving chocolate in the worst way. She had a vision in her mind of those biscuits where the chocolate coating was so thick you could spend ten whole glorious minutes carefully nibbling it off, bit by bit, before just scoffing the rest. And then moving on to the next one.

All she needed was a few minutes of peaceful indulgence. It had been a stressful week, and they hadn't even started assembling the paper yet. In all probability, today was going to be an absolute nightmare, and that was assuming everyone turned up. Oddly, she felt confident that Betty would take care of the Ox and Reggie situation. The woman was a force of nature, and Stella reckoned under that bumbling exterior might be one of the sharpest people she had ever met.

She bent down to check in the cupboard under the sink that was normally reserved for cleaning products. She was growing desperate.

'Hello.'

The voice was so unexpected that she jumped and walloped the back of her head against the underside of the sink.

'Damn it! Again!' said Stella. 'Right in the same bloody place as last time.' She turned around, her hand in her hair, massaging the bump, and saw Banecroft standing in the doorway.

'Sorry. I didn't mean to startle you.'

'Boss,' she said, getting to her feet. 'I . . . Don't worry about it. How are you?'

'I'm fine.'

There was definitely something different about him, but she couldn't put a finger on what that was. His eyes seemed brighter, his smile un-Banecroftianly wide, his skin drenched in sweat as if he'd been running.

'Great. Only — you have been AWOL for a few days. We were all worried about you.'

'Yes, sorry about that. I had a few things to sort out, but everything is fine now.'

She had never noticed before how vividly green his eyes were. He'd also used the word 'sorry', sincerely, twice now, breaking his previous record by three.

'Great. That's great to hear.' She stood there awkwardly for a moment, not really knowing what to say or do. Then, some deep-rooted and rather British instinct kicked in. She pointed at the kettle behind her. 'I was just going to make myself a brew. Would you like one?'

'Yes, please.'

And now a 'please' too. Somewhere in the back of her mind, a frightened chimp had got hold of an alarm bell and was going to town with it.

'Right.' She turned round and busied herself putting on the kettle and fishing out the requisite mugs, tea bags, sugar and milk. 'Ox and Reggie got themselves into a spot of bother, but Betty and Grace are off sorting it out right now. I'm sure everything will be fine.'

'Yes,' said Banecroft. 'Everything is finally going to be fine for us.'

Everything was off. Really off. Like when they changed the person doing the voice of Kermit the Frog and, suddenly, he became just some green felt, wires and a stranger's hand.

She thought again about Banecroft's green eyes. She was almost sure she'd never seen them like that. Before she could follow her train of thought any further, something foul-smelling was pressed over her mouth. She struggled, but was held still as her world jerked sickeningly out of focus.

Stella felt herself being lowered gently to the floor. The last thing she heard before she passed out was Banecroft saying, 'Don't worry. Everything is going to be fine.' His voice was soft. 'You're going to be cured.'

CHAPTER 51

Hannah stopped at the gates of *The Stranger Times* and looked up at the building basking in the early morning sunlight. The Church of Old Souls, as it had been known, was an imposing if ramshackle affair. Part of her realized that this momentous feeling was ridiculous; it was not some dramatic return. She had been gone for only a few weeks after having worked here for just a few months.

Still, given all that had happened, it was fair to say that the flow of time round here, like everything else, didn't work in the normal way. That, and the fact that, under instruction, she had walked out on her job with hardly a word to anyone. Yes, she had done so for good reasons – very good reasons, in fact, given what she now knew about the Banecrofts – but that didn't make her any less nervous about coming back.

With all the mess at the Pinter Institute yesterday, it had been late by the time she had returned to Manchester last night, having been dropped off by a black-eyed and surly Stanley. It had made little sense to head straight to the office, other than to give Banecroft the news she had been instructed to impart. Or maybe that was just how she was justifying to herself her delay in doing so. Certainly this morning, she felt no more prepared for the conversation than she had last night.

It wasn't as if she and Banecroft had ever spoken about Charlotte, but anyone who was around the man for an extended amount of time would realize that there was a deep wound there that had not healed. As it turned out, someone had actively prevented it from doing so. She wasn't looking forward to being the one to tell Banecroft about that, not when it would extinguish whatever candle of hope he still held on to.

She steeled herself and walked towards the entrance with purpose. As she entered, the doors to the printing room flew open and out stomped Manny. When he saw her, a big smile spread across his face. He extended his arms and pulled her into a bear hug.

'Hannah!'

'Manny,' she said, 'you're up early and you are wearing trousers.'

He released her and looked out the door. 'It early?'

'Yes.'

'And you back?'

Hannah nodded. 'I am back.'

'From de shops.'

'What? No. I've been gone for weeks.'

Manny's face scrunched up in concentration. 'Were dem shops closed?'

'No, I . . . I sort of left and now I have come back.'

He nodded. 'But ya not gone ta de shops?'

'No.'

He scratched at his dreadlocks with both hands. 'Who we send de shops, then?'

Hannah shrugged. 'I don't know.'

'We really hankerin' for some dem Pringles.'

'Sorry.'

He gave her another cheery grin. ''S all right. We happy ta see you.' And with that, he turned and headed back into his lair.

'Well,' said Hannah to herself as she looked up the stairs, 'let's hope everyone else is too.'

She found reception empty – of people, at least. It was positively overflowing with boxes. She moved into the bullpen, which she was also alarmed to find empty. It looked the same as it had always done, save for an inexplicable amount of what looked like builders' dust at the end of the room. She took a deep breath and knocked on Banecroft's door, only to find that his office was also deserted.

Now she really was beginning to worry. It was almost nine o'clock on a Thursday morning; normally the place would be a hive of frantic activity as articles were finished, edited, accepted, rejected, screamed about, cut down, bumped up or, in Ox's case, reworked until they were written in something commonly recognized as English. Finding the place like the *Mary Celeste* was unnerving.

In a small part of Hannah's mind, she even wondered if perhaps the new assistant editor was so good that they'd managed to sort everything out the night before. She swiftly rejected that idea. Even if that was the case, it wouldn't explain where Banecroft was. It wasn't as if he would have taken everybody out for ice-cream.

Stella. She would check Stella's room.

It was only when Hannah drew close to the base of the church steeple that she heard it. The unmistakable sound of weeping. She stopped in front of the makeshift door.

'Stella, it's Hannah. Is everything OK?'

She received no response, but the sound of crying continued. 'All right, I'm coming in.'

Hannah pulled back the sheet of plywood and stopped dead. Stella was nowhere to be seen, but hunched over the desk in the corner sat a transparent figure with his head buried in his arms.

'Simon?'

He turned and looked at her. It was the oddest of sensations, seeing the distress on his face at the same time as being able to see through him to the wall behind.

'Is everything OK?'

'No.' His voice trembled. 'Nothing is OK. He took her and I couldn't stop them. He's not right. I couldn't stop him. I couldn't do a thing.'

Hannah took a couple of steps forward, a sense of panic rising in her chest. 'Stella? Somebody took Stella?'

Simon gave a tearful nod.

'Who? Who did that?'

As he told her, Hannah's mouth dropped open in horror. Something was very wrong indeed.

CHAPTER 52

Grace shuffled her feet. Her fallen arches meant that while she could happily walk considerable distances, she found it decidedly uncomfortable to stand in the same place for any length of time. By her watch, she and Betty had been waiting in the middle of a large tunnel with ten machine guns pointed at them for a good twenty minutes.

'Do you think this will be much longer?'

Betty shrugged. 'Hard to say, really.' She took a couple of steps towards one of the storm troopers, which resulted in the business ends of ten machine guns tracking her movement. 'Oh, do calm down. Fair warning, if either you or any of your amigos attempts to shoot us, I shall become positively tetchy. Now, be a good chap or lady – that outfit is not flattering – and use whatever little radio you have to ask if the boss will be much longer.'

The figure didn't move. Admittedly, from what Grace could tell, they weren't able to move their feet because of something Betty had done, but the rest of him or her remained resolutely still too.

'Fine,' said Betty, 'but this will go in my Yelp review.'

She cocked her head. From somewhere in the distance came the unmistakable sound of a metal door being opened.

'Never mind.' She returned to stand beside Grace and proffered the bag of wine gums. 'Fancy another one?'

'No, thank you,' said Grace. 'Four is my absolute limit. I'm trying to watch my weight.'

'Aren't we all? I admire your resolve, though. I am an absolute demon for the sweeties.'

Over Betty's shoulder, Grace could see the woman she recognized as Dr Carter striding down the tunnel, flanked by four more storm troopers. Short, even in high heels, she still walked with the kind of authority that assured the world that everyone else was smaller than her in the ways that really mattered. Betty hummed a tune under her breath that Grace surprised herself by correctly identifying as 'The Imperial March' from *Star Wars*.

Dr Carter stopped at the edge of the circle of gunmen and gave a tight smile. 'Elizabeth.'

'Veronica,' Betty replied. 'How wonderful of you to make the time to see us. You know my colleague, Grace.'

'We have met briefly. While I am, of course, thrilled to see you, can I enquire about what you are doing? You do realize you are trespassing?'

'Of course, but not without reason. In violation of principles laid out in the Accord, vis-à-vis the neutrality and protection of, among other institutions, *The Stranger Times*, you have three of my journalists. I would like them back, please.'

'I'm afraid I have no idea what you're talking about.'

'Really?'

Dr Carter paused then looked around her. 'Perhaps we could discuss this in private?'

'Where would you like to go? I must admit, I have a rather busy morning planned.'

Dr Carter raised an eyebrow and darted her eyes at the surrounding storm troopers. 'No, I meant . . .'

'Oh, right,' said Betty.

She clicked her fingers and several of the storm troopers lost their balance, taken by surprise that their feet were no longer glued to the floor.

'Thank you. You may all fall back.'

One storm trooper paused and looked at Dr Carter.

'I'm sorry. Did I stutter?' she asked archly.

The storm trooper gave a brief bob of their head and, as one, they all pulled back to forty feet away. Once they were in position, Dr Carter moved closer to Betty, inclined her head and lowered her voice. 'And perhaps your colleague could also possibly take a little walk?'

Betty shook her head. 'No. Grace was keen to get out of the office and stretch her legs, so she shall stay here for the duration. Anything you would like to say to me, you can say in front of her.'

Dr Carter's eyes darted over to Grace and then back to Betty. 'Very well. May I ask how you found out about this place?'

Betty laughed. 'You can certainly ask.'

'Fine. I'm afraid your colleagues were trespassing, and the Accord does not protect them from matters covered by common law.'

'I see. So, you will be handing them over to the police?'

Dr Carter gave another tight smile. 'Eventually.'

Betty nodded. 'Fair enough. Thank you for your time.' She took a few steps back the way they had come and then stopped.

'Oh, by the way, in my new role as the assistant editor of *The Stranger Times*, I really shouldn't do this, but would you like a little preview of tomorrow's front page?' She drew her hand through the air as if laying out a headline. '*Massive secret facility found under central Manchester.* I mean, we're going to have to work that up into something snappier, obviously. It's my first week. I'm not a hundred per cent sure how these things work. Still, it should generate lots of interest, don't you think?'

'You wouldn't dare.'

'Wouldn't I?' said Betty, the lightness dropping from her tone. 'And don't for one second think I won't also be mentioning that the organization responsible is using this location because it thinks situating it under a high-population area makes it safer. Effectively using thousands of innocent people as a human shield.'

Dr Carter rolled her eyes. 'Oh, please. Spare me the moral superiority. Fine – you can have your staff back. The three of them are waiting down the tunnel. Although, interestingly, it appears two of them had never met the third one before now. Funny that.' She took a step towards Betty and lowered her voice. 'I do worry that focusing on nonsense like this is distracting you from more important tasks.'

Betty pursed her lips and took a long look at Dr Carter. 'It was you, wasn't it?'

'I don't know what you're talking about.'

'The tip-off. About Banecroft and . . . let us say, his issues.'

'The man has more issues than your esteemed publication has ever published, so you might need to narrow it down.' Dr Carter rolled out her irritating giggle. 'Still, a tip-off? That doesn't sound like something I would do.'

Betty raised her eyebrows and nodded. 'Well, regardless – that situation has been dealt with.'

'Has it? And you're entirely sure of that, are you?'

The two women looked at each other for a long while, and then Betty spun on her heel and started to walk away in a hurry. 'Grace, with me,' she shouted over her shoulder.

Grace had to run to catch up with her, past the storm troopers who were now stood in a line against the far wall, well out of their way.

'Is walking this fast necessary?'

'I'm afraid it is.'

As they rounded the corner, Grace was relieved to see a trio of men standing there, two of whom she recognized. She guessed the rather shell-shocked-looking third man was Tony Dawson. She hadn't seen him without a bag over his head.

'So, how have you found getting out of the office?' Betty asked her.

'Largely terrifying,' replied Grace.

Betty barked a laugh. 'Oh, Grace, I do enjoy you.'

'I am delighted to hear it as I fully expect you to pay for the parking ticket I will most certainly have been issued by now.'

CHAPTER 53

Hannah felt like screaming.

She had called everyone she could think of – Grace, Ox, Reggie, not to mention Stella and Banecroft, of course, and nobody had answered. Hell, she'd even tried to get in touch with DI Tom Sturgess. In fact, every one of her calls had gone straight to voicemail.

The irony wasn't lost on her that for the past few weeks voice-mail would have been all any of them would have got when they had tried to ring her. It was as if this were some sort of reverse nightmare. She wondered momentarily whether it all might be an elaborate practical joke to get her back, but there are some things you don't joke about.

She'd even attempted to ask Manny, for all the good that had done. He was confused by every one of her questions. He then tried to tell her about some kind of flying statue. When this was all over, they were going to have to have a serious talk about his 'glaucoma medicine'.

Not for the first time, Hannah wondered exactly how the guardian angel that lived within him worked. It seemed to excel at spotting certain kinds of dangers, but it had been powerless to stop the peculiar torture that had been inflicted on Banecroft. She tried not to think of Banecroft as a danger. He wasn't. What he was, was a terribly confused man – but it hadn't stopped him either. In any case, even if she figured out where to look, the guardian angel would prevent Manny from leaving the building, so she would still be entirely on her own. Admittedly, that thought was currently redundant, as she had no idea where to even start.

She stood in the middle of reception, desperately trying to come up with some course of action. Was there any point searching Banecroft's office? Stella's room? Going through whatever the hell was in all these boxes? She'd searched for Simon, but he was nowhere to be seen now. Ghosted by a ghost.

Hannah's heart leaped as she heard heavy footsteps below. A man's intimidatingly fierce bellow reached her before he did.

'Banecroft! I want a word.'

When the man appeared at the top of the stairs, Hannah realized that, if anything, the voice had undersold him. He was so tall that he had to crouch down to get through the door. His salt-and-pepper beard was the same length as his hair, which reached all the way down his back, and his tattoos, snaking out from under the dark vest he wore, covered every inch of his arms and torso. He looked like a man capable of throwing a car over a ditch if you were to annoy him. One look at his angry face was worth a thousand no parking signs.

He glanced at Hannah then scanned the room. 'Where the hell is he?'

'Not here,' she said firmly, trying to sound more in control than she felt.

'You wouldn't be lying to me, would you?'

'No. By any chance, are you John Mór?'

He gave her another look. 'I might be.'

Hannah folded her arms and glared at him. After a moment, he looked away, suddenly a little sheepish. 'Yes. Sorry.'

'I'm Hannah Willis, the assistant editor. While I've heard a lot about you from the others, we haven't met before. Now, please tell me why you're here?'

John Mór straightened up. 'I'd rather discuss that with Banecroft.' He made to take a step around her, but Hannah blocked his path.

'And I told you he is not here. I need to find him, because I guarantee whatever you think is important, what I am dealing with is far more critical, so stop being such a bloody man and tell me why you're here.'

John Mór took a step backwards and looked down at Hannah again. He considered her for a moment then spoke in a calmer tone of voice. 'Yesterday, he went to see poor Yvonne Braithwaite in Stockport, and literally forced her into doing a séance for him. Something that is exceptionally unnatural. She hurt herself doing it. Her Alan called me this morning and I've come straight from there. The poor woman is in bits. What the hell is he playing at?'

'Oh God,' said Hannah, more to herself than anyone else. 'The bloody fool. He found another way.'

'What does that mean?'

'Never mind. I am sorry to hear about your friend, but a lot is going on here that you don't understand. All you need to know is — Banecroft is not himself. Somebody got to him. He's taken Stella and I need to find them both, fast, before something far worse happens.'

'You've lost me.'

'And I'm afraid I don't have the time to explain it all now. Did this woman . . .'

'Yvonne.'

'Yvonne,' repeated Hannah, 'say anything about what happened during this séance or whatever it was?'

John Mór paused.

'Look, if I'm full of crap, you can come back later and just revert to your plan A, which, I assume, was walloping Banecroft. But right now, I need you to get on board with the fact that I might not be lying, and if I am not, this is literally a life-and-death situation. Now, what did they say?'

John Mór stretched his neck and looked around, seemingly coming to a decision. 'All right. She mentioned that there were three words.' He started patting his pockets. 'They made little sense to me, so I wrote them down. I've got them here somewhere.' He pulled a torn piece of notepaper out of his back pocket. 'This is them. Flesh. Loves. Enter.'

'You're sure?' said Hannah, taking out her phone.

Three words. Three words. Three words. It had to be. She'd edited the stupid bloody article about the app and the man's claim of persecution for the supposedly unfounded rumour concerning his love of trout.

'That's what she said,' confirmed the big man.

Hannah had downloaded the app to check the story, so swiftly tapped it open and typed in the words. After a couple of seconds, it showed a location.

'Where's Swinton?' she asked hurriedly.

'Not far. It's over near Worsley.'

'It has to be that,' she said, more to herself. She looked up at John Mór. 'Have you got a car?'

'Jeep.'

Hannah pushed him back towards the stairs. 'Come on, then. You're driving.'

'All right. But you'll explain on the way?'

'You'd better be a fast enough driver that I don't have time to.'

CHAPTER 54

Almost there.

They were almost there now.

Stella didn't weigh much really, but moving her unconscious form all the way from the car back to Charlotte at the lake was still a bit of a hike. As Banecroft struggled on, carrying her in an awkward version of a fireman's lift, he kept repeating the same words over and over. 'It's OK. Everything is going to be great. Charlotte will be back. You will be cured.'

That was how she had put it. *Cured*. It was all so simple. It would take away the burden that Stella hated, while providing the power to set Charlotte free.

They were through the fence now and, in the distance, he could see the water glimmering in the sunlight. Soon, all of this would be over and they would be together.

He stumbled as he made his way across the fairway, but regained his footing. His legs were aching, but the rest of him was awash with a feeling of ecstasy. When he got within thirty yards of the water, he sensed a change in the air's texture. It was as if he was pushing through an invisible membrane. Then, there she was, standing in the middle of the lake, sculpted to perfection from the water, beckoning him. Charlotte. His Charlotte.

Banecroft staggered forward and laid Stella down on the grass bank. His fingers gently brushed her hair away from her forehead as she mumbled something.

'Don't worry,' he responded. 'This will all be over soon. You will be cured.'

Charlotte moved closer to him. 'Vincent, darling – you've done so well. Now, you must wrap her in the bindings.'

He looked around to see what she meant. There, on the bank, was a neatly folded pile of white linen. He started wrapping Stella's body.

★

Hannah already had her door open as John Mór pulled his jeep in behind the Jag parked up outside the school.

'That's Banecroft's car,' she shouted.

A man in a hi-vis jacket came running out of the school gates. 'Whoa, whoa, whoa!' he hollered. 'You cannot park here.'

Hannah disappeared around the side of the building while John Mór looked at the jeep, looked at the man and tossed him the keys. As he set off after Hannah, the incredulous shout of the man followed behind them. 'It's not valet parking, fella!'

★

Banecroft had finished binding Stella. He'd been gentle. He'd tied her legs together, but her arms were still free to move around. And now her whole body was covered except for her face. She looked like a sleeping Egyptian mummy.

'Wonderful,' said Charlotte, drifting beside him on the water, the afternoon sun visible through her liquid form. 'Lower her in now. Carefully.'

Banecroft did as instructed, picking up Stella and pushing her tenderly into the pond's waters. It felt as if it was helping, cradling her as it took possession.

'And you're absolutely sure—' started Banecroft.

'It is done.' Charlotte turned around abruptly and cut him off in a voice that didn't sound right.

Then, with a splash, the figure disappeared. Somewhere deep inside Banecroft an unsettled feeling grew. No, everything was OK. Everything was—

Startled by the sound of someone clapping behind him, he spun around to see three figures walking towards him. Where had they come from? Two of them he recognized. One was Tamsin Baladin, who only a few days ago had been sitting across from him in his office. Her expression was hard to read, resolutely stony-faced.

The second member of the trio was a man he had seen only once before. He did not know his name, but he was freakishly tall – nearly seven feet – completely bald, and had a distinctive hooked nose. He wore a suit that wouldn't be out of place on a funeral director, and the last and only time Banecroft had seen him, he'd been pushing a wheelchair in which a sickly teenage boy had been seated.

In the middle of the trio, in stark contrast to the sombre

demeanour of his colleagues, strode a middle-aged man whose long, flowing blonde hair matched his Californian tan. Dressed in a white linen shirt and cream slacks, he was the one doing the clapping, while favouring Banecroft with a wide, white-toothed grin.

'Vincent Banecroft in the flesh.' His accent went with the tan. 'Dominic Johnson of the Beverly Hills Johnsons.' He patted his own chest. 'Charmed, I'm sure. This truly is an honour. So nice to finally meet you. I mean, I've been playing around in there' – he tapped his index finger against his forehead – 'for quite some time, but nothing beats in person, don't you think?'

Banecroft couldn't think. Couldn't breathe. It was as if cold deathly hands had gripped his throat. He stood there looking at them blankly, his brain unable to process what was happening. Gone completely were the feelings of joy and elation, only to be replaced with . . . nothing. He was empty. A massive wave of exhaustion rippled through his body and his legs buckled.

'Uh-uh,' said Johnson, with an admonishing shake of his head. He made some gestures with his left hand and a flurry of roots tore out of the ground, wrapped themselves around Banecroft's entire body and held him in a standing position. 'Don't you wuss out on me now. I need you fully awake and here for the whole thing, Vinnie. I put an awful lot of work into this, and I want you to really appreciate it. Speaking of which . . .'

The man was standing in front of Banecroft now, his TV-perfect grin and unblemished skin filling Banecroft's field of vision. He placed his hands on either side of Banecroft's head and looked into his eyes. Banecroft saw the fires of his own personal hell burning brightly there.

'How about, to use a biblical metaphor, we remove those scales from your eyes?'

Banecroft clenched his eyes shut and screeched at the sky as a shuddering jolt of white-hot pain coursed through his whole being. It was as if every molecule of his body was being ripped asunder. It ceased as quickly as it had started as Johnson's hands fell away.

Johnson's breath was warm on his face as the man laughed giddily. 'If you thought that was torture, wait until you see what's coming next.'

It was then that reality came brutally crashing in on Banecroft from all sides. His eyes flew open. The man's tanned face was now a matter of inches from his.

'Oh God,' he groaned. 'Stella.'

Johnson turned round and spoke excitedly to his colleagues. 'Oh, yes! I swear I saw the exact moment in his eyes when it hit. It's the little things that make it all worthwhile.'

'Oh Jesus,' said Banecroft. 'Please don't—' He was silenced as the roots wrapped themselves across his mouth.

'That's enough talk from you for a little while, I think.' The jovial tone had vanished from Johnson's voice. In its place was an unmistakable growl of hatred. 'There will be plenty of time for futile begging and pleading later. First, though, if you'll permit me, I'd like to remind you of how we got here. I appreciate you might be a little bewildered.'

Johnson pulled a photograph from his pocket and held it in front of Banecroft's face. He blinked to clear some of the tears. A teenage boy beamed a cheeky grin at the camera.

'This is my son, Daniel,' Johnson explained. 'Do you recognize him? Admittedly, he looked a little different when you met. By then, the cancer had really ravaged his body. I had to go to great lengths to find a way of saving him because thanks to this pathetic peace deal, I'm not supposed to have children. I am a Founder – the apex – and yet they have decreed to neuter me. How unnatural is that?

'Still, despite the obstacles, I did find a way to save him. My boy, my sweet innocent boy, would have lived for ever if you'd have only let that Moretti fool complete the procedure and make him a Founder. But no, you had to intervene.'

Johnson pulled the picture away, and his face appeared before Banecroft again.

'On that day, in that shitty warehouse, you signed his death warrant. And your own.'

Flecks of spittle now rested on Johnson's lower lip and in the corner of his mouth. His voice was strained and, as he worked himself into a frenzy, his restraint was visibly deteriorating.

'And yes, for him to live others would have had to die. Guess what? That's the same for everybody in some way or another. Nobody wants to admit it, but there's only so much to go around, and you get what you take. And what you took' – they were eyeball to eyeball now and Banecroft could feel Johnson's hatred like a physical presence scorching his skin – 'was . . . my . . . son.'

After a moment, Johnson pulled himself away and stood back, as if to concentrate on regaining his composure.

'Now, obviously in this situation, as a loving parent, I have the right, nay the duty, of revenge. The problem is, of course, that there really isn't a like for like here, is there? You don't have any kids and your beloved wife is already dead. As luck would have it, though' – he waved a hand at the freakishly tall man – 'Xander here is terribly resourceful and found a solution. You see, wifey dear got caught up in a little self-improvement scheme and when she died, she left a little bit of herself behind. A remnant is what they call it. Not enough to live, but more than enough to mess with you.'

As he spoke, Johnson took a small bottle of what looked like hand sanitizer out of his pocket, squeezed out a small amount and proceeded to clean his hands.

'Ever heard of sirens, Vincent? I don't mean the nee-naw-nee-naw-here-come-the-feds type. I mean the ones who supposedly lured sailors to their deaths with their songs? Or so the myths would have it. Thing is, that isn't really how it works. What they do is feed on memories. In the old days, they'd sneak on to ships and steal memories, then use those memories to lure the sailors on to the rocks. You know what they say – nostalgia is more addictive than crack.'

Johnson reached up and clapped Xander on the back. The tall man looked extremely uncomfortable.

'We didn't need to steal yours, though,' Johnson continued. 'Not to brag, but we sorta broke new ground here, with how we got inside that head of yours. I put all my considerable powers into making this happen – to get you right here, right now.'

He stepped back and gestured towards Stella, who was still floating on the surface of the water.

'Xander doesn't know exactly what your friend is, but that nut job Moretti reckoned she was something special. This little pond here – we've made it something special too.' He leaned in again, so his face was back in front of Banecroft's. 'It's going to allow me to drain every drop of power out of your little protégée. Oh, and the cure? It will kill her' – he moved in to Banecroft's ear and spoke softly – 'but only after the most indescribable, excruciating pain. And you will get to watch every . . . last . . . second.'

He slapped Banecroft playfully on the cheek. 'So, what do you say? Shall we get going?'

Xander stepped forward into Banecroft's eyeline and Banecroft could see that he was holding a large glass jar half full of a brown liquid. 'Sir?'

'Oh, of course,' said Johnson cheerfully. 'We should get our little siren friend out of there first.'

Xander stepped over to the water's edge, squatted down and opened the jar. A guttural noise left his mouth and, moments later, something inky black and eel-like leaped out of the pond and into the jar.

'Yes,' said Johnson. 'Not as attractive in their proper form, are they?'

Banecroft stood there, bound tightly by the roots and trapped in a hell of his own making. His mind raced, desperate for any chance to stop this, but there was nothing.

Xander stepped away and Johnson took his place beside Banecroft. He closed his eyes, dipped his head and stretched out his arms. For several seconds it seemed as if nothing was happening, then Banecroft caught sight of a tiny flash of golden light zipping across the water. Then there was another. And another.

More and more. Like fish being drawn into a frenzy after a scattering of bait.

Suddenly, Johnson held out his right arm and a swirling fount of gold surged from the water and into his hand. He turned to Banecroft, an ecstatic look on his face. 'Oh my, what is this? So much more than I could have hoped for!'

Then Stella's eyes opened, and she screamed.

CHAPTER 55

Hannah completed a three hundred and sixty-degree turn on the spot. There was no sign of Banecroft, Stella, or anything else out of the ordinary.

'I don't get it.'

John Mór bent over beside her, his hands on his knees, and panted heavily. He clearly wasn't a fan of cardio. 'Where exactly is that map thing telling you to go?'

Hannah waved her hand around. 'Here. Well, technically, over by that pond, but there's nothing and nobody there. We can't be in the wrong place. We saw Banecroft's car.'

A cheerful-looking man in shorts and a T-shirt was walking near by with his two dogs: one a sleek mix of lurcher and greyhound, the other a lumbering Labrador. As he strolled by, he used a chucker to throw a tennis ball for the lurcher mix to chase, while the Lab sauntered behind him, happily destroying a football he had found somewhere.

'Excuse me, sir,' said Hannah. 'By any chance have you noticed anything unusual around here?'

The man picked up the tennis ball, threw it as far as he could and the lurcher mix tore after it. 'Actually, now that you mention it, I have.'

'What exactly?'

The dog brought the ball back. It was dropped, picked up and thrown again.

'Up the far end of the course, there is a lake where migrating ducks stop and have their babies . . .'

The ball came back. Dropped. Picked up. Thrown.

'Someone has put up a sign saying, "Fuck the ducks". I mean, who has a problem with ducks?'

The ball came back. Dropped. Picked up. Thrown.

'And who has the time to waste putting up that kind of sign?'

The ball came back. Dropped. Picked up. Thrown.

'And who is it for? The ducks can't read it.'

The ball came back. Dropped. Picked up. Thrown.

Hannah was about to attempt to redirect him, but John Mór jumped in, placed a hand on her arm and said, 'Thanks. You've been a big help.'

'No worries,' said the man, walking away. 'Come on, Archie. Come on, Hudson. With me.'

'I was going to . . .' started Hannah, but stopped when she saw the excited look on John Mór's face. 'What?'

'The ball,' he said. 'You weren't watching the ball. The fella threw it that way.' He pointed towards the pond. Then his arm rotated about thirty degrees to the left. 'But it ended up over there.'

'I see,' said Hannah, who really didn't.

'Practitioners. Powerful practitioners can do this thing where they create a shield around an area where you can't see or hear what's happening inside it and it deflects things away from it. Physical objects don't pass through, and people, if they try to walk towards it, end up going around it without even realizing.'

Hannah pointed at the pond. 'Are you telling me there's something there that we are not seeing?'

'Exactly.'

'So how do we get in there?'

John Mór grabbed her hand. 'It doesn't work as well if you know it's there. Keep your eyes fixed on the pond and keep walking towards it.'

The two of them did just that, moving at a slow, steady pace. Hannah felt nothing at first and then . . . Yes, there it was. She met some resistance. It was as if the air was thicker somehow.

'That's the barrier,' whispered John Mór beside her. 'Keep going.'

Hannah felt a little queasy but kept walking forwards. A strange sensation came over her, as if her whole body popped instead of just her ears. And then they were through.

She gasped as John Mór pulled her quickly to the ground.

'What the . . .'

'We need to stay low,' hissed the big man. 'Jesus, what in the hell is going on here?'

Hannah looked. And shook her head in disbelief. Ahead of them, three people were standing near to the water's edge. One, a blonde man, was holding out his arms as what appeared to be a river of golden light flowed from the surface of the water to him. The very air around them seemed to hum, and Hannah could feel the hairs on the back of her neck standing on end. A weird tangle of roots looked to have sprung up from the ground beside the man.

As she took in the other two individuals present, her heart sank. One of them was Tamsin Baladin, which was just puzzling, but the other – the tall, bald man . . .

'Oh God.'

'What?' John Mór looked at her.

'I've seen the giant before. He was with the boy when that thing happened a few months ago. When we stopped that Moretti guy from—' Hannah's heart leaped into her mouth. 'Those roots . . .'

'Ye gods. That's Banecroft!' finished John Mór.

'Which means . . .' Hannah scanned the water, desperate for it not to be true. But then she saw her. 'Oh no.' Dread filled her. She pulled at John Mór's arm. 'Look! There, in the water . . . That's Stella.'

John Mór grunted and drew himself into a crouched position. He reached down and pulled an odd-looking dagger from each of his boots. 'I'll loop around the back. Try to take them by surprise.'

'Will that work?'

'Someone that powerful?' He nodded in the direction of the blonde-haired man. 'It had better work because nothing else will.'

'I had to ask. What should I do?'

John Mór shrugged. 'Plans are over-rated. Something will come to you.'

★

Tamsin Baladin didn't know what to make of all of this. Johnson's plan, given what was now happening, had undeniably worked. By severing the link with Simon Brush, that Betty woman had nearly ruined the whole thing but, irony of ironies, their secret weapon had turned out to be Banecroft himself. His stubborn determination meant he had offered them a new way in just when the old one had gone.

Still, the need for such vengeance was performative and inefficient. If the goal was just to get rid of Banecroft, that could easily have been done. If it had been getting the girl, similarly, there were far easier ways. Now, here they were in broad daylight, carrying out this crazy ritual.

The odd thing about it was that for all the power the Founders possessed individually, they were notoriously paranoid about being exposed like this. They were immortal, not invincible. They could live for ever, but they could also be killed, and from the little Dr Carter had given her by way of explanation, their deaths were not like that of normal people. She'd made some reference to each of them knowing with certainty that they would burn for eternity in a very real hell should they die. It was probably hyperbole, but even so, if there was a sliver of truth to it, all of this – she looked at Johnson – was sheer vanity.

As the American drew power from the girl, he kept whooping and hollering with joy. They had not known what she was, but apparently, whatever the answer was to that question, it was good news. Johnson was undeniably powerful, but his right-hand man, Xander, might prove more useful in the long run. Still, Tamsin had helped to make all of this happen, and that would surely raise her standing, which was the whole point after all: to get her to where she wanted to be in the shortest time imaginable.

She caught a flash of movement out of the corner of her eye, spun around and yelped. A massive, tattooed man, holding vicious-looking blades about his head in each hand, was charging straight for Johnson. The man himself, all his attention focused on the pond, seemed oblivious, but Xander had kept his wits about him. As the tattooed man leaped, Xander threw out his hands and held the attacker frozen in mid-air a few feet behind Johnson.

'Sire,' he said, the strain visible on his face.

No response.

'Sire,' he repeated more loudly.

Johnson, eyes wide, his face a picture of euphoria as the power flowed through him, shook his head. 'Not. Now.'

'Sire, we are under attack.'

This got Johnson's attention. He looked around. 'Who in the hell?'

The big tattooed man, held motionless mid-strike, with no other option, smiled. 'Welcome to Manchester.'

Before anyone could say anything else, there came a further distraction in the form of a splash. Tamsin turned to see a woman, that wretched ex-assistant editor of *The Stranger Times*, had thrown herself into the water. Her face now contorted into a rictus of agony.

'Get her out of there,' roared Johnson.

'I can't, sire,' said Xander. 'Not without releasing . . .' He looked back at the large, tattooed man. 'Can't you . . .'

'I cannot sever the connection while the girl is still alive.'

Tamsin felt that golden gaze of his fall on her.

'Baladin – get in there.'

★

It was as if she had been electrocuted, only the sensation was continuous. Hannah felt her mouth fill with blood from where she had bitten her tongue. The pond was shallow – the water only came up to her waist – but her lower half was spasming from the energy flowing through it. She did not know what had made her do it, but it had been the only thing that had gone through her mind. When in doubt, jump right in.

Stella lay floating in the water about ten feet away from her.

Hannah took a step towards her bound figure. The pain was excruciating.

She knew she must focus on Stella and took another step.

★

Tamsin looked at the water and then back at Johnson, who was staring at her with those mad eyes.

'Do it. Now,' he roared.

Out of the pocket of her jacket she pulled the flick knife she had carried since she was sixteen years old, took a few steps back to give herself a run-up, sprinted and launched herself into the water. She had been a long-jumper in school, but her form on landing was poor. As her legs hit the water, her body jerked wildly as the pain coursed through it.

*

Another step. *Focus*. Every inch further put more of her body in the water and her agony increased. Hannah had to hope against hope that she wouldn't pass out from the pain. *Focus*.

*

Knowing that failure meant death, Tamsin regathered herself and waded forward. She was only a few feet behind Hannah now. Her trembling hand held the blade out in front of her.

*

Nearly there. Hannah took another step. Her eyes were streaming with tears. *One. More. Step*.

*

Tamsin jabbed the blade forward. Just too short, but closer. Ever closer.

*

Hannah felt something in the water in front of her. Stella's hand. She grabbed it and pulled it towards her. Then Stella was in her arms. Her body was encased in some kind of binding. She looked down into Stella's face, her younger colleague's eyes open but staring into nothing, her mouth wide in a perpetual silent scream.

'Stella. It's me – Hannah. You've got to fight this. Please. Fight. You must—'

Hannah cried out in agony as she felt something sharp jab into the side of her neck. She grabbed Stella tighter as she felt herself begin to fall; the pain was winning, was overwhelming her. The last thing she saw before she lost consciousness seemed to be someone's blood – she couldn't quite work out whose – mingling with the water.

★

Tamsin turned to Johnson and yelled, 'I got her. I'm coming . . . out.' The pain was excruciating. And then, suddenly, it stopped.

She looked back to where the others were standing. The golden river of light running from the water to Johnson had become a trickle, and his face had transformed. His mouth and eyes were wide in disbelief.

'This . . . No. This is impossible.'

The roots holding Banecroft up fell away, and he crumpled to the ground.

Light of a different hue flickered from behind Tamsin, and she turned and gasped.

The girl, Stella, was standing in the middle of the pond, her eyes glowing bright blue. She looked around her and then down at the water, which was now red with Hannah's blood. And then she fixed her eyes on Johnson.

The voice that came next was not a single voice. It sounded

like a thousand-strong legion chanting in unison. 'You want what I have . . .'

Tamsin was dimly aware of Xander running in one direction, and the large, tattooed man running in the other, dragging a dazed-looking Banecroft away with him.

That left Johnson standing alone. His face became a mask of terror as, suddenly, the golden light started to flow back in the opposite direction, drawing him towards the water's edge as it did so. As Tamsin looked on, his face grew gaunt, and he seemed to shrivel before her eyes as he stumbled to his knees. He began to age impossibly fast, like one of those stop-motion animations brought to life.

As he fell, Stella rose and rose, until she hung in the air above the pond.

'. . . And you can take it,' she cried, throwing out her arms. 'Take all of it.'

The stream of gold stopped abruptly, and then, like a building collapsing or a devastating avalanche, a wave of blue light ripped out of the girl. It didn't hit Johnson so much as eviscerate him.

The shockwave flung Tamsin out of the water and towards the bank, which she hit with a sickening crack as a bone in her arm broke.

And then she ran. Ran for all she was worth and did not look back.

Hannah came to, with the concerned faces of Stella and John Mór peering over her.

'There she is,' said John Mór in a kind voice.

Stella touched Hannah's face: 'Are you OK?'

'Am I OK? Are you . . . Wait, what the hell happened?'

'You've got a stab wound at the top of your shoulder, back of the neck,' said John Mór. 'Nothing too serious. Not to worry you, but an inch to the right and it would've been the jugular and . . . Well, it wasn't that. I've stopped the bleeding, but you're going to need stitches.'

'Right,' said Hannah, sitting up. 'I meant . . .'

She trailed off as she took in her surroundings. There in front of her was an enormous trench carved out of the landscape. It was as if a massive digger had ripped through it, destroying earth, rocks, trees – everything in its path – and left behind a long smoking fissure fifty metres in width and a couple of hundred metres long.

'Yeah,' admitted John Mór. 'Things got a little intense.'

Hannah looked back up at Stella, whose expression lay somewhere between terrified and embarrassed. She was just a teenage kid who had no idea how to explain what had just happened.

A thought struck Hannah and she looked around. 'Banecroft. Where is . . .'

John Mór moved and pointed to where Banecroft was sitting under a tree, staring at the ground. 'If anything, he is more confused than the rest of us.'

Hannah nodded. 'Well, we should probably get everybody back to the office. After all, we have a newspaper due out tomorrow.'

CHAPTER 56

Banecroft sat on the decrepit sun lounger that someone had left on the roof of the offices of *The Stranger Times* and watched the sunset. It was beautiful if you were into that kind of thing. He was not in the mood for beauty, though. He reached down for the bottle of whiskey that was by his side, picked it up and then remembered it was empty.

'Presumably,' said Hannah, appearing from the door behind him, 'now that the well has run dry, you might finally come back downstairs.'

'I suppose I will have to, eventually.'

Hannah perched against one of the stone bollards. 'You've been up here all day. By the way, we are still nipping and tucking but it looks like we're putting out a newspaper tomorrow, no thanks to you.'

He gave her a look.

'Yeah,' said Hannah, 'I had a think about it, and I decided you are much more likely to respond to a kick up the arse than a pat on the shoulder.'

'I thought you didn't work here any more?'

She peered over the edge of the roof. 'Actually, I do. Before she left, Betty's second-last act as assistant editor was to rehire me as her replacement.'

'Do I want to know what the last act was?'

'She took your blunderbuss. She said she's getting it cleaned and serviced, and then she'll send it back to you.'

'That is a violation. Admittedly, not the worst one I've suffered of late, but a violation nonetheless. I cannot stand that woman.'

'Really?' said Hannah with a smile. 'She speaks highly of you.'

'So where did you disappear to?'

'Mrs Harnforth had me investigating the Pinter Institute.'

'That new-age, mumbo-jumbo crapshoot run by that wacky actress woman?'

'Yes, although it turned out she wasn't really the one in charge.'

'Why was that kind of place of interest to Mrs Harnforth? And why was she getting you to go behind my back to investigate it?'

Hannah paused, turned away for a few seconds, then looked back. 'Charlotte had gone there.'

'No, she definitely . . .' Banecroft stopped himself. 'Well, I guess I didn't know my wife as well as I thought I did. I'm sure she had her reasons for keeping it private.'

Banecroft listened in silence as Hannah took him through exactly what had been going on at the Pinter Institute. When she'd finished, he sat there for a long time before saying so quietly she could barely hear him, 'So it was this remnant, a little piece of Charlotte, that they got hold of and used against me?'

Hannah nodded. 'The good news is all of that is over now.'

His voice became a whisper. 'And she really is dead.'

'I'm sorry. For what it's worth, from the explanation I got from Mrs H, she'll be at peace now. Or, you know, whole.'

Banecroft nodded.

'So, it's time for you to come back downstairs.'

Banecroft hung his head. 'I wouldn't know what to say to them.'

'Just go with the greatest hits,' said Hannah. 'Admonish Ox for his terrible spelling. Tell Reggie to hurry up and get to the point.'

His voice faltered. 'And Stella?'

'What Stella needs right now more than anything is an editor. She seems pretty determined to get better at this journalism lark and I don't think any of the rest of us are up to teaching her now, do you?'

'I did the worst thing imaginable to the poor girl.'

'No,' said Hannah firmly, 'you didn't. They did. You weren't you. She knows that better than anyone.'

'That's the thing, though – I was me. A desperate, stupid, blinded version of me, but me nonetheless. I don't think I can be here any more.'

'Crap. Total crap.'

Banecroft turned to Hannah and raised an eyebrow.

'You think you're the only person round here who's broken?' she asked. 'Look around – we all are. I just got off an excruciating phone call with a certain detective inspector in the Greater Manchester Police, explaining how I haven't gone back to my husband. He, in turn, seemed confused about what day it was – possibly because of that eyeball thing living in his head, which, if we tell him about it, will kill him stone dead.

'Before that, I rang my soon-to-be ex-husband who, I'm relieved to say, has resumed trying to strong-arm me into not taking what I'm entitled to from our divorce, which means he's back to being his normal self – aka a monumental arsehole – which, incredibly, is better than the alternative.'

Hannah took a deep breath. 'My point is, as messed up as it might sound, right here is exactly where you need to be and, even harder to believe, we need you.' She pointed off into the distance. 'Do you seriously think there aren't going to be ramifications to what happened today? Stella killed a Founder and, while we can plead self-defence, I have no idea how they will respond to that. Is it even safe for her to be here any more? Whatever else she is, Stella is first and foremost a scared kid who doesn't understand what is happening to her and why, and she needs to be protected.

'You want to make it up to her? Fine. Then that's what you do. I don't care if you feel like doing it or not, or if you have any idea where to start, it's fake-it-until-you-make-it time. You think you owe her an apology – damn right you do, but words aren't going to cut it. This demands actions, and I don't mean running away or falling on your sword. You've taken one hell of a kicking, and some very low blows to boot. Now, at the risk of using every fighting metaphor I know in one go, get your arse up off the mat and get back in there.'

'Are you done?'

'No,' said Hannah, standing up. 'Here's your report. Seeing as Ox and Reggie apparently spent most of the week either distracted or kidnapped—'

'How did—'

'Doesn't matter. It happened and we found ourselves seriously short on articles. Luckily, circumstances have helped us out there. I don't know if you've heard, but earlier today a meteor hit an abandoned golf course over in Swinton. The authorities, and I think we know who they really are in the circumstances, have closed off the entire area. As it happens, we have exclusive photographs of the impact site. They were only taken on John Mór's mobile phone but they're still impressive, if I do say so myself. So that's pages one, two and three sorted. Also, the mysterious Dex Hex who used to write a column for this newspaper has sadly passed away—'

'Really?'

'No. Although, in a way, yes. There was a bloke pretending to be him, but he's now back with his sister and he seems awfully keen to get out of the conspiracy business entirely. Anyway, as a tribute to the late great Dex Hex, we're doing a four-page special and reprinting all the bizarre theories he proposed over the years. It isn't technically news, but it is an entertaining read.'

Banecroft couldn't help himself. 'That will still leave us pretty short.'

'Ah, but that brings us to our other exclusive. We have a three-page interview with a ghost, written by our own junior reporter.'

'Is that . . .'

'Simon? Yes. Stella did a great job of interviewing him. By the way, you know how Stella has told us very little about her past? It turns out we probably need to ask more questions. Like, for example, are you aware the kid has no second name? She's down there right now, trying to come up with one. I was going to give her the byline for that article, but she said it should have Simon's name on it. Which brings me all the way back to my original point. You need to get your arse downstairs now.'

Banecroft clambered to his feet messily and gave a jaunty mock salute. 'Aye, aye, assistant captain.'

'Excellent,' said Hannah, turning on her heel and heading back towards the fire exit. 'Trust the process.'

'What?'

'Nothing. Come on.'

CHAPTER 57

Grace finished lighting the candles around the desk, Reggie burned a bit of incense and Ox produced a foil container of curry from the Tandoori Palace – it had been Simon's favourite take-away, apparently. As far as Hannah was aware, none of this was necessary, but everyone had felt like they wanted to do something. Even Manny had come up and whispered a few words before taking a seat in the corner.

When all that was done, Stella laid out a copy of that week's *The Stranger Times*, hot off the press, and opened it to the pages that featured Simon's exclusive interview. That done, she retreated and sat back on the far side of the room with the rest of them in line: Manny, Ox, Banecroft, Reggie, Hannah, Stella and Grace.

Reggie leaned over to Hannah and whispered, 'Are we sure this is going to work?'

She glanced at Stella, whose eyes were set resolutely forward, and then gave a brief nod. And so, for the first time ever, the staff of *The Stranger Times* all sat in silence.

It only took about fifteen minutes in the end. In its way, it was odd how naturally it happened. Simon's ghost wasn't there, and then it was. Sitting at the desk, reading the newspaper. Ox made to stand, but Hannah waved him back into his seat.

Eventually, Simon looked up. 'Look,' he said, a quiver of excitement in his voice. 'My name is on an article in *The Stranger Times*.'

At that, Stella stood and everyone else followed her lead. 'You deserve it,' she said.

They all walked a few steps closer.

In the air behind Simon, a dull glimmer of light came into being and hung there. He took one last look down at the paper, smiled, then turned and looked behind him. 'I guess this is my time to move on,' he said, getting to his feet.

Reggie spoke in a croaky voice. 'What comes next?'

Simon smiled and shrugged. 'I don't know. I'm sure it'll be an adventure. I always wanted to go on one of those.'

Banecroft stepped forward abruptly and cleared his throat awkwardly. 'I . . . I wanted to say how incredibly sorry I am.'

Simon shook his head. 'You have nothing to be sorry for.'

As he turned and took a step towards the light, the brightness grew. Then he stopped and tilted his head upwards for several seconds before turning back round.

He looked directly at Banecroft. 'She wants you to know it's all OK. She says you can let her go now and . . .' His face scrunched up in concentration. 'She says, "I've had worse." Does that make sense?'

Banecroft held his hand to his mouth and nodded. A juddering sob escaped his lips. Hannah could see the tears rolling down his face, but beneath them, a smile.

'Right, then,' announced Simon. 'Best be cracking on.'

This time, he spun round and rushed towards the light. It grew so bright that Hannah had to squint and hold up a hand to shield her eyes.

Simon stood there, waving cheerfully. 'And remember,' he said, 'every failure is just an opportunity to succeed the next time.'

And then he was gone.

EPILOGUE 1

Hannah woke breathing hard, her sheets soaked with sweat again.

Every night since the incident on the golf course it had been the same. The same nightmare.

That's what it had to be – a nightmare. A stupid dream conjured up by her subconscious. She kept telling herself that.

She climbed out of bed and padded into the kitchen to get herself a glass of water. After draining it, she leaned against the sink and looked out the window at the night staggering towards morning. The first rays of dawn were touching the sky. Maybe she could grab a shower and go in early? Exhausted as she was, it felt like the easier option rather than going back to sleep again, knowing that thing was lurking there, waiting for her.

The dream played on repeat every night. Sometimes two or three showings.

Stella, standing in the middle of Oxford Road in a torrential downpour, laughing maniacally. Abandoned cars strewn all around her, a couple of police cars among them. A white van has run into the traffic lights outside Sainsbury's and smoke is coming from under the bonnet. A black Hackney cab, turned upside down, rocks back and forth. Over near the Palace Theatre, a double-decker bus is in flames. With a motion of Stella's hand, a tendril of blue energy wraps itself around one of the cars, picks it up and tosses it into the distance. After a couple of seconds comes the sound of an explosion.

And then the dream ends the same way, every time.

Hannah looks into Stella's face, which is contorted into a mask of fury as she screams at her friend, 'Run, Hannah, run!'

Then she wakes up.

It's just a dream. Just. A. Dream.

EPILOGUE 2

Red's.

The best of the best.

The finest BBQ food available in Manchester, if not England, possibly the world. Stanley hadn't ever visited the American Deep South, so that was a hell of a leap to make, but still, it was good. Really good.

The waitress had offered him the menu but he'd waved it away. He knew what he wanted. He'd known what he'd wanted three days ago when he'd made the reservation.

'The bin lid,' he confirmed.

The waitress paused. 'Are you expecting someone else?'

'No, but I'll take the bin lid for two.'

'Right. That's a lot of—'

'I know.'

She shrugged. 'If you're sure. Drink?'

'Diet Coke, please.'

'Just the one?'

'Yes.'

She departed then returned with the drink. Stanley sat there, staring straight ahead, thinking happy thoughts. The most incredible meal imaginable was on its way – pork ribs, brisket, XXXL smoked wings, cheese and jalapeño sausage, smoked chicken, chopped pork, garlic chilli greens, giant onion rings, meaty BBQ pit beans, slaw and fries – all presented on a bin lid for reasons Stanley didn't understand or care to know.

This was going to be great.

This was going to be absolutely fantastic.

Best. Meal. Ever.

After about thirty minutes, the waitress and a couple of her associates returned with a silver dustbin lid laden with the most glorious display of BBQ known to man. They placed it down in front of him, and the waitress gave him a cheery 'bon appétit' before disappearing.

Stanley picked up his knife and fork. Where to start? The smoked wings? No. The ribs? He settled on the chicken. Can't go wrong with chicken. He carefully sliced off a piece and raised the fork to his lips . . .

In crashed the image again. The top of Anton Lasherf's skull resting on top of his full English breakfast.

Stanley drew the fork away and took a few deep breaths. Mind over matter. He could do this. He could absolutely do this.

Damn it. He threw down the cutlery and grabbed a rib with his bare hands. He pulled it towards his mouth and . . . Before his lips could make contact, he felt his stomach spasm and he quelled a retch.

Stanley set down the rib and burst into tears.

This was it. His last chance – gone. If this place didn't work, nothing would.

Two minutes later, the waitress pulled herself away from her conversation with the maître d' and followed Stanley as he hurried towards the door. 'Is everything OK, sir?'

'No,' said Stanley. 'Nothing is OK. Everything is terrible. Turns out I'm a bloody vegetarian.'

FREE STUFF!

Hello, C. K. (or Caimh) here. Thanks very much for reading *Love Will Tear Us Apart* – I hope you enjoyed it, although if you didn't, well done for hate-reading all the way to the end.

If you wish to head to thestrangertimes.co.uk you can sign up for my newsletter and I won't be able to stop you. You'll even get a collection of *Stranger Times* short stories for doing so – FREE! I am also powerless to prevent you from checking out *The Stranger Times* podcast, which features over thirty episodes of weird tales from *The Stranger Times* world written by me, as it turns out I seriously need a hobby.

Before that, though, up next are the acknowledgements for this book, written by *The Stranger Times*'s resident past-life regression expert, Maximillian Winters.

Acknowledgements

The author wishes to thank the following people for their invaluable contribution to making this book a reality:

Editor Simon Taylor, who in a past life was a court jester to Henry VIII. His medieval existence was tragically cut short when he over-estimated his lord and master's sense of humour regarding his dating history.

Judith Welsh, managing editor, who was the Egyptian queen Cleopatra, world-renowned for her wisdom, beauty and tactical savvy. Her passing resulted in a massive decline in the donkey-milk industry, from which it has never truly recovered.

Rebecca Wright, copy editor, who was also Queen Cleopatra. In fact, scientific research has shown that 24 per cent of human beings were Cleopatra in a past life. People think this proves that past-life regression is nonsense, but actually, Cleopatra suffered from the most extreme case of multi-personality disorder ever recorded, so it all makes perfect sense. Please stop asking about it.

Cover-design maestro Marianne Issa El-Khoury, who was the unknown artist responsible for the much better picture that the *Mona Lisa* was looking at when old Leonardo quickly banged out her portrait.

Production master Phil Evans, who has been all the greatest Phils in history. Unfortunately, space does not permit us to name them all here.

Marketeer Sophie Bruce, previously Lady Minerva Happenstance, who was credited with pre-modifying 'Britain' with the word 'Great'. Arguably, it's the greatest piece of marketing ever conceived.

PR guru Tom Hill, formerly the Greek courier Pheidippides, who invented the marathon in his determination to spread the word of a glorious victory. Historians now believe Pheidippides would have survived if he hadn't been required to consume quite so much wine and cheese at the various events along his path to glory.

Audiobook narrator Brendan McDonald and engineer/producer Paul Fegan. Brendan was King Tamba of Banaras, famous for having the largest harem in history. Paul was Sussondi, the queen of said harem. I do hope the discovery of this information doesn't make it weird for them in that rather small studio.

Uber agent Ed Wilson was previously the cricketer Fred Trueman. Annoyingly for all concerned, not the legendary Fred Trueman, but a man of the same name who enjoyed a career in the sport largely because teams didn't want to admit they'd signed him in error. He is most famous in his own right for once being attacked by an irate pigeon while fielding.

Finally, the author wishes to thank Elaine, Diller and Jackson, who were Martha and the two hairiest Vandellas in a former life.

ABOUT THE AUTHOR

Born in Limerick and raised in Dublin, C. K. (Caimh) McDonnell is a former stand-up comedian and TV writer. He performed all around the world, had several well-received Edinburgh shows and supported acts such as Sarah Millican on tour before hanging up his clowning shoes to concentrate on writing. He has also written for numerous TV shows and been nominated for a Kid's TV BAFTA.

His debut novel, *A Man With One of Those Faces* – a comic crime novel – was published in 2016 and spawned *The Dublin Trilogy* books and the spin-off *McGarry Stateside* series. They have been Amazon bestsellers on both sides of the Atlantic. As C. K. McDonnell, he is the author of *The Stranger Times* contemporary comic fantasy series.

Caimh lives in Manchester. To find out more, visit whitehairedirishman.com

Read on for an exclusive look at the
first pages of the fourth book in
The Stranger Times series . . .

RELIGHT MY FIRE

PROLOGUE

And with a gasp, she was awake.

The first thing she became aware of was the torpid thumping of her heartbeat reverberating through her body.

Shyanne blinked repeatedly, trying to bring the world into focus. It was a world she did not recognize. She was in a room with what seemed to be discoloured metal walls, and there was no other furniture except for the metal chair she was sitting on.

No. Not sitting on, strapped to.

She looked down at her hands. Metal clasps were securing her forearms to the arms of the chair. She tried to move her feet, but something was holding them in place, too. And her chest – there was something across her chest. She drew her head back and looked down. There was a metal restraint there too. Beneath it, she could see that she was wearing a green hospital gown.

Two cannulas were inserted into the top of her right arm; one tube was attached to a blue IV and the other to a green. They led off to something behind her she couldn't see.

Incongruous plinky-plonky music was being piped into the room from unseen speakers. It was the kind of stuff wellness spas played during massages in the mistaken belief it provided ambiance.

The cloying sound from the tinny speakers was joined by a female voice. 'Test 31. 11.22 a.m. Subject has regained consciousness. Seems relatively alert.' The tone changed from clinical to irritated. 'Do you have to eat that in here?'

'What?' came a gruff male voice. 'I've not had me breakfast. I've got to do the clean-up after and—'

Shyanne tried to speak, but she couldn't. The noise coming from her throat was no more than a wheezy rasp.

'At least use a plate. You're leaving crumbs everywhere. You un-hygienic toad.'

Shyanne gagged, worked her jaw and desperately tried to locate her voice. The slow drumbeat of her heart picked up pace ever so slightly as she did so.

She finally spoke, her voice croaky. 'Hello?'

'And do your flies up, you awful worthless lump of ineptitude.'

The response to this was an unintelligible grumble.

'I can hear you!' shouted Shyanne, finding her voice at last.

The voices stopped, then the woman spoke in a sniping whisper. 'The mic is live? You blithering idiot!'

'Have you got it on mute?'

'Of course, I've—'

'Please talk to me,' pleaded Shyanne. 'What's going on?'

The voices stopped squabbling and after a moment, the female voice came through, louder now, speaking in a slow, measured tone. 'OK, Shyanne. You're all right. Relax. Everything is fine.'

'Where am I?'

'You are safe. There was an accident, but you are OK now.'

An image flashed into Shyanne's mind. She was looking down at a supermarket shopping trolley, trying to lean on the handle as it rolled away from her and she stumbled to the ground. 'I don't . . .'

'For the record,' said the voice, 'can you please tell me your full name?'

'I . . .' Shyanne scanned the room again. The tempo of the drumbeat kicked up another notch. 'Where am I?'

'You are in a hospital. Just relax and let me help you. Now, what is your full name?'

'Shyanne Jane Rivers,' she said, almost on auto pilot. She looked down again. 'Wait, why am I strapped to this chair?'

'It's just a precaution,' answered the voice. 'Now, what are your parents' names?'

'Martin and Philomena Rivers' – she paused – 'only, Mum is dead.'

'Excellent. I mean – and are you married?'

'Yes, to Kieran. Oh God, where's Kieran? I need to speak to Kieran.'

'He's waiting outside.'

The tempo picked up once more. 'The kids? Someone needs to pick the kids up. Sarah's at ballet and Tom's at . . . his friend's house . . .' The friend? How could she not remember Tom's friend's name? 'I . . . I can't remember but Kieran will know. Tell him to get the kids.'

'Your children are with Kieran. Everything is fine. Try to remain calm.'

'I want to see them.'

'You will soon.'

'I . . .' Shyanne strained against the restraints. 'Let me go. This . . . What kind of hospital is this?'

'You're fine. You became confused, Shyanne, and we just need to make sure you're OK, and then the restraints will be removed and you can see your—'

'Confused? What do you mean confused?' The tempo nudged up again, the drumbeat growing ever faster. Louder now too. 'How am I confused?'

'That's not important,' said the voice. 'The sooner you answer our questions, the sooner you can get out of here. Now, what is your date of birth?'

'The seventeenth of June, 1981. What hospital is this?'

'We're a private clinic. Where did you go to school?'

'St Martin's Primary and . . . Wait, why do you need to know that?'

'We're just testing your memory. Relax. These are just standard questions. Please, take a deep breath and calm yourself.'

Shyanne tried to comply with the instruction. It felt weird though, drawing the breath in. Like something was very wrong. Like she hadn't been doing it until she'd been instructed to do so.

'Can you tell me the last place you went on holidays?'

'Mexico.'

She scanned the room again. There were no windows, and everything was metal. Why was everything metal?

'OK, Shyanne, did you have any pets when—'

'What's that smell?'

'I'm sorry?'

Shyanne tried to concentrate as the thumping of her heartbeat threatened to drown out her thoughts. 'It smells of petrol in here. Or something like petrol.'

'Just a moment.' Shyanne heard a soft click and then the voice spoke again. 'Interesting. Subject reports olfactory functionality, which is—'

'Why did you refer to me as the subject?'

'I . . .' The voice stopped and then could be heard hissing off-mic. 'The stupid mute button doesn't work. You had one job.'

'It was working yesterday,' whined the male voice.

'Sorry about that, Shyanne,' said the female voice again, back to sounding detached and reasonable. 'Nothing to worry about.'

'Let me out!' screamed Shyanne.

'You need to remain calm.'

'Stop telling me to stay calm. Let me out!' The drumbeat was frantic now, her frenetic pulse thundering in her ears.

'Shyanne, if you want to see your—'

'Let me out!' she yelled at the top of her lungs, while rocking back and forth, straining every sinew against the metal constraints. 'Let me out! OUT! OUT!'

'Just—'

Shyanne screamed again. No words this time. Just wild, visceral rage. Then she turned her head, wrapped her teeth around the tubes that were pumping God knows what into her right arm and wrenched them out.

The flesh of her left forearm was sliced open from where it had worked against the restraint and her entire arm was hanging at an unnatural angle. Like it was broken, but there was no pain. No blood.

It meant she could pull it out. She tilted her back and roared. Freedom. Of a sort.

The female voice gave a resigned sigh. '11.24 a.m. – Test 31 terminated.'

Shyanne screeched primal fury at the soot-marked ceiling, as the rhythm of her heart consumed her world, no longer individual beats but one continuous indistinguishable wall of sound.

She waved her free left arm about, her hand dangling at a sickening angle as she screamed with everything she had.

Some small remaining part of her mind was dimly aware of a clicking noise somewhere behind her.

Then.

A pause of a couple of seconds.

And . . .

Ignition.

CHAPTER 1

The thing about life is that it is fundamentally impossible.

Not that Wayne Grainger didn't believe in the whole theory-of-evolution thing; it was just that he had realized we'd all been looking at it from the wrong end. We were the result. The result could believe in itself because it was self-evident. Nobody thought about it from the other end of the equation. Imagine being that single-celled organism however many million, billions of years ago and somebody pulled you aside and said, 'All right, champ, I'm going to level with you; we need you to get your shit together and fast because you and your descend-ants are going to have to evolve into sponges or something, then fish, then those fish are going to have to decide that water is so last millen-nium, grow legs and go for a beach holiday. You'll then become mammals with nipples – nipples are like crazy important and pretty fun, and then you're going to need to become monkeys, and then, here's the hard bit, stop being monkeys, which is tough as it's clearly the most fun stop on the trip, but you've got places to be and things to avoid being eaten by because, oh yeah, did we mention all the way along everything else has evolved into other stuff designed to kill you in like a hundred different why-you-don't-go-outside-in-Australia kind of ways? One of those evolutionary bros will be a *T-Rex*, which will be the size of a triple-decker bus, which doesn't seem like a fair fight, does it? But don't worry, they'll all get wiped out in a mass-extinction event and, heads up, keep an eye out for those big-boss moments too, and run away from any large, rapidly approaching bright lights in the sky or massive sheets of ice heading your way. You don't want it too hot or too cold. You'll basically need to Goldilocks the shit out of this, and, assuming you avoid that part of the evolutionary assault course, you'll need to pick up the pace, because "team you" needs to be evolving into Homo basic, who'll learn how to use simple tools – just like those lads in school who sat at the back of the bus and the teachers pretended not to be afraid of. Then, eventually, you're going to end up evolving into man, proper man, with Crocs, orgasms, iPhones and student debt, and one day you'll go to university to study film, while trying to continue evolving by telling people to call you Zack, but Daniel bloody Wallace from your old school will turn up and make sure everyone knows you're really a Wayne. So, the point is, little single-celled organism guy, that's the evolutionary slalom run you and the progeny have got ahead of you, and the question is, are you up for this?'

They'd have reasonably said, 'No, thanks, that sounds like a total nightmare. Entirely impossible.' And they would be right. From their perspective, life is so utterly unbelievably improbable as to be fundamentally impossible.

The thing is, once you realize life is fundamentally impossible, it is a wonderfully freeing thing. It being impossible means that the impossible is not impossible. *Ipso facto*, *QED*.

Jeez, whatever was in that tablet he'd scored from Deano was good. Wayne needed to write this stuff down. He'd been meant to take it when they went out later, but he didn't like the idea of not knowing what was coming. He'd had an awful experience with vodka in sixth-form college and he really did not want to shit himself again. The social stink of that had not washed off. Daniel Wallace had only kept schtum about it after Wayne had slipped him fifty quid, but it didn't feel like a long-term solution. He had been considering leaning into it and becoming a total party monster, but he wasn't sure he had the constitution for it.

Still, now he knew anything was possible.

Wayne had always secretly believed, deep down, that he could fly. The old him knew that was nonsense, the new him was more of a free-thinker. Wayne couldn't fly, but maybe Zack could? Mankind had been stuck in the mud for quite some time now. A bit of evolution was required and maybe he was the man for the job.

Some small part of his brain was also aware that he was not the first person to take drugs and decide he could fly. So yes, he was going up to the top of a thirty-two-storey building, but he wasn't going to jump off it. He wasn't an idiot. Doing it up there just meant distractions would be kept to a minimum. It felt like he was meeting the sky halfway.

Deano had nabbed the security code for the roof when the window cleaners had been in a couple of weeks ago. The view from up there was absolutely mental. They'd gone up last Monday for a quick recce.

Wayne stopped at the top of the stairs, gathered himself and punched in the code. After a moment, the light turned green and the door buzzed open. This was a sign from the universe. It was behind him all the way on this one. He could feel it in his bones.

The sight of Manchester lit up and laid out before him wasn't any less breathtaking the second time around. Up this high, how could you not feel like a god?

With a gust of wind, the door slammed shut behind him. He looked at it. The first time they'd come up here, Deano had wedged the door open. Why had he done that? There was a code panel thing on this side too, wasn't there? He had a sudden sinking feeling that he might not have been paying total attention to everything Deano had told him. Along with Zack's strong, reassuring voice in his head, telling him he could fly, there was now another little, distinctly Wayne voice inform-ing him he might be in the shit here. Maybe he should try to open the door now? See if he was in trouble in the unlikely event he couldn't fly?

No, screw that, no negative thoughts. Only forward.

Positivity.

He positioned himself in the centre of the rooftop and closed his eyes. The razor-edged autumn wind whipped at his skin and there was a taste of rain in the air. He didn't recall there being any wind when he'd trudged home from lectures an hour ago, but then again, he was one hundred and nine metres above the earth now. It was another world up here. A world of freedom. A world of flight. It's evolution, baby!

He just needed to think flighty thoughts. There was no point in jumping in the air. Jumping in the air was something somebody who was trying to fly would do. Wayne – no, Zack already *knew* he could fly. He just needed to let it happen. His body would simply decide that gravity was more of a guideline than a hard and fast rule, and would act accordingly.

He stood there and centred himself. He didn't actually know what that meant, but he'd heard people say it and it sounded like something he should be doing. Last Friday, that Zara chick had been telling them all about how she was into Zen and all that. Wayne had tried to bluff that he was too, but he needed to get a book from the library and really nail that shit down. Zen dude and party animal were his two current life choices, but he was leaning towards the former. He was pretty sure that achieving spiritual enlightenment would be great for getting laid.

He slowed his breathing and listened to the wind. He had to become one with the magnificent, impossible universe.

Reinvent.

Evolve.

Fly.

★

As time ticked by, he was fighting to hold on to his positive state of mind, but the little voice, his inner Wayne, was back, pointing out to Zack that he probably should have put on something warmer than a retro Nirvana T-shirt if he was going to stand on a freezing-cold rooftop in October, in Manchester, like a twat. He tried to ignore Wayne, but the longer he stood there, trying to think flighty thoughts, the more his buzz was wearing off and the more Wayne-y he felt. His mind kept coming back to how the door had blown closed and how he didn't have his phone with him. Jesus, the code had better work on this side too, or he was going to be in all kinds of shit. They couldn't kick you out after just a couple of weeks, could they? That was assuming he didn't die of hypothermia first, of course. If he did, his mum was going to hit the roof.

He was on the roof.

He needed to get down off the roof fast and not tell anyone about this and . . .

Wayne opened his eyes.

Only he wasn't Wayne any more.

Wayne had been standing on the roof, Zack was now hovering above it.

Wayne was earthbound, but Zack, Zack could fly.

He reckoned he was a good ten feet above the rooftop. He glanced down at his feet, dumbfounded that they were floating below him. He tentatively moved the left one. Nope, it wasn't in contact with anything.

HOLY SHIT!

Adrenalin surged through his body.

This was it.

This was IT!

He'd known it. He'd always known it. Impossible was just a word. He was Zack and he could bloody well fly! This'd show Johnny and his crappy guitar a thing or two. Best of luck dominating the next halls party now, closing your eyes when you sing 'Wonderwall' like a bellend. And Daniel Wallace could jog on as well. Nobody would care that the flying guy had needed to phone his dad to pick him up and bring a pair of spare trousers because he'd defecated in his other pair while drunk.

This was going to get him laid. He'd been putting in the groundwork with Susan, but screw that. This was a game-changer. Her best mate, the unattainable Zen-filled Zara, was now definitely in his sights. Sod it. Why not both of them? Zack was nothing if not a convention-defying dude. The guy who directed the *Thor* movies had done something like that. He'd seen it on Insta. Two smoking-hot women at the same time in, like, a relationship-thing. Unattainable was just a word. Just like impossible. Words that did not apply to the Zack he now definitely was.

It says something of the workings of the teenaged male mind that a mere minute after achieving the dream of flight, he was almost entirely focused on sex.

So focused, in fact, that he was oblivious to his surroundings. His environment was irrelevant now. He had mastered it. He had made gravity his bitch.

Zack turned his head, drinking in the view. The view he was now experiencing in a way that nobody in the history of the world had experienced before him.

He was a legend.

A god.

He was probably going to meet Beyoncé.

Christ, what do you say to Beyoncé? She was Beyoncé, after all, whereas all he could do was fly.

He was not paying any attention to the wind or to the fact that it had been steadily nudging him in a particular direction.

Eventually, the now teeny-tiny whisper that was all that remained of Wayne made itself heard, and he looked down.

He was now no longer hovering over the roof. He had drifted and was about one hundred and twenty or so metres above Hulme Street.

His mind might now believe that he could fly, but apparently his bladder didn't share its confidence.

As a stream of rapidly cooling urine leaked down his leg, his belief dripped away with it.

The thing about making gravity your bitch is that the bitch can bite back.

CHAPTER 2

As soon as the lecturer had wrapped up with his humorous 'enjoy your Thursday night, but not too much' bit, Stella had shoved her notebook in her bag, jammed her headphones on and headed for the door. She told herself her hurry was because she needed to get back to work, but that was only partly true. Hannah had been back as assistant editor of *The Stranger Times* for a couple of months now and while things were, well, not exactly running smoothly, they were certainly running more efficiently than they had done in all the time Stella had been there.

Hannah had managed to force a bit of forward planning into proceedings, which meant there was less of a panicked rush to get stuff done on a Thursday night for publication the following day. Vincent Banecroft still screamed, shouted, reprimanded, belittled and occasionally eviscerated his staff, but connoisseurs of his moods had noted a reduction in their intensity. It was like having a hurricane downgraded to a tropical storm – better, but still not kite-flying weather. He said all the same mean things, but they were delivered at a less ear-splitting volume. Maybe it was because of Hannah's organizational improvements or perhaps it was because of 'the other thing'.

Speaking of things, the whole uni thing had been Banecroft's idea. He'd been saying for a while that Stella was going to be sent on a training course. Then, what happened happened and a few weeks later she was suddenly a 'non-assessed' student at Manchester Metropolitan

University studying for an undergraduate degree in Multimedia Journalism. Seemingly, Vincent Banecroft's guilt was a powerful motivator. From what she could glean from Hannah, through a combination of him cashing in whatever favours he was still owed on Fleet Street, some badgering, cajoling and outright blackmailing, plus enlisting some lady called Cathy who was, as Hannah put it, 'good with computers', Stella was now attending classes at Manchester's second most prestigious university. She wouldn't be taking exams or receiving any other form of official assessment but, as Banecroft seemed to believe, that was entirely irrelevant, as the only assessment that mattered was his.

Stella had also been informed that, should anyone ask, she had A levels in English, Maths and French. Not that it was her biggest concern, but why did they pick French? She didn't know a word of it. She was so freaked out by the prospect of someone trying to speak to her in the language, she'd downloaded an app and was trying to learn some words daily. So far, she had to hope that any chatty French people would primarily be interested in discussing where the library was, otherwise she was screwed.

As she exited through the revolving doors of the Business School, the cold autumnal air hit her like a slap to the face. From here, she could just point at the library, which made her newly learned French redundant. Having a lecture on a Thursday evening had been the cause of much moaning from her classmates, it being the big going-out night of the week. Lots of students were milling about in groups outside already, laughing, talking too loudly, enjoying life. It looked nice.

Pulling her hoodie around her, Stella was reminded yet again that she really needed to get some proper winter clothes because Manchester had proper winters. She turned on her music and the vocals of Robert Smith, assuring the world he was a love cat, filled her ears. The Cure were her current go-to – their brand of whimsical misery really appealed to her. She'd pointedly avoided mentioning it in the office as any of the olds getting excited about her listening to something they recognized would ruin it.

Stella had been terrified of being unmasked as a fraud until Reggie, Hannah and Ox had sat her down the night before uni started and given her a pep talk. It had gone along the lines of, don't worry about it, everyone starting university thinks they're a total fraud. People use it as an opportunity to 'reinvent' themselves all the time and—

Someone grabbed Stella's forearm from behind and she whirled around, crouching into a defensive stance, every sinew tensing. She felt 'the thing' inside her surge forward; that sickening crackle of power.

She was confronted by a startled Yvette – a girl from her course with a round cheerful face framed by blonde locks – standing there with her hands up, looking utterly mortified.

'Shit! Sorry, sorry, sorry,' Yvette apologized. 'I'm a total lemon. Didn't mean to startle you. Christ, good one, Yvette. Go around scaring the hell out of people.'

Stella took a step back and drew a deep breath to calm herself. 'Sorry,' she echoed, 'my bad. I'm very jumpy.'

'No, totally my fault. Shouldn't be grabbing women from behind like a muppet. I was lucky I didn't get a front-door key in the face. That was one of the things they mentioned in that self-defence session for female-identifying freshers last week. It was good, but also bloody terrifying. I mean, Jesus, right? Unbelievable. There are some scary people out there.'

Yes, thought Stella, and I'm one of them. An image flashed into her mind, unbidden, of a massive wave of blue energy surging out of her and ripping a scar in the earth, but she pushed it away.

'Don't worry about it. Too much coffee,' said Stella, trying to muster a smile. She didn't actually drink the stuff, but had learned it was an acceptable excuse for all manner of jumpiness. Her heart rate was slowing down, still punk speed, but now at the more melodic end of the spectrum.

'Right, well, I just wanted to catch you because a couple of us are heading up to check out Canal Street this evening and we wondered if you wanted to join? I mean, it's the Gay Village but you don't have to be – although obviously great if you are. Aisha is, and she's coming, I think. Plus Bea reckons she might be bi. I mean, not that any of it matters. It's more, yeah, y'know, just wanted to see if you'd fancy it?'

Yvette talked like that all the time. Just a stream of consciousness babbling forth before she finally hit the buffers of a question. She asked a lot of questions. Stella suspected she used them as a braking mechanism.

'I'd love to,' said Stella, 'but I'm afraid I've got to get back to the office. Publication night.'

'Right,' said Yvette. 'Yeah, of course. They keep you busy.'

Stella stretched her face into a mock grimace. 'Deadlines.'

'God, yeah, you're doing, like, proper journalism. Amazing.'

What had helped with Stella's imposter syndrome was the first few practical sessions they'd had, where she'd edited copy and then formatted pages using Adobe InDesign. Stella had actually shown her lecturer, John, a couple of easier ways to format articles across two pages. She'd honestly not been trying to show off. It was all just stuff she'd picked up through work and hadn't thought it was much of a big deal, but John had been blown away.

Her plan had been to try to keep *The Stranger Times* thing quiet, but once she was asked directly where she'd gained her experience, she'd had to fess up. The other students had seemed mostly impressed, but it was hard to tell. Stella had little experience with people her own age. Or, rather, people she thought might be her age.

Yvette gave a disappointed nod. 'Sure, some other time, then? We could do something earlier in the week, when you haven't got that deadline monkey on your back?'

'Yeah, that'd be good. Enjoy your night out.'

They said their farewells and Stella moved off, heading out onto Oxford Road. She hadn't eaten, and she wanted to pick up some snacks from the SPAR before heading back to the office and facing whatever inevitable last-minute changes Banecroft wanted to make.

On the very first day of class, Yvette had plonked herself beside

Stella, opened with 'you weren't at induction', and started talking a mile a minute. She was chatty with everyone, but she seemed determined that she and Stella should be friends. A part of Stella wondered if maybe this was a blonde girl from the home counties looking to snap up a Black friend to show how cool she was on the all-important Instagram feed. That was probably unfair. Stella just wasn't good at trusting people.

The SPAR was busy with students stocking up on booze for preloading. Stella had read about the concept in an article. Apparently, the way some younger people were economizing during the cost-of-living crisis was by getting hammered before they went out. Getting thrown out of a club before you'd even got in was a thing now. As was not drinking at all, increasingly. Two very distinct approaches to life. Stella was definitely in the second camp. Getting out of control was her idea of hell. It wasn't Hallowe'en until Tuesday, but fancy dress was already heavily in evidence. Last night, she'd seen a White girl who had blacked-up as Crazy Eyes from *Orange Is the New Black*. She didn't even know where to start with that.

Bag of Revels, bottle of Prime, sweet chilli crisps and egg mayo roll purchased, Stella headed off down Hulme Street.

She had yet to figure out how to cope with all of this. She hadn't gone to university to 'reinvent' herself, largely because she was still trying to invent herself. That's why Yvette freaked her out. The girl was a never-ending stream of questions, and Stella didn't have good answers.

'So, where are you from, Yvette? Surrey? Cool! What, me? Oh, no idea. I mean, I know I was being kept in a sort of boarding-school-cum-prison, then I busted out, got on the first train I found, then another one, and then I was in Manchester. I headed for a weird old church building because, I dunno, something drew me there, and I'm pretty sure someone was chasing me, but don't ask me who. The old church turned out to be the offices of *The Stranger Times*, which I discovered when the editor pointed a blunderbuss at me as I was trying to climb in his office window in the middle of the night. Then they took me in like a lost cat and I sort of live/work there now.

'That's not even the weirdest part, because I don't know my age, birthday, where I was born, who the hell my parents are – essentially who I am. None of it. I don't even have a full set of memories. It's like I didn't have a childhood. Not in a chained-to-a-radiator, raising-seven-siblings way, more in a there's-a-great-big-gaping-hole-where-a-life-should-be way, and I've got nothing but a few snatches of random memories that could all come from the same couple of weeks.

'Even weirder, it's only really dawned on me recently how strange that is. Like I didn't know what I didn't know. Like I wasn't properly alive. As if I don't really exist, or at least I didn't until about a year ago when I hopped on that train. And, oh yeah, I killed a man a couple of months ago at a disused golf course because I have this massive, terrifying, uncontrollable power inside me that freaks everybody out, most of all me, and I know nothing about it. I was acting in self-defence as the arsehat in question was trying to, I guess you'd say, drain me of my power or something, before inevitably killing me and a few of my friends, but yes, it does still mean I wake up screaming and I have far more golf-course-related issues than you'd expect from a girl my age, which reminds me, did I mention I don't know my age? Anyway, enough about me. What bands are you into?'

Yeah, as much as Hannah's heart was in the right place, telling Stella to go and have a normal life, that wasn't happening anytime soon. She hadn't gone to that self-defence class Yvette had mentioned because she didn't have to worry about defending herself in the way other women did. Heaven help any sex pest who came at her, because if she let rip what was inside her, they'd end up a pile of randomized rapey atoms floating away in the light Mancunian breeze. Not that Stella wasn't in danger; she'd been kidnapped twice in about six months, after all. The second time had been by Banecroft, her mentor, because the aforementioned golf-course homicidal arsehat had got inside Banecroft's head and weaponized his grief following his wife's death.

Banecroft hadn't known what he was doing. Stella knew that on an intellectual level, but it hurt her emotionally. It was still a betrayal, albeit an understandable one. She knew it haunted him too, judging by the gross over-compensation of the vague promise of her receiving a couple of days' training being upgraded to a three-year degree course she had not even applied for.

Still, for all that, and for all the anxiety, Stella was happy to be there. She was a student, almost. She was doing what other people her age did, assuming the estimates of her age actually were accurate. As Ox had helpfully pointed out, Black don't crack – Stella could be thirty-four for all they knew. Regardless, perhaps things were finally calming down. Maybe, just maybe, she could start living a somewhat normal life.

Admittedly, it would be a certain approximation of normal. In the last six months, when not being kidnapped, she'd also discovered that magic was real, that there was this whole other world that existed just below the surface of the one most people knew, and it was populated with all manner of weird and wonderful creatures and characters, a lot of whom could kill you. And there really was a cabal of mega-powerful monsters who secretly ran the world, aka the Founders, although there was one less of them now since the incident just off the fourteenth fairway of Swinton golf course. All that, plus her job required her to write articles about a man from Bradford who claimed UFOs had stolen his dog and replaced her with an identical copy, a bunch of people in North Wales who had started a cult worshipping Tom Jones, and some dude who came into the office every Loon Day who was sexually attracted to cigarette machines.

Stella shoved a handful of Revels into her mouth. Yes, things were looking up. She decided to make a conscious effort to be more positive and see where it took her. Maybe she could start enjoying life and, who knew – a half-decent guy might fall from the sky and she could take a crack at having one of those relationship things she was always hearing about. Stranger things had happened, certainly to her. Not unlike

Yvette's friend Bea, Stella had recently done a self-audit and had come to the conclusion that she was regrettably heterosexual, which was a pain as men seemed to come in a few unimpressive variations on the same basic idiot model.

At a junction up ahead, she noticed a group of half a dozen students talking excitedly and waving their phones about. Stella had to admit that the cliché that people her assumed age were constantly taking selfies and filming themselves held a lot of water. Talk about obsessive behaviour. You couldn't walk through campus without passing somebody videoing themselves on their phone, sharing their every unfiltered thought with the world. She was not a fan of the digital part of the journalism course she was on. *The Stranger Times* didn't even have a website, which was weird but also kind of retro cool. They had a big old printing press, run by a stoned Rastafarian, which would rumble through the night, making the building shake as it pumped out the physical sheets of paper that was their product. She probably should hate the machine for keeping her awake, but it was in its way the most reassuring sound in the world to her. Another edition of *The Stranger Times* was almost out, and everything was right with the world.

As she approached the junction, the crowd grew bigger, with more people joining it. Stella had initially thought the students were holding their phones up searching for that perfect selfie angle, but that wasn't it. Their attention was fixed on something up in the sky. She tapped her headphones to pause the track and was just about to follow their gaze when the screaming started. Stella tried to focus on what they were looking at in the dark sky, but she couldn't. Belatedly, she realized it was because the object was coming rapidly towards her.

She froze as people scattered in every direction. With a blur of motion, something passed a couple of feet in front of her face before hitting the ground with a stomach-turning squelch and the shattering of bones. Thick wet matter splashed across her cheeks as she stumbled backwards. Blue lightning crackled around her fingers as her panic stirred the beast. She started to fall but hands grabbed her, holding her up.

Stella looked down at the ground.

A half-decent guy had fallen from the sky.

Introducing the outrageously
entertaining *Stranger Times* series . . .

THE STRANGER TIMES

Dedicated to reporting the weird and the wonderful
(but mostly the weird), *The Stranger Times* is Manchester's
go-to newspaper for the unexplained and inexplicable.

Well, that's the pitch. The reality is rather less auspicious. The
foul-tempered drunk of an editor thinks little (and believes less) of
the publication he edits. His staff are a bunch of misfits, each with a
secret or two to hide. And as for the new assistant editor Hannah
Willis, she's got a whole heap of problems of her own.

Then tragedy strikes in Hannah's first week on the job and suddenly
the team is forced to do some actual investigative journalism. What
they discover leads to a shocking realisation: some of the stories
they'd previously dismissed as nonsense are in fact terrifyingly real.

For it seems that Dark Forces are at work in our world . . .
and in Manchester in particular.

'Evocative of Terry Pratchett – which I think
is the highest compliment I can give'
ADAM KAY

'I loved this . . . hugely enjoyable'
JODI TAYLOR

'Ripping entertainment'
THE TIMES

The second laugh-out-loud adventure in the
brilliant *Stranger Times* series

THIS CHARMING MAN

Vampires do not exist. Everyone knows this.
So it's rather annoying when they start popping up
around Manchester . . .

Nobody is pleased about it. Not the Founders, the secret organisation
for whom vampires were invented as an allegory. Nor the Folk, the
magical people hiding in plain sight who only want a quiet life. And
not the people of Manchester either, because there is nothing more
irksome than being murdered by an allegory run amok.

Somebody needs to sort this out fast — step forward the
staff of the newspaper dedicated to reporting the
unexplained and inexplicable, *The Stranger Times*.
Although with all the kidnapping, precarious plumbing,
and ground-breaking swearing that's going on, they have
rather a lot on their plates already . . .

The fourth, furiously funny novel in the
fabulous bestselling *Stranger Times* series . . .

RELIGHT MY FIRE

Some comebacks can be murder . . .

Stella is enjoying life as an almost student.
Or at least she was until a man fell from the sky right in front of her,
leaving a big hole in the pavement for Manchester Council to fill.
The obvious question of how he ended up in the sky in the first
place has no obvious answers, which is where *The Stranger Times*
come in. This isn't just the hunt for another story though.
Dark powers think Stella was involved and the only way she and
the team can prove her innocence is to find out what is really
going on. What have dodgy gear, disturbed graves and a
decommissioned rock star got to do with all this?

And Vincent Banecroft has problems of his own. A tall, dark
but-definitely-not-handsome man has been sent to make
the *Times*'s editor atone for his sins. Once he finds out that this
means being banished to a Hellscape for all eternity,
Vincent is far from keen – not least because he has that
pale Irish skin that burns *really* easily . . .

Add territorial ghouls, homicidal felines, unstoppable gnomes
and a veritable *Who's Who* of undead celebrities that'd put a
royal wedding to shame, and you're looking at a wild few days
for *The Stranger Times*.